SHOCK WAVE

Now available for the first time
in an Archway edition.

From an island off the coast of Australia, a diamond tycoon heads a reign of terror. Governments worldwide are under his thumb, but he has never come up against the fury of a man like DIRK PITT®!

DIRK PITT

He is a man of action who lives by the moment and for the moment . . . without regret. A graduate of the Air Force Academy, son of a United States Senator, and Special Projects Director for the U.S. National Underwater and Marine Agency (NUMA), he is cool, courageous and resourceful—a man of complete honor at all times and of absolute ruthlessness whenever necessary. Pitt answers to no one but Admiral James Sandecker, the wily commander of NUMA, and trusts no one but the shrewd, street-smart Al Giordino, a friend since childhood and his partner in undersea adventure for twenty years.

Arthur Dorsett: An ugly, hulking giant of a man, head of the world's second largest diamond empire, he has the personality of a pit bull. His master plan will destroy the global diamond market—and net him billions. . . .

Maeve Fletcher: Dorsett's lovely blond daughter rebelled against laboring in her father's mines, changing her name and earning her master's degree in zoology without a penny of his fortune. But now her father has ordered her to spy on Dirk Pitt® and NUMA, seizing her twin six-year-old sons. . . .

Mason Broadmoor: A revered totem-pole carver of Canada's Haida Indian tribe, he smuggled Pitt into the Dorsett mine on Kunghit Island, where Pitt unlocked the key to the murderous blasting operations—and was captured by Dorsett's thugs. But Broadmoor's daring rescue gave him the ride of his life. . . .

Boudicca Dorsett: A towering beauty with the poise of a tigress, she is in charge of security operations for Dorsett Consolidated Mining Limited. Her physical strength far surpasses that of most men, and her cruel streak is rivaled only by her father's. . . .

Deirdre Dorsett: A glamorous woman with copper hair and the flair of a fashion model, she is vividly attractive to Dirk Pitt®, until he perceives that her sophistication conceals a heart as cold as polar ice. . . .

Hiram Yaeger: The iconoclastic chief of NUMA's computer network is filled with horror when a magnificent new graphics program targets the next area to be rocked by Dorsett's revolutionary mining technique. . . .

Books by Clive Cussler

INCA GOLD
SHOCK WAVE

Available from Archway Paperbacks
Published by Pocket Books

Clive Cussler

Shock Wave

A DIRK PITT® ADVENTURE

AN ARCHWAY PAPERBACK
Published by POCKET BOOKS
New York   London   Toronto   Sydney   Tokyo   Singapore

This book is a work of fiction. Names, characters, places and
incidents are products of the author's imagination or are used
fictitiously. Any resemblance to actual events or locales or persons,
living or dead, is entirely coincidental.

This is an abridged version of *Shock Wave,* first published in
hardcover by Simon & Schuster in 1996.

An Archway Paperback published by
POCKET BOOKS, a division of Simon & Schuster Inc.
1230 Avenue of the Americas, New York, NY 10020

ISBN: 0-671-02055-2

First Archway Paperback printing October 1998

10 9 8 7 6 5 4 3 2 1

DIRK PITT is a registered trademark of Clive Cussler.

AN ARCHWAY PAPERBACK and colophon are
registered trademarks of Simon & Schuster Inc.

Interior illustrations by Errol Beauchamp

Front cover illustration by Franco Accornero

Printed in the U.S.A.

IL 5+

Contents

Shock Wave

PROLOGUE

RAFT OF THE *GLADIATOR*

THE GLADIATOR

January 17, 1856
The Tasman Sea

THERE WERE FOUR CLIPPER SHIPS BUILT IN ABERDEEN, SCOT-
land, in 1854. One of them, the *Gladiator,* stood out
from the others. She was a big ship—1,256 tons, 198 feet
long, with a 34-foot beam, and three towering masts. She
was one of the swiftest of the clippers ever to take to the
water, but she was a dangerous ship to sail in rough
weather because of her too-fine lines. She was called a
"ghoster," because she could sail in the slightest breath
of wind.

Unfortunately, she was a ship destined for oblivion.

Her owners made her ready for the Australian trade
and emigrant business, and she was one of the few
clippers designed to carry passengers as well as cargo.
But as they soon discovered, there weren't many colo-
nists who could afford the fare, so she was sailing with
first- and second-class cabins empty. It was found to be
far more lucrative to obtain government contracts for
the transportation of convicts to the continent that
initially served as the world's largest jail.

The *Gladiator* was placed under command of one of
the hardest driving clipper captains, Charles "Bully"
Scaggs. He was aptly named. His aggressive methods

produced results. On her third homeward voyage, *Gladiator* set a sixty-three-day record that still stands for sailing ships. Many of the slower merchant ships took as long as three and a half months to make the voyage.

Locked belowdecks, the convicts were treated like a cargo of cattle. Some were hardened criminals, some were political dissidents, all too many were poor souls who had been imprisoned for stealing a few pieces of cloth or scraps of food. Skimpy bedding in small wooden berths, the barest of hygienic facilities and food with little nutrients was their lot for the months at sea. Their only luxuries were rations of sugar, vinegar and lime juice to ward off scurvy. They were guarded by a small detachment of ten men from the New South Wales Infantry Regiment, under the command of Lieutenant Silas Sheppard.

Doctors were required to serve on the convict ships, and the *Gladiator* was no exception. Surgeon-Superintendent Otis Gorman saw to the prisoners' general health and arranged for small groups of them to come on deck for fresh air and exercise whenever the weather permitted.

Bully Scaggs mostly ignored the unfortunates locked below his decks. Record runs were his stock in trade. His iron discipline and aggressiveness had paid off handsomely in bonuses from happy shipping owners while making him and his ship immortal in the legends of clipper ships.

This trip he smelled a new record and was relentless. Fifty-two days out of London, bound for Sydney with a cargo of trade goods and 192 convicts, 24 of them women, he pushed *Gladiator* to her absolute limits, seldom taking in sail during a heavy blow. His perseverance was rewarded with a twenty-four-hour run of an incredible 439 miles.

And then Scaggs' luck ran out. Disaster loomed over the astern horizon.

A day after *Gladiator*'s safe passage through the Bass Strait between Tasmania and the southern tip of Australia, the evening sky filled with ominous black clouds and the stars were blotted out as the sea grew vicious in proportion. Unknown to Scaggs, a full-blown typhoon was hurling itself upon his ship from the southeast beyond the Tasman Sea.

The tempest was to prove the most violent and devastating typhoon within memory of the South Sea islanders. The wind gained in velocity with each passing hour. A thirty-foot wave smashed into the stern and rolled over the ship, crushing the captain's cabin and tearing off the rudder. The deck was swept free of boats, helm, deckhouse and galley. The hatches were stove in, and water poured into the hold unobstructed.

Then one deadly, enormous wave suddenly battered the once graceful clipper ship into a helpless, crippled derelict. She was tossed like a block of wood, made unmanageable by the mountainous seas. Unable to fight the tempest, her unfortunate crew and cargo of convicts could only stare into the face of death as they waited in terror for the ship to take her final plunge into the restless depths.

Two weeks after the *Gladiator* failed to reach port, ships were sent out to retrace the known clipper passages through Bass Strait and the Tasman Sea, but they failed to turn up a trace of survivors or floating wreckage. Her owners wrote her off as a loss, the underwriters paid off, the relatives of the crew and convicts mourned their passing and the ship's memory became dimmed by time.

Almost three years were to pass before the mysterious disappearance was solved.

Incredibly, unknown to the maritime world, the *Gladiator* was still afloat after the terrible typhoon had passed on to the west. Somehow the ravaged clipper ship had survived. But the sea was entering between sprung planks in the hull at an alarming rate. By the following noon, there were six feet of water in the hold, and the pumps were fighting a losing battle.

Captain Bully Scaggs' flinty endurance never wavered. The crew swore he kept the ship from foundering by sheer stubbornness alone. He issued orders sternly and calmly, enlisting those convicts who hadn't suffered major injuries from having been knocked about by the constant battering of the sea to man the pumps while the crew concentrated on repairing the leaking hull.

The rest of the day and night was spent in an attempt to lighten the ship, throwing overboard the cargo and any tool or utensil that was not deemed absolutely necessary. Nothing helped. The water gained another three feet by the following morning.

By midafternoon an exhausted Scaggs bowed to defeat. Nothing he or anyone could do would save the *Gladiator*. And without boats there was only one desperate gamble to save the souls on board. He ordered Lieutenant Sheppard to release the prisoners and line them up on deck opposite the watchful eyes of his armed soldiers.

Bully Scaggs was a giant of a man. He stood six feet two inches tall, with eyes that were olive gray, peering from a face weathered by the sea and sun. A great shag of ink-black hair and a magnificent black beard framed his face. He spoke with a deep, vibrant voice that enhanced his commanding presence. In the prime of life, he was a hard-bitten thirty-nine years old.

As he looked over the convicts he was startled by the number of injuries, the bruises, the sprains, the heads wrapped with blood-soaked bandages. Fear and consternation were revealed on every face. An uglier group of men and women he'd never laid eyes on.

When the poor wretches saw the terrible damage above deck, they were overwhelmed with despair. The women began uttering cries of terror, all except one, Scaggs noted, who stood out from the rest.

His eyes briefly paused on the female convict, who was nearly as tall as most of the men. Her clothes appeared neat and clean, and her waist-length yellow hair had a brushed luster to it, unlike that of the other women, whose hair was unkept and stringy. She stood poised, her fear masked by a show of defiance as she stared back at Scaggs through eyes as blue as an alpine lake.

This was the first time Scaggs had noticed her. He refocused on the emergency at hand and addressed the convicts.

"Our situation is not promising," Scaggs began. "In all honesty I must tell you the ship is doomed, and with the sea's destruction of our boats, we cannot abandon her."

His words were greeted with a mixed reaction. Lieutenant Sheppard's infantrymen stood silent and motionless, while many of the convicts began to wail and moan. Expecting to see the ship go to pieces within moments, several of the convicts fell to their knees and begged the heavens for salvation.

Turning a deaf ear to their cries, Scaggs continued his address. "With the help of a merciful God, I will attempt to save every soul on this ship. I intend to build a raft of sufficient size to carry everyone on board until we are saved by a passing ship or drift ashore on the Australian mainland. We'll load ample provisions of food and water, enough to last us for twenty days."

"If you don't mind me asking, Captain, how soon do you reckon before we'd be picked up?"

The question came from a huge man with a contemptuous expression who stood head and shoulders above the rest. Unlike his companions he was fashionably dressed, with every hair on his head fastidiously in place.

Before answering, Scaggs turned to Lieutenant Sheppard. "Who's that dandy?"

Sheppard leaned toward the captain. "Name is Jess Dorsett."

Scaggs' eyebrows raised. "Jess Dorsett the highwayman?"

The lieutenant nodded. "The same. Made a fortune, he did, before the Queen's men caught up with him. The only one of this motley mob who can read and write."

Scaggs immediately realized that the highwayman might prove valuable if the situation on the raft turned menacing. The possibility of mutiny was very real. "I can only offer you all a chance at life, Mr. Dorsett. Beyond that I promise nothing."

"So what do you expect of me and my friends here?"

"I expect every able-bodied man to help build the raft. Any of you who refuse or shirk will be left behind on the ship."

"Hear that, boys?" Dorsett shouted to the assembled convicts. "Work or you die." He turned back to Scaggs. "None of us are sailors. You'll have to tell us how to go about it."

Scaggs gestured toward his first officer. "I have charged Mr. Ramsey with drawing up plans and framing the raft. A work party drawn from those of my crew not required to keep us afloat will direct the construction."

At six feet four, Jess Dorsett seemed a giant when standing among the other convicts. The shoulders beneath the expensive velvet coat stretched broad and powerful. His copper-red hair was long and hung loose over the collar of the coat. He had a large nose, high cheekbones and a heavy jaw. Despite two months of hardship, locked in the ship's hold, he looked as though he'd just stepped out of a London drawing room.

Before they turned from each other, Dorsett and Scaggs briefly exchanged glances. First Officer Ramsey caught the intensity. The tiger and the lion, he thought. He wondered who would be left standing at the end of their ordeal.

Fortunately, the sea had turned calm, since the raft was to be built in the water. The construction began with the materials being thrown overboard. The main framework was made up from the remains of the masts, lashed together with a strong rope. Heavy planking was nailed across the top for a deck and then surrounded by a waist-high railing. Two spare topmasts were erected fore and aft and fitted with sails, shrouds and stays.

When completed the raft measured eighty feet in length by forty feet wide, and though it looked quite large, by the time the provisions were loaded on board, it was a tight squeeze to pack in 192 convicts, 11 soldiers and the ship's crew, which numbered 28, including Bully Scaggs, for a total of 231. At what passed for the stern, a rudimentary rudder was attached to a makeshift tiller behind the aft mast.

Wooden kegs containing water, lime juice, brined beef and pork, as well as cheese, and several pots of rice and peas cooked in the ship's galley, were lowered on board between the masts and tied down under a large sheet of canvas that was spread over two thirds of the raft as an awning to ward off the burning rays of the sun.

The departure was blessed by clear skies and a sea as smooth as a millpond. The soldiers were disembarked first, carrying their muskets and sabers. Then came the convicts, who were all too happy to escape sinking with the ship. The ship's ladder was inadequate to support them all, so most came over the side, dangling from ropes. Several jumped or fell into the water and were recovered by the soldiers. The badly injured were low-

CLIVE CUSSLER

ered by slings. In two hours, all 203 were safely stationed
on the raft in positions assigned by Scaggs.

The crew came next, Captain Scaggs the last man to
leave the steeply slanting deck. He dropped a box
containing two pistols, the ship's log, a chronometer,
compass and a sextant into the arms of First Officer
Ramsey. Scaggs had taken a position fix before dropping
over the side and had told no one, not even Ramsey, that
the storm had blown the *Gladiator* far off the normal
shipping routes. They were drifting in a dead area of the
Tasman Sea, three hundred miles from the nearest
Australian shore, and what was worse, the current was
carrying them even farther into nothingness where no
ships sailed. He consulted his charts and determined
their only hope was to take advantage of the adverse
current and winds and sail east toward New Zealand.

Soon after settling in, everyone in their place on the
crowded deck, the raft's passengers found to their dismay that there was only enough space for forty bodies to
lie down at any one time. It was obvious to the seamen
from the ship that their lives were in great jeopardy; the
planked deck of the raft was only four inches above the
water. If confronted with a rough sea, the raft and its
unfortunate passengers would be immersed.

Scaggs hung the compass on the mast forward of the
tiller. "Set sail, Mr. Ramsey. Steer a heading of one-
fifteen degrees east-southeast."

"Aye, Captain. We'll not try for Australia, then?"

"Our best hope is the west coast of New Zealand."

"How far do you make it?"

"Six hundred miles," Scaggs answered as if a sandy
beach lay just over the horizon.

Jess Dorsett studied the tall woman with the golden
hair. She was sitting alone beside the forward mast. She

10

appeared not to notice the other female convicts, seldom conversing, choosing to remain aloof and quiet. She was, Dorsett decided, a woman of values.

Dorsett moved until he was at the imaginary line dividing the men from the women. The blond woman did not notice; her blue eyes were fixed on something only she could see in the distance.

"Looking for England?" he asked, smiling.

She turned and stared at him as if making up her mind whether to grace him with an answer. "You're the highwayman," was all she said.

"I was until my horse broke her leg and the Queen's men ran me down."

"And your name is Jess Dorsett." He was pleased that she knew who he was and wondered if she had inquired of him. "And you are . . . ?"

"Betsy Fletcher," she answered without hesitation.

"Betsy," Dorsett said with a flourish, "consider me your protector."

"I need no fancy highwayman," she said smartly. "I can fend for myself."

He motioned around the horde jammed on the raft. "You may well need a pair of strong hands before we see hard ground again."

Betsy Fletcher turned and pointed at some evil-looking clouds scudding in their direction before a freshening breeze. "Tell me, Mr. Dorsett, how are you going to protect me from that?"

The sea began to heap up uncomfortably, and the raft lurched and rolled as the waves began to sweep over the huddled mass of bodies. The storm was not half as strong as the typhoon that did in the *Gladiator,* but it soon became impossible to tell where the raft began and the sea left off. The waves rose ever higher as the whitecaps blew off their crests. Some tried to stand to get their heads above water, but the raft was pitching and rolling savagely. They fell back on the planking almost immediately.

The raft and its suffering passengers endured the storm through the night, pounded by the wash that constantly rolled over them. By the following morning the sea had begun to ease off, and the wind dwindled to a light southerly breeze.

When Scaggs was finally able to stand and appraise the total extent of the damage, he was shocked to find that not one keg of food or water had been spared from the violence of the sea.

"Any nearer to land, Captain?" asked Ramsey.

"I'm afraid not," Scaggs said gravely. "The storm drove us north and west. We're farther away from New Zealand than we were at this time two days ago."

"We won't last long in the Southern Hemisphere in the dead of summer without fresh water."

Scaggs gestured toward a pair of fins cutting the water fifty feet from the raft. "If we don't sight a boat within four days, Mr. Ramsey, I fear the sharks will have themselves a sumptuous banquet."

The sharks did not have long to wait. The second day after the storm, the bodies of those who succumbed from injuries sustained during the raging seas were slipped over the side and quickly disappeared in a disturbance of bloody foam.

The horror was only beginning. Dorsett was the first to have a premonition of the atrocities that the poor wretches on the raft would inflict upon themselves.

"They're up to something," he said to Betsy.

"Who are you talking about?" she asked through parched lips. She had covered her face with a tattered scarf, but her bare arms and her legs below the skirt were already burned and blistered from the sun.

"That scurvy lot of smugglers at the stern of the raft, led by the murderin' Welshman, Jake Huggins. He'd as soon slit your gullet as give you the time of day. I'll wager they're planning a mutiny."

Betsy looked at the bodies sprawled on the raft. "Why would they want to take command of this?"

"I mean to find out," said Dorsett as he began making his way over the convicts slouched about the damp planking, oblivious to everything around them while suffering from a burning thirst. He was one of the few who dared approach the conspirators, and he muscled his way through Huggins' henchmen. They ignored him as they muttered to themselves in low tones and cast fierce looks at Sheppard and his infantrymen.

"What brings you nosin' around, Dorsett?" grunted Huggins.

"I figured you could use a good man to help you take over the raft."

"You want to get in on the spoils and live a while longer, do you?"

"I've got nothing to lose by throwing in with you, Jake," Dorsett said with a tight smile. "When do we make our move?"

"One hour after dark. At my signal we attack the soldier boys and go for their muskets. Once we're armed we'll have no trouble with Scaggs and his crew."

Dorsett returned to Betsy's side but said nothing to her about the terror about to be unleashed by the convicts. He knew Huggins and his men were observing his every move, making certain he was not making a furtive effort to warn the *Gladiator*'s crew and the soldiers. His only opportunity would come with darkness, and he had to move before Huggins gave his signal to launch the horror. He lay as near to Betsy as the guard would allow and appeared to doze away the afternoon.

As soon as dusk covered the sea and the stars appeared, Dorsett left Betsy and snaked his way to within a few feet of First Officer Ramsey and hailed him in a hushed whisper.

"Ramsey, do not move or act as if you're listening to anyone."

"What is this?" Ramsey blurted under his breath. "What do you want?"

"Listen to me," Dorsett said softly. "Within the hour, the convicts, led by Jake Huggins, are going to attack the soldiers. If they are successful in killing them all, they will use their arms against you and your crew."

"Why should I believe the words of a common criminal?"

"You'll all be dead if you don't."

"I'll tell the captain," Ramsey said grudgingly.

"Just remind him it was Jess Dorsett who warned you."

Dorsett broke off and crawled back to Betsy. He removed his left boot, twisted off the sole and heel and removed a small knife with a four-inch blade. Then he sat back to wait.

A quarter-moon was beginning to rise over the horizon, giving the pitiful creatures on board the raft the look of ghostly wraiths, some of whom suddenly began rising to their feet and moving toward the prohibited area in the center.

"Kill the swine!" Huggins shouted, leaping forward and leading a surge of flesh toward the soldiers. Half out of their minds with thirst the mass of prisoners unleashed their hatred for authority and made a rush toward the middle of the raft from all sides.

A volley of musket fire cut holes in their ranks, and the unexpected resistance stunned them momentarily.

Ramsey had passed on Dorsett's alarm to Scaggs and Sheppard. The infantrymen, muskets loaded and bayonets fixed, waited along with Scaggs and his crew, who had been armed with the soldiers' sabers, the carpenter's hammers and hatchets, and any other weapon they could scrape up.

"Don't give 'em time to reload, boys!" Huggins roared. "Strike hard!"

The mass of maddened mutineers rushed forward again, met this time with thrusting bayonets and slashing sabers. Yet, nothing diminished their rage. They threw themselves against the cold steel, several of them grasping the sharpened blades in their bare hands.

The soldiers and sailors fought furiously. Every inch of the raft was occupied by men fighting savagely to kill each other. The bodies piled up, entangling the feet of combatants. Blood flowed on the deck planking, making it difficult to stand if not impossible to rise after falling.

Pierced by five saber wounds, Huggins staggered toward Dorsett, a large splintered board in an upraised hand. "Traitor!" he hissed.

Dorsett hunched and held the knife out in front of his body. "Step forward and die," he said calmly.

Infuriated, Huggins yelled back. "It is you who will feed the sharks, highwayman!" Then he put his head down and charged, swinging the board like a scythe.

At the instant Huggins lunged at him, Dorsett dropped to his hands and knees. Unable to check his momentum, the enraged Welshman stumbled over him and fell, crashing heavily to the deck. Before he could raise himself up, Dorsett had leaped on the immense back, reversed the knife in his hand and slashed Huggins' throat.

The bloody brawl raged on for another two hours. Scaggs and his seamen, Sheppard and his infantrymen, fought desperately, beating off every assault and then counterattacking. Again and again the mad rush was pushed back by the ever-thinning ranks of the defenders who desperately clung to the center of the raft. Sheppard went down, garroted by two convicts. Ramsey suffered severe contusions and Scaggs had two ribs broken.

By daylight the dead were seen sprawling grotesquely around on the raft. Ramsey made a rough count of the remaining survivors and was shocked to see that only 78 out of the 231 were still alive. In the senseless battle, 109 convicts had perished. Five of Sheppard's soldiers had vanished, presumably thrown overboard, and Ramsey counted 12 of the *Gladiator*'s crewmen dead or missing. It seemed inconceivable that so few could have subdued so many, but the convicts were not trained for combat as were Sheppard's infantrymen, or as physically toughened by hard work at sea as Scaggs' crew.

Ramsey came over and spoke to Dorsett. "The captain would like a word with you."

The highwayman accompanied the first officer to where Scaggs was lying, his back against the aft mast. Surgeon-Superintendent Gorman was binding up the captain's rib cage with a torn shirt. Before the dead were rolled into the sea, the ship's surgeon stripped the bodies of their clothes to use as bandages. Scaggs looked up at Dorsett, his face taut with pain.

"I want to thank you, Mr. Dorsett, for your timely warning. I daresay the honest people who are still left on this vessel owe their lives to you. When we reach New South Wales, I'll do my best to persuade the governor to commute your sentence."

"I'm grateful to you, Captain. I'm under your orders."

Scaggs stared at the small knife that was shoved into Dorsett's belt-sash. "Is that your only weapon?"

"Yes, sir. It performed admirably last night."

"Give him a spare saber," Scaggs said to Ramsey. "We're not through with those dogs yet."

"I agree," said Dorsett. "They'll not have the same fury without Jake Huggins to lead them, but they're too unhinged by thirst to give up. They'll try again after dark."

His words were prophetic. The convicts assaulted the defenders two hours after the sun set. The attack was not as fierce as the night before. Wraithlike figures reeled against each other, recklessly clubbing and slashing, the bodies of convicts, sailors and soldiers intermingling as they fell.

Fifty-two died that night. With the dawn, only twenty-five men and three women were left, out of the seventy-eight from the night before: sixteen convicts, including Jess Dorsett, Betsy Fletcher and two other women; two soldiers and ten of the *Gladiator*'s crew, including Captain Scaggs. First Officer Ramsey was among the dead. Surgeon-Superintendent Gorman was mortally wounded and passed on later that afternoon like a lamp that slowly runs out of oil. Dorsett had received a nasty gash in his right thigh, and Scaggs had suffered a broken collarbone to add to his broken ribs. Amazingly, Betsy had emerged with only minor bruises and cuts.

The convicts were thoroughly beaten; there wasn't one who didn't suffer from ugly wounds. The insane battle for the raft of the *Gladiator* was over.

By the tenth day of their grisly ordeal, another six had died. On day twelve they were down to eighteen. Those who could still move were in rags, their bodies covered with wounds from the massacre, faces disfigured by the burning sun, skin covered with sores from scraping against the constantly moving planking and immersion in saltwater. They were far beyond despondency, and their hollow eyes began to see visions. Two seamen swore they saw the *Gladiator,* dove off the raft and swam toward the imaginary ship until they went under.

Hallucinations conjured up every image from banquet

tables laden with food and drink, to populated cities or homes none had visited since childhood. Scaggs fancied he was sitting in front of a fireplace with his wife and children in his cottage overlooking the harbor at Aberdeen.

His navigational instruments having been lost over the side during the fighting, Scaggs had no idea of their position. He ordered his men to make an attempt at catching fish using twine and nails for hooks.

They had given up attempting to catch a meal when later that afternoon a large school of mullet passed under the raft. Before the school swam past, seven cigar-shaped bodies with forked tails were flopping on the waterlogged planks.

"God hasn't forsaken us," mumbled Scaggs, staring at the silvery fish. "Mullet usually inhabit shallow seas. I've never seen them in deep water."

"It's as though he sent them directly to us," murmured Betsy, her eyes wide at the sight of her first meal in nearly two weeks.

Another gift arrived with a rain squall that took nearly an hour to pass over and provided them with a catch of two gallons of water.

The air was stifling and the heat intolerable. The nights brought relief and cooler temperatures. But some of the raft's passengers could not endure the misery of one more day. Another five, four convicts and the last soldier, quietly slipped into the sea and perished quickly.

By the fifteenth day, only Scaggs, Dorsett, Betsy Fletcher, three sailors and four convicts, one a woman, were left alive. They were beyond caring. Death seemed unavoidable. The spark of self-preservation had all but gone out. The mullet was long gone, and the lack of water and the torrid heat made it impossible to hold out for more than another forty-eight hours before the raft would float empty of life.

Then an event occurred that diverted attention from the unspeakable horrors of the past two weeks. A large greenish-brown bird suddenly appeared out of the sky, circled the raft three times and then lit with a flutter on a yardarm of the forward mast.

"What kind of strange bird is that?" Betsy asked. Her tongue was so swollen her voice was like a whisper.

"It's a kea," Scaggs murmured. "One of my former officers kept one."

"Do they fly over the oceans like gulls?" asked Dorsett.

"No, they're a species of parrot that lives on New Zealand and the surrounding islands. I never heard of one flying over water unless . . ." Scaggs paused. "Unless it's another message from the Almighty." His eyes took on a distant look as he painfully rose to his feet and peered at the horizon. "Land!" he exclaimed with joy. "Land to the west of us."

Everyone turned their eyes westward and saw a large island with two low mountains, one on each end, and a forest of trees between. For a long moment no one spoke. Almost all the haggard survivors struggled to their knees and prayed to be delivered on the beckoning shore.

Another hour passed before Scaggs determined that the island was growing larger. "The current is pushing us toward it," he announced gleefully. "It's a miracle, a miracle. I know of no island on any chart in this part of the sea."

The unexpected promise of continued life revived what little strength they had left and inspired them to take action. Scaggs and his few seamen set a sail made from the tattered awning, while Dorsett and the remaining convicts tore up planks and feverishly used them as paddles. Then, as if to guide them, the parrot took wing and flew back toward the island.

Dorsett turned and looked toward the shore. A beautiful white sandy beach beckoned less than a quarter of a mile away. Then he heard a nearby shout.

The tall fin of a great white shark was circling the wreckage in search of new prey.

It wasn't fair, Dorsett screamed inside his mind. To have endured suffering beyond imagination only to have salvation snatched from their fingertips by the jaws of death was an injustice. He clutched Betsy tightly in his arms and watched with morbid terror as the fin stopped circling, headed in their direction and slowly slipped beneath the surface. His heart froze as he waited helplessly for the jagged teeth to snap shut on his body.

Then, without warning, the second miracle occurred.

The calm waters of the lagoon under them abruptly turned into a boiling cauldron. Then a great fountainlike gush burst into the air, followed by the great white shark. The murderous beast thrashed about wildly, its awesome jaws snapping like a vicious dog's at a huge sea serpent that was coiled around it.

Everyone clutching the floating wreckage stared dumbstruck at the life-and-death struggle between the two monsters of the deep.

From his position on his scrap of raft, Scaggs had a good seat to observe the struggle. The body of the enormous eel-like creature stretched from a blunt head to a long, tapering tail. Scaggs estimated the length of the body to be sixty to sixty-five feet, with the circumference of a large flour barrel. The mouth on the end of the head opened and closed spasmodically, revealing short fang-like teeth. The skin appeared smooth and was a dark brown on the upper surface of the body, almost black, while the belly was an ivory white. Scaggs had often heard tales of ships sighting serpentine sea monsters, but had laughed them off as the visions of sailors after drinking too much rum in port. Frozen in awe, he was not laughing now as he watched the once-feared white shark writhe violently in a futile attempt to shake off its deadly attacker.

Despite its tremendous strength and its frenzied convulsions, it could not shake the death grip. Revolving around in complete circles with great speed, shark and serpent writhed beneath the surface before reappearing in an explosion of spray that beat the water into froth again.

The serpent then began biting into the shark's gill slits. After another few minutes, the gargantuan combat faded, the shark's agonized struggle ceased and the two monsters slowly sank out of sight in the deepest part of the lagoon. The hunter had become the meal of another hunter.

Scaggs wasted no time after the epic battle in pulling the bedraggled convicts from the water onto the small piece of the raft that still hung together. Stunned by what they had witnessed, the pitifully few survivors finally reached the white sandy beach and staggered ashore, carried at last from their nightmare world to a Garden of Eden as yet unknown to European mariners.

A stream of pure water was soon found that ran from the volcanic mountain that rose above the southern end of the island. Five different varieties of tropical fruit grew in the forested area, and the lagoon was teeming with fish. Their perils over, only eight out of the original 231 who set out on the raft of the *Gladiator* lived to tell about the horrors of their fifteen days adrift in the sweltering emptiness of the sea.

According to Captain Scaggs, only he and two others were cast up on an uninhabited island, where they survived extreme hardships for over two years until they could build a vessel with tools and materials salvaged from the wreckage of another unfortunate ship that was driven ashore a year later with the loss of her entire crew. They constructed the hull of their craft from wood cut from the native trees they found growing on the island.

The tiny piece of land where the men existed for over two years cannot be precisely plotted since Scaggs lost all his navigational instruments at the time of the sinking. His best reckoning puts the uncharted island approximately 350 miles east-southeast of Sydney, an area other ships' captains claim is devoid of land.

Another twenty years were to pass before the true story of what happened on the raft of the *Gladiator*—and the event that took place on the island—would be told.

THE LEGACY

September 17, 1876
Aberdeen, Scotland

AFTER SCAGGS' RETURN TO ENGLAND AND A BRIEF REUNION with his wife and children, Carlisle & Dunhill offered him command of their newest and finest clipper ship, the *Culloden,* and sent him to engage in the China tea trade. After six more grueling voyages, in which he set two records, Bully Scaggs retired to his cottage in Aberdeen. Tough as the beams inside his ships, Scaggs took his last voyage at fifty-nine.

After the death of his beloved wife, Lucy, and with his children grown with families of their own, he maintained his love for the sea by sailing in and around the firths of Scotland in a small ketch he'd built with his own hands. It was after a brief voyage through bitterly cold weather, to visit his son and grandchildren at Peterhead, that he took sick.

A few days before he died, Scaggs sent for his longtime friend and former employer, Abner Carlisle. A respected shipping magnate, who built a sizable fortune with his partner, Alexander Dunhill, Carlisle was a leading resident of Aberdeen. Carlisle was a thin, wiry man, completely bald. He had kindly eyes and walked with a noticeable limp, caused by a fall off a horse when he was a young man.

25

He was shown into Scaggs' house by the captain's daughter, Jenny, whom Carlisle had known since she was born. She embraced him briefly and took him by the hand.

"Good of you to come, Abner. He's been asking for you every half hour."

She led Carlisle upstairs and through an open door into a bedroom with a large window that overlooked Aberdeen Harbor. "Father, Abner Carlisle is here."

An old man, ravaged by three decades of a hard life at sea, Scaggs lay unmoving on the bed. As bad as Scaggs looked, Carlisle couldn't help but marvel at the fire that still burned in those olive-gray eyes.

"I don't have much time for idle chatter," Scaggs said. "I asked you to come to hear my deathbed confession and do me a personal favor."

He paused for a moment, then went on.

"I lied about the *Gladiator*," he said.

"She sank in a typhoon," Carlisle said. "What was there to lie about?"

"She sank in a typhoon all right, but the passengers and crew didn't go down to the bottom with her."

Carlisle was silent for several moments, then he said carefully, "Charles Bully Scaggs, you're the most honest man I have ever known. Are you sure it isn't the sickness that's making you say crazy things?"

"Trust me now when I say I've lived a lie for twenty years in repayment of a debt."

Carlisle stared at him curiously. "What is it you wish to tell me?"

"A story I've told no one." Scaggs leaned back on his pillow and stared beyond Carlisle, far into the distance at something only he could see. "The story of the raft of the *Gladiator*."

* * *

Jenny returned half an hour later with tea. It was dusk, and she lit the oil lamps in the bedroom. "Father, you must try to eat something. I've made your favorite fish chowder."

"I've no appetite, Daughter."

"Abner must be starved, listening to you all afternoon. I'll wager he'll eat something."

"Give us another hour," ordered Scaggs. "Then make us eat what you will."

As soon as she was gone, Scaggs continued with the saga of the raft.

"When we finally got ashore there were eight of us left. Of the *Gladiator's* crew, only myself, Thomas Cochran, the ship's carpenter, and Alfred Reed, an able seaman, survived. Among the convicts there was Jess Dorsett, Betsy Fletcher, Marion Adams, George Pryor and John Winkleman. Eight out of the 231 souls who set sail from England."

"You'll have to excuse me, dear old friend," said Carlisle, "if I appear skeptical. Scores of men murdering each other on a raft in the middle of the ocean, then being saved from being devoured by a man-eating shark through the intervention of a sea serpent that kills the shark. An unbelievable tale to say the least."

"You are not listening to the ravings of a dying man," Scaggs assured him weakly. "The account is true, every word of it."

For the next half hour, Scaggs told of how they drank their fill in a stream with sweet and pleasant water that ran from one of the small volcanic mountains. He described the large turtles that were caught in the lagoon, thrown on their backs and butchered with Dorsett's knife, the only tool among them. Then using a hard stone found at the water's edge and the knife as flint, they built a fire and cooked the turtle meat. Five different kinds of fruit that Scaggs had never seen before were picked from trees in the forest. He recounted how the survivors passed the next few days gorging themselves until they regained their strength.

"After the calamity on the raft, the island must have seemed like paradise," said Carlisle.

"She was the most beautiful island I've seen in my many years at sea," Scaggs agreed. "A magnificent emerald on a sapphire sea, she was." He hesitated as if envisioning the jewel rising out of the Pacific. "We soon settled into an idyllic way of life. I designated those to be in charge of certain services and appointed times for fishing, the construction and repair of shelter, the harvesting of fruit and other edibles, and the maintenance of a constant fire for cooking as well as to signal any ship that might pass by. Tranquillity reigned on the island when John Winkleman married Marion Adams and Jess married Betsy."

"Married?" Carlisle snorted in righteous indignation. "How was that possible?"

"Have you forgotten, Abner?" Scaggs said with a grin cracking his thin lips. "As a ship's captain I was empowered to perform the ceremony."

"By not actually standing on the deck of your ship, I must say you stretched matters a bit."

"I have no regrets. We all lived in harmony until ship's carpenter Thomas Cochran and I sailed away."

"Why didn't the rest come with you?"

"Best they stayed on the island. I offered to plead for their release with the governor, but they didn't dare take the chance, and rightly so. As soon as they'd have landed in Australia, the penal constables would have grabbed the children and distributed them as orphans. Betsy gave birth to two boys in as many years as well as nursing Marion's child. Dorsett and Betsy were devoted to each other. They'd likely never have seen their boys and each other again. I promised them that as long as I lived they'd remain forgotten along with the lost souls of the *Gladiator*."

"Haven't you ever wondered how they made out?"

"No need to wonder," Scaggs replied slyly. "I know."

Carlisle's eyebrows raised. "I'd be grateful for an explanation."

"Four years after I departed, an American whaler sighted the island and stood in to fill her water casks. Jess and Betsy met the crew and traded fruits and fresh fish for cloth and cooking pots. They told the captain of the whaler that they were missionaries who were stranded on the island after their ship had been wrecked. Before long, other whalers began stopping by for water and food supplies. One of the ships traded Betsy seeds for hats she'd woven out of palms, and she and Jess began tilling several acres of arable land for vegetables."

"How do you know all this?"

"They began sending out letters with the whalers."

"They're still alive?" asked Carlisle, his interest aroused.

Scaggs' eyes saddened. "Jess died while fishing six years ago. A sudden squall capsized his boat. Betsy said it looked as if he struck his head and drowned. Her last letter, along with a packet, arrived only two days ago. You'll find it in the center drawer of my desk. She wrote that she was dying from some sort of disease of the stomach."

Carlisle rose and crossed the bedroom to a worn captain's desk that Scaggs had used on all his voyages after the *Gladiator* went down. He pulled a small packet wrapped in oilskin from the drawer and opened it. Inside he found a leather pouch and a folded letter. He returned to his chair, slipped on his reading glasses and began reading aloud.

My Dear Captain Scaggs,

I pray you are in good health. This will be my last letter to you as I have a malady of the stomach, or so the doctor aboard the whaling ship *Amie & Jason* tells me. So I will soon be joining my Jess.

I have a last request that I pray you will honor. In the first week of April of this year, my two sons and Marion's daughter, Mary, departed the island on board a whaler whose captain was sailing from here to Auckland for badly needed repairs to his hull after a brush with a coral reef. There, the children were to book passage on a ship bound for England and then eventually make their way to you in Aberdeen.

I have written to ask you, dearest friend, to take them under your roof upon their arrival and arrange for their education at the finest schools England has to offer. I would be eternally grateful, and I know Jess would share the same sentiments, rest his dear departed soul, if you will honor my request.

I have included my legacy for your services and whatever cost it takes to see them through school. They are very bright children and will be diligent in their studies.

With deepest respect I wish you a loving farewell.

Betsy Dorsett

One final thought. The serpent sends his regards.

Carlisle peered over his glasses. " 'The serpent sends his regards.' What nonsense is that?"

"The sea serpent who saved us from the great white shark," answered Scaggs. "Turned out he lived in the lagoon. I saw him with my own eyes on at least four other occasions during my time on the island."

Carlisle looked at his old friend as if he were drunk, then thought better of pursuing the matter. "She sent young children alone on a long voyage from New Zealand to England?"

"Not so young," said Scaggs. "The oldest must be going on nineteen."

"If they left the island the early part of April, they may come knocking on your door at any time."

"Providing they did not have to wait long in Auckland to find a stout ship that made a fast passage."

"You're in an impossible situation."

"What you really mean is, how can a dying man carry out an old friend's dying wish?"

"You're not going to die," said Carlisle, looking Scaggs in the eye.

"Oh yes I am," Scaggs said firmly. "You're a practical businessman, Abner. Nobody knows that better than me. That's why I asked to see you before I take my final voyage."

"You want me to take in Betsy's children."

"They can live in my house until you drop their anchor in the best educational institutions money can buy," Scaggs said.

"They'll need the proper clothes and private tutors to bring them up to proper learning levels. I hope you're not asking *me* to provide for total strangers."

Scaggs pointed to the leather pouch.

Carlisle held it up. "Is this what Betsy sent you to educate her children?"

Scaggs nodded slightly. "Open it."

Carlisle loosened the strings and poured the contents into his hand. He looked up at Scaggs incredulously. "Is this some sort of joke? These are nothing but ordinary stones."

"Trust me, Abner. They are not ordinary."

Carlisle held up one about the size of a prune in front of his spectacles and peered at it. The surface of the stone was smooth and its shape was octahedral, having eight sides. "This is nothing but some sort of crystal. It's absolutely worthless."

"Take the stones to Levi Strouser."

"The gem merchant?"

"Show the stones to him."

"Precious gems, they're not," said Carlisle firmly.

"Please . . ." Scaggs barely got the word out. The long conversation had tired him.

"As you wish, old friend." He pulled out his pocket watch and looked at the time. "I'll call on Strouser first thing in the morning and return to you with his appraisal."

"Thank you," Scaggs murmured. "The rest will take care of itself."

True to his word, Carlisle took the stones to Strouser & Sons the very next day.

Strouser laid a sheet of white paper on the desktop and poured the contents of the pouch in a pile in the center. He counted the stones. There were eighteen. He took his time and carefully scrutinized each one through his loupe, a small magnifier used by jewelers. Finally, he held up the largest and the smallest stones, one in each hand.

"If you will kindly be patient, Mr. Carlisle, I would like to conduct some tests on these two stones. I'll have one of my sons serve you a cup of tea."

"Yes, thank you. I don't mind waiting."

Nearly an hour passed before Strouser returned to the room with the two stones.

"May I ask where these stones came from?" Strouser asked.

"I cannot tell you the exact location," Carlisle answered honestly. "Why? Is there a value to the stones?"

"You do not know what they are?" Strouser asked in astonishment.

"I am not an expert in minerals. My business is shipping."

Strouser held out his hands over the stones like an ancient sorcerer. "Mr. Carlisle, these are diamonds! The finest uncut stones I have ever seen."

Carlisle covered his amazement nobly. "What do they weigh?"

"Well," Strouser began, "the smallest you have here weighs 60 carats in the rough." He paused to hold up the largest specimen. "This one weighs out at over 980 carats, making it the largest known uncut diamond in the world."

"What do you think they will be worth?" was Carlisle's question.

Strouser stared down at the ordinary-looking stones, visualizing them as sparkling crystals. "If these stones came from an unlimited source that can be easily exploited, the owners are about to launch an empire of extraordinary wealth."

"If you will forgive me for saying so, your appraisal sounds a bit fanciful."

Strouser looked across the desk at Carlisle and smiled. "Trust me when I say these stones, when cut and faceted, could sell in the neighborhood of one million pounds."*

"That much?" Carlisle blurted.

Strouser lifted the huge 980-carat stone to the light, holding it between his fingers as if it were the Holy Grail. When he spoke it was in a voice of adoring reverence. "Perhaps even more, much more."

---

*Approximately $7 million U.S. at that time, or close to $50 million on today's market.

PART I

DEATH FROM NOWHERE

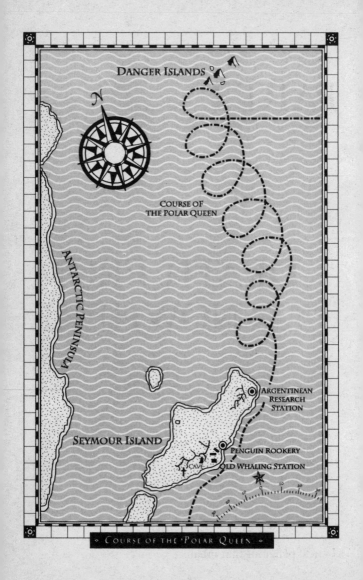

COURSE OF THE POLAR QUEEN

January 14, 2000
Seymour Island,
Antarctic Peninsula

1

THERE WAS A CURSE ABOUT THE ISLAND. A CURSE PROVEN by the graves of men who set foot on the forbidding shore, never to leave. Seymour Island made up the largest ice-free surface on or near the whole continent of Antarctica. It was a singularly ugly place, inhabited only by few varieties of lichen and a rookery of Adélie penguins.

The majority of the dead, buried in shallow pits pried from the rocks, came from a Norwegian Antarctic expedition after their ship was crushed in the ice in 1859. They survived two winters before their food supply ran out, finally dying off one by one from starvation. Lost for over a decade, their well-preserved bodies were not found until 1870, by the British while they were setting up a whaling station.

The restless ghosts of the explorers and sailors that roamed the forsaken ground could never have imagined that one day their resting place would be crawling with accountants, attorneys, plumbers, housewives and retired senior citizens who showed up on luxurious pleasure ships to gawk at the inscribed stones and ogle the comical penguins that inhabited a piece of the shoreline.

Perhaps, just perhaps, the island would lay its curse on these intruders too. . . .

The impatient passengers aboard the cruise ship *Polar Queen* saw nothing ominous about Seymour Island. Safe in the comfort of their floating palace, they felt only excitement at a new experience, especially since they were among the first wave of tourists ever to walk the shores of Seymour Island.

Many had traveled Europe and the Pacific, seen the usual exotic places travelers flock to around the world. Now they wanted something more, something different; a visit to a destination few had seen before, a remote place they could set foot on and brag about to friends and neighbors afterward.

As they clustered on the deck near the boarding ladder in happy anticipation of going ashore, aiming their telephoto lenses at the penguins, Maeve Fletcher walked among them, checking the bright orange insulated jackets passed out by the ship's cruise staff, along with life jackets for the short trip between the ship and shore.

Maeve was three years shy of thirty, with a master's degree in zoology. Energetic and in constant motion, she towered above the women and stood taller than most of the men. Her hair, braided in two long pigtails, was as yellow as a summery iris. She stared through eyes as blue as the deep sea, from a strong face with high cheekbones. Her lips always seemed parted in a warm smile, revealing a tiny gap in the center of her upper teeth. Tawny skin gave her a robust outdoorsy look.

This trip there were ninety-one paying passengers on board, and Maeve was one of four naturalists who were to conduct the excursions on shore. Maeve was scheduled to accompany the first party of twenty-two visitors to the island. She checked off the list of names as the excited travelers stepped down the boarding ladder to a waiting Zodiac, the versatile rubber float craft designed by Jacques Cousteau. As she was about to follow the last passenger, the ship's first officer, Trevor Haynes, stopped her on the boarding ladder.

"Tell your people not to be alarmed if they see the ship sailing off," he told her.

She turned and looked up the steps at him. "Where will you be going?"

"There is a storm brewing a hundred miles out. The captain doesn't want to risk exposing the passengers to any more rough water than necessary. Nor does he want to disappoint them by cutting short the shore excursions. He intends to steam twenty kilometers up the coast and drop off another group at the seal colony, then return in about two hours to pick you up and repeat the process."

"Putting twice the number ashore in half the time."

"That's the idea. That way, we can pack up and leave and be in the relatively calm waters of the Bransfield Strait before the storm strikes here. You have your portable communicator should you encounter a problem."

Maeve held up the small unit that was attached to her belt. "You'll be the first to know."

"Say hello to the penguins for me."

"I shall."

As the Zodiac skimmed over water that was as flat and reflective as a mirror, Maeve lectured her little band of intrepid tourists on the history behind their destination. "Seymour Island was first sighted by James Clark Ross in 1842. Forty Norwegian explorers, castaway when their ship was crushed in the ice, perished here in 1859. We'll visit the site where they lived until the end and then take a short walk to the hallowed ground where they are buried."

"Are those the buildings they lived in?" asked a lady who must have been pushing eighty, pointing to several structures in a small bay.

"No," answered Maeve. "What you see are what remains of an abandoned British whaling station. We'll visit it just before we take a short hike around that rocky point you see to the south, to the penguin rookery."

"Does anyone live on the island?" asked the same lady.

"The Argentineans have a research station on the northern tip of the island."

"How far away?"

"About thirty kilometers."

They could see the bottom clearly now, naked rock with no growth to be seen anywhere. Their shadow followed them about two fathoms down as they cruised through the bay.

Maeve felt a tinge of regret she couldn't quite understand as the yellow-and-white *Polar Queen* grew smaller in the distance. For a brief moment she experienced the apprehension the lost Norwegian explorers must have felt at seeing their only means of survival disappear. She quickly shook off any feelings of uneasiness and began leading her party across the gray moonscape to the cemetery.

She allotted them twenty minutes to pick their way among the tombstones, shooting rolls of film of the inscriptions. Then she herded them around a vast pile of giant bleached whale bones near the old station while describing the methods the whalers used to process the whales.

"After the danger and exhilaration of the chase and kill," she explained, "came the rotten job butchering the huge carcass and rendering the blubber into oil. 'Cutting in' and 'trying out,' as the old-timers called it."

Next came the antiquated huts and rendering building. The whaling station was still maintained and monitored on an annual basis by the British and was considered a museum of the past. Furnishings, cooking utensils in the kitchen, along with old books and worn magazines, were still there just as the whalers left them when they finally departed for home.

"Please do not disturb any of the artifacts," Maeve told the group. "Under international law nothing may be removed." She took a moment to count heads. Then she said, "Now I'll lead you into the caves dug by the whalers, where they stored the oil in huge casks before shipping it to England."

From a box left at the entrance to the caves by expedition leaders from previous cruises, she passed out flashlights. "Is there anyone who suffers from claustrophobia?"

One woman who looked to be in her late seventies raised her hand. "I'm afraid I don't want to go in there."

"Anyone else?"

The woman who asked all the questions nodded. "I can't stand cold, dark places."

"All right," said Maeve. "The two of you wait here. I'll conduct the rest a short distance to the whale-oil storage area. We won't be more than fifteen minutes."

She led the group through a long, curving tunnel carved by the whalers to a large storage cavern stacked with huge casks that had been assembled deep inside the rock and later left behind. After they entered she stopped and gestured at a massive rock at the entrance.

"The rock you see here was cut from inside the cavern and acts as a barrier against the cold and to keep competing whalers from pilfering surplus oil that remained after the station closed down for the winter. This rock weighs as much as an armored tank, but a child can move it, providing he or she knows its secret." She paused to step aside, placed her hand on a particular place on the upper side of the rock and easily pushed it to close the entrance. "An ingenious bit of engineering. The rock is delicately balanced on a shaft through its middle. Push in the wrong spot and it won't budge."

Everyone made jokes about the total darkness broken only by the flashlights as Maeve moved over to one of the great wooden casks. One had remained half full, and she held a small glass vial under a spigot and filled it with a small amount of oil. She passed the vial around, allowing the tourists to rub a few drops between their fingers.

"Amazingly, the cold has prevented the oil from spoiling, even after nearly a hundred and thirty years. It's still as fresh as the day it came from the cauldron and was poured into the cask—"

Maeve was abruptly cut off by the scream of an elderly woman who frantically clutched the sides of her head. Six other people followed suit, the women crying out, the men groaning.

Maeve ran from one to the other, stunned at the look of intense pain in their eyes. "What is it?" she shouted. "What's wrong? Can I help you?"

Then suddenly it was her turn. A daggerlike thrust of pain plunged into her brain, and her heart began to pound erratically. Instinctively her hands pressed her temples. Then she was struck by a tidal wave of dizziness rapidly followed by great nausea. She fought an overwhelming urge to vomit before losing all balance and falling down.

No one could understand what was happening. The air became heavy and hard to breathe. The beams of the flashlights took on an unearthly bluish glow. There was no vibration, no shaking of the earth, and yet dust began to swirl inside the cavern.

Everyone began to sag and fall to the ground. One moment people stared at death from an unknown source. Then inexplicably, an instant later, the excruciating agony and vertigo began to ease. As quickly as it had come on, it faded and disappeared.

Maeve felt exhausted to her bones. She leaned weakly against the cask of whale oil, eyes closed, vastly relieved at being free of pain.

No one found the voice to speak for nearly two minutes. Finally, a man, who was cradling his stunned wife in his arms, looked up at Maeve. "What was that?"

Maeve slowly shook her head. "I don't know," she answered dully.

With great effort she made the rounds, greatly cheered at finding everyone still alive. They all appeared to be recovering with no lingering effects. Maeve was thankful that none of the more elderly had suffered permanent damage, especially heart attacks.

"Please wait here and rest while I check the two ladies at the entrance of the tunnel and contact the ship." She swung open the massive door and walked through the portal until the beam of her flashlight vanished around a curve in the tunnel.

As soon as Maeve reached daylight again, she couldn't help wondering if it had all been a hallucination. The sea was still calm and blue. The sun had risen a little higher in a cloudless sky. And the two ladies who had preferred to remain in the open air were lying sprawled on their stomachs, each clutching at nearby rocks as if trying to keep from being torn away by some unseen force.

She bent down and tried to shake them awake but stiffened in horror when she saw the sightless eyes and the gaping mouths. They were dead.

Maeve ran down to the Zodiac, which was still sitting with its bow pulled onto the shoreline. The crewman who had brought them ashore was also lifeless, the same appalling expression on his face. In numbed shock, Maeve lifted her portable communicator and began transmitting. *"Polar Queen,* this is land expedition one.

We have an emergency. Please answer immediately. Over."

There was no reply.

She tried again and again to raise the ship. Her only response was silence. It was as if *Polar Queen* and her crew and passengers had never existed.

2

MAEVE CONTINUED HER FUTILE ATTEMPTS TO MAKE CONTACT every half hour until eleven o'clock in the evening. As the polar sun dipped toward the horizon, she stopped hailing on the ship's channel to conserve the transmitter's batteries. The portable radio's range was limited to ten kilometers, and no other ship or passing aircraft was within five hundred kilometers of picking up her calls for help. The nearest source of relief was the Argentinean research station on the other end of the island, but unless freak atmospheric conditions stretched her signals, they would not have received them either. In frustration, she gave up and planned to try again later.

Where was the ship and crew? she wondered constantly. Was it possible they had encountered the same murderous phenomenon and suffered harm? She did not wish to dwell on pessimistic thoughts. For the time being she and her party were secure. But without food or bedding for warmth, she did not see how they could hold out very long. A few days at most. The ages of her excursion group were on the high side. The youngest couple were in their late sixties, while the rest ranged through the seventies to the oldest, a woman of eighty-three.

Maeve finally gave up hope of seeing the ship anytime soon and began to plan for the worst by making preparations for the excursion members to bed down for the next ten hours. She decided her group would stand a better chance of surviving the bitter cold and life-threatening wind by remaining in the cavern.

Four of the younger men helped her pull the Zodiac farther ashore and tie it down to prevent it from being blown inland by the increasing winds. Next they sealed all but a small opening of the tunnel entrance with rocks to minimize any frigid gusts that might sweep through into the cavern. She did not want to seal them off completely from the outside by closing the rock door. Then she gathered everyone around and ordered them to huddle together for mutual warmth.

There was nothing left to do, and the hours of waiting for rescue seemed like an eternity. They tried to sleep but found it all but impossible. The numbing cold slowly began to penetrate their clothing, and the wind outside turned into a gale that found its way through the air hole in the stone barrier they'd erected at the tunnel entrance.

Only one or two complained. Most bore the ordeal stoically. Some were actually excited at experiencing a real adventure. Two of the Aussie husbands, big men who had made their fortune as partners in a construction firm, teased their wives and cracked sarcastic jokes to keep everyone's spirits up. They seemed as unconcerned as if they were waiting to board a plane. They were all good people in their twilight years, Maeve thought. It would be a shame, no, a crime, if they were to all die in that icy hellhole.

She lay there, staring at the fog that formed in the cavern from the heavy concentrated breathing, and tried to picture her sons, twins, now only six years old, watched over by friends, while she earned badly needed money with the cruise line. What would become of them if she died? She prayed that her father would never get his hands on them. People's lives mattered little to him. Nor was money a driving force. He considered it merely a tool. Power to manipulate, that was his passion. Maeve's two sisters shared their father's callousness toward others. Fortunately, she took after her mother, a gentle lady who was driven to suicide by her cold and abusive husband when Maeve was twelve.

After the tragedy, Maeve never considered herself part of the family. None of them had forgiven her for leaving the fold and striking out on her own under a new name with nothing but the clothes on her back. It was a decision she had never regretted.

She awakened, listening for a sound, or rather the lack of it. The wind was no longer whistling into the tunnel from outside. The storm was still brewing, but there was a temporary break in the frigid wind. She returned and roused two of the men.

"I need you to accompany me to the penguin rookery," she told them. "They're not hard to capture. I'm breaking the law, but if we are to stay healthy until the ship returns, we must put nourishment in our stomachs."

They made for the rookery, which was about two kilometers around the point encircling the north part of the bay. Though the wind had died, the sleet made their way miserable. They could hardly see more than three meters in front of them.

The wind howled, biting into their exposed faces. The thought of them all trekking to the Argentinean research station crossed Maeve's mind. But she quickly dismissed it. Few would survive the thirty-kilometer journey through the storm. Better than half the aged tourists would quickly perish along the way. Maeve had to consider all prospects, the feasible and the impractical. She might make it. She was young and strong. But she could not bring herself to desert the people who were depending on her. Sending the men who trudged beside her was a possibility. The nagging problem as she saw it was what would they find when they arrived?

The sleet had slackened, and their vision increased to nearly fifty meters. Overhead, the sun appeared as a dim orange ball with a halo of varied colors like a round prism. They rounded the spur of rock encompassing the bay and curved back to the shoreline containing the penguin rookery. Maeve did not relish the thought of killing penguins even as a means to stay alive. They were such tame and friendly creatures.

As she and the Australian men walked closer, it struck Maeve as odd that none of the birds stood on their little feet, tail feathers extended as props to keep from falling over backward. They were scattered all about, most lying on their backs as if they had toppled over.

"Something's not right," she said. "None are standing."

Maeve ran to the edge of the rookery and looked down at the penguins lying on the outer edge. She was struck by the absence of sound. None moved nor showed interest in her approach. She knelt and studied one. It lay limp on the ground, eyes staring sightless at her. Her face was stricken as she looked at the thousands of birds that showed no sign of life. She stared at two leopard seals, the natural predator of penguins, whose bodies washed back and forth in the small surge along the rock-strewn beach.

"They're all dead," she muttered in shock. This can't be real, she thought wildly. She stood absolutely still. She could not see what caused the mass death, but she could feel it. The crazy idea that every living thing in the rest of the world had died from the mysterious malady suddenly struck her mind. Is it possible we're the only ones left alive on a dead planet? she wondered in near panic.

One of the men bent over and picked up a penguin. "Saves us the trouble of having to slaughter them."

"Leave them be!" Maeve shouted at him.

"Why?" the man replied indignantly. "We've all got to eat."

"We don't know what killed them. They might have died from some sort of plague."

The other man nodded. "The little lady knows what she's talking about. Whatever disease killed these birds could do us in too. I don't know about you, but I don't aim to be responsible for my wife's death."

"But it wasn't a disease," the other man argued. "Not what killed those little old ladies and that sailor lad. It was more like some fluke of nature."

Maeve stood her ground. "I refuse to gamble with lives. *Polar Queen* will be back. We haven't been forgotten."

"If the captain is trying to give us a good scare, he's doing a fine job of it."

Maeve was in no mood to argue. She turned her back on the killing ground and set off toward the storage cavern. The two men followed, their eyes searching over a menacing sea for something that wasn't there.

3

WITHOUT ANY SIGN OF THE ARRIVAL OF THE *POLAR QUEEN*, the once-cheerful excursion that came ashore to experience the wondrous isolation of the Antarctic had become a nightmare for the vacation travelers. And to add to Maeve's desperation, the batteries of her portable communicator had finally gone dead.

Anytime now, Maeve knew she could expect the older members of the party to succumb to the harsh conditions inside the cave.

At first they joked and told stories, treating their ordeal as merely a bonus adventure. They sang songs, mostly "Waltzing Matilda," and attempted word games. But soon lethargy set in, and they became quiet and unresponsive. Bravely, they accepted their suffering without protest.

Now, hunger overcame any fear of diseased meat, and Maeve stopped a mutiny by finally relenting and sending the men out to bring in several dead penguins. One of the men was an avid hunter. He produced a Swiss army knife and expertly skinned and butchered the meat. By filling their bellies with protein and fat they would add fuel to maintain their body heat.

Outside, the storm went from bad to worse and it

began to snow, a rare occurrence on the peninsula during summer. Hope of a chance discovery was destroyed as the storm mounted in intensity. Four of the elderly were near death from exposure, and Maeve suffered bleak discouragement as all control began to slip through her frozen fingers. She blamed herself for the three that were already dead, and it affected her badly.

Maeve knew she must see the terrible trial through to its final outcome, but she didn't think she had the strength to continue carrying twenty lives on her shoulders. She felt exhausted and didn't want to struggle anymore. Dimly, through her listlessness, she heard a strange sound unlike the cry of the wind. It came to her ears as though something were pounding the air. Then it faded. Only her imagination, she told herself. It was probably nothing but the wind changing direction and making a different howl through the air vent at the tunnel entrance.

Then she heard it again briefly before it died. She struggled to her feet and stumbled through the tunnel. A snowdrift had built up against the wind barrier and nearly filled the small opening. She removed several rocks to widen a passage and crawled outside into an icy world of wind and snow.

Something seemed to be moving out there, a vague shape with no substance and yet darker than the opaque veil that fell from the sky.

She took a step and pitched forward. For a long moment she thought of just lying there and going to sleep. The urge to give it all up was overwhelming. But the spark of life refused to diminish and blink out. She lifted herself to her knees and stared through the wavering light. She caught something moving toward her, and then a gust obliterated it. A few moments later it reappeared, but closer this time. Then her heart surged.

It was the figure of a man covered in ice and snow. She

51

waved excitedly and called to him. He paused as if listening, then turned and began walking away.

This time she screamed. The figure turned and stared through the drifting snow in her direction. She waved both arms frantically. He waved back and began jogging toward her.

"Please don't let him be a mirage or a delusion," she begged the heavens.

And then he was kneeling in the snow beside her, cradling her shoulders in arms that felt like the biggest and strongest she had ever known. "Oh, thank God. I never gave up hoping you'd come."

He was a tall man, wearing a turquoise parka with the letters NUMA stitched over the left breast, and a ski mask with goggles. He removed the goggles and stared at her through a pair of incredible opaline green eyes that betrayed a mixture of surprise and puzzlement. His deeply tanned face seemed oddly out of place in the Antarctic.

"What in the world are you doing here?" he asked in a husky voice tinged with concern.

"I have twenty people back there in a cavern. We were on a shore excursion. Our cruise ship sailed off and never returned."

He looked at her in disbelief. "You were abandoned?"

She nodded and stared fearfully into the storm. "Did a worldwide catastrophe occur?"

His eyes narrowed at the question. "Not that I'm aware of. Why do you ask?"

"Three people in my party died under mysterious circumstances. And an entire rookery of penguins just north of the bay has been exterminated down to the last bird."

If the stranger was surprised at the tragic news, he hid it well. He helped Maeve to her feet. "I'd better get you out of this blowing snow."

"You're American," she said, shivering from the cold.

"And you're Australian."

"It's that obvious?" Maeve asked.

"You pronounce *a* like *i.*"

She held out a gloved hand. "You don't know how glad I am to see you, Mr. . . . ?"

"My name is Dirk Pitt."

"Maeve Fletcher."

He ignored her objections, picked her up and began carrying her, following her footprints in the snow toward the tunnel. "I suggest we carry on our conversation out of the cold. You say there are twenty others?"

"That are still alive."

Once inside the tunnel he set her on her feet and pulled off his ski mask. His head was covered by a thick mass of unruly black hair. His green eyes peered from beneath heavy dark eyebrows, and his face was craggy and weathered from long hours in the open but handsome in a rugged sort of way.

A minute later, Pitt was greeted by the tourists like a hometown football hero who had led the team to a big victory. Seeing a stranger suddenly appear in their midst had the same impact as winning a lottery. He marveled that they were all in reasonably fit shape, considering their terrible ordeal. The old women all embraced and kissed him like a son while the men slapped his back until it was sore. Everybody was talking and shouting questions at once. Maeve introduced him and related how they met up in the storm.

"Where did you drop from, mate?" they all wanted to know.

"A research vessel from NUMA—the National Underwater & Marine Agency. We're on an expedition trying to discover why seals and dolphins have been disappearing in these waters at an astonishing rate. We were flying over Seymour Island in a helicopter when the

53

snow closed in on us, so we thought it best to land until it blew over."

"There're more of you?"

"A pilot and a biologist who remained on board. I spotted what looked like a piece of a Zodiac protruding from the snow. I wondered why such a craft would be resting on an uninhabited part of the island and walked over to investigate. That's when I heard Miss Fletcher shouting at me."

"Good thing you decided to take a walk when you did," said the eighty-three-year-old great-grandmother to Maeve.

"I thought I heard a strange noise outside in the storm. I know now that it was the sound of his helicopter coming in to land," Maeve said.

"An incredible piece of luck we stumbled into each other in the middle of a blizzard," said Pitt. "I didn't believe I was hearing a woman's scream. I was sure it was a quirk of the wind until I saw you waving through a blanket of snow."

"Where is your research ship?" Maeve asked.

"About forty kilometers northeast of here."

"Did you by chance pass our ship, *Polar Queen?*"

Pitt shook his head. "We haven't seen another ship for over a week."

"Any radio contact?" asked Maeve. "A distress call, perhaps?"

"We talked to a ship supplying the British station at Halley Bay, but have heard nothing from a cruise ship."

"She couldn't have vanished into thin air," said one of the men in bewilderment. "Not along with the entire crew and our fellow passengers."

"We'll solve the mystery as soon as we can transport all you people to our research vessel. I can only squeeze five or six of you at a time into the helicopter, so we'll have to make several trips," explained Pitt. "Because we set down a good three hundred meters away, I'll return to the craft and fly it closer to the entrance to your cave so you won't have to suffer the discomfort of trekking through the snow."

"Nothing like curbside service," Maeve said, feeling as if she had been reborn. "May I go with you?"

"Feel up to it?"

She nodded. "I think everyone will be glad to not have me ordering them around for a little while."

Al Giordino sat in the pilot's seat of the turquoise NUMA helicopter and worked on a crossword puzzle. No taller than a floor lamp, he had a body as solid as a barrel on two legs, with a pair of construction derricks for arms. His ebony eyes occasionally glanced into the snow glare through the cockpit windshield, then seeing no sign of Pitt, they refocused on the puzzle.

A close friend of Pitt's since elementary school, when they had gotten into a fistfight, they had played on the same high school football team, Giordino as a tackle, Pitt as quarterback. They had been inseparable during their years together in the Air Force before volunteering for an assignment to help launch the National Underwater & Marine Agency, a temporary assignment that had lasted the better part of fourteen years.

"What's a six-letter word for fuzzballed goondorpher that eats stinkweed?" he asked the man sitting behind him in the cargo bay of the aircraft, which was packed with laboratory testing equipment. The marine biologist from NUMA looked up from a specimen he'd collected earlier and raised his brows quizzically.

"There is no such beast as a fuzzballed goondorpher."

"You sure? It says so right here."

After three months at sea together, Roy Van Fleet had

55

become too smart to fall for Giordino's con jobs. "On second thought, it's a flying sloth from Mongolia. See if 'slobbo' fits."

Realizing he had lost his easy mark, Giordino looked up from the puzzle again and stared into the falling snow. "Dirk should have been back by now."

"How long has he been gone?" asked Van Fleet.

"About forty-five minutes."

Giordino screwed up his eyes as a pair of vague shapes took form in the distance. "I think he's coming in now." Then he added, "There must have been funny dust in that cheese sandwich I just ate. I'd swear he's got someone with him."

"Not a chance. There isn't another soul within thirty kilometers."

"Come see for yourself."

By the time Van Fleet had capped his specimen jar and placed it in a wooden crate, Pitt had thrown open the entry hatch and helped Maeve Fletcher climb inside.

She pushed back the hood on her orange jacket, fluffed out her long golden hair and smiled brightly. "Greetings, gentlemen. You don't know how happy I am to see you."

Van Fleet's face registered total incomprehension. Giordino, on the other hand, simply sighed in resignation. "Who else," Giordino asked, "but Dirk Pitt could tramp off into a blizzard on an uninhabited backwater island in the Antarctic and discover a beautiful girl?"

4

LESS THAN AN HOUR AFTER PITT ALERTED THE NUMA research vessel *Ice Hunter,* Captain Paul Dempsey braved an icy breeze and watched as Giordino hovered the helicopter above the ship's landing pad. Except for the ship's cook busily preparing hot meals in the galley, and the chief engineer, who remained below, the entire crew, including lab technicians and scientists, had turned out to greet the first group of cold and hungry tourists to be airlifted from Seymour Island.

Captain Dempsey had grown up on a ranch in the Beartooth Mountains astride the Wyoming-Montana border. He ran away to sea after graduating from high school and worked the fishing boats out of Kodiak, Alaska. He fell in love with the icy seas above the Arctic Circle and eventually passed the examination to become captain of an ice-breaking salvage tug. No matter how high the seas or how strong the wind, Dempsey never hesitated to take on the worst storms the Gulf of Alaska could throw at him after he'd received a call from a ship in distress. During the next fifteen years, his daring rescues of innumerable fishing boats, six coastal freighters, two oil tankers and a Navy destroyer created a legend that resulted in a bronze statue beside the dock at

Seward, a source of great embarrassment to him. Forced into retirement when the oceangoing salvage company became debt ridden, he accepted an offer from the chief director of NUMA, Admiral James Sandecker, to become captain of the agency's polar research ship, *Ice Hunter*.

Dempsey's trademark, a chipped briar pipe, jutted from one corner of his mouth. He was broad shouldered and thick waisted, and he presented a distinguished appearance. Gray haired, clean shaven, a man given to telling good sea stories, Dempsey might have been taken for a jovial captain of a cruise ship.

He stepped forward as the wheels of the chopper settled onto the deck. Beside him stood the ship's physician, Dr. Mose Greenberg. Tall and slender, he wore his dark brown hair in a ponytail. His blue-green eyes twinkled.

Dr. Greenberg, along with four crewmen bearing stretchers for any of the elderly passengers who found it difficult to walk on their own, ducked under the revolving rotor blades and opened the rear cargo door. Dempsey moved toward the cockpit and motioned to Giordino to open the side window.

"Is Pitt with you?" asked Dempsey loudly above the swoosh of the blades.

Giordino shook his head. "He and Van Fleet stayed behind to examine a pack of dead penguins."

"How many of the cruise ship's passengers were you able to carry?"

"We squeezed in six of the oldest ladies who had suffered the most. Four more trips ought to do it. Three to transport the remaining tourists and one to bring out Pitt, Van Fleet, the guide and the three dead bodies."

Dempsey motioned into the miserable mixture of snow and sleet. "Can you find your way back in this soup?"

"I plan to beam in on Pitt's portable communicator."

"How bad off are these people?"

"Better than you might expect for senior citizens who've suffered three days and nights in a frigid cave. Pitt said to tell Dr. Greenberg that pneumonia will be his main worry. The bitter cold has sapped the older folk's energy, and in their weakened condition their resistance is real low."

Dempsey tucked a blanket around the eighty-three-year-old woman, who was being lifted to the deck on a stretcher. "Welcome aboard," he said with a warm smile. "We have hot soup and coffee and a soft bed waiting for you in our officers' quarters."

"If it's all the same to you," she said sweetly, "I'd prefer tea."

"Your wish is my command, dear lady," Dempsey said gallantly. "Tea it is."

"Bless you, Captain," she replied, squeezing his hand.

The gale had slackened considerably by the time Pitt, along with Maeve Fletcher and Van Fleet, reached the penguin rookery. The storm had carried the carcasses of those nearest the shoreline out to sea. But by Pitt's best calculation a good forty thousand of the dead birds still lay scattered amid the small stones and rocks, like black-and-white gunnysacks filled with wet grain.

Giant petrels, the vultures of the sea, began arriving to feast upon the dead penguins. Majestic as they soared gracefully through the air, they were merciless scavengers of meat from any source.

"Not exactly a sight I care to remember," said Pitt.

Van Fleet was stunned. He turned to Maeve, his eyes unbelieving. "Now that I see the tragedy with my own eyes I find it hard to accept so many of the poor creatures dying within such a concentrated space in the same time period."

"Whatever the phenomenon," said Maeve, "I'm certain it also caused the death of my two passengers and the ship's crewman who brought us ashore."

Van Fleet knelt and studied one of the penguins. "No indication of injury, no obvious signs of disease or poison. The body appears fat and healthy."

Maeve leaned over his shoulder. "The only nonconformity that I found was the slight protrusion of the eyes."

"Yes, I see what you mean. The eyeballs seem half again as large."

Pitt looked at Maeve thoughtfully. "When I was carrying you to the cave, you said the three who died did so under mysterious circumstances."

She nodded. "Some strange force assaulted our senses, unseen and nonphysical. I have no idea what it was. But I can tell you that for at least a full five minutes it felt like our brains were going to explode. The pain was excruciating."

"From the bodies you showed me," said Van Fleet, "the cause of death appears to be cardiac arrest."

"Any connection with the huge school of dolphins we found out in the Weddell Sea or the pod of seals washed up just across the channel on Vega Island, all deader than petrified wood?" Pitt asked Van Fleet.

The marine biologist shrugged. "Too early to tell without further study. There does, however, appear to be a definite link."

"Dolphins, seals, birds, and humans," Pitt said softly. "They're all vulnerable to this scourge."

Van Fleet nodded solemnly. "Not to mention the vast numbers of squid and sea turtles that have washed ashore throughout the Pacific and the millions of dead fish found floating off Peru and Ecuador in the past two months."

Van Fleet got to his feet. He appeared badly shaken.

"If we don't determine whether the cause is from natural disturbances or human intervention of some kind, and do it damned quick, we may be looking at oceans devoid of all life."

"Not just oceans. You're forgetting this thing also kills on land," Maeve reminded him.

For a long minute no one said a word, each trying to comprehend the potential catastrophe that lay somewhere in and beyond the sea. Finally, Pitt broke the silence.

"It would appear," he said, a pensive look on his craggy face, "that we have our work cut out for us."

5

PITT STUDIED THE SCREEN OF A LARGE MONITOR THAT
displayed a computer-enhanced satellite image of the
Antarctic Peninsula and the surrounding islands. He
leaned back, rested his eyes a moment and then stared
through the tinted glass on the navigation bridge of *Ice
Hunter* as the sun broke through the clouds. The time
was eleven o'clock on a summer's evening in the Southern Hemisphere, and daylight remained almost constant.

The passengers from *Polar Queen* had been fed and
bedded down in comfortable quarters provided by the
crew and scientists, who doubled up. Doc Greenberg
examined each and every one and found no permanent
damage or trauma. He was also relieved to find only a
few cases of mild colds but no evidence of pneumonia.
In the ship's biolaboratory, two decks above the ship's
hospital, Van Fleet, assisted by Maeve Fletcher, was
performing examinations of the penguins and seals they
had airlifted from Seymour Island in the helicopter.

Pitt ran his eyes over the huge twin bows of the *Ice
Hunter*. She was not your garden-variety research ship
but one of a kind, the first scientific vessel entirely
computer designed by marine engineers working with

input from oceanographers. She rode high on parallel hulls that contained her big engines and auxiliary machinery. Her space-age rounded superstructure abounded with technical sophistication and futuristic innovations. She was sleek and almost fragile looking, but that was a deception. She was born to ride smooth in choppy waves and weather the roughest sea. Her radically designed triangular hulls could cut through and crush an ice floe four meters thick.

Admiral James Sandecker, the feisty director of the National Underwater & Marine Agency, followed her construction from the first computerized design drawing to her maiden voyage around Greenland. He took great pride in every centimeter of her gleaming white superstructure and turquoise hulls. Sandecker was a master of obtaining funds from Congress, and nothing had been spared in *Ice Hunter*'s construction nor her state-of-the-art equipment. She was without argument the finest polar research ship ever built.

Pitt turned and refocused his attention on the image beamed down from the satellite.

He felt almost no exhaustion. It had been a long and tiring day, but one filled with every emotion, happiness and satisfaction at having saved the lives of over twenty people and sorrow at seeing so many of nature's creatures lying dead almost as far as the eye could see. This was a catastrophe beyond comprehension. Something sinister and menacing was out there. A hideous presence that defied logic.

His thoughts were interrupted by the appearance of Giordino and Captain Dempsey as they stepped out of the elevator that ran from the observation wing above the navigation bridge down through fifteen decks to the engine room.

"Any glimpse of *Polar Queen* from the satellite cameras?" asked Dempsey.

"Nothing I can positively identify," Pitt replied. "The snow is blurring all imaging."

"What about radio contact?"

Pitt shook his head. "It's as though the ship were carried away by aliens from space. The communications room can't raise a response. And while we're on the subject, the radio at the Argentinean research station has also gone dead."

"Whatever disaster struck the ship and the station," said Dempsey, "must have come on so fast none of the poor devils could get off a distress call."

"Have Van Fleet and Fletcher uncovered any clues leading to the cause of the deaths?" asked Pitt.

"Their preliminary examination shows that the arteries ruptured at the base of the creatures' skulls, causing hemorrhaging. Beyond that, I can tell you nothing."

"Looks like we have a thread leading from a mystery to an enigma to a dilemma to a puzzle with no solution in sight," Pitt said philosophically.

"If *Polar Queen* isn't floating nearby or sitting on the bottom of the Weddell Sea," Giordino said thoughtfully, "we might be looking at a hijacking."

"Not a likely scenario," Pitt said evenly. "I can't think of one solid reason why terrorists would hijack a cruise ship in the Antarctic."

"So what's your guess?"

"I believe she's either drifting or steaming in circles within two hundred kilometers of us," Pitt said. "Al and I will conduct a search for the second group from the air," Pitt said, contemplating the image on the monitor. "If we can't find any sign of their presence, we'll push on and check on the people manning the Argentinean research station. For all we know they could be dead too."

6

PITT AND GIORDINO TOOK OFF AT FOUR O'CLOCK IN THE morning, when most of the crew of *Ice Hunter* were still sleeping. The weather had returned to milder temperatures, calm seas and crystal-clear blue skies, with a light five-knot wind out of the southwest. With Pitt at the controls, they headed toward the old whaling station before swinging north in search of the second group of excursionists from *Polar Queen*.

Pitt leveled out at fifty meters and flew above the waterline, staring out the windscreen for any sign of the excursionists' landing site. Giordino gazed out his side window, scanning the open-water pack ice for any glimpse of *Polar Queen*, occasionally making a mark on a folded chart that lay across his lap. He checked the airspeed against his watch. "Twenty kilometers from the whaling station, and no sign of passengers from the cruise ship."

Pitt nodded in agreement. "Certainly nothing I can see that resembles a human."

"Maeve Fletcher said they were supposed to put the second party ashore at a seal colony."

"The seals are there all right," Pitt said, gesturing below. "Must be over eight hundred of them, all dead."

Giordino raised up in his seat and peered out the port window as Pitt banked the helicopter in a gentle descending turn to give him a better view. The yellow-brown bodies of big elephant seals packed the shoreline for nearly a kilometer. From fifty meters in the air, they looked like they were sleeping, but a sharp look soon revealed that not one moved.

"It doesn't look like the second excursion group left the ship," said Giordino.

There was nothing more to see, so Pitt swung the aircraft back on a course over the surf line. "Next stop, the Argentinean research station."

"It should be coming into view any minute now."

"I'm not looking forward to what we might find," said Pitt uneasily.

"Look on the bright side." Giordino smiled tightly. "Maybe everybody decided to pack it up and go home."

"Wishful thinking on your part," Pitt replied. "The station is highly important for its work in atmospheric sciences. It's one of five permanently occupied survey stations that measure the behavior and fluctuations of the Antarctic ozone hole."

"What's the latest news on the ozone layer?"

"Weakening badly in both Northern and Southern Hemispheres," Pitt answered seriously. "The plant and animal life in those regions received the most harmful dose of ultraviolet radiation ever recorded."

"Which means we'll have to pile on the suntan lotion," Giordino said sarcastically.

"That's the least of the problem," said Pitt. "Small overdoses of ultraviolet radiation badly damage every agricultural product from potatoes to peaches. If the ozone values drop a few more percentage points, there will be a disastrous loss of food crops around the world—"

"There!" Giordino abruptly cut in and pointed. They

were coming over a shoulder of rock that sloped toward the sea. "Looks more like a frontier town than a scientific base."

The Argentinean research and survey station was a complex of ten buildings, constructed with solid steel portal frames that supported dome roofs. The hollow walls had been thickly filled with insulation against the wind and frigid cold. The antenna array for gathering scientific data on the atmosphere festooned the domed roofs like the leafless branches of trees in winter. Giordino tried one last time to get somebody on the radio while Pitt circled the buildings.

He settled the helicopter neatly beside the largest of the six buildings, the rotor blades whipping the snow into a shower of ice crystals. The place looked eerily deserted. The blanket of white gave it a ghostly look indeed, thought Pitt.

"We'd better take along the shovels stored in the cargo bay," he said. "It looks like we're going to have to dig our way in."

They exited the aircraft and trudged through snow up to their thighs until they reached the entrance to the central building. About two meters of snow had drifted against the door. Twenty minutes later they had removed enough to pull the door half ajar.

Giordino gave a slight bow and smiled grimly. "After you."

This was an old routine they had practiced many times. Pitt led the way while Giordino covered any unexpected movement from the flanks and rear. One behind the other they stepped into a short tunnel ending at an interior door that acted as an additional cold barrier. Once through the inside door, they continued on down a long corridor that opened into a combination recreation and dining room.

They did not have to go far to discover their first resident.

The odd thing about him was that he didn't look like he was dead. He knelt on the floor, clutching the top of a table, staring open-eyed at Pitt and Giordino as if he had been expecting them.

The frightening part about him, the part that made the nape of Pitt's neck tingle, was the expression of abject fear and agony on the face that was frozen by the cold into a mask of white marble. The eyes bulged, and the mouth was oddly twisted open as if in a final scream. Pitt could tell this man was not stiffened by rigor mortis; he was frozen solid.

Giordino stepped around a serving counter and entered the kitchen. He returned within thirty seconds. "There are two more in there."

"Worst fears confirmed," said Pitt heavily. "Had just one of the station's people survived, he'd have maintained the auxiliary motors to run the generators for electrical heat and power. That's what we've got to do now."

Pitt turned to Giordino. "Find the generating room, fuel the auxiliary motors, restart them and turn on the electrical power. Then head for the communications center and report to Dempsey while I check out the rest of the station."

Pitt found the rest of the Argentinean scientists where they had died. Several had fallen in the lab and instrument center, three grouped around a spectrophotometer that was used to measure the ozone. Pitt counted sixteen corpses in all, four of them women, sprawled in various compartments about the station.

Their bodies were fixed in odd, unnatural positions. None lay on the floor as if they had simply fallen. Most looked as if they had suddenly lost their balance and were desperately clinging to something to keep upright.

As he walked in deep contemplation toward the communications room, a theory began unfolding in his mind. His thoughts were rudely interrupted when he entered and was greeted by a cadaver perched on a desk.

"How did *he* get there?" Pitt asked calmly.

"I put him there," Giordino said matter-of-factly without looking up from the radio console. "He was sitting on the only chair in the room and I figured I needed it worse than he did."

"He makes a total of seventeen."

"The toll keeps adding up."

"You get through to Dempsey?"

"He's standing by. Do you want to talk to him?"

Pitt leaned over Giordino and spoke into the satellite telephone that linked him with almost any point of the globe. "This is Pitt. You there, skipper?"

"Go ahead Dirk, I'm listening."

"Has Al filled you in on what we've found here?"

"A brief account. As soon as you can tell me there are no survivors, I will alert Argentinean authorities."

"Consider it done. Unless I missed one or two in closets or under beds, I have a body count of seventeen."

"Seventeen," Dempsey repeated. "I read you. Can you determine the cause of death?"

"Negative," Pitt answered. "The apparent symptoms aren't like anything you'd find in your home medical guide. We'll have to wait for a pathologist's report."

"You might be interested to know that Miss Fletcher and Van Fleet have pretty well eliminated viral infections and chemical contamination as the cause of death for the penguins and seals."

"Everyone at the station vomited before they died. Ask them to explain that."

"I'll make a note of it. Any sign of the second shore party?"

"Nothing. They must still be on board the ship."

"Very strange."

"So what are we left with?"

Dempsey sighed defeatedly. "A big fat puzzle with too many missing pieces."

"On the flight here we passed over a seal colony that was wiped out. Have you determined how far the scourge extends?"

"The British station two hundred kilometers to the south of you on the Jason Peninsula and a U.S. cruise ship that's anchored off Hope Bay have reported no unusual events nor any evidence of mass creature destruction. By taking into account the area in the Weddell Sea where we discovered the school of dead dolphins, I put the death circle within a diameter of ninety kilometers, using the whaling station on Seymour Island as a center point."

"We're going to move on now," Pitt notified him, "and make a sweep for *Polar Queen*."

"Make sure that you keep enough fuel in reserve to return to the ship."

"I will," Pitt assured Dempsey. "An invigorating swim in ice water is something I can do without."

Giordino closed down the research station's communications console, and then they hurried toward the entrance. As they rose from the station, Giordino studied his chart of the Antarctic Peninsula.

"Where to?" Giordino asked.

"We'll check out the islands north of here as far as Moody Point at the tip of the peninsula. Then we'll curve east and work out to sea until we converge with the *Ice Hunter*."

Giordino drew the course Pitt requested on the chart. After a few minutes he propped it against the instrument panel so Pitt could view his markings. "If your intuition is on target, the only chance *Polar Queen* has for striking hard ground between here and the South Atlantic is on one of three small islands that are little more than pinnacles of exposed rock."

"What are they called?"

"Danger Islands."

"They sound like the setting of an adolescent pirate novel."

Giordino thumbed through a coastal reference manual.

"Ships are advised to give these islands a wide berth," he said.

"High basalt palisades rising sharply from rough waters. Then it lists the ships that have piled up on them." He looked up from the chart and reference manual and gave Pitt a very narrow look. "Not exactly a place where kids would play."

7

THEY SKIRTED DUNDEE ISLAND, NOT FAR BELOW THE EX-
treme tip of the peninsula. Directly ahead of them
Moody Point curled toward the Danger Islands. They
found the sea suddenly transformed into an unbroken
mass of white-capped swells marching in from the Drake
Passage. A buffeting wind sprang up and caused the
helicopter to sway like a toy locomotive hurtling around
a model train layout.

The peaks of the three Danger Islands came into view,
their rock escarpments rising out of a sea that writhed
and thrashed around their base. They rose so steeply that
even seabirds couldn't get a foothold on their sheer
walls.

"No ship could live long in that bedlam," said Pitt.

"No shallow water around those pinnacles," Giordino
observed. "The water looks to drop off a hundred
fathoms within a stone's throw of the cliffs."

"According to the charts, it drops over a thousand
meters in less than three kilometers."

They circled the first island in the chain. There was no
sign of floating debris on the tormented sea. They flew
across the channel separating this island from the next,
looking down on the rushing white-capped surge that

reminded Pitt of the spring floodwaters gushing down the Colorado River through the Grand Canyon. No ship's captain would be crazy enough to take his vessel within a cannon shot of this place.

"See anything?" Pitt asked Giordino as he struggled to keep the helicopter stable against the unpredictable winds that tried to slam them against the towering cliffs.

"A seething mass of liquid only a white-water kayaker could love. Nothing more."

Pitt completed the circumference and dipped the craft toward the third and outermost island. This one looked dark and evil, with slitty eyes, small rock protrusions for horns and a sharp beard below smirking lips.

"Now that's what I call repugnant," said Pitt.

A moment later, Pitt swung the helicopter on a parallel course with the wave-swept palisades and began circling the barren island. Suddenly, Giordino stiffened and peered intently through the front windscreen. "Look over the top of that high ridge dead ahead," he told Pitt.

Pitt studied the strange rock formation that trailed from the main mass and led into the sea like a man-made breakwater. "That blob of white snow beyond the ridge?"

"That ain't no blob of snow," Giordino said firmly.

Pitt suddenly realized what it was. "I've got it now!" he said with mounting excitement. It was smooth and white and shaped like a triangle with the top cut off. The upper rim was black, and there was some sort of painted emblem on the side. "A ship's funnel! And there's her radar mast sticking up forty meters forward. You made a good call, pal."

"If it's *Polar Queen*, she must have struck the cliffs on the other side of that spur."

But that was an illusion. When they flew over the natural seawall jutting into the sea it became apparent that the cruise ship was floating undamaged a good five hundred meters from the island. It was incredible, but there she was without a scratch.

"She's still clear!" Giordino shouted.

"Not for long," Pitt said. In an instant he took in the dire situation. The *Polar Queen* was steaming in large circles, her helm somehow jammed hard to starboard. They had arrived less than thirty minutes before her arc would bring her in collision with the sheer rocks, crushing her hull and sending everyone on board into deep, icy water.

"There are bodies on her deck," said Giordino soberly.

A few lay scattered about the bridge deck. Several had fallen on the sundeck near the stern. A Zodiac, still attached to the gangway, was dragged along through the swells, two bodies lying on its bottom. That no one was alive was obvious by the fact they were all covered with a thin coating of snow and ice.

"Two more revolutions and she'll kiss the rock," said Giordino.

"We've got to get down there and somehow turn her about."

"Not in this wind," said Giordino. "The only open space is the roof over the bridge-deck quarters. That's a tricky landing I wouldn't want to try. Once we dump airspeed and hover prior to setting down, we'll have as much control as a dry leaf. A sudden downdraft and we'll end up in the mess down there."

Pitt unsnapped his safety harness. "Then you drive the bus while I go down on the winch."

"That's crazy. You'd be whipped around like a yo-yo on a string."

"You know any other way to get on board?"

Pitt already wore thermal underwear made from heavy nylon pile to retain his body heat and shield him

from frigid temperatures. Over this he pulled on a
diver's dry suit, specially insulated for polar waters. He
strapped on a quick-release harness and tightened the
chin strap to the heavy crash-type helmet that contained
his radio headset. He looked through the compartment
that held Van Fleet's lab equipment and into the cockpit.
"Do you read me okay?" he asked Giordino through the
tiny microphone in front of his lips.

"A little fuzzy around the edges. But that should clear
once you're free of the engine's interference."

Pitt adjusted his helmet's face mask and pulled on his
gloves. He took the remote control unit to the winch
motor in one hand, turned and pulled open the side
entry hatch. If he hadn't been dressed for the abrupt
blast of polar frigidity he would have been frozen into a
Popsicle within a few seconds. He leaned out the door
and gazed at *Polar Queen.*

She was circling in closer and closer to her death. Only
fifty meters separated her from destruction on this pass.
The uncompromising rock walls of the outermost Danger Island seemed to beckon to her. There wasn't much
time left. She was beginning her final circuit, which
would bring her into collision with an immovable object.

"Throttling back," Giordino said, announcing the
start of his run over the ship.

"Exiting now," Pitt informed him. Pitt pressed the
release button to reel out the cable. As soon as he had
enough slack to clear the doorway he stepped into space.

The rush of wind took him in its grasp and strung his
body out behind the underside of the helicopter. The
rotor blades thumped above him, and the sound of the
turbine exhaust came through his helmet and earphones.
Whirling through the chilly air, Pitt felt the same sensation as that felt by a bungee jumper after the initial
recoil. He focused his concentration onto the ship, which
looked like a toy boat floating on a blanket of blue in the

near distance. The superstructure of the ship rapidly grew until it filled most of his vision.

"Coming up on her," Giordino's voice came over the earphones. "Mind you don't slam into the railing and slice yourself into little pieces."

"And don't you bloody your nose on those rocks," Pitt shot back.

Those were the last words between them. From now on it was all by sight and gut instinct. Pitt had let himself down until he was almost fifteen meters below and behind the chopper. He fought against the pull and momentum that worked to twist him in circles, using his outstretched arms like the wings and ailerons of an aircraft. He felt himself drop a few meters as Giordino reduced speed.

Giordino eased back on the throttle as far as he dared. One more notch and all control would belong to the winds. He was flying with every shred of experience he'd gained during many thousands of hours in the air. Despite the wind buffeting, if he maintained his present course, he could drop Pitt dead center onto the sundeck.

They were flying toward the lee side of the island, and the winds abated slightly. Then he was over the icy crest and was struck by the full force of the wind, which threw the aircraft on its tail, the rotor blades in a perpendicular position. Giordino threw the helicopter around to a level position on a reverse course and beat back over the ship, his eyes darting as he looked out the window for a glimpse of Pitt.

Giordino did not know that Pitt had released his harness and made a perfect drop from a height of only three meters directly into the center of the sundeck's open swimming pool. He didn't spot him at first. He shouted into his microphone. "Did you make it down okay? Make yourself known, buddy."

Pitt waved his arms and replied. "I'm here in the swimming pool."

Giordino was dazed. "You fell in the pool?"

"I've a good notion to stay here," Pitt replied happily. "The heater is still on and the water is warm."

"I strongly suggest you get to the bridge," Giordino said. "She's coming out of the backstretch and into the far turn. I give her no more than eight minutes before you hear a big scraping noise."

Pitt needed no further encouragement. He hoisted himself out of the pool and took off at a dead run along the deck to the forward companionway. The bridge was only one deck above. He took the companionway four steps at a time, threw open the door of the wheelhouse and rushed inside. A ship's officer was lying on the deck, dead, his arms clutching the base of the chart table.

Pitt hurriedly scanned the ship's automated navigation systems console. The yellow light indicated that the electronic control was on manual override. Feverishly he dashed outside onto the starboard bridge wing. It was empty. He turned and rushed back across the wheelhouse onto the port bridge wing. A body hunched over the ship's exterior control panel. He wore a foul-weather jacket with no markings but a cap with enough gold braid to show that he was surely the captain.

"Can you drop the anchors?" asked Giordino.

"Easier said than done," Pitt replied irritably. "Besides, there is no flat bottom."

"You'd better be quick," Giordino's anxious voice came over the earphones.

Pitt sneaked a fast glance in awe at the sinister walls that seemed to stretch above his head into the upper atmosphere. Pitt estimated that the ship would strike on her starboard bow in another four minutes.

Pitt tried to pull the captain away from the control

panel, but he wouldn't budge. The hands clasped around the base refused to give. Pitt gripped the body under the armpits and heaved with all his strength. Suddenly the captain was free. Pitt threw him off to the side, found the chrome lever that controlled the helm and pushed it hard against the slot marked PORT to increase the angle of turn away from calamity.

For nearly thirty seconds it seemed nothing was happening, then with agonizing slowness the bow began to swing away from the boiling surf. It was not nearly quick enough. A ship can't turn in the same radius as a big semitrailer. It takes almost a kilometer to come to a complete stop, much less cut a sharp inside turn.

Above the ship, Giordino looked down with a sinking sensation. From his vantage point it didn't seem the ship was turning. He saw no chance for Pitt to escape once the ship rammed into the island. Leaping into the boiling water meant only a futile struggle against the incredible power of a surging sea, an impossible situation at best.

"I'm coming in for you," he apprised Pitt.

"Stay clear," Pitt ordered. "You can't feel it up there, but the air turbulence this close to the precipice is murderous—" Pitt broke off in horror as the *Polar Queen* was caught broadside by a giant comber that rolled over her like an avalanche. The ship descended ever deeper as if she were continuing a voyage to the bottom far below.

8

THE TORRENT CAME WITH A ROAR LOUDER THAN THUNDER and flung Pitt to the deck. He held his breath as the icy water surged over and around him. He clung desperately to the pedestal of the control console to keep from being swept over the side into the maelstrom. He thought his arms were being pulled from their sockets as he clung for his life.

Then *Polar Queen* struggled up and burst through the back of the wave, her bow forging another ten meters to port. She was refusing to die, game to fight the sea to the bitter end.

The next comber struck like an express train before colliding with the backwash from the last one. Bludgeoned by the impact from two sides, the ship was tossed upward until her hull was visible almost to the keel. Her twin screws rose into the air, throwing white water that reflected the sun like sparks of a fireworks pinwheel. She hung suspended for a terrible moment, finally dropping into a deep trough before she was struck by the next breaker in line.

Again and again the cruise ship heeled over as the waves rolled against the sides of her hull. There was no stopping her now. She was through the worst of it and shook off the endless swells as though she were a dog shaking water off its coat. The hungry sea might take her another time, but more likely she would end up at the scrappers thirty or more years from now. But this day she still sailed the brutal waters.

"You pulled it off! You really pulled it off!" shouted Giordino as though he didn't believe his eyes.

Pitt sagged against the bridge-wing railing and felt suddenly tired. He looked up as the turquoise helicopter hovered over the wheelhouse. "How's your fuel?" he asked Giordino.

"Enough to make *Ice Hunter* with a few liters to spare," Giordino answered.

"See you soon," Giordino signed off. He did not envy Pitt for even one second as he swung the helicopter into a turn and set a course for the *Ice Hunter*.

Pitt removed his helmet and watched as the turquoise helicopter flew low across the blue ice-cold sea. He watched until it became a speck on the golden-blue horizon. A fleeting sense of loneliness shrouded him as he gazed around the empty ship. How long he stood gazing across the decks devoid of life, he never recalled. He stood there as if stalling, his mind blank.

He was waiting for some sort of sound besides the slap of the waves against the bow and the steady beat of the engines. Maybe he waited for a sound that indicated the presence of people, voices or laughter. Maybe he waited for some sign of movement from something other than the ship's pennants flapping in the breeze. More likely he was seized by foreboding about what he would most certainly find.

At last he pulled his mind back on track and entered the wheelhouse. He set the engines on half speed and plotted an approximate course toward an interception point with *Ice Hunter*. Then he programmed the coordinates into the navigation computer and engaged the automated ship's control system, linking it with the radar to self-steer the ship around any passing icebergs. Assured the ship was in no further danger, he stepped from the wheelhouse.

Though mentally prepared, he still found it hard to believe there was no life on board. That death had swept through the ship like a gust of wind was foreign to everything he'd ever experienced.

Suddenly he paused, cocked an ear and listened. Piano music was drifting from somewhere within the ship. Then, as suddenly as the music began, it stopped.

Pitt tried to write off the intriguing discovery with a dozen different logical solutions. But subconsciously, a fear began to grow. Unthinkingly, he began to look over his shoulder every so often. He worked forward into the ship's lounge. A Steinway grand piano was situated beside a small wooden dance floor.

Then he noticed a woman, sitting on the carpet in one corner of the lounge. Her chin was on her knees, head cradled in her arms. Dressed in a fashionable short-sleeved leather jacket and wool slacks, she was not in a contorted position, nor did she appear to have vomited like all the others.

Pitt's nerves reacted by sending a cold shiver up his spine. His heart sprinted from a slow steady beat to a rapid pace. Gathering control over his initial shock, he moved slowly across the room until he stood looking down on her.

He reached out and touched her cheek with a light exploring fingertip, experiencing an incredible wave of relief as he felt warmth. He gently shook her by the shoulders and saw her eyelids quiver open.

At first she looked at him dazed and uncomprehending, and then her eyes flew wide, she threw her arms around him and gasped. "You're alive!"

"You don't know how happy I am to see you are too," Pitt said softly, his lips parted in a smile.

Abruptly, she pulled back from him. "No, no, you can't be real. You're all dead."

"You needn't be afraid of me," he said in a soothing tone.

She stared at him through wide brown eyes rimmed red from weeping. She looked as if she were about to fall over on her side, so he quickly bent down and lifted her into a leather chair next to a table.

After she'd gasped a few breaths of air, she looked up at Pitt. "My name is Deirdre Dorsett," she whispered.

"Go on," he prompted. "That's a start. Are you one of the passengers?"

She shook her head. "An entertainer. I sing and play the piano in the lounge."

"That was you playing."

"Call it a reaction from shock. Shock at seeing everyone dead, shock at thinking it would be my turn next. I can't believe I'm still alive."

"Where were you when the tragedy occurred?" Pitt asked.

"Two of the passengers were celebrating their fiftieth anniversary with friends who accompanied them on the cruise. The night before their private party, the kitchen staff had carved a heart out of ice. I volunteered to bring the ice carving from the storage freezer."

"You were in the freezer?"

She nodded silently.

"Then what did you do?"

She closed her eyes very tightly, then pressed her hands against them and whispered. "I was only in there for a few minutes. When I came out I found everyone on the ship dead."

"Exactly how many minutes would you say?" Pitt asked softly.

Slowly she lowered her hands and stared vacantly at the surface of the table. "I don't know, I have no way of knowing exactly how long I was in there. All I remember is it took me a little while to wrap the ice carving in a couple of towels so I could get a good grip on it and carry it without freezing my fingers."

"You were very lucky," he said. "Yours is a classic example of being in the right place at the right time. If you had stepped from the freezer two minutes before you did, you'd be as dead as all the others. You were doubly lucky I came on board the ship when I did."

"Are you one of the crew? You don't look familiar."

It was obvious to him she was not fully aware of the *Polar Queen*'s near brush with the Danger Islands. "I'm sorry, I should have introduced myself. My name is Dirk Pitt. I'm with a research expedition. We found your excursion party where they had been abandoned on Seymour Island and came looking for your ship after all radio calls went unanswered."

"That would have been Maeve Fletcher's party," she said quietly. "I suppose they're all dead too."

"Two passengers and the crewman who took them ashore," he answered. "Miss Fletcher and the rest are alive and well."

For a brief instant her face took on a series of expressions. Shock was followed by anger culminating in a slow change to happiness. Her eyes brightened and she visibly relaxed. "Maeve is all right," she said with relief.

The sunlight came through the windows of the lounge and shone on her hair. Pitt sensed a strange mood change in her.

"Why . . . ?" she asked numbly, gesturing around her. "Why did they all have to die?"

"I can't be totally certain," Pitt said in a voice solemn with rage and pity, "but I think I have a good idea."

9

PITT SEARCHED THE REST OF THE *POLAR QUEEN* FOR OTHER survivors, then allowed himself a short catnap while Deirdre Dorsett stood watch, ready to wake him lest the ship run down some poor trawler fishing for ice-water cod. Then he picked up the phone and called Admiral Sandecker over a satellite link to give him an update on the situation.

The receptionist at NUMA headquarters put him straight through on Sandecker's private line. Though they were a third of the globe apart, Pitt's time zone in the Antarctic was only one hour ahead of Sandecker's in Washington, D.C.

"Good evening, Admiral."

"Have you rendezvoused with *Ice Hunter?*" Sandecker was short on greetings.

"Yes, sir. Captain Dempsey is only a few hundred meters off my starboard beam. He's sending a boat across to put a salvage crew on board and take off the only survivor."

"How many casualties?" asked Sandecker.

"After a preliminary search of the ship," answered Pitt, "I've accounted for all but five of the crew. Using a passenger list from the purser's office and a roster of the crew in the first officer's quarters, we're left with 20 passengers and two of the crew still among the living, out of a total of 202."

"That tallies to 180 dead."

"As near as I can figure."

"Since it is their ship, the Australian government is launching a massive investigation into the tragedy. A British research station with an airfield is situated not far to the southwest of your position, at Duse Bay. I've ordered Captain Dempsey to proceed there and transport the survivors ashore. The cruise line owners, Ruppert & Saunders, have chartered a Qantis jetliner to fly them to Sydney."

"Speaking of *Polar Queen,*" said Pitt. "What do we do with her?"

"Ruppert & Saunders are also sending a crew to sail her back to Adelaide, accompanied by a team of Australian government investigators, who will examine her from funnel to keel before she reaches port."

"You might be interested in learning that dead marine life in your area has tapered off," the admiral continued. "Fishermen and research-station support vessels have reported finding no unusual fish or mammal kills in the past forty-eight hours. Whatever the killer is, it has moved on. Now we're beginning to hear of massive amounts of fish and unusually high numbers of sea turtles being washed up on beaches around the Fiji Islands."

"Sounds suspiciously like the plague has a life of its own."

"It doesn't stay in one place," said Sandecker grimly. "The stakes are high. Unless our scientists can systematically eliminate the possible causes and home in on the one responsible damned quick, we're going to see a loss of sea life that can't be replenished, not in our lifetime."

"Do our lab people have any suspects on this one?" inquired Pitt.

"Not on this end," replied Sandecker. "We were hoping the biologists on board *Ice Hunter* might have come up with something."

"If they have, they're keeping it a secret from me."

"Do you have any notions on the subject?" asked Sandecker. "Something juicy that I can give the hounds from the news media who are parked in our lobby nearly two hundred strong."

A shadow of a smile touched Pitt's eyes. There was a private understanding between them that nothing of importance was ever discussed over a satellite phone. The mere mention of the news media meant that Pitt was to dodge the issue. "They're drooling for a good story, are they?"

"The tabloids are already touting a ship of the dead from the Antarctic triangle."

"Are you serious?"

"I'll be happy to fax you the stories."

"I'm afraid they'll be disappointed by my hypothesis."

"Care to share it with me?"

There was a pause. "I think it might be an unknown virus that is carried by air currents."

"A virus," Sandecker repeated mechanically. "Not very original, I must say."

"Forgive me, Admiral, I'm not thinking straight."

"You sound like a man wandering in a fog. As soon as Dempsey sends a crew on board, you head for *Ice Hunter* and get some sleep."

"Thank you for being so understanding."

"Simply a matter of appreciating the situation. We'll speak later." A click, and Admiral Sandecker was gone.

* * *

Deirdre Dorsett went out onto the bridge wing and waved wildly as she recognized Maeve Fletcher standing at the railing of *Ice Hunter*.

"Maeve!" she cried.

Maeve stared across the water, searching the decks of the cruise ship for the female calling her name. Then her eyes locked on the figure standing on the bridge wing, waving. For half a minute she stared, bewildered. Then as she recognized Deirdre, her face took on the expression of someone walking in a graveyard at night who was suddenly tapped on the shoulder.

"Deirdre?" she shouted the name questioningly.

"Oh, Maeve, you can't know how happy I am to see you alive."

"I'm shocked to see you too," said Maeve, slowly taking rein of her senses.

"Were you injured while ashore?" Deirdre asked as if concerned.

"A mild case of frostbite, nothing more." Maeve gestured to the *Ice Hunter* crewmen who were lowering a launch. "I'll hitch a ride and meet you at the foot of the gangway."

"I'll be waiting." Deirdre smiled to herself and stepped back into the wheelhouse, where Pitt was talking over the radio to Dempsey. He nodded and smiled at her before signing off.

"Dempsey tells me Maeve is on her way over."

Deirdre nodded. "She was surprised to see me."

"A fortunate coincidence," said Pitt, "that two friends are the only members of the crew still alive."

Deirdre shrugged. "We're hardly what you'd call friends."

He stared curiously into brown eyes that glinted from the sun's rays that shone through the forward window. "You dislike each other?"

"A matter of bad blood, Mr. Pitt," she said matter-of-factly. "You see, despite our different last names, Maeve Fletcher and I are sisters."

10

THE SEA WAS THANKFULLY CALM WHEN *ICE HUNTER*, TRAILED
by *Polar Queen,* slipped under the sheltering arm of
Duse Bay and dropped anchor just offshore from the
British research station. From his bridge, Dempsey
instructed the skeleton crew on board the cruise ship to
moor her a proper distance away so the two ships could
swing on their anchors with the tides without endanger-
ing each other.

Still awake and barely steady on his feet, Pitt had not
obeyed Sandecker's order that he have a peaceful sleep.
There were still a hundred and one details to be attended
to after he turned over operation of *Polar Queen* to
Dempsey's crew. First he put Deirdre Dorsett in the boat
with Maeve and sent them over to *Ice Hunter*. Then he
spent the better part of the sunlit night making a
thorough search of the ship, finding the dead he had
missed on his brief walk-through earlier. Only when
Polar Queen was safely anchored under the protecting
arm of the bay did he hand over command and return to
the NUMA research ship. Giordino and Dempsey
waited in the wheelhouse to greet and congratulate him.
Giordino took one look at Pitt's exhausted condition

and quickly poured him a cup of coffee from a nearby pot that was kept brewing at all times in the wheelhouse. Pitt gratefully accepted, sipped the steaming brew and stared over the rim of the cup toward a small craft with an outboard motor that was chugging toward the ship.

Representatives from Ruppert & Saunders climbed aboard the lowered gangway and quickly climbed to the bridge, where Pitt, Dempsey and Giordino awaited them. One man cleared the steps three at a time and pulled up short, surveying the three men standing before him. He was big and ruddy and wore a smile a yard wide.

"Captain Dempsey?" he asked.

Dempsey stepped forward and extended his hand. "I'm he."

"Captain Ian Ryan, Chief of Operations for Ruppert & Saunders."

"Happy to have you aboard, Captain."

Ryan looked apprehensive. "My officers and I are here to take command of *Polar Queen.*"

"She's all yours, Captain," Dempsey said easily. "If you don't mind, you can send back my crew in your boat once you're aboard."

"The directors of the company have asked me to express our deepest thanks and congratulations for your efforts in saving our passengers and ship," Ryan said.

Dempsey turned to Pitt and Giordino and introduced them. "These are the gentlemen who found the survivors on Seymour Island and kept your company's ship from running onto the Danger Island rocks."

Ryan pumped their hands vigorously, his grasp strong and beefy. "A remarkable achievement, absolutely remarkable."

Pitt's movements were purely out of habit as he took a shower and shaved for the first time since before he and

Giordino took off to find *Polar Queen*. He came within an eye blink of sagging to his knees and drifting asleep under the soothing splash of the warm water. Too tired even to dry his hair, he tucked a bath towel around his waist and stumbled to his queen-sized bed—no tight bunk or narrow berth on this ship—pulled back the covers, stretched out, laid his head on the pillow and was gone.

His unconscious mind didn't register the knock on his cabin door. Normally alert to the tiniest peculiar sound, he did not awaken or respond when the knock came a second time.

"Mr. Pitt, are you in there?"

Maeve moved in cautiously. The excuse for her barging in like this was to properly thank Pitt for saving her life.

Startled, she caught her reflection in a mirror above a desk that folded from the wall just outside the bedroom. Her cheeks were flushed like those of a young girl waiting for her date to the high school prom to show up. It was a condition she'd seldom experienced before. Maeve turned away, angry at herself. She couldn't believe she was entering a man's quarters without being invited. She hardly knew Pitt. He was little more than a stranger. But Maeve was a lady used to striking out on her own.

Her father, the wealthy head of an international mining operation, had raised Maeve and her sisters as if they were boys, not girls. There were no dolls or fancy dresses or debutante balls. His departed wife had given him three daughters instead of sons to continue the family's financial empire, so he simply ignored fate and trained them to be tough. By the time she was eighteen, Maeve could kick a soccer ball farther than most men in her college class, and she once trekked across the outback of Australia from Canberra to Perth with only a dog, a domesticated dingo, for company, an accomplishment her father rewarded her for by pulling her out of school and putting her to work in the family mines alongside of hard-bodied male diggers and blasters. She rebelled. This was no life for a woman with other desires. She ran away to Melbourne and worked her way through university toward a career in zoology. Her father made no attempt to bring her back into the family fold. He merely abolished her claim to any family investments and pretended she never existed after her twins were born.

Maeve stared down at the personal things casually thrown among a stack of papers and a nautical chart. She peeked furtively into a cowhide wallet fat with assorted credit cards, business and membership cards. How strange, she thought, there were no pictures. She laid the wallet back on the desk and studied the other items strewn about. There was a well-worn, orange-faced Doxa dive watch with a heavy stainless-steel band, and a mixed set of house and car keys. That was all.

Hardly enough to give her an insight into the man who owned them, she thought. This seemed to be a man who walked a lonely path, leaving nothing behind.

"See something you like, little sister," came a quiet, husky voice from behind her.

Maeve spun and stared at Deirdre, who leaned casually against the doorway. "What are you doing here?" she demanded in a whisper.

"I might ask the same of you, dear sister," Deirdre answered with a challenging smile as she closed the door to the bedroom.

"The ship's scientists asked me to remain on board and make out a report of my experience with the death plague."

"And I remained because I thought we might kiss and make up," Deirdre said.

"There was a time I might have believed you. But not now."

"I admit there were other considerations."

"How did you manage to stay out of my sight during the weeks we were at sea?"

"Would you believe I remained in my cabin with an upset stomach."

"That's so much rot," snapped Maeve. "You have the constitution of a horse. I've never known you to be sick."

"Aren't you the least bit amazed at my miraculous survival?" Deirdre asked.

Maeve stared into her eyes, confused and uncertain. "You told everyone you were in the freezer."

"Rather good timing, don't you think?"

"You were incredibly lucky."

"Luck had nothing to do with it," Deirdre contradicted. "What about yourself? Didn't it ever occur to you how you came to be in the whaling station caves at exactly the right moment?"

"What are you implying?"

"You don't understand, do you?" Deirdre said. "Did you think Daddy was going to forgive and forget after you stormed out of his office, swearing never to see any one of us again? He especially went mad when he heard that you had legally changed your name to that of our great-great-great-grandmother. Fletcher, indeed. Since you left, he's had your every movement observed from the time you entered Melbourne University until you were employed by Ruppert & Saunders."

Maeve stared at her with anger and disbelief that faded as something began to dawn slowly in her mind. "He was that afraid that I would talk to the wrong people about his business operations?"

"Whatever unorthodox means Daddy has used to further the family empire was for your benefit as well as Boudicca and myself."

"Boudicca!" Maeve spat. "Our sister, that hateful creature."

"Think what you may," Deirdre said. "Boudicca has always had your best interests at heart. It was Boudicca who talked Daddy into sparing your life by insisting I go along on the voyage."

"Sparing my life?" Maeve looked lost. "You're not making sense."

"Who do you think arranged for the ship's captain to send you ashore with the first excursion?"

"You?"

"Me."

"It was my turn to go ashore. The other lecturers and I worked in sequence."

Deirdre shook her head. "If they had stuck to the proper schedule, you'd have been placed in charge of the second shore party that never got off the ship."

"So what was your reasoning?"

"An act of timing," said Deirdre. "Daddy's people calculated that the phenomenon would appear when the first shore party was safe inside the whaling station storage caves."

Maeve felt the deck reeling beneath her feet, and the color drained out of her cheeks. "No way he could have predicted the terrible event," she gasped.

"A smart man, our father," Deirdre said calmly as if she were gossiping with a friend over the telephone. "If not for his advance planning, how do you think I knew when to lock myself in the ship's freezer?"

"How could he possibly know when and where the plague would strike?" she asked skeptically.

"Our father," Deirdre said, baring her teeth in a savage smile, "is not a stupid man."

Maeve's fury seethed throughout her body. "If he had any suspicions, he should have given a warning and averted the slaughter," she snapped.

"Daddy has more important business than to fuss over a boatload of dismal tourists."

"I swear I'll see that you all pay for your callousness."

"You'd betray the family?" Deirdre shrugged sarcastically, then answered her own question. "Yes, I believe you would."

"Bet on it."

"Never happen, not if you want to see your precious sons again."

"Sean and Michael are where Father will never find them."

"Call in the dogs if you have a mind to, but hiding the twins with that teacher in Perth was not really all that clever."

"You're bluffing."

"Your flesh-and-blood sister, Boudicca, merely persuaded the teacher and his wife, the Hollenders as I recall their name, to allow her to take the twins on a picnic."

Maeve trembled and felt she was going to be sick as the full enormity of the revelation engulfed her. "You have them?"

"Daddy is taking very good care of them on our private island. He's even teaching them the diamond trade. Cheer up. The worst that can happen is that they suffer some type of accident. You know better than anybody the risks children run, playing around mining tunnels. The bright side is that if you stand with the family, your boys will someday become incredibly wealthy and powerful men."

"Like Daddy?" Maeve cried in outrage and fear. "I'd rather they die."

"They could do worse," said Deirdre, gloating over Maeve's helplessness. "String along your friends from NUMA for a few days, and keep your mouth shut about what I've told you. Then we'll catch a flight for home."

She walked to the door and turned. "I think you'll find Daddy most forgiving, providing you ask forgiveness and demonstrate your loyalty to the family." Then she stepped onto the outside deck and out of sight.

PART II

WHERE
DREAMS
COME FROM

N

KOMANDORSKIE OSTROVA
(COMMANDER ISLANDS)

KUNGHIT
ISLAND

North Pacific
Ocean

NORTH
AMERICA

HAWAIIAN
ISLANDS

W

E

AUSTRALIA

South Pacific Ocean

ISLA DE PASCUA
(EASTER ISLAND)

GLADIATOR
ISLAND

NEW ZEALAND

◦ ACOUSTIC CONVERGENCE ◦

11

ADMIRAL SANDECKER SELDOM USED THE LARGE BOARD ROOM for conferences. He reserved it mainly for visiting congressmen and -women, and respected scientists, foreign and American. For internal NUMA business, he preferred a smaller workroom just off his office. It was an extremely comfortable room, uniquely his own, sort of a hideaway for him to hold informal but confidential meetings with his NUMA directors.

All four walls and ceiling were richly paneled in a satiny teak, and there were paintings of United States naval actions hung in ornate frames.

There was a beautifully detailed painting of the epic battle between John Paul Jones in the woefully armed *Bonhomme Richard* and the new British fifty-gun frigate, *Serapis.* Next to it the venerable American frigate *Constitution* was demasting the British frigate *Java.* On the opposite wall the Civil War ironclads *Monitor* and *Virginia,* better known as the *Merrimac,* slugged it out.

After Sandecker's retirement, a former President of the United States picked him to organize and establish a newly funded government agency dedicated to research of the sea. Beginning in a rented warehouse with a staff of fewer than a dozen people, including Pitt and Giordino, Sandecker had built NUMA into a huge organization that was the envy of oceanographic institutions around the world, manned by two thousand employees, and with a huge budget rarely questioned and almost always approved by Congress.

Sandecker stepped into the conference room in a cloud of smoke as if he were a magician materializing on a fog-shrouded stage.

He walked to the head of the table and smiled benignly at the two men seated to his left and right. "Sorry to keep you so late, gentlemen, but I wouldn't have asked you to work overtime unless it was important."

Hiram Yaeger, the chief of NUMA's computer network and overseer to the world's most expansive data library on marine sciences, leaned his chair back on two legs and nodded toward Sandecker. Whenever a problem needed solving, Sandecker always started with Yaeger. Rudi Gunn was his organizational wizard.

Sandecker slid into one of the leather chairs, dropped an ash from his cigar into a dish made from an abalone shell and flattened a chart of the Weddell Sea and the Antarctic Peninsula on the surface of the table. He tapped his finger on a marked circle with a series of small red crosses drawn within its circumference and labeled by number.

"Gentlemen, you're all familiar with the tragic situation in the Weddell Sea, the latest in a series of kill sites. Number one is the position where *Ice Hunter* found the dead dolphins. Two, the seal kills off South Orkney Island. Three, Seymour Island, the site of mass slaughter of men, women, penguins and seals. And four, the approximate position of *Polar Queen* when the scourge struck."

Yaeger studied the perimeter of the circle. "Looks to be about ninety kilometers in diameter."

"Not good," Gunn said, a deep frown creasing his forehead. "That's twice the size of the last kill zone, near Chirikof Island off the Aleutians."

"The count was over three thousand sea lions and five fishermen in that disaster," said Sandecker. He lifted a small remote control from the table, aimed it at a panel in the far wall and pressed a button. A large screen slowly dropped from the ceiling. He pressed another button and a computer-generated chart of the Pacific Ocean appeared in three-dimensional holograph. Several blue, neonlike globes, displaying animated fish and mammals, were projected seemingly from outside the screen and spaced in different areas of the chart. The globe over Seymour Island off the Antarctic Peninsula as well as one near Alaska included human figures. "Until three days ago," Sandecker continued, "all the reported kill zones have been in the Pacific. Now with the sea around Seymour Island, we have a new one in the South Atlantic."

"That makes eight appearances of the unknown plague in the past four months," said Gunn. "The occurrences seem to be intensifying. I've got thirty scientists working on the problem, and they have yet to stumble on a clue indicating a source."

"Something killed them," Sandecker burst out. "The skipper died in the wheelhouse, his hands gripped on the helm, while the crew went down on deck in the act of bringing in their nets. People just don't drop dead without cause, certainly not hardy men in their twenties and thirties."

"Maybe we're looking in the wrong place. It has to be something we haven't considered," Yaeger said.

Sandecker idly stared at his cigar smoke as it spiraled toward the paneled ceiling. He seldom laid all his cards on the table, preferring to turn them over slowly, one at a time. "I was talking to Dirk just before our meeting."

"Anything new at his end?" asked Gunn.

"Not from the biologists on board *Ice Hunter,* but Dirk has a theory, pretty farfetched he admits, but one none of us had thought of."

"I'd like to hear it," said Yaeger.

"He came up with a type of pollution."

Gunn looked at Sandecker, his eyes skeptical. "What type of pollution could he possibly suggest that we missed?"

Sandecker grinned like a sniper sighting through his scope. "Noise," he answered flatly.

"Noise," repeated Gunn. "What kind of noise?"

"He thinks there might be deadly sound waves that travel through water for hundreds, perhaps thousands of miles, before they surface and kill everything within a certain radius." Sandecker paused and studied his subordinates for their reaction.

Oddly, there was not a hint of doubt on Gunn's face. He peered intently at the projected image of the Pacific Ocean for a few moments. Then he said, "I think Dirk is onto something."

"I'm happy to hear another vote," said Sandecker. "When he first laid it on me, I thought Dirk's mind was sluggish from exhaustion. But the more I considered his theory, the more I came to believe in its possibilities."

"Word has it," said Yaeger, "that he single-handedly saved *Polar Queen* from running onto the rocks."

Gunn nodded. "It's true. After Al dropped him from a helicopter onto the ship, he steered it away from certain destruction. After tonight it will be the lead news story on every TV news program around the world."

Sandecker nodded at Yaeger. "Hiram, you delve into your library and extract every piece of data dealing with underwater acoustics. Search out any experiments, commercial or military, involving high-energy sound waves through water, their cause and effects on humans and underwater mammals."

"I'll start on it immediately," Yaeger assured him.

Gunn and Yaeger rose from their chairs and left the conference room. Sandecker sat there, slouched in his chair and puffing on his cigar. His eyes moved from sea battle to sea battle, lingering for several moments on each before moving to the next. Then he closed his eyes tightly as he collected his thoughts.

It was the uncertainty of the dilemma that clouded his mind. After a while, he opened his eyes and stared at the computer-generated chart of the Pacific Ocean. "Where will it strike next?" he spoke aloud to the empty room. "Who will it kill?"

January 22, 2000
Near Howland Island,
South Pacific

12

To the crew lining the rails of *Mentawai*, an Indonesian freighter bound from Honolulu to her next port of call, Jayapura in New Guinea, the sight of an awkward-looking craft in the middle of the ocean was highly unusual if not downright remarkable. The *Tz'u-hsi*, named after the last Chinese dowager empress, was the second home of Hollywood actor Garret Converse, the biggest box-office action hero on the silver screen. The junk was twenty-four meters in length with a beam of six meters, built from top to bottom of cedar and teakwood. Converse had installed every amenity for the crew's accommodations and the latest in navigational technology. No expense was spared. Few yachts were as luxuriously embellished. A master adventurer in the mode of Errol Flynn, Converse had sailed *Tz'u-hsi* from Newport Beach on a round-the-world cruise and was now running on the final leg across the Pacific, passing within fifty kilometers of Howland Island, Amelia Earhart's destination when she disappeared in 1937.

As the two ships plodded past each other on opposite courses, Converse hailed the freighter over the radio.

"Greetings from the junk *Tz'u-hsi*. What ship are you?"

The freighter's radio operator replied, "The freighter *Mentawai* out of Honolulu. Where are you bound?"

"Christmas Island, and then to California."

"I wish you clear sailing."

"The same to you," Converse answered.

The captain of *Mentawai* watched the junk slip astern and then nodded toward his first officer. "I never thought I'd see a junk this deep in the Pacific."

The first officer, a man of Chinese descent, nodded disapprovingly. "I crewed on a junk when I was a young boy. They're taking a great risk sailing through the breeding grounds of typhoons. Junks are not built for heavy weather. They ride too high and have a tendency to roll crazily. Their huge rudders are easily broken off by a rough sea."

"They're either very brave or very mad to tempt the fates," said the captain, turning his back on the junk as it grew smaller in the distance. "As for me, I feel more comfortable with a steel hull and the solid beat of engines under my decks."

Eighteen minutes after the freighter and junk crossed paths, a distress call was heard by the United States container carrier *Rio Grande,* bound for Sydney, Australia, with a cargo of tractors and agricultural equipment. The radio room was directly off the spacious navigation bridge, and the operator had only to turn to address the second officer, who stood the early morning watch.

"Sir, I have a distress signal from the Indonesian cargo freighter *Mentawai.*"

The second officer, George Hudson, picked up the ship's phone, punched a number and waited for an answering voice. "Captain, we've picked up a distress signal."

Captain Jason Kelsey was about to take his first forkful

of breakfast in his cabin when the call came from the bridge. "Very well, Mr. Hudson. I'm on my way. Try and get her position."

Kelsey wolfed down his eggs and ham, gulped half a cup of coffee and walked through a short passageway to the navigation bridge. He went directly to the radio room.

The operator looked up. "Very strange signal, Captain." He handed Kelsey a notepad.

Kelsey read the message aloud. "All ships come quick. Freighter *Mentawai* forty kilometers south-southwest of Howland Island. Come quick. All are dying." He looked up. "Nothing more? No coordinates?"

The radio operator shook his head. "They went dead, and I haven't been able to raise them again."

"Any other ships responding?" Kelsey asked the radio operator.

"We're the only one who attempted a reply, sir."

Kelsey stared at the deck. "We should be able to reach her in a shade less than two hours."

Sherman continued staring at the message in bewilderment. "If this isn't some kind of hoax, it's very possible that all we'll find are corpses."

They found *Mentawai* a few minutes after eight in the morning. Unlike *Polar Queen,* which had continued steaming under power, the Indonesian freighter appeared to be drifting. She looked peaceful and businesslike. Smoke curled from her twin funnels, but no one was visible on the decks, and repeated hails through a loudspeaker from the bridge of *Rio Grande* brought no response.

"Quiet as a tomb," said First Officer Sherman ominously.

"She's surrounded by a sea of dead fish," muttered Kelsey.

"I don't much like the look of it."

"You'd better collect a boarding party and investigate," ordered Kelsey.

"Yes, sir. On my way."

Second Officer Hudson was peering at the horizon through binoculars. "There's another ship about ten kilometers off the port bow."

"Is she coming on?" asked Kelsey.

"No, sir. She seems to be moving away."

"That's odd. Why would she ignore a ship in distress? Can you make her out?"

"She looks like a fancy yacht, a big one with sleek lines. The design you see moored in Monaco or Hong Kong."

Kelsey moved to the threshold of the radio-room doorway and nodded to the operator. "See if you can raise that boat in the distance."

After a minute or two, the radio operator shook his head. "Not a peep. They've either closed down, or they're ignoring us."

Twenty minutes passed before Sherman called over to the *Rio Grande.* "Captain Kelsey?"

"Go ahead, Mr. Sherman. What have you found?"

"All dead, sir, every one of them, including two parakeets found in the chief engineer's cabin and the ship's dog, a beagle."

"Any clue as to the cause?"

"Food poisoning seems the most obvious. They look like they threw up before they died."

"Be careful of toxic gas." Kelsey was abruptly cut off as *Mentawai's* hull shuddered from an explosion from deep inside her bowels. The hatches above the cargo holds were thrown skyward as flame and smoke erupted from below. There was another deep rumble inside the freighter, followed by the screeching sound of tearing metal.

No one on board *Rio Grande* could believe the freighter could go so quickly. They stared in horror at the wreckage mixed with wisps of smoke that swirled around her watery crypt, hurtling toward eternal darkness at the bottom of the sea.

Kelsey stood there for nearly a full minute, the grief and outrage etched in his face. Somehow a tiny thought in the back of his mind finally mushroomed and emerged through the shock. He turned from the whirlpool of death, picked up a pair of binoculars and stared through the forward windows at the yacht vanishing in the distance. Now only a white speck against a blue sky and an azure sea, it was moving away at great speed. The mysterious vessel had not ignored the distress signal, he realized. It had come and gone and was now purposely running away from the disaster.

13

THE ATMOSPHERE IN THE *ICE HUNTER'S* DINING ROOM HAD A strange mood of subdued festivity. The occasion was a farewell party thrown by the crew and scientists for the survivors of the *Polar Queen* tragedy. Roy Van Fleet and Maeve had been working day and night, shoulder to shoulder, for the past three days, examining the remains of the penguins, seals and dolphins collected for study and filling notebooks full of observations.

Late the next evening, the ship would dock at the Chilean port of Punta Arenas in Tierra del Fuego, where Maeve and Deirdre would take a commuter flight to Santiago. From there they could book a direct flight to Australia.

The *Ice Hunter's* chef did himself proud with an incredible gourmet dinner featuring filets of deep-sea cod with mushroom and wine sauce.

Dr. Mose Greenberg made a long speech laced with bad jokes about everyone on board. He might have kept on for another hour if Dempsey hadn't signaled for the chef to bring out a cake especially baked for the occasion. It was shaped like the continent of Australia, with icing picturing the more notable landmarks including Ayres Rock and Sydney Harbor. Maeve was truly touched, and tears moistened her eyes. Deirdre appeared bored with it all.

As captain, Dempsey sat at the head of the longest table, the women sitting in honor at his elbows. Because he was head of NUMA's special-projects division, Pitt was allotted the chair at the opposite end of the table. He tuned out the conversations flowing around him and focused his attention on the two sisters.

He slipped a hand below the table and touched the folded fax in his pants pocket. Overcome by curiosity, he had communicated with St. Julien Perlmutter, a close family friend. Pitt had put in a call and asked his friend to check on the ladies' family background. Perlmutter faxed him a brief report in less than an hour with a promise of a more in-depth account within two days.

These were no ordinary women from common circumstances. Maeve and Deirdre's father, Arthur Dorsett, was head of a diamond empire second only to De Beers and the sixth richest man in the world.

The section of the report that struck him as odd was a drawing of the Dorsett corporate hallmark that Perlmutter included. Instead of the obvious, a diamond on some sort of background, the Dorsett logotype was a serpent undulating through the water.

The ship's officer on duty came up alongside Pitt and spoke softly. "Admiral Sandecker is on the satellite phone and would like to talk to you."

"Thank you, I'll take the call in my cabin."

Unobtrusively, Pitt pushed back his chair, rose and left the dining room, unnoticed by all except Giordino.

Pitt exhaled a deep breath, removed his shoes and unlimbered in his leather chair. "Admiral, this is Dirk."

"About time," Sandecker grunted. "I require the services of you and Giordino here in Washington. How soon can you fly off *Ice Hunter* for Punta Arenas?"

"We're within the helicopter's range now," said Pitt. "We can lift off within the hour."

"I've arranged for a military jet transport to be waiting for your arrival at the airport."

Sandecker was never one to let the grass grow under his feet, Pitt thought. "Then Al and I will see you sometime tomorrow afternoon."

The dishes were cleared and the party in the ship's dining room had become loud with laughter as everyone competed in telling shaggy dog stories. On one wall nearby, a ship's phone rang, and the first officer answered. Without a word, he nodded in Dempsey's direction. The captain caught the gesture, came over and took the call. He listened a moment, hung up the receiver and started for the open passageway leading to the stern deck.

"Are you all joked out?" Van Fleet called after him.

"I have to stand by for the helicopter's departure," he answered.

"What's the mission?"

"No mission. Pitt and Giordino have been ordered back to Washington by the admiral, posthaste. They're flying off to the mainland to catch a military transport."

Maeve overheard and grabbed Dempsey by the arm. "When are they leaving?"

He was surprised by the sudden strength of her grip. "They should be lifting off about now."

Maeve felt as if a giant hand had suddenly reached inside her and squeezed her heart. Anguish filled her body. She rushed out the door onto the deck. Pitt had only lifted the helicopter a scant three meters off the pad when she came running into view. She could clearly see both men through the helicopter's large windows. Giordino looked down, saw her and waved. Pitt had both hands busy and could only respond with a warm grin and a nod.

He expected to see her smile and wave in return, but her face seemed drawn in fear. She cupped her hands and cried out to him, but the noise of the turbine exhaust and thumping rotor blades drowned out her words. He could only shake his head and shrug in reply.

Maeve shouted again, this time with lowered hands as if somehow willing her thoughts into his mind. Too late. The helicopter shot into the air vertically and dipped over the side of the ship. She sagged to her knees on the deck, head in her hands, sobbing, as the turquoise aircraft flew over the endless marching swells of the sea.

Giordino looked back through his side window and saw Maeve slumped on the deck, Dempsey walking toward her. "I wonder what the fuss was all about," he said curiously.

"What fuss?" asked Pitt.

"Maeve . . . she acted like a Greek mourner at a funeral."

Concentrating on controlling the helicopter, Pitt had missed Maeve's unexpected display of grief. "Maybe she hates good-byes," he said, feeling a wave of remorse.

"She tried to tell us something," Giordino said vaguely, reliving the scene in his mind.

"How could you hear anything over the chopper's racket?"

"I couldn't. It was all in the way she formed the words with her mouth."

Pitt grinned. "Since when do you read lips?"

"I'm not kidding, pal," Giordino said in dead seriousness. "I know the message she tried to get across to us."

Pitt knew from long years of experience and friendship that when Giordino turned profound he worked purely from essentials. "Spit it out. What did she say?"

Giordino slowly turned and looked at Pitt, his deep-set black eyes reflective and somber at the same time. "I could swear she said 'Help me.'"

14

THE TWIN-ENGINED BUCCANEER JET TRANSPORT TOUCHED down smoothly and taxied to a quiet corner of Andrews Air Force Base, southeast of Washington. Fitted out comfortably for high-ranking Air Force officers, the aircraft flew nearly as fast as the most modern fighter plane.

As the flight steward, in the uniform of an Air Force master sergeant, carried their luggage to a waiting car and driver, Pitt scolded himself for not returning to *Ice Hunter* shortly after liftoff. If Giordino had interpreted her message correctly, Maeve was in some sort of trouble. The possibility that he had deserted her when she was calling out to him gnawed at his conscience.

His thoughts were broken as the car rolled over the driveway in front of the tall green, solar-glassed building that housed NUMA's headquarters. The visitors' parking lot was covered with television transmitter trucks and vans.

"I'll run you into the underground parking area," said the driver. "The news media are starved for details of the cruise ship massacre. The Australians tried to put a tight lid on it, but all hell broke loose after the surviving passengers talked when they reached Chile. They were glowing in their praise of how you guys rescued them and saved the cruise ship from going on the rocks. The fact that two of them were daughters of diamond king Arthur Dorsett naturally excited the exposé rags."

The car stopped in front of a security guard stationed in front of a small alcove that led to a private elevator. They signed an entry form and took the elevator to the tenth floor. When the doors opened they stepped into a vast room that was Hiram Yaeger's electronics fiefdom from which the computer wizard directed NUMA's vast data systems network.

Yaeger looked up from a huge horseshoe-shaped desk in the middle of the room and smiled broadly. He jumped to his feet and came from behind the desk, vigorously shaking Pitt's and Giordino's hands. "Good to see you two scoundrels back in the building. It's been as dull as an abandoned amusement park since you skipped to the Antarctic."

"Always good to be back on a floor that doesn't rock and roll," said Pitt. He glanced about the room crowded with electronic data systems and a crew of technicians. "Are the admiral and Rudi Gunn on hand?"

"Waiting for you in the private conference room," answered Yaeger. "We assumed you and Al would go there first."

"I wanted to catch you before we all sat down."

"What's on your mind?"

"I'd like to study your data on sea serpents."

Yaeger raised his eyebrows. "You did say *sea serpents?*"

Pitt nodded. "They intrigue me. I can't tell you why."

"It may surprise you to learn I have a mountain of material on sea serpents and lake monsters."

"Forget the legendary creatures swimming around in Loch Ness and Lake Champlain," said Pitt. "I'm only interested in the seagoing variety."

Yaeger shrugged. "Since most of the sightings are on inland waters, that cuts the search by eighty percent. I'll have a fat file on your desk tomorrow morning."

"Thank you, Hiram. I'm grateful as always."

When Pitt and the others entered the conference room, Sandecker and Gunn were studying the region where the latest case of unexplained death was projected on the holographic chart. The admiral and Gunn stepped forward to greet them. For a few minutes they all stood in a tight little huddle and deliberated the turn of events. Gunn anxiously probed Pitt and Giordino for details, but they were both extremely tired, and they condensed the wild series of incidents into brief descriptions.

Sandecker knew better than to crowd them. Full reports could be written at a later time. He motioned to the empty chairs. "Why don't you sit down, and we'll get to work."

Gunn pointed toward one of the blue globes that seemed to float over one end of the table. "The latest kill zone," he said. "An Indonesian freighter called *Mentawai,* with a crew of eighteen."

"There is something else to consider," said Gunn. "The captain of the American container ship that found *Mentawai* reported a luxury yacht speeding from the site. He can't swear to it in court, but he's certain the yacht closed with *Mentawai* before he arrived, after responding to the freighter's distress call. He also thinks the crew of the yacht are somehow responsible for the explosives that wiped out his boarding party."

"Did he get a description of the yacht?" asked Pitt.

"By the time Kelsey concentrated his attention on it, the yacht was too distant to identify. His second officer, however, observed it earlier through binoculars before it widened the gap. Fortunately, he's an amateur artist who enjoys sketching ships and boats while in port."

"He drew a picture of it?"

"He admits to taking a few liberties. The yacht was pulling away from him, and his view was mostly of the stern quarter. But he managed to give us a good enough likeness to trace the hull design to her builders."

Sandecker nodded toward Giordino. "Al, why don't you act as lead investigator on this one?"

"I'll get on the trail after a shower and a change of clothes." Pitt was doodling on a notepad and spoke to Yaeger without looking up. "Suppose you tell me, Hiram. Did my idea of killer sound waves have any merit?"

"A great deal, as it turns out," replied Yaeger. "The acoustics experts are still working out a detailed theory, but it looks as if we're looking at a *killer* that travels through water."

"Can you make a case for high-intensity sound waves that kill?" Pitt asked.

Yaeger shrugged. "We're on shaky ground, but this is the best lead we have at the moment. The only joker in the deck is that sound waves intense enough to kill could not come from an ordinary sound source."

"Any idea where these sound rays originate?" asked Sandecker.

"Yes, as a matter of fact, we do. By borrowing the global monitoring system of hydrophones placed by the Navy around the oceans to track the Soviet submarine fleet during the Cold War, we've managed to trace the source of the destructive sound waves to four different points in the Pacific Ocean." Yaeger paused to pass printed copies of the chart to everyone seated at the table. "Number one, by far the strongest, appears to emanate from Gladiator Island, the exposed tip of a deep ocean range of volcanic mountains that surfaces midway between Tasmania and New Zealand's South Island. Number two is almost on a direct line toward the

Komandorskie Islands, off the Kamchatka Peninsula in the Bering Sea."

Pitt rose from the table and moved until he was almost standing inside the three-dimensional chart of the ocean. "A bit unusual for the acoustic sources to all stem from islands." He turned and stared at Yaeger. "Are the islands inhabited?"

Yaeger handed Pitt a small folder. "We've gleaned the usual encyclopedia of data on the islands. Geology, fauna, inhabitants. Gladiator Island is privately owned. The other three are leased from foreign governments for mineral exploration. These have to be considered forbidden zones."

"One more question," Pitt said. "Except for the mineral exploration companies, what do the islands have in common?"

"Diamonds."

Sandecker stared at Yaeger. "Diamonds, you say?"

"Yes, sir." Yaeger checked his file. "The operations on all four islands are either owned or run by Dorsett Consolidated Mining Limited of Sydney, Australia. Second only to De Beers as the world's largest diamond producer."

Pitt felt as if someone had walked up and suddenly punched him in the stomach. "Arthur Dorsett," he said quietly, "the chairman of Dorsett Consolidated Mining, happens to be the father of the two women Al and I rescued in the Antarctic."

"Of course," said Gunn, suddenly seeing the light. "Deirdre Dorsett." Then a quizzical look came into his eyes. "But the other lady, Maeve Fletcher?"

"Deirdre's sister, who took an ancestral grandmother's name," explained Pitt.

Sandecker turned to Pitt. "This strikes me as more than a mere coincidence."

Giordino came right back. "I can't help wondering

what one of the world's richest diamond merchants will have to say when he learns his diggings came within a hair of killing off his darling daughters."

"We may have a blessing in disguise," said Gunn. "If Dorsett's mining operations are somehow responsible for an acoustic death plague, Dirk and Al have the credentials to walk up to his front door and ask questions. The man has every reason to act the role of a grateful father."

"From what I know of Arthur Dorsett," said Sandecker, "he's so reclusive, he won the hermit trophy from Howard Hughes. As with De Beers diamond mining operations, Dorsett's properties are heavily guarded against thievery and smuggling. He is never seen in public and he has never granted an interview to the news media. We're talking about a very private man. I doubt seriously that saving his daughters' lives will make a dent in this guy. He's as hard-nosed as they come."

Yaeger motioned toward the blue globes on the holographic chart. "People are dying out there. Surely he'll listen to reason should his operations be somehow responsible."

"Arthur Dorsett is a foreign national with an immense power base." Sandecker spoke slowly. "We have to consider him innocent of any wrongdoing until we have proof. For all we know at the moment, the scourge is a product of nature. As for us, we're committed to working through official channels. That's my territory. I'll start the ball rolling with the State Department and the Australian ambassador. They can set up a dialogue with Arthur Dorsett and request his cooperation in an investigation."

"That could take weeks," argued Yaeger.

"Why not save time," said Giordino, "cut through the red tape, and see if his mining technology is somehow behind the mass murders?"

"Not a simple exercise, snooping around diamond mines," said Pitt. "They're notoriously well guarded against poachers and any intruders out for a quick buck scavenging for stones. Security around diamond-producing mines is notoriously heavy. Penetrating high-tech electronic systems will require highly trained professionals."

"A Special Forces team?" Yaeger put on the table.

Sandecker shook his head. "Not without presidential authority."

"What about the President?" asked Giordino.

"Too soon to go to him," answered the admiral. "Not until we can produce hard evidence of a genuine threat to national security."

Pitt spoke slowly as he contemplated the chart. "The Kunghit Island mine seems the most convenient of the four. Since it's in British Columbia and practically on our doorstep, I see no reason why we can't do a little exploring on our own."

Sandecker eyed Pitt shrewdly. "I hope you're not laboring under the impression our neighbors to the north might be willing to turn a blind eye to an intrusion?"

"Why not? Considering that NUMA found a very profitable oil site off Baffin Island for them several years ago, I figure they won't mind if we take a canoe trip around Kunghit and photograph the scenery."

"Is that what you think?"

Pitt looked at the admiral like a kid expecting a free ticket to the circus. "I may have overstated my case slightly, but yes, that's the way I see it."

"All right," Sandecker finally sighed. "Do your trespassing. But just remember, if you get caught by Dorsett's security people, don't bother to call home. Because nobody will answer the phone."

15

A ROLLS-ROYCE SEDAN ROLLED SOUNDLESSLY TO A STOP
beside an ancient aircraft hangar that stood in a weed-
grown field on the far perimeter of Washington's International Airport.

The Rolls was a model known as the Silver Dawn. The
chassis came out of the factory in 1955 and was fitted
with a custom body by the coach-builders Hoopers &
Company. The front fenders tapered gracefully into the
body at the rear until the skirted wheels and sides were
perfectly smooth. The engine was a straight six with
overhead valves, which carried the car over the roads as
quietly as the ticking of an electric clock. Speed with a
Rolls-Royce was never a factor. When questioned about
horsepower, the factory merely stated that it was ade-
quate.

St. Julien Perlmutter's chauffeur stepped around the
car and opened the door for him. "Shall I wait?"

"No, I'm having dinner here. Enjoy yourself for a few
hours. Then return and pick me up at eleven-thirty."

Mulholland helped Perlmutter from the car and escorted him to the entry door of the hangar. The door was
stained and layered with dust. The camouflage was well
conceived. Anyone who happened to pass the run-

down–appearing hangar would assume it was simply a deserted building scheduled for demolition. Perlmutter rapped on the door with his cane. After a few seconds there was an audible click, and the door opened as if pulled by a ghostly hand.

"Enjoy your dinner," said Mulholand as he slid a cylindrical package under Perlmutter's arm and held up the handle of a briefcase for him to grasp. Then he turned and walked back to the Rolls.

Perlmutter stepped into another world. Instead of dust, grime and cobwebs, he was in a brilliantly lit, brightly decorated and spotless atmosphere of gleaming paint and chrome. Nearly four dozen classic automobiles, two aircraft and a turn-of-the-century railroad car sat in restored splendor on a highly polished concrete floor. The door closed silently behind him as he walked through the incredible display of exotic machinery.

A J2X Allard, clearly Pitt's pride and joy, was parked near the door. It was a low red car with twin bucket seats and no upholstery. The small curved racing windscreen offered almost no protection from the airstream. There were no bumpers, and the front wheels were covered by motorcycle fenders. The spare tire was hung on the right side of the body between the fender and the door.

Built in England in 1952, and installed with big American V-8 engines, Allards cleaned up at the sports car races until the Mercedes 300 SL coupes came along. Nowadays, Pitt drove it exclusively when he was home.

Pitt stood on a balcony that extended from an apartment and which ran across one end of the hangar a good ten meters above the concrete floor. He sent down an antique freight elevator with ornate wrought-iron screens around it. As soon as it jangled to a stop, Perlmutter stepped in and the elevator carried him up to Pitt's apartment.

At the landing they greeted each other like the old friends they were. "Good to see you, Julien."

"Always happy to dine with my tenth son." It was one of Perlmutter's jokes. He was a bachelor, and Pitt was the only son of Senator George Pitt of California.

Perlmutter paused to sniff the air. "Is that herring I smell?"

Pitt nodded. "You're eating basic German farmhand fare tonight. Corned beef hash with salt herring and steamed spiced sauerkraut preceded by lentil soup with pork liver sausage."

"Sounds wonderful. You'll make some woman a happy wife with your masterful cooking."

"I'm afraid a love of cooking won't make up for all my failings."

As soon as Pitt cleared the dishes, Perlmutter moved into the living room, opened his briefcase and laid a thick sheaf of papers on the coffee table. When Pitt joined him, he was glancing at the pages, checking his notations.

Pitt settled in a leather sofa beneath staggered shelves that held a small fleet of ship models, replicas of ships that Pitt had discovered over the years. "So what have you got on the renowned Dorsett family?"

"Would you believe this represents a shallow scratch on the surface?" Perlmutter replied, holding up the thick volume of over a thousand pages. "From what I've researched, the Dorsett history reads like a dynasty out of an epic novel."

"What about the current head of the family, Arthur Dorsett? How did he get his start?"

"For that story we have to go back 144 years," Perlmutter said. "We begin with an epic of the sea that was recorded by the captain of a clipper ship and published by his daughter after he died. During a voyage in January of 1856, while he was transporting convicts to the Australian penal colony at Botany Bay, an inlet south of the present city of Sydney, his ship ran afoul of a violent typhoon while beating north through the Tasman Sea. The ship was called the *Gladiator,* and she was skippered by one of the most famous clipper captains of the era, Charles 'Bully' Scaggs."

"Iron men and wooden ships," murmured Pitt.

"They were that," agreed Perlmutter. "Anyway, Scaggs and his crew must have labored like demons to save the ship from one of the worst storms of the century. But when the winds died and seas calmed, *Gladiator* was little more than a derelict. Her masts were swept over the side, her superstructure was destroyed and her hull was taking on water. The ship's boats were gone or smashed, and Captain Scaggs knew his ship had only hours to live, so he issued orders for the crew and any convicts handy as carpenters to dismantle what was left of the ship and build a raft."

"Probably the only option open to him," Pitt commented.

"Two of the convicts were Arthur Dorsett's ancestors," Perlmutter continued. "His great-great-grandfather was Jess Dorsett, a convicted highwayman, and his great-great-grandmother was Betsy Fletcher, who was given a twenty-year sentence to the penal colony for stealing a blanket."

Pitt gave a small laugh. "Crime certainly didn't pay in those days."

"Most Americans don't realize that our own colonies were also a dumping ground for England's criminals until the Revolutionary War. Many families would be surprised to learn their ancestors landed on our shores as convicted criminals."

"Were the ship's survivors rescued from the raft?" asked Pitt.

Perlmutter shook his head. "The next fifteen days became a saga of horror and death. Storms, thirst and starvation, and a mad slaughter between the sailors, a few soldiers and the convicts decimated the people clinging to the raft. When it finally drifted onto the reef of an uncharted island and went to pieces, legend has it the survivors were saved from a great white shark by a sea serpent while swimming to shore."

"Which explains the Dorsett hallmark. It came from the hallucinations of near-dead people."

"I wouldn't be surprised. Only eight of the original 231 poor souls who left the ship staggered onto a beach—six men and two women more dead than alive. Two years later, Captain Scaggs and his remaining seaman, luckily for him the *Gladiator*'s carpenter, built a boat out of the remains of a French naval sloop that was driven on the rocks by a storm with the loss of all hands. Leaving the convicts behind on the island, they sailed across the Tasman Sea to Australia."

"Scaggs deserted Dorsett and Fletcher?"

"For a very good reason. The enchantment of living on a beautiful island was preferred to the prison camps at Botany Bay. And because Scaggs felt he owed his life to Dorsett, he told the penal colony authorities that all the convicts had died on the raft so the survivors could be left in peace."

"So they built a new life and multiplied."

"Exactly," said Perlmutter. "Jess and Betsy were married by Scaggs and had two boys, while the other two convicts produced a girl. In time they built a little family community and began trading food supplies to whaling ships that began making Gladiator Island, as it later became known, a regular stopover during their long voyages."

"What became of Scaggs?" asked Pitt.

"He returned to the sea as master of a new clipper ship

owned by a shipping company called Carlisle & Dunhill. After several more voyages to the Pacific, he retired and eventually died, twenty years later, in 1876."

"Where do diamonds enter the picture?"

"Patience," said Perlmutter like a schoolteacher. "A little background to better understand the story. The shipwrecked convicts unknowingly found not one, but two phenomenally rich underground pipes in volcanic mounds on opposite ends of Gladiator Island. The stones they found, which were freed from the rock by centuries of rain and wind, simply appeared to be 'pretty things,' as Betsy Fletcher referred to them in a letter to Scaggs. Actually, uncut and unpolished diamonds are dull-looking stones with almost no sparkle. They often feel and look like an oddly shaped bar of soap. It was not until 1866, after the American Civil War, that a U.S. Navy vessel on an exploratory voyage to find possible sites for deepwater ports throughout the South Pacific stopped at the island to take on water. On board was a geologist. He happened to see the Dorsett children playing a game with stones on the beach and became curious. He examined one of the stones and was amazed as he identified it as a diamond of at least twenty carats. When the geologist questioned Jess Dorsett as to where the stone came from, the cagey old highwayman told him he brought it with him from England."

"And that timely little event launched Dorsett Consolidated Mining."

"Not immediately," said Perlmutter. "After Jess died, Betsy sent her two boys, Jess Junior and Charles, no doubt named after Scaggs, and the daughter of the other two convicts, Mary Winkleman, to England to be educated. She wrote Scaggs for his help and included a pouch of uncut diamonds to pay for this undertaking, which the captain turned over to his friend and former employer, Abner Carlisle. Acting on behalf of Scaggs, who was on his deathbed, Carlisle had the diamonds faceted and polished, later selling them on the London exchange for nearly one million pounds, or about seven million dollars, in the currency of the time."

"A tidy sum for college tuition for those days," Pitt said consideringly. "The kids must have had a ball."

Perlmutter shook his head. "You're wrong this time. They lived frugally at Cambridge. Mary attended a proper girl's school outside of London. She and Charles married soon after he took his degree, and they returned to the island, where they directed the mining operations in the dormant volcanos. Jess Junior remained in England and opened the House of Dorsett in partnership with a Jewish diamond merchant from Aberdeen by the name of Levi Strouser. The London end of the business, which dealt in the cutting and sale of diamonds, had luxurious showrooms for retail sales, elegant offices on the upper floors for larger wholesale trading and a vast workshop in the basement, where the stones from Gladiator Island were cut and polished. The dynasty prospered, helped in no small measure by the fact that the diamonds that came out of the island pipes were a very rare violet-rose color and of the highest quality."

"The mines have never played out?"

"Not yet. The Dorsetts have been very shrewd in holding back much of their production in cooperation with the cartel to hold up the price."

"What about offspring?" asked Pitt.

"Charles and Mary had one boy, Anson. Jess Junior never married."

"Anson was Arthur's grandfather?" Pitt asked.

"Yes, he ran the company for over forty years. He was probably the most decent and honest of the lot. Anson was satisfied to run and maintain a profitable little empire. Never driven by greed like his descendants, he gave a great deal of money to charity. Any number of libraries and hospitals throughout Australia and New Zealand were founded by him. When he died in 1910, he left the company to a son, Henry, and a daughter, Mildred. She died young in a boating accident. Rumors circulated that she was murdered by Henry, but no investigations were made. Henry's money made sure of that. Under Henry, the family launched a reign of greed, jealousy, cruelty and ravenous power that continues to this day."

"Henry Dorsett died sometime in the late seventies, didn't he?"

Perlmutter smiled. "History repeated itself. At the age of sixty-eight, he fell off his yacht while in Monaco and drowned. It was whispered that Arthur got him drunk and shoved him into the bay."

"What's the story on Arthur?"

Perlmutter checked his file of papers, then peered over the lenses of his reading glasses. "Born on Gladiator Island in 1941, the only child of Henry and Charlotte Dorsett. He was educated by his mother, never going to school on the mainland until the age of eighteen, when he entered the Colorado School of Mines in Golden, Colorado. He was a big man, towering half a head above his classmates, yet he took no interest in sports, preferring to probe around the old ghost mines that are scattered throughout the Rocky Mountains. After graduating with a degree as a mining engineer, he worked the De Beers diggings in South Africa for five years before returning home and taking over as superintendent of the family mines on the island. During his frequent trips to the Dorsett headquarters building in Sydney, he met and married a lovely young girl, Irene Calvert, who was the daughter of a professor of biology at the university at Melbourne. They had three daughters."

"Maeve, Deirdre and . . ."

"Boudicca."

"Maeve and Deirdre are twenty-seven and thirty-one years of age. Boudicca is thirty-eight."

"Admiral Sandecker knows something of Arthur Dorsett and says he's impossible to reach," said Pitt.

"Very true. He is never seen in public, never socializes, has no friends. His entire life revolves around the business. He even has a secret tunnel for entering and leaving the Sydney headquarters building without being seen. He has cut Gladiator Island off from the outside world completely. To his way of thinking the less known about Dorsett mining operations the better."

"Do his daughters work within the company?"

"Two of them are said to be employed by dear old Dad, the other one . . ."

"Maeve," Pitt offered.

"Maeve cut herself off from the family, put herself through university and came out a marine zoologist. Something of her mother's father must have come through in her genes."

"And Deirdre and Boudicca?"

"The gossipmongers claim the two are worse than the old man. Deirdre is a conniving schemer with larceny in her veins. Boudicca is rumored to be quite ruthless and as cold and hard as ice from the bottom of a glacier."

A distant look reflected in Pitt's eyes. "What is it about diamonds that gives them so much allure? Why do men and women kill for them? Why have nations and governments risen and fallen because of them?"

"Besides their beauty after being cut and polished, diamonds have unique qualities. They happen to be the hardest known substance in the world. Rub one against silk and it produces a positive electrostatic charge. Expose it to the setting sun and it will later glow in the dark with an unearthly phosphorescence. No, my young friend. Diamonds are more than a myth. They are the ultimate creator of illusions."

16

AFTER HE LEFT THE NUMA BUILDING, GIORDINO SIGNED out one of the agency's turquoise cars and drove to his recently purchased condominium in Alexandria, along the Potomac River.

He threw his dirty clothes in the washer and took a quick shower. Then he packed an overnight bag and drove to Dulles International, where he caught an early evening flight to Miami. Upon arrival, he rented a car, drove to the city's port area and checked into a dockside motel. Next he checked the Yellow Pages for marine architects, copying the names, addresses and phone numbers of those who specialized in private motor yachts. Then he began to call.

The first four, who had already left for home, responded with answering machines, but the fifth picked up the call. Giordino was not surprised. He had expected that one of them would be conscientiously working late, creating the construction plans for some rich man's floating home away from home.

"Mr. Wes Wilbanks?" inquired Giordino.

"Yes, this is Wes. What can I do for you this time of night?" The voice had a soft Southern drawl.

"My name is Albert Giordino. I'm with the National

Underwater & Marine Agency. I need your help in identifying the manufacturer of a boat."

"Is it docked here in Miami?"

"No, sir. It could be anywhere in the world."

"Sounds mysterious."

"More than you know."

"I'll be in the office tomorrow at around ten."

"This is a matter of some urgency," Giordino said with quiet authority.

"Okay, I'll be wrapping up in about an hour. Why don't you drop by then? Do you have the address?"

"Yes, but I'm a stranger to Miami."

Wilbanks gave Giordino directions. The architect's office was only a few blocks away, so Giordino grabbed a fast dinner at a small Cuban café and set off on foot, following the directions he'd received over the phone.

The man who opened the door was quite tall and dressed in shorts and a flowered shirt.

"Mr. Giordino, Wes Wilbanks. I'm real pleased to meet you."

"Thank you for seeing me."

Wilbanks led him into an office with a hardwood floor, shelves covering one wall stacked with books on yacht and small-boat design. The other wall was filled with half-hull models that Giordino assumed were built from Wilbanks' plans. The middle of the room contained a large antique drafting table. A desk with a computer sat nestled on a bench in front of a picture window overlooking the port.

Giordino laid the sketches from the second officer of the container ship *Rio Grande* on the drafting table. "I know this isn't much to go on, but I'm hoping you might point me toward the manufacturer."

Wilbanks studied the drawings, tilting his head from side to side. After a solid minute, he rubbed his chin and peered over the sketch paper. "At first glance it looks like a basic design from any one of a hundred boatbuilders. But I do believe whoever observed the boat and sketched it was fooled by the angle from which he viewed it. Actually, I believe there are two hulls, not one, mounting a futuristic pod that gives it a space-age look. I've always wanted to create something like this but have yet to find a customer willing to stray very far from conventional designs.

"Tell you what, drop back by my office about ten in the morning. I should have something for you."

"I'm grateful for your help."

Giordino shook Wilbanks' hand, then took a long walk along the waterfront before returning to his motel room, where he read a mystery novel before finally falling asleep.

At ten o'clock on the nose the next morning, Giordino entered Wilbanks' studio. The boat architect was studying a set of plans. He held them up and grinned.

"After you left last night," he said, "I refined the sketches you gave me and ran off scaled plans. Then I reduced the size and faxed them to San Diego and Germany. Because of the difference in time, Heinklemann had responded before I came in this morning. Glastec replied to my inquiry only twenty minutes before you walked in."

"Were they familiar with the boat in question?" asked Giordino impatiently.

"The good news is that one of Heinklemann's engineers saw and studied your boat when it was moored in Monaco about nine months ago. He reports the manufacturer was a French firm, a new one in the industry I wasn't aware of. Jusserand Marine out of Cherbourg."

"Then we can fax them a set of your plans," said Giordino, his hopes on the rise again.

"No need." Wilbanks waved him off. "Though the subject never came up, I assumed your real reason for tracing the boat manufacturer was to learn the identity of the owner."

"I have no reason to deny it."

"The Heinklemann engineer who spotted the boat in Monaco was also kind enough to include the owner's name in the fax. He mentioned that he inquired only after he noticed that the crew looked more like a band of Mafia toughs than polished seamen maintaining and sailing a luxury yacht."

"Mafia toughs?"

"He claimed they all packed guns."

"The name of the owner?"

"A woman, a wealthy Australian. Her family made a fortune in diamond mining. Her name is Boudicca Dorsett."

17

While Pitt was on a flight to Ottawa, Canada, Giordino called his plane and briefed him on the mystery yacht.

"There is no doubt?" asked Pitt.

"Not in my book," replied Giordino. "It's almost a dead certainty the boat that fled the death scene belongs to the Dorsett family."

"The plot thickens."

"You might also be interested in learning that the admiral asked the Navy to conduct a satellite search of the central and eastern belt of the Pacific Ocean. The yacht was discovered and tracked. It made a brief layover in Hawaii and then continued on toward your goal."

"What does the yacht look like?"

"Unlike any boat you've ever seen before. Strictly a space-age design."

"I'll keep an eye out for it," Pitt promised.

"I know it's a waste of breath saying this," Giordino said cynically, "but stay out of trouble."

"I'll wire if I need money." Pitt laughed as he hung up, thankful that he had a caring friend like Albert Cassius Giordino.

After landing and renting a car, Pitt took the bridge across the Rideau River into Ottawa, the Canadian capital city. The weather was colder than the inside of a refrigerator, and the landscape appeared ugly and barren without leaves on the trees.

As he drove across the bridge over the Ottawa River and into the small city of Hull, he glanced at his map and memorized the streets leading to a group of three upscale buildings that housed several government offices. The one he was looking for was Environment Canada, a department of the government that corresponded to the U.S. Environmental Protection Agency in Washington.

A security guard at a gatehouse gave him directions and waved him through. Pitt slipped the car into a slot in the visitors' parking lot and entered the building. A quick glance at the building directory, and he was into the elevator and on his way up to Environment Canada's offices.

A receptionist nearing retirement looked up and forced a thin smile. "May I help you?"

"My name is Pitt. I have an appointment with Mr. Edward Posey."

"One moment." She dialed a number, announced his arrival and then nodded. "Please take the hallway down to the doorway at the end."

Pitt thanked her and did as he was told. A pretty red-haired secretary met him at the door and ushered him into Posey's office.

A short man with glasses and a beard rose from his chair, leaned over the desk and pressed Pitt's extended hand. "A pleasure to see you again, Dirk."

"I need a favor, Ed."

Posey nodded to a chair. "Sit down, sit down. What exactly can I do for you?"

"I'd like your permission to investigate the mining activities being conducted at Kunghit Island."

"You talking about Dorsett Consolidated's operations?"

Pitt nodded. "The same. NUMA has reason to believe their excavating technology is having a devastating effect on sea life as far away as the Antarctic."

Posey gave him a thoughtful look. "This have anything to do with that Australian cruise ship and its dead passengers?"

"Any connection is purely circumstantial at this date."

"But you have your suspicions?" Posey inquired.

"We do."

"Natural Resources Canada is who you should talk to."

"I don't think so. If your government operates anything like mine, it would take an act of Parliament to allow an investigation onto land that is legally leased by a mining company. Even then, Arthur Dorsett is too powerful to allow that to happen."

"Why don't you simply go on the property with a bona fide team of Canadian environmental engineers and blow the whistle on any shady operations?"

Pitt shook his head. "A waste of time. Dorsett's foreman would only close down the mine until they left. Better to investigate when their guard isn't up."

Posey stared past Pitt out the window for several seconds. Then he shrugged. "Okay, I'll arrange for you to work under contract with Environment Canada to investigate the kelp forest around Kunghit Island. You're to study any possible damage to the kelp from chemicals running into the sea from the mining operations. How does that sound?"

"Thank you," Pitt said sincerely.

"One more thing," said Posey. "I strongly advise you take along one of the local Indians as a guide. That will give you more of an official look. Environment Canada works closely with the tribes to prevent pollution and save forested land. A researcher and a local fisherman working on a project for the government should dilute any doubts by Dorsett security."

"Do you have a name in mind?" asked Pitt.

"Mason Broadmoor. A very resourceful guy. I've hired him before on a number of environmental projects."

"An Indian with the name of Mason Broadmoor?"

"He's a member of the Haida who live on the Queen Charlotte Islands of British Columbia. Most of them took British names generations ago. They're excellent fishermen and are familiar with the waters around Kunghit Island."

"Is Broadmoor a fisherman?"

"Not really. But he's very creative."

"Creative at what?"

Posey hesitated for a few moments, straightened some papers on his desk and then stared at Pitt rather sheepishly.

"Mason Broadmoor," he said finally, "carves totem poles."

18

ARTHUR DORSETT STEPPED OUT OF THE PRIVATE ELEVATOR to his penthouse suite as he did every morning at precisely seven o'clock. He was a giant of a man, brawny shoulders brushing the sides of the door frame as he ducked under the lintel. He had the hairy, muscular build of a professional wrestler. Coarse and wiry sandy hair swirled about his head like a thicket of brambles. His face was ruddy and as fierce as the black eyes that stared from beneath heavy, scraggly brows. He walked with an odd rocking motion, his shoulders dipping up and down like the walking beam of a steam engine.

His skin was rough and tanned by long days in the sun, working in the open mines, driving his miners for higher production, and he could still fill a muck bucket with the best of them. A huge mustache curled downward past the corners of lips that were constantly stretched open like a moray eel's, revealing teeth yellowed from long years of pipe smoking. He radiated contempt and arrogance. Arthur Dorsett was an empire unto himself who followed no laws but his own.

Dorsett shunned the limelight, a difficult feat with his incredible wealth and the $400 million jewelry trade building he built in Sydney. The building housed the offices of diamond brokers, traders, and merchants, cutting and faceting laboratories and a polishing factory. Known as a major player among diamond producers, Arthur Dorsett also played a highly secret role behind the scenes of the colored gemstone market.

He strode into the large anteroom, past four secretaries without acknowledging their presence, into an office that was located in the center of the building, with no windows to allow a magnificent panoramic view of modern Sydney sprawling outward from its harbor. Too many men who had been crossed in business deals with Dorsett gladly would have hired a sniper to take him out. He entered through a steel door into an office that was plain, with walls two meters thick. The entire room was one gigantic vault where Dorsett directed the family mining ventures and where he had collected and now displayed the largest and most opulent stones dug from his mines and faceted by his cutting workshops. Hundreds of incredibly beautiful stones were laid out on black velvet in glass cases. It was estimated this one room alone held diamonds worth close to $1.2 billion.

Dorsett sat down behind his desk, a huge monstrosity built of polished lava rock with mahogany drawers. He pressed a button on a console that alerted his head secretary that he was now in his office.

She came back over the intercom almost immediately. "Your daughters have been waiting nearly an hour."

Indifferent, Dorsett replied with a voice that was as hard as the diamonds in the room. "Send the little darlin's in." Then he sat back to watch the parade, never failing to enjoy the physical and personal differences of his daughters.

Boudicca, a statuesque giantess, strode through the doorway with the self-assurance of a tigress entering an unarmed village. Far taller than her sisters, she towered over all but a very few men. Only slightly shorter than her father, she had his black eyes, but more ominous and veiled than fierce. She wore no makeup, and a flood of reddish-blond hair fell to her hips, loose and flowing. Her expression was half contemptuous, half evil. She easily dominated anyone in her presence except, of course, her father.

Deirdre seemed to float into the room, poised and nonchalant. Undeniably glamorous, she knew exactly what she was capable of doing. She and Boudicca dutifully sat down in two of three chairs placed in front of Dorsett's desk.

Maeve followed her sisters, moving as gracefully as pond reeds in a light breeze. Her long blond hair was soft and glowing, her skin flushed red and her blue eyes blazing with anger. She moved in a straight line between her seated sisters, chin up firmly, staring deeply into her father's eyes, which reflected intrigue and corruption.

"I want my boys!" she snapped. It was not a plea but a demand.

"Sit down, girl," her father ordered, picking up a briar pipe and pointing it like a gun.

"No!" she shouted. "You abducted my sons, and I want them back or I'll turn you and these two over to the police, but not before I've exposed you all to the news media."

He looked at her steadily, calmly appraising her defiance. Then he called his secretary over the intercom. "Will you please connect me with Jack Ferguson?" He smiled at Maeve. "You remember Jack, don't you?"

"That sadistic ape you call your superintendent of mines. What about him?"

"I thought you'd like to know. He's baby-sitting the twins."

The anger fled from Maeve's face and was replaced with alarm. "Not Ferguson?"

"A little discipline never hurt growing boys."

She started to say something, but the intercom buzzed and Dorsett held up his hand for silence. He spoke through a speakerphone on his desk. "Jack, you there?"

There was the sound of heavy equipment in the background as Ferguson replied over his portable phone. "I'm here."

"Are the boys nearby?"

"Yes, sir. I've got them loading muck that's spilled from the cars."

"I'd like you to arrange an accident—"

"No!" Maeve screamed. "My God, they're only six years old. You can't murder your own grandchildren!"

"I don't consider them my grandchildren," Dorsett roared back.

Maeve was overcome with sickening fear. It was a battle she could not win. Her sons were in deadly danger, and she saw clearly that her only hope of saving them was to submit to her father's will. Somehow she had to stall for time until she devised a plan to save her boys. Nothing else mattered. If only she had gotten her plight across to the man from NUMA. He might have thought of a way to help her. But he was thousands of kilometers away.

She sagged into an empty chair, beaten but still defiant, her emotions in upheaval. "What do you want from me?"

"I want you to return to the United States and work with their National Underwater & Marine Agency. Watch them carefully. Observe their methods in attempting to discover the cause of the unexplained deaths. If they begin to get close to an answer, do what you can to stall them."

"You're mad," she gasped, stunned at what she'd heard. "You'd murder your own flesh and blood as if it meant nothing—"

"Oh, but you're very wrong, dear sister," Boudicca

interrupted. "Twenty billion dollars is far more than nothing."

"What insane scheme have you hatched?" asked Maeve.

"If you hadn't run away from us, you'd know," said Deirdre nastily.

"Daddy is going to collapse the world diamond market," revealed Boudicca as unruffled as if she were describing a new pair of shoes.

Maeve stared at him. "That's impossible. Even you can't dictate the diamond market."

"You're dead wrong, Daughter," said Dorsett smugly. He sat back, folded his huge hands across his chest and nodded. "I've had our mining crews working three shifts, twenty-four hours a day for the past ten years. In another month I will have accumulated a stockpile of over $2 billion worth of stones. If my instincts are right, the market will reach bottom in thirty days before it rebounds. I intend to attack when it's down."

"What are you doing in the mines that causes death throughout the ocean?" demanded Maeve.

"About a year ago, my engineers developed a revolutionary excavator using high-energy pulsed ultrasound to carve through the blue clay that contains the major deposits of diamonds. Apparently, the subterranean rock under the islands we mine creates a resonance that channels into the surrounding water. Though a rare event, it occasionally converges with the resonance from our other mining operations, near Siberia, Chile, and Canada. The energy intensifies to a level that can kill animals and humans. However unfortunate, I cannot allow these aberrant side effects to throw off my time schedule."

"Don't you understand?" pleaded Maeve. "Don't you care about the sea life and hundreds of people your greed has killed? How many more must die before this madness is satisfied?"

"Only after I have destroyed the diamond market will I stop," Dorsett said coldly. He turned to Boudicca. "Where is the yacht?"

"I sent it on to Kunghit Island after I debarked in Honolulu and flew home. My chief of security there has informed me that the Canadian Mounties are becoming suspicious. They've been flying over the island, taking photographs and asking questions of the nearby inhabitants. With your permission, I would like to rejoin the yacht. Your geophysicists are also predicting another convergence approximately five hundred kilometers west of Seattle. I should be standing by to remove any possible wreckage to frustrate investigation by the American Coast Guard."

"Take the company jet and return as soon as possible."

"You know where the deaths will occur next?" Maeve demanded in dismay. "You must warn ships to stay out of the area."

"Not a practical idea," Boudicca answered, "letting the world in on our secret. Besides, Daddy's scientists can only give rough estimates for where and when the sound waves will strike."

Maeve stared at her sister, her lips slowly tightening. "You had a pretty good idea when you put Deirdre on the *Polar Queen* to save my life."

Boudicca laughed. "Is that what you think?"

"That's what she told me."

"I lied to keep you from informing the NUMA people," said Deirdre. "Sorry, sister dear, father's engineers made a slight miscalculation in time. The acoustic plague was estimated to strike the ship three hours earlier."

"Three hours earlier . . ." Maeve murmured as the

awful truth slowly dawned on her. "I would have been on the ship."

"And you would have died with the others," said Deirdre as if disappointed.

"You meant for me to die!" Maeve gasped, contempt and horror in her expression.

Her father looked at her as if he were examining a stone he'd picked up at his mine. "You turned your back on your sisters and me. To us, you no longer existed. You still don't."

19

A STRAWBERRY-RED FLOATPLANE WITH CHINOOK CARGO Carriers painted in white block letters on the side of the fuselage rocked gently in the water beside a refueling dock near the Shearwater Airport in British Columbia. A short, brown-haired man with an unsmiling face, dressed in an old-fashioned leather flight suit, was holding a gas nozzle in one of the wing tanks. He looked down and examined the man who walked casually along the dock, carrying a backpack and a large black case. He was dressed in jeans with a skier's down vest. A cowboy hat was set square on his head. When the stranger stopped beside the aircraft and looked up, the pilot nodded at the wide-brimmed hat.

"A Stetson?"

"No, it was custom-made by Manny Gammage out of Austin, Texas."

The stranger studied the floatplane. It looked to have been built prior to 1970. "A de Havilland, isn't she?"

The pilot nodded. "De Havilland Beaver, one of the finest bush planes ever designed."

"An oldie but goody."

"Canadian-built in 1967. She'll lift over four thousand

kilograms off a hundred meters of water. Revered as the workhorse of the North. Over a hundred of them are still flying."

"Don't see big radial engines much anymore."

"You a friend of Ed Posey?" the pilot asked abruptly.

"I am," answered Pitt without introducing himself.

"A bit breezy today."

"About twenty knots, I should judge."

"You a flyer?"

"I have a few hours in the air."

"Malcolm Stokes."

"Dirk Pitt."

"I understand you want to fly to Black Water Inlet."

Pitt nodded. "Ed Posey told me that's where I could find a totem carver by the name of Mason Broadmoor."

"I know Mason. His village sits at the lower end of Moresby Island, across the Houston Stewart Channel from Kunghit Island."

"How long a flight?"

"An hour and a half across Hecate Strait. Should get you there in time for lunch."

"Sounds good," said Pitt.

Stokes gestured at the black case. "What you got in there, a trombone?"

"A hydrophone, an instrument for measuring underwater sound."

Without further discussion, Stokes capped the fuel tank and inserted the nozzle back into the gas pump as Pitt loaded his gear on board. After untying the mooring lines and pushing the plane away from the dock with one foot, Stokes made his way to the cockpit.

"Care to ride up front?" he asked.

Pitt smiled inwardly. He saw no passenger seats in the cargo section. "Don't mind if I do."

Pitt strapped himself into the copilot's seat as Stokes started and warmed up the big single radial engine and checked his gauges. Already the receding tide had carried the aircraft three meters from the dock. After a visual check of the channel for other boats or planes, Stokes eased the throttle forward and took off, banking the Beaver over Campbell Island and heading west. As they climbed, Pitt recalled the report Hiram Yaeger had given him before leaving Washington.

The Queen Charlotte Islands are made up of about 150 islands running parallel to the Canadian mainland 160 kilometers to the east. The total area of the islands comes to 9,584 square kilometers. The population of 5,890 is made up mostly of Haida Indians, who invaded the islands in the eighteenth century. The Haida used the abundant red cedars to build huge dugout canoes and multifamily plank houses supported by massive portal poles, and to carve splendid totem poles as well as masks, boxes and dishes.

The economy is based on lumber and fishing as well as the mining of copper, coal and iron ore. In 1997, prospectors working for Dorsett Consolidated Mining Ltd., found a kimberlite pipe on Kunghit Island, the southernmost island in the Queen Charlotte chain. After drilling a test hole, 98 diamonds were found in one 52-kilogram sample. Although Kunghit Island was part of the South Moresby National Park Reserve, the government allowed Dorsett Consolidated to file a claim and lease the island. Dorsett then launched an extensive excavation operation and closed off the island to all visitors and campers. It was estimated by New York brokers C. Dirgo & Co. that the mine could bring out as much as $2 billion in diamonds.

"May I ask about your game plan?" asked Stokes.

"Nothing complex," Pitt answered. "I hope to infiltrate the mine, hiring Mason Broadmoor as a guide to get me on the island, providing he's willing."

"If I know Mason, he'll jump at the chance. His

brother was fishing near the island about a year ago. One of Dorsett Consolidated's security boats ordered him away. Since the family had been fishing those waters for generations, he refused. They beat him pretty badly and burned his boat. When we investigated, Dorsett's security people claimed that Broadmoor's boat exploded and they rescued him."

"His word against twenty of them."

"More like eight, but you get the picture."

"Now it's your turn," said Pitt kindly. "How am I supposed to help you?"

Stokes pointed out his window at a forested island with a great dirt scar in the middle of it. "Kunghit Island. They carved a small runway for air transport to ferry in men and supplies. I'll fake engine trouble and we'll drop in. While I tinker under the cowling, you regale the security guards with your tales of derring-do under the sea."

Pitt stared at Stokes dubiously. "What do you hope to accomplish besides antagonizing Dorsett's security enforcers?"

"I have my reasons for wanting to land. Reason one. To allow the cameras encased in the floats to take close-up pictures during landing and takeoff."

"Somehow I have the impression they hate uninvited visitors. What makes you think we won't be stood against a privy and shot?"

"Reason two," said Stokes, brushing off Pitt's objections. "My superiors are hoping for just such an event. Then they can come swooping in here and close them down."

"Naturally."

"Reason three. We have an undercover agent working in the mines. We're hoping he can pass me information while we're on the ground."

"We're just full of devious little plots, aren't we?" said Pitt.

"In a more serious vein, if worse comes to worst, I'll let Dorsett's security people know I'm a Mountie. They're not so stupid as to risk invasion by a small army of law officers running about the place searching for the body of one of their finest."

"You *did* notify your team and superiors we'd be dropping in?"

Stokes looked hurt. "Any disappearance is timed to make the evening newspapers. Not to worry, Dorsett's mine executives abhor bad publicity."

"When exactly do we pull off this marvel of Royal Mounted Police planning?"

Stokes pointed down to the island again. "I should begin my descent in about five minutes."

Pitt could do little but sit back and enjoy the view. Below he could see the great volcanic cone with its central pipe of blue ground that contained the rough diamonds. What looked like a giant bridge of steel girders stretched over the open core, with a myriad of steel cables that raised and lowered the excavated debris. Once they reached the top, the buckets then moved horizontally like ski gondolas across the open pit to buildings where the diamonds were extracted from the tailings, which were then dumped onto a huge mound that enclosed the diggings. The mound also acted as an artificial barrier to discourage anyone from entering or leaving, a reality Pitt found obvious from the total absence of any entrances except one, a tunnel that opened to a road that led to a dock on a small bay. He knew from his map that the bay was called Rose Harbour. As he watched, a tug with an empty barge in tow was pulling away from the dock and heading toward the mainland.

A series of prefabricated buildings grouped between the mound and the pit were apparently used for offices and living quarters for the miners. The enclosure, easily two kilometers in diameter, also accommodated the narrow airstrip with a hangar. The entire mining operation looked like a gigantic scar on the landscape from the air.

"That's one big pockmark," said Pitt.

Without looking down, Stokes said, "That pockmark, as you call it, is where dreams come from."

Stokes leaned out his fuel mixture and starved his big 450-horsepower Pratt & Whitney R-985 Wasp engine until it began to miss and backfire. Already, a voice was coming over the radio warning him away from the property, but he ignored it. "I have a fuel blockage and must borrow your airstrip for an emergency landing. Sorry for the inconvenience, but it can't be helped." Then he switched off the radio.

"Don't you just hate dropping in unannounced?" said Pitt.

Stokes was concentrating on landing the plane, with the engine coughing and barely turning over, and did not reply. He lowered a pair of small wheels through the forward center of the two large pontoons and lined up with the runway. A crosswind caught the plane, and Stokes overcompensated. Pitt tensed slightly as he observed that Stokes lacked full control. The Mountie was reasonably competent but hardly an expert pilot. The landing was rough, and he almost ground-looped.

Before the plane rolled to a stop in front of the airstrip's hangar, it was surrounded by nearly ten men in blue combat fatigues, holding Bushmaster customized M-16 assault rifles with suppressors. A tall, gaunt man in his early thirties and wearing a combat helmet stepped up on one of the floats and opened the door. He entered the aircraft and made his way to the cockpit. Pitt noticed the guard rested his hand on a holstered nine-millimeter automatic.

"This is private property, and you are trespassing," he said in a perfectly friendly voice.

"Sorry," said Stokes. "But the fuel filter clogged. The second time this month. It's this damned stuff they're passing off as gas nowadays."

"How soon can you make repairs and be on your way?"

"Twenty minutes, no more."

"Please hurry," said the security official. "You'll have to remain by your plane."

"May I borrow a bathroom?" Pitt asked politely.

The security guard studied him for a moment, then nodded. "There's one in the hangar. One of my men will escort you."

"You don't know how grateful I am," Pitt said as if in minor agony. He jumped out of the plane and set off toward the hangar with a security guard close at his heels. Once inside the metal structure, he turned as if waiting expectantly for the guard to direct him to the door leading to the bathroom. It was a ploy; he'd already guessed the correct door, but it gave him a brief instant to glance at the aircraft resting on the hangar floor.

A Gulfstream V, the latest development in business jets, was an imposing aircraft. Unlike the earlier Learjet—so eagerly purchased and flown by the rich and famous—whose interior barely had enough room to turn around in, the G V was spacious, giving passengers plenty of elbowroom and enough height for most tall men to stand up straight. Capable of cruising 924 kilometers per hour at an altitude of just under 11,000 meters, with a range of 6,300 nautical miles, the aircraft was powered by a pair of turbofan jets built by BMW and Rolls-Royce.

Dorsett spared no expense for his transportation fleet,

thought Pitt. An aircraft like this cost upward of $33 million.

Parked just in front of the main hangar door, menacing and sinister in dark blue-black paint, were a pair of squat-looking helicopters. Pitt recognized them as McDonnell Douglas 530 MD Defenders, a military aircraft designed for silent flying and high stability during abnormal maneuvers. A pair of 7.62-millimeter guns were mounted in pods under the fuselage. An array of tracking gear sprouted from the underside of the cockpit. These were scout models specially modified for tracking diamond smugglers or other unwelcome intruders on the ground.

After he came out of the bathroom, he was motioned by the guard into an office. The man who sat at a desk was small, thin. He turned from a computer monitor and studied Pitt, his deep-set eyes gray and unreadable. Pitt found the man slimy and repellant.

"I am John Merchant, chief of security for this mine," he said with a distinctive Australian accent. "May I see some identification, please?"

Silently, Pitt handed over his NUMA ID and waited.

"Dirk Pitt." Merchant rolled the name on his tongue and repeated it. "Dirk Pitt. Aren't you the chap who found an immense cache of Inca treasure in the Sonoran Desert a few years ago?"

"I was only one member of the team."

"Why have you come to Kunghit?"

"Better you ask the pilot. He's the one who landed the plane on your precious mining property. I'm only a passenger along for the ride."

"Malcolm Stokes is an inspector with the Royal Canadian Mounted Police. He's also a member of the Criminal Investigation Directorate." Merchant gestured toward his computer. "I have an entire data file on him. It's you who are in question."

"You're very thorough," said Pitt. "Taking into account your close contacts in the Canadian government, you probably already know I'm here to study the effects of chemical pollution on the local kelp and fish populations. Would you care to see my documents?"

"I already have copies."

Pitt was tempted to believe Merchant, but he knew Posey well enough to trust his confidence. He decided Merchant was lying. It was an old Gestapo ploy, to make the victim think the accuser knew all there was to know. "Then why bother to inquire?"

"To find if you are in the habit of inaccurate statements."

"Am I under suspicion for some hideous crime?" asked Pitt.

"My job is to apprehend smugglers of illicit diamonds before they traffic their stones to European and Middle Eastern clearinghouses. Because you came here uninvited, I have to consider your motives."

Pitt observed the reflection of the guard in the windows of a glass cabinet. He was standing slightly behind Pitt, to his right, automatic weapon held across his chest. "Since you know who I am and claim to have documentation for my purpose for coming to the Queen Charlotte Islands, you cannot seriously believe that I'm a diamond smuggler." Pitt rose to his feet. "I've enjoyed the conversation, but I see no reason to hang around."

"I regret that you must be detained temporarily," Merchant said, brisk and businesslike.

"You have no authority."

"Because you are a trespasser on private property under false pretenses, I have every right to make a citizen's arrest."

Not good, Pitt thought. If Merchant dug deeper and connected him to the Dorsett sisters and the *Polar Queen,* then no lies, no matter how creative, could explain his presence here. "What about Stokes? Since you claim you know he's a Mountie, why not turn me over to him?"

"I prefer turning you over to his superiors," Merchant said almost cheerfully, "but not before I can investigate this matter more thoroughly."

Pitt didn't doubt now that he would not be allowed off the mining property alive. "Is Stokes free to leave?"

"The minute he finishes his unnecessary repairs to the aircraft. I enjoy observing his primitive attempts at surveillance."

"It goes without saying that he'll report my seizure."

"A foregone conclusion," said Merchant dryly.

Outside the hangar came the popping sound of an aircraft engine firing up. Stokes was being forced to take off without his passenger. If he was going to act, Pitt figured that he had less than thirty seconds. He noted an ashtray on the desk with several cigarette butts and assumed Merchant smoked. He threw up his hands in a gesture of defeat.

"If I'm to be detained against my wishes, do you mind if I have a cigarette?"

"Not at all," said Merchant, pushing the ashtray across the desk. "I may even join you."

Pitt had stopped smoking years before, but he made a slow movement as if to reach in the open breast pocket of his shirt. He doubled up his right hand into a fist and clasped it with his left. Then in a lightning move, pulling with one arm and pushing with the other for extra strength, he jammed his right elbow into the security guard's stomach. There came an explosive gasp of agony as the guard doubled over.

Merchant's reaction time was admirable. He pulled a small nine-millimeter automatic from a belt holster and unsnapped the safety in one well-practiced motion. But before the muzzle of the gun could clear the desktop, he found himself staring down the barrel of the guard's automatic rifle, now cradled in Pitt's steady hands, lined up on Merchant's nose. The security chief felt as though he were staring through a tunnel with no light at the other end.

Slowly, he placed his pistol on the desk. "This will do you no good," he said acidly.

Pitt grabbed the automatic and dropped it in his coat pocket. "Sorry I can't stay for dinner, but I don't want to lose my ride."

Then he was through the door and sprinting across the hangar floor. He threw the rifle in a trash receptacle, cleared the door and slowed to a jog as he passed through the ring of guards. They stared at him suspiciously, but assumed their boss had allowed Pitt to leave. They made no move to stop him as Stokes opened the throttle and the floatplane began moving down the runway. Pitt leaped onto a float, yanked open the door against the wash from the propeller and threw himself inside the cargo bay.

Stokes looked dumbfounded as Pitt slipped into the copilot's seat. "Where did you come from?"

"The traffic was heavy on the way to the airport," Pitt said, catching his breath.

"They forced me to take off without you."

"What happened to your undercover agent?"

"He didn't show. Security around the plane was too tight."

"You won't be happy to learn that Dorsett's security chief, a nasty little jerk called John Merchant, has you pegged as a snooping Mountie from the CID."

"So much for my cover as a bush pilot," Stokes muttered as he pulled back on the control column.

Pitt slid open the side window, stuck his head into the prop blast and looked back. The security guards appeared to be wildly scurrying about like ants. Then he saw something else that caused a small knot in his stomach. "I think I made them mad."

"Could it be something you said?"

Pitt pulled the side window closed. "Actually, I beat up a guard and stole the chief of security's side arm."

"That would do it."

"They're coming after us in one of those armed helicopters."

"I know the type," Stokes said uneasily. "They're a good forty knots faster than this old bus. They'll overhaul us long before we can make it back to Shearwater."

"They can't shoot us down in front of witnesses," said Pitt. "How far to the nearest inhabited community on Moresby Island?"

"Mason Broadmoor's village. It sits on Black Water Inlet, about sixty kilometers north of here. If we get there first, I can make a water landing in the middle of the village fishing fleet."

His adrenaline pumping, Pitt gazed at Stokes through eyes flashing with fire. "Then go for it."

20

PITT AND STOKES QUICKLY BECAME AWARE THEY WERE IN A
no-win situation from the very start. They had little
choice but to take off toward the south before banking on
a 180-degree turn for Moresby Island to the north. The
McDonnell Douglas Defender helicopter, manned by
Dorsett's security men, had merely to lift vertically off
the ground in front of the hangar, turn northward and
cut in behind the slower floatplane even before the chase
shifted into first gear. The de Havilland Beaver's airspeed indicator read 160 knots, but Stokes felt as if he
were flying a glider as they crossed the narrow channel
separating the two islands.

"Where are they?" he asked without taking his eyes
from a low range of cedar- and pine-covered hills directly ahead and the water only a hundred meters below.

"Half a kilometer back of our tail and closing fast,"
Pitt answered.

"Just one?"

"They probably decided knocking us down was a
piece of cake and left the other chopper home."

"But for the extra weight and air drag of our floats, we
might be on equal footing."

"Do you carry any weapons in this antique?" asked Pitt.

"Against regulations."

"A pity you didn't hide a shotgun in the floats."

"Unlike your American peace officers, who think nothing of packing an arsenal, we're not keen to wave guns around unless there is a life-threatening situation."

Pitt glanced at him incredulously. "What do you call this mess?"

"An unforeseen difficulty," Stokes answered stoically.

"Then all we have is the nine-millimeter automatic I stole, against two heavy machine guns," said Pitt. "You know, I downed a chopper by throwing a life raft into its rotor blades a couple of years ago."

Stokes turned and stared at Pitt, unable to believe the incredible calm. "Sorry. Except for a pair of life vests, the cargo bay is bare."

"They're swinging around on our starboard side for a clear shot. When I give the word, drop the flaps and pull back the throttle."

"I'll never pull out if I stall her at this altitude."

"Coming down in treetops beats a bullet in the brain and crashing in flames."

"I never thought of it quite like that," Stokes said grimly.

Pitt watched intently as the blue-black helicopter pulled parallel to the floatplane and seemed to hang there, like a hovering falcon eyeing a pigeon. They were so close that Pitt could discern the expressions on the faces of the pilot and copilot. They were both smiling. Pitt opened his side window and held the automatic out of sight under the frame.

"No warning over the radio?" said Stokes disbelievingly. "No demand we return to the mine?"

"These guys play tough. They wouldn't dare kill a

Mountie unless they've got orders from someone high up in Dorsett Consolidated."

"I can't believe they expect to get away with it."

"They're sure going to try," Pitt said quietly, his eyes locked on the gunner. "Get ready." He was not optimistic. Their only advantage, which was really no advantage at all, was that the 530 MD Defender was better suited for ground attack than air-to-air combat.

Stokes held the control column between his knees as one hand embraced the flap levers and the other gripped the throttle. He found himself wondering why he placed so much trust in a man he had known less than two hours. The answer was simple. In all his years with the Mounties he had seen few men who were in such absolute control of a seemingly hopeless situation.

"Now!" Pitt shouted, raising and firing off the automatic in the same breath.

Stokes rammed the flaps to the full down position and slapped back the throttle. The old Beaver, without the power of its engine and held by the wind resistance against the big floats, slowed as abruptly as if it had entered a cloud of glue.

At almost the same instant, Stokes heard the rapid-fire stammer of a machine gun and the thump of bullets on one wing. He also heard the sharp crack of Pitt's automatic. This was no fight, he thought as he frantically threw the near-stalling plane around in the air, this was a high school quarterback facing the entire defensive line of the Arizona Cardinals football team. Then suddenly, for some inexplicable reason the shooting stopped. The nose of the plane was dropping, and he pushed the throttle forward again to regain a small measure of control.

Stokes stole a glance sideways as he leveled out the floatplane and picked up speed. The helicopter had veered off. The copilot was slumped sideways in his seat behind several bullet holes in the plastic bubble of the cockpit. Stokes was surprised to find that the Beaver still responded to his commands. What surprised him even more was the look on Pitt's face. It was sheer disappointment.

"I missed," Pitt muttered.

"What are you talking about? You hit the copilot."

Pitt, angry at himself, stared at him. "I was aiming at the rotor assembly."

"You timed it perfectly," Stokes complimented him. "How did you know the exact instant to give me the signal and then shoot?"

"The pilot stopped smiling."

Stokes let it go. They weren't out of the storm yet. Broadmoor's village was still thirty kilometers away.

"They're coming around for another pass," said Pitt.

"No sense in attempting the same dodge."

Pitt nodded. "I agree. The pilot will be expecting it. This time pull back on the control column and do an Immelmann."

"What's an Immelmann?"

Pitt looked at him. "You don't know? How long have you been flying?"

"Twenty-one hours, give or take."

"Oh, that's just great," Pitt groaned. "Pull up in a half loop and then do a half roll at the top, to end up going in the opposite direction."

"I'm not sure I'm up for that."

"Don't the Mounties have qualified professional pilots?"

"None who were available for this assignment," Stokes said stiffly. "Think you might hit a vital part of the chopper this time?"

"Not unless I'm amazingly lucky," Pitt replied. "I'm down to three rounds."

There was no hesitating on the part of the Defender's pilot. He angled in for a direct attack from above and to the side of his helpless quarry. A well-designed attack that left little room for Stokes to maneuver.

"Now!" Pitt yelled. "Put your nose down to gain speed and then pull up into your loop."

Stokes' inexperience caused hesitation. He was barely coming to the top of the loop in preparation for the half roll when the 7.62-millimeter shells began smashing into the floatplane's thin aluminum skin. The windshield burst into a thousand pieces as shells hammered the instrument panel. The Defender's pilot altered his aim and raked his fire from the cockpit across the fuselage. It was an error that kept the Beaver in the air. He should have blasted the engine.

Pitt fired off his final three rounds and hurled himself forward and down to make himself as small a target as possible in an act that was pure illusion.

Remarkably, Stokes had completed the Immelmann, late to be sure, but now the Beaver was headed away from the helicopter before its pilot could swing his craft around 180 degrees. Pitt shook his head in dazed incredulity and checked his body for wounds. Except for a rash of small cuts on his face from slivers that had flown off the shattered windshield, he was unscathed. The Beaver was in level flight, and the radial engine was still roaring smoothly at full revolutions. The engine was the only part of the plane that hadn't been riddled with bullets. He looked at Stokes sharply.

"Are you okay?"

Stokes slowly turned and gazed at Pitt through unfocused eyes. "I think the bastards just shot me out of my pension," he murmured. He coughed and then his lips were painted with blood that seeped down his chin and trickled onto his chest. Then he slumped forward against his shoulder harness, unconscious.

Pitt took the copilot's control wheel in his hands and immediately threw the floatplane around into a hard 180-degree bank until he was heading back on a course toward Mason Broadmoor's village. His snap turn caught the helicopter's pilot off guard, and a shower of bullets sprayed the empty air behind the floatplane's tail.

He wiped away the blood that had trailed into one eye and took stock. Most of the aircraft was stitched with over a hundred holes, but the control systems and surfaces were undamaged and the big 450 Wasp engine was still pounding away on every one of its cylinders.

Now what to do?

The first plan that ran through his mind was to make an attempt at ramming the helicopter. But that's all it could have been, an attempt. The Defender was far more nimble in the air than the lumbering Beaver with its massive pontoons. He'd stand as much chance as a cobra against a mongoose, a fight the mongoose never failed to win against the slower cobra. Only when it came up against a rattlesnake did the mongoose go down to defeat. The crazy thought running through Pitt's mind became divine inspiration as he sighted a low ridge of rocks about half a kilometer ahead and slightly to his right.

There was a path toward the rocks through a stand of tall Douglas fir trees. He dove between the trees, his wingtips brushing the needles of the upper branches. To anyone else it would have seemed like a desperate act of suicidal madness. The gambit misled the Defender's pilot, who broke off the third attack and followed slightly above and behind the floatplane, waiting to observe what looked like a certain crash.

Pitt kept the throttle full against its stop and gripped the control wheel with both hands, eyes focused on the wall of rocks that loomed ahead. The airstream blasted through the shattered windshield, and he was forced to turn his head sideways in order to see. Fortunately, the gale swept away the trickling blood and the tears that it pried from his squinting eyes.

He flew on between the trees. There could be no misjudgment, no miscalculation. He had to make the right move at the exact moment in time. A tenth of a second either way would spell certain death. The rocks were rushing toward the plane as if driven from behind. Pitt could clearly see them now, gray-and-brown jagged boulders with black streaks. He didn't have to look to see the needle on the altimeter registering on zero or the needle on the tachometer wavering far into the red. The old girl was hurtling toward destruction just as fast as she could fly.

"Low!" he shouted into the wind rushing through the smashed windshield. "Two meters low!"

He barely had time to compensate before the rocks were on him. He gave the control column a precisely measured jerk, just enough to raise the plane's nose, just enough so the tips of the propeller whipped over the ridge, missing the crest by centimeters. He heard the sudden crunch of metal as the aluminum floats smashed into the rocks and tore free of the fuselage. The Beaver shot into the air, as graceful as a soaring hawk released from its tether. Unburdened by the weight of the bulky floats, which lay smashed against the rocks, and with the drag on the aircraft decreased by nearly half, the ancient plane became more maneuverable and gained another thirty knots in airspeed. She responded to Pitt's commands instantly, without a trace of sluggishness as she chewed the air, fighting for altitude.

Now, he thought, a grin on his lips, I'll show you an Immelmann. He threw the aircraft into a half loop and then snapped it over in a half roll, heading on a direct course toward the helicopter. "Write your will, sucker!" he shouted, his voice drowned out by the rush of wind and the roar of the engine's exhaust. "Here comes the Red Baron."

Too late the chopper's pilot read Pitt's intentions. There was nowhere to dodge, nowhere to hide. The last thing he expected was an assault by the battered old floatplane. But here it was closing on a collision course at almost two hundred knots. It came roaring at him at a speed he didn't believe possible. He made a series of violent maneuvers, but the pilot of the old floatplane anticipated his moves and kept coming on. He angled the helicopter's nose toward his opponent in a wild attempt to blast the punctured Beaver out of the sky before the imminent crash.

Pitt saw the helicopter turn head-on, saw the flash from the guns in the pods, heard the shells punching into the big radial engine. Oil suddenly spurted from under the cowling, streaming onto the exhaust stacks and causing a dense trail of blue smoke to streak behind the plane. Pitt held up a hand to shield his eyes from the hot oil splattering against his face in stinging torrents from the airstream.

The sight that froze in his memory a microsecond before the impact was the expression of grim acceptance on the face of the helicopter's pilot.

The prop and engine of the floatplane smashed squarely into the helicopter just behind the cockpit in an explosion of metal and debris that sheared off the tail rotor boom. Deprived of its torque compensation, the main body of the helicopter was thrown into a violent lateral drift. It spun around crazily for several revolutions before plummeting like a stone, five hundred meters to the ground. Unlike special-effects crashes in motion pictures, it didn't immediately burst into flames after crumpling into an unrecognizable mass of smoldering wreckage. Nearly two minutes passed before flames flickered from the debris and a blinding sheet of flame enveloped it.

Pieces of the Beaver's shattered propeller spun into the sky like a fireworks pinwheel. The cowling seemed to burst off the engine and fluttered like a wounded bird into the trees. The engine froze and stopped as quickly as if Pitt had turned off the ignition switch. He wiped the oil from his eyes, and all he could see over the exposed cylinder heads was a carpet of treetops. The Beaver's airspeed fell off, and she stalled as he braced himself for the crash. The controls were still functioning, and he tried to float the plane down into the upper tree limbs.

He almost made it. But the outer edge of the right wing collided with a seventy-meter-tall red cedar, throwing the aircraft into an abrupt ninety-degree turn. Now totally out of control and dead in what little sky was left, the plane plunged into a solid mass of trees. The left wing wrapped itself around another towering cedar and was torn away. Green pine needles closed over the red plane, blotting it out from any view from above. The trunk of a fir tree, half a meter wide, rose in front of the battered aircraft. The propeller hub struck the tree head-on and punched right through it. The engine was pulled from its mountings as the upper half of the tree fell across the careening aircraft and knocked off the tail section. What remained of the wreckage plowed into the moist compost earth of the forest floor before finally coming to a dead stop.

For the next few minutes the ground below the trees was as silent as a cemetery. Pitt sat there, too stunned to move. He stared dazedly through the opening that was once the windshield. He noticed for the first time that the entire engine was gone and wondered vaguely where it went. At last his mind began to come level again, and he reached over and examined Stokes.

The Mountie shuddered in a fit of coughing, then shook his head feebly and regained a small measure of consciousness. He stared dumbly over the instrument panel at the pine branches that hung into the cockpit. "How did we come down in the forest?" he mumbled.

"You slept through the best part," Pitt muttered, as he tenderly massaged a gang of bruises.

Pitt didn't require eight years of medical school to know Stokes would surely die if he didn't get to a hospital. Quickly, he unzipped the old flying suit, ripped opened the Mountie's shirt and searched for the wound. He found it to the left of the breastbone, below the shoulder. There was so little blood and the hole was so small, he almost missed it. This wasn't made by a bullet, was Pitt's first reaction. He gently probed the hole and touched a sharp piece of metal. Puzzled, he looked up at the frame that once held the windshield. It was smashed beyond recognition. The impact of a bullet had driven a splinter from the aluminum frame into Stokes' chest, penetrating the left lung. Another centimeter and it would have entered the heart.

Stokes coughed up a wad of blood and spit it out the open window. "Funny," he murmured, "I always thought I'd get shot in a highway chase or in a back alley."

"No such luck."

"How bad does it look?"

"A metal splinter in your lung," Pitt explained. "Are you in pain?"

"More of a throbbing ache than anything else."

Pitt stiffly rose out of his seat and came around behind Stokes. "Hang on, I'll get you out of here."

Within ten minutes, Pitt had kicked open the crumpled entry door and carefully manhandled Stokes' deadweight outside, where he gently laid him on the soft ground. It took no small effort, and he was panting heavily by the time he sat next to the Mountie to catch his breath. Stokes' face tightened in agony more than once, but he never uttered so much as a low moan. On the verge of slipping into unconsciousness, he closed his eyes.

Pitt slapped him awake. "Don't black out on me, pal. I need you to point the way to Mason Broadmoor's village."

Stokes' eyes fluttered open, and he looked at Pitt questioningly, as if recalling something. "The Dorsett helicopter," he said between coughs. "What happened to those jokers who were shooting at us?"

Pitt stared back at the smoke rising above the forest and grinned. "They went to a barbecue."

21

PITT HAD EXPECTED TO TRUDGE THROUGH SNOW IN JANUARY on Kunghit Island, but only a light blanket of the white stuff had fallen on the ground, and much of that had melted since the last storm. He pulled Stokes along behind him on a travois, a device used for hauling burdens by American Plains Indians. He couldn't leave Stokes, and to attempt carrying the Mountie on his back was inviting internal hemorrhaging, so he lashed two dead-branch poles together with cargo tie-down straps he scrounged in the wreckage of the aircraft. Rigging a platform between the poles and a harness on one end, he strapped Stokes to the middle of the travois. Then throwing the harness end over his shoulders, Pitt began dragging the injured Mountie through the woods. Hour followed hour, the sun set and night came on as he struggled north through the darkness, setting his course by the compass he'd removed from the aircraft's instrument panel, an expedient he had used several years previously when trekking across the Sahara Desert.

Every ten minutes or so Pitt asked Stokes, "You still with me?"

"Hanging in," the Mountie repeated weakly.

"I'm looking at a shallow stream that runs to the west."

"You've come to Wolf Creek. Cross it and head northwest."

"How much farther to Broadmoor's village?"

Stokes replied in a hoarse murmur. "Two, maybe three kilometers."

"Keep talking to me, you hear?"

Pitt readjusted the harness straps, which were cutting into his chest, and pulled Stokes across the stream. After plodding through the underbrush for a kilometer, he came to a faint path that led in the direction he was headed. The path was grown over in places, but it offered relatively free passage, a godsend to Pitt after having forced his way through woods thick with shrubs growing between the trees.

Twice he thought he'd lost the path, but after continuing on the same course for several meters, he would pick it up again. Despite the freezing temperature, his exertions were making him sweat. He dared not allow himself to stop and rest. He kept up a one-way conversation with the Mountie, fervently trying to keep him from drifting into a coma from shock. Concentrating on keeping one foot moving ahead of the other, Pitt failed to recognize anything strange.

Stokes whispered something, but Pitt couldn't make it out. He turned his head, cocked an ear and paused. "You want me to stop?" Pitt asked.

"Smell it . . . ?" Stokes barely whispered.

"Smell what?"

"Smoke."

Then Pitt had it too. He inhaled deeply. The scent of wood smoke was coming from somewhere ahead. Soon his ears picked up the sound of a small gas engine, of a chain saw cutting into wood. The wood smell became stronger, and he could see smoke drifting over the tops of the trees in the early light of dawn. His heart was pounding under the strain, but he wasn't about to quit this close to his destination.

The sun rose but remained hidden behind dark gray clouds. A light drizzle was falling when he stumbled into a clearing that touched the sea and opened onto a small harbor. He found himself staring at a small community of log houses with corrugated metal roofs. Smoke was rising out of their stone chimneys. Tall cylindrical totem poles were standing in different parts of the village, carved with the features of stacked animal and human figures. A small fleet of fishing boats rocked gently beside a floating dock, their crews working over engines and repairing nets. Several children, standing under a shed with open sides, were observing a man carving a huge log with a chain saw. Two women chatted as they hung wash on a line. One of them spotted Pitt, pointed and began shouting at the others.

Overcome by exhaustion, Pitt sank to his knees as a crowd of a dozen people rushed toward him. One man, with long straight black hair and a round face, knelt down beside Pitt and put an arm around his shoulder. "You're all right now," he said with concern. He motioned to three men who gathered around Stokes and gave them an order. "Carry him into the tribal house."

Pitt looked at the man. "You wouldn't by chance be Mason Broadmoor?"

Coal-black eyes stared at him curiously. "Why, yes, I am."

"Boy," said Pitt as he sagged bone weary to the soft ground, "am I ever glad to see you."

The nervous giggle of a little girl roused Pitt from a light sleep. Tired as he was, he'd only slept four hours. He opened his eyes, stared at her a moment, gave her a bright smile and crossed his eyes. She ran out of the room, yelling for her mother.

He was in a cozy room with a small stove radiating wondrous heat, lying in a bed made up of bear and wolf hides. He smiled to himself at the recollection of Broadmoor standing in the middle of an isolated Indian village with few modern conveniences, calling over his satellite phone for an air ambulance to transport Stokes to a hospital on the mainland.

Pitt had borrowed the phone to contact the Mountie office at Shearwater. At the mention of Stokes' name, he was immediately put through to an Inspector Pendleton, who questioned Pitt in detail about the events commencing the previous morning. Pitt ended the briefing by giving Pendleton directions to the crash site so the Mounties could send in a team to retrieve the cameras inside the pontoons, if they had survived the impact.

A seaplane arrived before Pitt had finished a bowl of fish soup that was thrust on him by Broadmoor's wife. Two paramedics and a doctor examined Stokes and assured Pitt the Mountie had every chance of pulling through. Only after the seaplane had lifted off the water on its flight back to the mainland and the nearest hospital had Pitt gratefully accepted the loan of the Broadmoor family bed and fallen dead asleep.

Broadmoor's wife entered from the main living room and kitchen. A woman of grace and poise, stout yet supple, Irma Broadmoor had haunting coffee eyes and a laughing mouth. "How are you feeling, Mr. Pitt? I didn't expect you to wake up for another three hours at least."

"I'm most grateful for your hospitality."

"You must be hungry. That bowl of fish soup wasn't enough for a big man like you. What would you like to eat?"

"A can of beans will be fine."

"People sitting around a campfire eating canned beans

in the north woods is a myth. I'll grill some salmon steaks. I hope you like salmon."

"I do indeed."

"While you're waiting, you can talk to Mason. He's working outside."

Pitt pulled on his socks and hiking boots, ran his hands through his hair and faced the world. He found Broadmoor in the open shed, chiseling away on a five-meter-long red cedar log that lay horizontal on four heavy-duty sawhorses. Broadmoor was attacking it with a round wooden mallet shaped like a bell and a concave chisel called a fantail gouge. The carving was not far enough along for Pitt to visualize the finished product. The faces of animals were still in the rough stage.

Broadmoor looked up as Pitt approached. "Have a good rest?"

"I didn't know bearskins were so soft."

Broadmoor smiled. "Don't let the word out or they'll be extinct within a year."

"Ed Posey told me you carved totem poles. I've never seen one in the works before."

"My family have been carvers for generations. Totems evolved because the early Indians of the Northwest had no written language. Family histories and legends were preserved by carving symbols, usually animals, on red cedar trees."

"Do they have religious significance?" asked Pitt.

Broadmoor shook his head. "They were never worshiped as icons of gods, but respected more as guardian spirits."

"What are the symbols on this pole?"

"This is a mortuary pole, or what you might call a commemorative column. The pole is in honor of my uncle, who passed away last week. When I finish the carvings, they will illustrate his personal crest, which was an eagle and a bear, along with a traditional Haida figure of the deceased. After completion it will be erected, during a feast, at the corner of his widow's house."

"As a respected master carver, you must be booked up for many months in advance."

Broadmoor shrugged modestly. "Almost two years."

"Do you know why I'm here?" Pitt asked, and the abrupt question caught Broadmoor with the mallet raised to strike the fantail gouge.

The wood-carver laid his tools aside and motioned for Pitt to follow him to the edge of the harbor, where he stopped beside a small boathouse that extended into the water. He opened the doors and stepped inside. Two small craft floated within a U-shaped dock.

"Are you into Jet Skis?" asked Pitt.

Broadmoor smiled. "I believe the term is now water-craft."

Pitt studied the pair of sleek Duo 300 WetJets by Mastercraft Boats. High-performance craft that could seat two people, they were vividly painted with Haida animal symbols. "They look like they can almost fly."

"Over water, they do. I modified their engines to gain another fifteen horsepower. They move along at almost fifty knots." Broadmoor suddenly changed the subject. "Ed Posey said you wanted to circle Kunghit Island with acoustic measuring equipment. I thought the watercraft might be an efficient means of conducting your project."

Broadmoor picked up a pebble at the waterline and threw it far out into the deep green water. "The company has a small fleet of boats patrolling the waters around the island," he said finally. "They're armed and have been known to attack fishermen who venture too close."

"It seems Canadian government officials didn't tell me all I needed to know," said Pitt.

"I guess they figured since you were under their license to do field research, you wouldn't be harassed by the mine's security."

"Your brother. Stokes mentioned the assault and burning of his boat."

He pointed back toward the partially carved totem pole. "Did he also tell you they killed my uncle?"

Pitt shook his head slowly. "No. I'm sorry. You think Dorsett's security people murdered him."

"I know they murdered him," Broadmoor said, anger in his eyes.

"What about the law?"

Broadmoor shook his head. "Inspector Stokes only represents a token investigative force. After Arthur Dorsett sent his prospecting geologists swarming all over the islands until they found the main diamond source on Kunghit, he used his power and wealth to literally take over the island from the government. Never mind that the Haida claim the island as tribal sacred ground. Now it is illegal for any of my people to set foot on the island without permission or to fish within four kilometers of its shore. We can be arrested by the Mounties who are paid to protect us."

"I see why the mine's chief of security has so little regard for the law."

"Merchant, 'Dapper John' as he's called," Broadmoor said, pure hatred in his round face. "Lucky you escaped. Chances are you'd have simply disappeared. Many men have attempted to search for diamonds in and around the island. None were successful and none were ever seen again."

"Has any of the diamond wealth gone to the Haida?" Pitt asked.

"So far not one bit," answered Broadmoor. "Whether wealth from the diamonds will come to us has become more a legal than a political issue. We've negotiated for years in an attempt to get a piece of the action, but Dorsett's attorneys have stalled us in the courts."

He paused and stared into Pitt's eyes as if trying to read something. "What is your interest, Mr. Pitt? Do you want to shut the mine down?"

Pitt nodded. "I do, providing I can prove their excavation is causing the acoustic plague responsible for the mass killing of humans and sea life."

He looked at Pitt. "I will take you inside the mining property."

Pitt considered the offer briefly. "You have a wife and children. No sense in risking two lives. Put me on the island and I'll figure a way to get over the mound without being seen."

"Can't be done. Their security systems are state-of-the-art. A squirrel can't get past them, as proven by their little bodies that litter the mound, along with those of hundreds of other animals that inhabited the island before Dorsett's mining operation gutted what was once a beautiful environment. And then there are the Alsatian police dogs that can smell out a diamond-smuggling intruder at a hundred meters."

"There's always the tunnel."

"You'll never get through it alone."

"Better that than your wife becoming another widow."

"You don't understand," Broadmoor said patiently; his eyes burned with consuming flames of revenge. "The mine pays my tribal community to keep their kitchen stocked with fresh fish. Once a week my neighbors and I sail to Kunghit and deliver our catch. At the docks we load it on carts and transport the fish through the tunnel to the office of the head cook. He serves us breakfast, pays us in cash—not nearly what the catch is worth—

and then we leave. You've got black hair. You could pass for a Haida if you wear fisherman's work clothes and keep your head down. The guards are more concerned with diamonds smuggled out of camp than fish coming in. Since we only deliver and take nothing, we're not suspect."

"Are there no good paying jobs for your people at the mine?"

Broadmoor shrugged. "To forget how to fish and hunt is to forget independence. The monies we make stocking their kitchen goes toward a new school for our children."

"There's a small problem. Dapper John Merchant. We've met and struck up a mutual dislike. He had a close look at my face," Pitt said. "Do you know any miners you can trust to describe the excavation procedures?"

"All the mine workers are Chinese, illegally brought in by criminal syndicates. None speak English. Your best hope is an old mining engineer who hates Dorsett Consolidated with a passion."

"Can you contact him?"

"I don't even know his name. He works the graveyard shift and usually eats breakfast about the same time we deliver our fish. We've talked a few times over a cup of coffee. He's not happy about the working conditions. During our last conversation, he claimed that in the past year over twenty Chinese workers have died in the mines."

"If I can get ten minutes alone with him, he might be of great help in solving the acoustics enigma."

"No guarantee he'll be there when we make the delivery," said Broadmoor.

"I'll have to gamble," Pitt said thoughtfully. "When do you deliver your next catch?"

"The last of our village fleet should be docking within a few hours. We'll ice and crate the catch later this evening and be ready to head for Kunghit Island at first light."

Pitt wondered if he was physically and mentally primed to lay his life on the line again. Then he thought of the hundreds of dead bodies he'd seen on the cruise ship, and there wasn't the slightest doubt about what he must do.

22

SIX SMALL FISHING BOATS, PAINTED IN A VARIETY OF VIVID colors, sailed into Rose Harbour, their decks stacked with wooden crates filled with fish packed in ice. The diesel engines made a soft chugging sound through tall exhaust stacks as they turned the shafts to the propellers. A low mist covered the water and turned it a gray green. The sun was half a globe on the eastern horizon, and the wind was less than five knots.

Broadmoor came up to Pitt, who was sitting in the stern, watching the gulls that dipped and soared over the boat's wake in hope of a free meal. "Time to go into your act, Mr. Pitt."

Pitt could never get Broadmoor to call him Dirk. He nodded and pretended to carve a nose on a half-finished mask the Haida had loaned him. He was dressed in yellow oilskin pants with suspenders that were slung over a heavy woolen sweater knitted by Irma Broadmoor. He wore a stocking cap pulled down over his thick, black eyebrows. Indians are not known for five o'clock shadows so he had given his face a close shave. He did not look up as he lightly scraped the dull side of the knife over the mask, staring out of the corners of his eyes at the long dock—not a small pier but a true landing stage for big ships, with anchored pilings—that loomed larger as the boats entered the harbor. A tall crane moved on rails along one side of the dock to unload heavy equipment and other cargo from oceangoing ships.

A large craft with unusually smooth lines and a globular-shaped superstructure, unlike any luxury yacht Pitt had ever seen, lay moored to the dock. Her twin high-performance fiberglass hulls were designed for speed and comfort. She looked capable of skimming the sea at over eighty knots. Going by Giordino's description of a seagoing, space-age design, this was the boat seen running from the freighter *Mentawai*. Pitt looked for the name and port, normally painted across the transom, but no markings marred the beauty of the yacht's sapphire-blue hull.

Most owners are proud of their pet name for their boat, Pitt thought, and its port of registry. He had a pretty good idea why Arthur Dorsett didn't advertise his yacht.

His interest kindled, he stared openly at the windows with their tightly drawn curtains. The open deck appeared deserted. None of the crew or passengers were about this early in the morning. He was about to turn his attention from the yacht and focus on half a dozen uniformed security guards standing on the dock, when a door opened and a woman stepped out onto the deck.

She was Amazon tall, strikingly beautiful. Shaking her head, she tossed a long, unbrushed mane of red-blond hair out of her face. Her gaze swept over the little fishing fleet, then fell on Pitt when she caught him openly staring at her.

The everyday, devil-may-care Pitt would have stood up, swept off his stocking cap and bowed. But he had to play the role of an Indian, so he looked at her expressionless and merely nodded a respectful greeting. She turned away and dismissed him as if he were simply another tree in the forest, while a uniformed steward approached and held out a cup of coffee on a silver tray. Shivering in the cold dawn, she returned inside the main salon.

"She's quite impressive, isn't she?" said Broadmoor, smiling at the look of awe on Pitt's face.

"I have to admit she's unlike any woman I've ever seen."

"Boudicca Dorsett, one of Arthur's three daughters. She shows up unexpectedly several times a year on that fancy yacht of hers."

So this was the third sister, Pitt mused. Perlmutter had described her as ruthless and as cold and hard as ice from the bottom of a glacier.

"Boudicca is director of the company's security organization. I'm told she travels from mine to mine, inspecting the systems and personnel for any weaknesses," Broadmoor told him.

"Dapper John Merchant will be particularly vigilant while she's probing for cracks in his security precautions," said Pitt. "He'll take special pains to ensure his guards look alert to impress his boss."

"We'll have to be extra cautious," Broadmoor agreed. He nodded toward the security guards on the dock, waiting to inspect the fishing boats. "Look at that. Six of them. They never sent more than two on any other delivery. The one with the medallion around his neck is in charge of the dock. Name is Crutcher. He's a mean one."

Pitt gave the guards a cursory glance to see if he recognized any that had gathered around the floatplane during his intrusion with Stokes. The tide was out, and he had to stare up at the men on the dock. He was especially apprehensive about being recognized by the guard he'd laid out in John Merchant's office. Luckily, none looked familiar.

They carried their weapons slung over one shoulder, muzzle pointing forward in the general direction of the Indian fishermen. It was all for show and intimidation, Pitt quickly perceived. Crutcher, a cold-faced, arrogant man, stepped up to the edge of the dock as Broadmoor's helmsman eased the fishing boat along the pilings. Broadmoor cast a line that fell over the guard's combat boots.

"Hi there, friend. How about tying us up?"

The cold-faced guard kicked the rope off the dock back onto the boat. "Tie up yourself," he snapped.

A dropout from a Special Forces team, that one, Pitt thought as he caught the line. He scrambled up a ladder onto the dock, and purposely brushed against Crutcher as he looped the line around a small bollard.

Crutcher lashed out with his boot and kicked Pitt upright, then grabbed him by his suspenders and shook him violently. "You stinking fish head, mind your manners."

Broadmoor froze. It was a trick. The Haida were a quiet people, not prone to quick anger. He thought with fearful certainty that Pitt would shake himself loose and punch the contemptuous guard.

But Pitt didn't bite. He relaxed his body, rubbed a hand over a blossoming bruise on his buttocks and stared at Crutcher with an unfathomable gaze. He pulled off his stocking cap as if in respect, revealing a mass of black hair whose natural curls had been greased straight. He shrugged with a careless show of deference.

"I was not careful. I'm sorry."

"You don't look familiar," said Crutcher coldly.

"I make this trip twenty times," Pitt said quietly. "I've seen you lots before. Your name is Crutcher. Three deliveries back, you punched my gut for unloading the fish too slow."

The guard studied Pitt for a moment, then gave a short

laugh. "Get in my way again, and I'll boot your butt across the channel."

Pitt registered a look of friendly resignation and joined the fishermen and began passing crates of salmon up to one of Broadmoor's crew, who stacked them on flatbed trailers that were hitched to a small tractor vehicle with eight drive wheels. The crates were heavy, and Pitt's biceps and back soon ached in protest. He gritted his teeth, knowing the guards would suspect he didn't belong if he couldn't heave the ice-filled fish crates around with the ease of the Haida.

Two hours later the trailers were loaded, then four of the guards and the crews of the fishing boats piled aboard as the train set off toward the mining operation's mess hall. They were stopped at the tunnel entrance, herded into a small building and told to strip to their underwear. Then their clothes were searched and they were individually X-rayed. All passed scrutiny except one Haida who absentmindedly carried a large fishing knife in his boot. Pitt found it strange that instead of merely confiscating the knife, it was returned and the fisherman sent back to his boat. The rest were allowed to dress and reboard the trailers for the journey to the excavation area.

"I would think they'd search you for concealed diamonds when you came out rather than entering," said Pitt.

"They do," explained Broadmoor. "We go through the same procedure when we exit the mine. They X-ray you going in as a warning that it doesn't pay to smuggle out a handful of diamonds by swallowing them."

The arched concrete tunnel that penetrated the mound of mine tailings was about five meters high by ten wide, ample room for large trucks to transport men and equipment back and forth from the loading dock. The length stretched nearly half a kilometer, the interior brightened by long rows of fluorescent lighting. Side tunnels yawned about halfway through, each about half the size of the main artery.

"Where do those lead?" Pitt asked Broadmoor.

"Part of the security system. They circle the entire compound and are filled with detection devices."

"The guards, the weapons, the array of security systems. Seems like overkill, just to prevent a few diamonds from being smuggled off the property."

"Only the half of it. They don't want the illegal laborers escaping to the mainland."

They emerged at the other end of the tunnel amid the busy activity of the mining operation. The driver of the tractor curled the train of trailers onto a paved road that circled the great open pit that was the volcanic chute. He pulled up beside a loading dock that ran along a low concrete building in the shape of a quonset hut, and stopped.

A man wearing the white attire of a chef under a fur-trimmed overcoat opened a door to a warehouse where foodstuffs were stored. He threw a wave of greeting to Boardmoor. "Good to see you, Mason. Your arrival is timely. We're down to two cases of cod."

"We've brought enough fish to grow scales on your workers." Broadmoor turned and said in a low voice to Pitt, "Dave Anderson, the head cook for the miners."

"The frozen-food locker is open," said Anderson. "Mind how you stack the crates. I found salmon mixed in with flounder your last trip. It screws up my menus."

"Brought you a treat. Fifty kilos of moose steaks."

"You're okay, Mason. You're the reason I don't buy frozen fish from the mainland," the cook replied with a wide smile. "After you've stored the crates, come on into the mess hall. My boys will have breakfast waiting for your people. I'll write a check as soon as I've inventoried your catch."

The wooden crates of fish were stacked in the frozen-food locker, and the Haida fishermen, followed by Pitt, thankfully tramped into the warmth of the mess hall. They walked past a serving line and were dished up eggs, sausages, and flapjacks. As they helped themselves to coffee out of a huge urn, Pitt looked around at the men sitting at the other tables. The four guards were conversing under a cloud of cigarette smoke near the door. Close to a hundred Chinese miners from the early morning graveyard shift filled up most of the room. Ten men who Pitt guessed to be mining engineers and superintendents sat at a round table that was set off in a smaller, private dining room.

"Which one is your disgruntled employee?" he asked Broadmoor.

Broadmoor nodded toward the door leading into the kitchen. "He's waiting for you outside by the garbage containers."

Pitt stared at the Indian. "How did you arrange that?"

Broadmoor smiled shrewdly. "The Haida have ways of communicating that don't require fiber optics."

Pitt did not question him. Now was not the time. Keeping a wary eye on the guards, he casually walked into the kitchen. None of the cooks or dishwashers looked up as he moved between the ovens and sinks through the rear door and dropped down the steps outside. The big metal garbage containers reeked of stale vegetables in the sharp, crisp air.

He stood there in the cold, not sure what to expect.

A tall figure moved from behind a container and approached him. He was wearing a yellow jumpsuit. The bottoms of the legs were smeared with mud that had a strange bluish cast to it. A miner's hard hat sat on his head, and his face was covered by what Pitt took for a mask with a breathing filter. He clutched a bundle under one arm. "I understand you're interested in our mining operation," he said quietly.

"Yes. My name is—"

"Names are unimportant. We don't have much time if you are to leave the island with the fishing fleet." He unfolded a jumpsuit, a respirator mask and a hard hat and handed them to Pitt. "Put these on and follow me."

Pitt said nothing and did as he was told. He did not fear a trap. The security guards could have taken him anytime since he set foot on the dock. He dutifully zipped up the front of the jumpsuit, tightened the chin strap of the hard hat, adjusted the respirator mask over his face and set out after a man he hoped could show him the source behind the violent killings.

23

PITT FOLLOWED THE ENIGMATIC MINING ENGINEER ACROSS A road into a modern prefabricated building that housed a row of elevators that transported the workers to and from the diggings far below. Two larger ones carried the Chinese laborers but the smaller one on the end was for the use of company officials only. The lift machinery was the latest in Otis elevator technology. The elevator moved smoothly, without sound or sensation of dropping.

"How deep do we go?" asked Pitt, his voice muffled by the breathing mask.

"Five hundred meters," replied the miner.

"Why the respirators?"

"When the volcano we're standing in erupted in the distant past, it packed Kunghit Island with pumice rock. The vibration that results from the excavating process can churn up pumice dust, which wreaks havoc with the lungs."

"Is that the only reason?" asked Pitt slyly.

"No," replied the engineer honestly. "I don't want you to see my face. That way, if security gets suspicious, I can pass a lie-detector test, which our chief of security uses with the frequency of a doctor giving urine tests."

"Dapper John Merchant," Pitt said, smiling.

"You know John?"

"We've met."

The older man shrugged and accepted Pitt's claim without comment.

As they neared the bottom of the run, Pitt's ears were struck by a weird humming sound. Before he could ask what it was, the elevator stopped and the doors slid open. He was led through a mine shaft that opened onto an observation platform perched fifty meters above the vast excavation chamber below. The equipment at the bottom of the pit was not the typical type of machinery one might expect to encounter in a mine. No cars filled with ore pulled over tracks by a small engine, no drills or explosives, no huge earth-moving vehicles. This was a well-financed, carefully designed and organized operation that was run by computers aided in a small way by human labor. The only obvious mechanization was the huge overhead bridge with the cables and buckets that lifted the diamond-bearing blue rock-clay to the surface and carried it to the buildings where the stones were extracted.

The engineer turned and stared at him through green eyes over the mask. "Mason did not tell me who you are or who you represent. And I don't want to know. He merely said you were trying to trace a sound channel that travels underwater and kills."

"That's true. Untold thousands of various forms of sea life and hundreds of people have already died mysteriously in the open sea and along shorelines."

"You think the sound originates here?"

"I have reason to believe the Kunghit Island mine is only one of four sources."

The engineer nodded knowingly. "Komandorskie in the Bering Sea, Easter Island, Gladiator Island in the Tasman Sea, being the other three."

"You guessed?"

"I know. They all use the same pulsed ultrasound excavation equipment as we do here." The engineer swept his hand over the open pit. "We used to dig shafts, in an attempt to follow the largest concentration of diamonds. Much like miners following a vein of gold. But after Dorsett scientists and engineers perfected a new method of excavating that produced four times the production in one third the time, the old ways were quickly abandoned."

Pitt leaned over the railing and stared at the action across the bottom of the pit. Large robotic vehicles appeared to ram long shafts into the blue clay. Then came an eerie vibration that traveled up Pitt's legs to his body. He gazed questioningly at the engineer.

"The diamond-bearing rock and clay are broken up by high-energy pulsed ultrasound." The engineer paused and pointed to a large concrete structure with no obvious windows. "See that building on the south side of the pit?"

Pitt nodded.

"A nuclear generating plant. It takes an enormous amount of power to produce enough energy at ten to twenty bursts a second to penetrate the rock-hard clay and break it apart."

"The crux of the problem."

"How so?" asked the engineer.

"The sound generated by your equipment radiates into the sea. When it converges with the energy pulses from the other Dorsett mines scattered around the Pacific, its intensity increases to a level that can kill animal life within a large area."

"An interesting concept as far as it goes, but a piece is missing."

"You don't find it plausible?"

The engineer shook his head. "By itself, the sound energy produced down below could not kill a sardine three kilometers from here. The ultrasound drilling equipment uses sound pulses with acoustic frequencies of 60,000 to 80,000 hertz, or cycles per second. These frequencies are absorbed by the salts in the sea before they travel very far."

Pitt stared into the eyes of the engineer, trying to read where he was coming from. "How do I know you're not trying to throw me off the track?"

Pitt could not see the tight smile behind the respirator mask, but he guessed it was there. "Come along," said the engineer. "I'll show you the answer to your dilemma." He stepped back into the elevator, but before he pushed the next button on the panel, he handed Pitt an acoustic-foam helmet. "Take off your hard hat and set this over your head. Make certain it's snug or you'll get a case of vertigo. It contains a transmitter and receiver so we can converse without shouting."

"Where are we headed?" asked Pitt.

"An exploratory tunnel, cut beneath the main pit to survey the heaviest deposit of stones."

The doors opened and they stepped out into a mine shaft carved from the volcanic rock and shored up with heavy timbers. Pitt involuntarily lifted his hands and pressed them against the sides of his head. Though all sound was muffled, he felt a strange vibration in his eardrums.

"Do you hear me all right?" asked the engineer.

"I hear you," answered Pitt through the tiny microphone. "But through a humming sound."

"You'll get used to it."

"What is it?"

"Follow me a hundred meters up the shaft and I'll show you your missing piece."

Pitt trailed in the engineer's footsteps until they reached a side shaft, only this one held no shoring timbers. The volcanic rock that made up its rounded sides was almost as smooth as if it had been polished by some immense boring tool.

"A Thurston lava tube," Pitt said. "I've seen them on the big island of Hawaii."

"Certain lavas such as those basaltic in composition form thin flows called pahoehoe that run laterally, with smooth surfaces," clarified the engineer. "When the lava cools closer to the surface, the deeper, warmer surge continues until it flows into the open, leaving chambers, or tubes as we call them. It is these pockets of air that are driven to resonate by the pulsed ultrasound from the mining operation above."

"What if I remove the helmet?"

The engineer shrugged. "Go ahead, but you won't enjoy the results."

Pitt lifted the acoustic-foam helmet from his ears. After half a minute he became disoriented and reached out to the wall of the tube to keep from losing his balance. Next came a mushrooming sensation of nausea. The engineer reached over and replaced the helmet on Pitt's head. Then he circled an arm around Pitt's waist to hold him upright.

"Satisfied?" he asked.

Pitt took a long breath as the vertigo and nausea quickly passed. "I had to experience the agony. Now I have a mild idea of what those poor souls suffered before they died."

The engineer led him back to the elevator. "Not a pleasant ordeal. The deeper we excavate, the worse it becomes. The one time I walked in here without protecting my ears, my head ached for a week."

As the elevator rose from the lava tube, Pitt fully

recovered except for a ringing in his ears. He knew it all now. He knew the source of the acoustic plague. He knew how it worked to destroy. He knew how to stop it—and was buoyed by the knowledge.

"I understand now. The air chambers in the lava resonate and radiate the high-intensity sound pulses down through rock and into the sea, producing an incredible burst of energy."

"There's your answer." The engineer removed his helmet and ran a hand through a head of thinning gray hair. "The resonance added to the sound intensity creates incredible energy, more than enough to kill."

"Why did you risk your job and maybe your life showing me this?"

The engineer's eyes burned, and he shoved his hands deep into the pockets of his jumpsuit. "I do not like working for people I cannot trust. Men like Arthur Dorsett create trouble and tragedy. This whole operation stinks, as do all his other mining operations. These poor Chinese laborers are driven until they drop. They're fed well but paid nothing and forced to slave in the pit eighteen hours a day. Twenty have died in the past twelve months from accidents, because they were too exhausted to react and move out of the way of the equipment. Why the need to dig diamonds twenty-four hours a day when there is a worldwide surplus of the stones? De Beers may head a repugnant monopoly, but you have to give them credit. They hold production down so prices remain high. No, Dorsett has a rotten scheme to harm the market. I'd give a year's pay to know what's going on in his mind. Someone like you, who understands the horror we're causing here, can now work to stop Dorsett before he kills another hundred innocent souls."

The elevator reached the surface level and stopped in the main lift building. The engineer stepped outside, glancing at a Ford van that drove past. Pitt followed him around the corner of the mess hall and behind the garbage containers.

The engineer nodded at Pitt's jumpsuit. "Your gear belongs to a geologist who's down with the flu. I'll have to return it before he discovers it missing and wonders why."

"Great," Pitt muttered. "I probably contacted his flu germs from the respirator."

"Your Indian friends have returned to their boats." The engineer gestured at the food-storage loading dock. The tractor and trailers were gone. "The van that just passed by the elevator building is a personnel shuttle. It should return in a couple of minutes. Hail the driver and tell him to take you through the tunnel."

Pitt stared at the old engineer dubiously. "You don't think he'll question why I didn't leave with the other Haida?"

The old engineer took a notebook and a pencil from a pocket of his jumpsuit and scribbled a few words. He tore off the sheet of paper, folded it and passed it to Pitt. "Give him this. It will guarantee your safe passage. I have to return to work before Dapper John's muscle boys begin to ask questions."

Pitt shook his hand. "I'm grateful for your help. You took a terrible risk by revealing Dorsett Consolidated secrets to a perfect stranger."

"If I can prevent future deaths of innocent people, any risk on my part will have been well worth it."

"Good luck," said Pitt.

Five minutes later, the van appeared and Pitt waved it to a stop. The driver, in the uniform of a security guard, stared at Pitt suspiciously. "Where did you come from?" he asked.

Pitt handed him the folded note and shrugged wordlessly.

The driver read the note, wadded it up, tossed it on the floor and nodded. "Okay, take a seat. I'll run you as far as the search house at the other end of the tunnel."

As the driver closed the door and shifted the van into drive, Pitt took a seat behind him and casually leaned down and picked up the crumpled note.

It read,

This Haida fisherman was in the john when his friends unknowingly left him behind. Please see that he gets to the dock before the fishing fleet departs.

C. Cussler
Chief Foreman

24

THE DRIVER STOPPED THE VAN IN FRONT OF THE SECURITY building, where Pitt was explored from head to feet by X ray for the second time that morning. The doctor in charge of anatomical search nodded as he completed a checklist.

"No diamonds on you, big boy," he said, stifling a yawn.

"Who needs them?" Pitt grunted indifferently. "You can't eat stones. They're a curse of the white man. Indians don't kill each other over diamonds."

"You're late, aren't you? Your tribesmen came through here twenty minutes ago."

"I fell asleep," said Pitt, hurriedly throwing on his clothes.

He took off at a dead run and rushed onto the dock. Fifty meters from the end he came slowly to a stop. Concern and misgiving coursed through him. The Haida fishing fleet was a good five kilometers out in the channel. He was alone with nowhere to go.

A large freighter was unloading the last of its cargo across the dock from the Dorsett yacht. He dodged around the big containers that were hoisted from the cargo holds on wooden skids and tried to lose himself amid the activity while moving toward the gangway in an attempt to board the ship. One hand on the railing and one foot on the first step was as far as he got.

"Hold it right there, fisherman." The calm voice spoke from directly behind him. "Missed your boat, did you?"

Pitt slowly turned around and froze as he felt his heart double its beat. The sadistic Crutcher was leaning against a crate containing a large pump as he casually puffed on the stub of a cigar. Next to him stood a guard with the muzzle of his M-1 assault rifle wavering up and down Pitt's body. It was the same guard Pitt had struck in Merchant's office. Pitt's heart went on triple time as Dapper John Merchant himself stepped from behind the guard, staring at Pitt with the cold authority of one who holds men's lives in the palms of his hands.

"Well, well, Mr. Pitt, you are a stubborn man."

"I knew he was the same one who punched me the minute I saw him board the shuttle van." The guard grinned wolfishly as he stepped forward and thrust the gun barrel into Pitt's gut. "A little payback for hitting me when I wasn't ready."

Pitt doubled over in sharp pain as the narrow, round muzzle jabbed deeply into his side, badly bruising but not quite penetrating the flesh. He looked up at the grinning guard and spoke through clenched teeth. "A social misfit if I've ever seen one."

The guard lifted his rifle to strike Pitt again, but Merchant stopped him. "Enough, Elmo. You can play games with him after he's explained his persistent intrusion." He looked at Pitt apologetically. "You must excuse Elmo. He has an instinctive drive to hurt people he doesn't trust."

Pitt desperately tried to think of some way to escape. But except for jumping in the icy water and expiring from hypothermia or—and this was the more likely option of the two—being blasted into fish meal by Elmo's automatic rifle, there was no avenue open.

"You must have an active imagination if you consider me a threat," Pitt muttered to Merchant as he stalled for time.

Merchant leisurely removed a cigarette from a gold case and lit it with a matching lighter. "Since we last met, I've run an in-depth check on you, Mr. Pitt. To say you are a threat to those you oppose is a mild understatement. You are not trespassing on Dorsett property to study fish and kelp. You are here for another, more ominous purpose. I rather hope you'll explain your presence in vivid detail without prolonged theatrical resistance."

"A pity to disappoint you," said Pitt, between deep breaths. "I'm afraid you won't have time for one of your sordid interrogations."

Merchant was not easily fooled. But he knew that Pitt was no garden-variety diamond smuggler. A tiny alarm went off in the back of his mind when he saw the utter lack of fear in Pitt's eyes. He felt curious yet a trifle uneasy. "I freely admit I thought more highly of you than to expect a cheap bluff."

Pitt stared upward and scanned the skies. "A squadron of fighters from the aircraft carrier *Nimitz*, bristling with air-to-surface missiles, should be whistling over at any moment."

"A bureaucrat with an obscure governmental agency with the power to order an attack on Canadian soil? I don't believe so."

"You're right about me," said Pitt. "But my boss, Admiral James Sandecker, has the leverage to order an air strike."

For an instant, a brief eye blink in time, Pitt thought Merchant was going to buy it. Hesitation clouded the security chief's face. Then he grinned, stepped forward and wickedly backhanded Pitt across the mouth with a gloved hand. Pitt staggered backward, feeling the blood springing from his lips.

"I'll take my chances," Merchant said drily. He wiped a speck of blood from his leather glove with a bored expression of distaste. "No more stories. You will speak only when I ask for answers to my questions." He turned to Crutcher and Elmo. "Escort him to my office. We'll continue our discussion there."

Crutcher pushed a flat-handed palm into Pitt's face and sent him staggering across the dock. "I think we'll walk instead of ride to your office, sir. Our nosy friend could use a little exercise to soften him up . . ."

"Hold on there!" came a sharp voice from the deck of the yacht. Boudicca Dorsett was leaning against the rail, watching the drama below on the dock. She tossed her long hair over her shoulders and gestured to the gangway leading from the dock to the yacht's promenade deck. "Bring your intruder on board."

Merchant and Crutcher exchanged indulgent glances before hustling Pitt on board the yacht. Elmo prodded him viciously in the lower back with the assault rifle, forcing him through a teak doorway into the main salon.

Boudicca sat on one edge of a desk carved from driftwood with an Italian-marble top.

"Nice place you have here," Pitt said impassively.

"Shut your mouth in front of Ms. Dorsett," Elmo snapped, raising the butt of his weapon to strike Pitt again.

Pitt whirled on his feet, knocked away the approaching rifle with one hand and rammed his other fist into Elmo's gut. The guard groaned in pain and anger and doubled over, dropping the rifle, both hands clutched at the point of impact.

Pitt scooped up the rifle from the salon's thick carpet before anyone could react and calmly handed the weapon to a stunned Merchant. "I'm tired of being on the receiving end of this cretin's sadistic habits. Please keep him under control."

Boudicca remained calm and aloof, staring at Pitt with renewed curiosity. She looked at Merchant. "Where did he come from?" she demanded. "Who is this man?"

"He penetrated our security by posing as a local fisherman. In reality he's an American agent."

"Why is he snooping around the mine?"

"I was taking him back to my office for the answers when you called us to come aboard," replied Merchant.

She rose to her full height and stood taller than any man in the salon. "Your name, please, and your business here," she said to Pitt.

Merchant began to answer. "His name is—"

"I want *him* to tell me," she cut Merchant off.

"So you're Boudicca Dorsett," Pitt said, brushing off her question and returning her gaze. "Now I can say I know all three."

She searched his face for a moment. "All three?"

"Arthur Dorsett's lovely daughters," answered Pitt.

Anger at being toyed with flashed in her eyes. She took two steps, reached out, grasped Pitt's upper arms and squeezed as she leaned forward, crushing him against one wall of the salon. There was no expression in the giantess' black eyes as they stared unblinkingly into Pitt's, almost nose to nose. She said nothing, only stood there increasing the pressure and pushing upward until his feet were barely touching the carpet.

Pitt resisted by tensing his body and flexing his biceps, which felt as if they were clamped in ever-tightening vises. He could not believe anyone could be so strong. His muscles began to feel as if they were mashed to pulp. He clenched his teeth and bleeding lips together to fight the rising pain. The restricted blood flow was numbing and turning his hands white when Boudicca finally released her grip and stepped back.

"Now then, before I encircle your throat, tell me who you are and why you're prying into my family's mining operation."

Pitt stalled for a minute while the pain subsided and feeling returned to his lower arms and hands. He was stunned by the woman's inhuman strength. Finally, he gasped out, "Is that any way to treat the man who rescued your sisters from certain death?"

Her eyes widened questioningly, and she stiffened. "What are you talking about? How do you know my sisters?"

"My name is Dirk Pitt," he said slowly. "My friends and I saved Maeve from freezing to death and Deirdre from drowning in the Antarctic."

"You?" The words seemed to boil from her lips. "You're the one from the National Underwater & Marine Agency?"

"The same," Pitt replied.

Merchant gazed blankly at Boudicca. "He must be lying."

"Would you like me to describe them in detail?" asked Pitt carelessly. "Maeve is tall, blond, with incredibly blue eyes." He paused to point at a portrait of a young blond woman, wearing an old-fashioned dress with a diamond the size of a quail's egg set in a pendant around her neck. "That's her in the painting."

"Not even close." Boudicca smirked. "That happens to be a portrait of my great-great-great-grandmother."

"Neither here nor there," Pitt said with feigned indifference, unwilling to tear his eyes away from the incredible likeness of Maeve. "Deirdre, on the other hand, has brown eyes and red hair and walks like a runway model."

After a long pause, Boudicca said, "He must be who he says he is."

"That doesn't explain his presence here," Merchant persisted.

"I told you during our last meeting," said Pitt. "I came here to study the effects of the chemicals and pollution flowing into the sea from the mine."

Merchant smiled thinly. "An inventive story, but far from the truth."

Pitt could not relax for a moment. He was in the company of dangerous people, cunning and shrewd. He had felt his way, assessing the reaction to his line of approach, but he realized it was only a matter of a minute or two before Boudicca figured out his game. It was inevitable. She had enough pieces to fill in the borders of the puzzle. He decided he could better control the situation by telling the truth.

"The gospel you want, the gospel you'll get. I'm here because the pulsed ultrasound you use to excavate for diamonds causes an intense resonance that channels great distances underwater. When undersea conditions are optimal these pulses converge with those from your other mining operations around the Pacific and kill any living organism in the area. But of course I'm not telling you anything you don't already know."

He'd caught Boudicca off balance. She stared at Pitt as if he had stepped off an alien spaceship. "You're quite good at creating a scene," she said hesitantly. "You should have gone into the movies."

"I've considered it," said Pitt. "As I was saying, you know more about the horrors of the acoustic plague, as it's come to be called, than I do, Ms. Dorsett. The same killer that came frighteningly close to killing your sisters. So it would be foolish of me to waste my time attempting to enlighten you."

"I don't have the vaguest idea of what you're talking

about." She turned to Merchant and Crutcher. "This man is dangerous. He is a menace to Dorsett Consolidated Mining. Get him off my boat and do with him whatever you think is necessary to ensure he doesn't bother us again."

Pitt made one last toss of the dice. "Surely you haven't forgotten the *Mentawai*. Now there was a sloppy job. You mistimed your explosives and blew up the boarding party from the *Rio Grande* who were investigating what appeared to be an abandoned ship. Unfortunately for you, your yacht was seen fleeing the scene and later identified."

"A most intriguing tale." There was scorn in Boudicca's voice, but a scorn disputed by a deep foreboding in her face. "You might almost say spellbinding. Are you quite finished, Mr. Pitt, or do you have an ending?"

"An ending?" Pitt sighed. "It hasn't been written yet. But I think it's safe to say that very soon Dorsett Consolidated Mining Limited will be only a memory."

He had gone one step too far. Boudicca began to lose control. Her anger swelled, and she came close to Pitt, her face tight and cold. "My father can't be stopped. Not by any legal authority or any government. Not in the next twenty-seven days. By then, we'll have closed down the mines of our own accord."

"Why not do it now and save countless many lives?"

"Not one minute before we're ready."

"Ready for what?"

"A pity you can't ask Maeve."

"Why Maeve?"

"Deirdre tells me that she became quite friendly with the man who saved her."

"She's in Australia," said Pitt.

Boudicca shook her head and showed her teeth. "Maeve is in Washington, working as an agent for our father, feeding him whatever information NUMA has collected on the deathly sound waves. Nothing like having a trusted relative in the enemy camp to keep one out of trouble."

"I misjudged her," Pitt said brusquely. "She led me to believe that protecting sea life was her life's work."

"Any moral indignation flew out the window when she learned my father was holding her twin sons as insurance."

"Don't you mean hostages?" The mist began to lift. Pitt began to see that Arthur Dorsett's machinations went far beyond mere greed. The man was a bloodthirsty cutthroat, a predator who thought nothing of using his own family as pawns.

Boudicca disregarded Pitt's remark and nodded at John Merchant. "He's yours to dispose of as you will."

"Before we bury him with the others," said Crutcher with seeming anticipation, "we'll persuade him to fill in any details he might have purposely left out."

"So I'm to be tortured and then executed," Pitt said nonchalantly, while his mind desperately created and discarded a dozen useless plans for escape.

"You've condemned yourself by coming here," said Boudicca. "If, as you say, officials of NUMA suspected our excavation operations were responsible for sending deadly sound waves throughout the ocean, there would have been no need for you to clandestinely spy on Dorsett property. The truth is, you have learned the answers within the past hour and have yet to pass them on to your superiors in Washington. I compliment you, Mr. Pitt. Slipping through our security and entering the mine was a masterstroke. You could not have done it alone. Explanations will be forthcoming after Mr. Merchant motivates you to share your secrets."

She nailed me good, Pitt thought in defeat. "You *will* give Maeve and Deirdre my best wishes."

"Knowing my sisters, they've probably already forgotten you."

"Deirdre maybe, not Maeve. Now that I've met all of you, it's evident that she's the most virtuous of the three."

Pitt was surprised at the look of hatred that flashed in Boudicca's eyes. "Maeve is the outcast. She has never been close to the family."

Pitt grinned, a natural grin, mischievous and challenging. "It's easy to see why."

Boudicca stood up, looking even taller due to the heels of her boots, and stared down at Pitt, enraged at the laughter she read in his opaline green eyes. "By the time we close the mine, Maeve and her sons will be gone." She spun around and glared at Merchant. "Get this scum off my boat," she said. "I don't want to see him again."

"You won't, Ms. Dorsett," said Merchant, motioning for Crutcher to push Pitt from the salon. "I promise, this will be your last look at him."

With Pitt between them and Elmo bringing up the rear, Merchant and Crutcher escorted their captive down the gangway and walked across the dock toward a waiting van. As they passed by the large containers of supplies and equipment that had been off-loaded from the cargo ship, the loud exhaust from the diesel engines operating the cranes drowned out a dull thud. Only when Crutcher suddenly crumpled to the planking of the dock did Pitt spin around in a defensive crouch, just in time to see Merchant's eyes roll up into his head before he dropped like a sack of sand. Several steps behind them, Elmo lay stretched out like a dead man, which he was.

The whole operation hadn't taken ten seconds from the killing blow to the back of Elmo's neck to the concussion of John Merchant's skull.

Mason Broadmoor grabbed Pitt's arm with his left

hand, his right still gripping a massive steel wrench. "Quick, jump!"

Confused, Pitt hesitated. "Jump where?"

"Off the dock, you idiot."

Pitt needed no further urging. Five running steps and they both flew through the air and landed in the water a few meters in front of the bow of the cargo ship. The ice-cold water shocked every nerve ending in Pitt's body before his adrenaline took over and he found himself swimming beside Broadmoor.

"Now what?" he gasped, breathing steam over the icy water while shaking the water from his face and hair.

"The watercraft," answered Broadmoor after snorting water from his nose. "We sneaked them off the fishing boat and hid them under the pier."

"They were on the boat? I didn't see them."

"A hidden compartment I built myself," Broadmoor said, grinning. "You never know when you'll need to skip town ahead of the sheriff." He reached one of the Duo 300 WetJets that were floating beside a concrete piling and climbed aboard. "You know how to ride a watercraft?"

"Like I was born on one," said Pitt, pulling himself aboard and straddling the seat.

"If we keep the cargo ship between us and the dock, we should be blocked from their line of fire for a good half kilometer."

They punched the starters, the modified engines roared to life, and with Broadmoor less than a meter in the lead, they burst from under the dock as if shot from a cannon. They stuck the noses of their watercraft in a hard turn and sliced around the bows of the cargo ship, using the hull as a shield. The engines accelerated with no hint of hesitation. Pitt never looked back. He hunched over the handlebars and pressed the trigger throttle to its stop, half expecting a hail of gunfire to pepper the water around him at any second. But their getaway was clean. They were far out of range before the rest of John Merchant's security team was alerted.

Pitt couldn't know with any certainty, but he estimated he was whipping over the sea at close to sixty knots. It was almost like riding a high-performance motorcycle over water.

He jumped Broadmoor's wake, pulled even until they were hurtling across the water virtually side by side and shouted, "We'll be dead meat if they come after us!"

"Not to worry!" Broadmoor yelled back. "We can outrun their patrol boats!"

Pitt turned and peered over his shoulder at the rapidly receding island. He spotted the remaining Defender helicopter rising above the mound surrounding the mine. In less than a minute it was sweeping across the channel, taking up the chase and following their wakes.

"We can't outrun their helicopter," Pitt informed Broadmoor loudly.

In contrast to a grim-faced Pitt, Mason Broadmoor looked as enthusiastic and bright eyed as a boy warming up for his first track meet. His brown features were flushed with excitement. He stood on the footrests and glanced back at the pursuing aircraft. "They don't stand a chance," he said, grinning. "Follow in my wake."

Pitt stuck the nose of his watercraft into the rooster tail shooting up behind the front-runner and hung in the foaming wake, as they ran flat out through a cauldron of waves thrashing against a fortress of offshore rocks.

To Pitt it looked as if they were on a direct course toward the wave-hammered cliffs. He gripped the handlebars, braced his feet in the padded footwells and hung on to keep from being pitched off.

Broadmoor cut around a huge rock. Pitt followed.

They rocketed over the crest of a huge roller and smashed down in the trough before ascending on the back of the next one.

The helicopter was almost upon them, but the pilot stared in dumb fascination at the suicidal course set by the two men on the watercraft. Wary of his own danger, he pulled the aircraft up in a steep vertical climb and swept over the palisades. He banked sharply to come around for another look but the watercraft had already been out of sight for a critical ten seconds. When he circled back over the water, his quarry had vanished.

A tiny crevice in the lower face of the cliffs suddenly yawned open like the eye of a needle, no wider than two meters. Broadmoor swept into the narrow opening and was gone.

Pitt grimly followed, swearing that the ends of his handlebars brushed the sides of the entrance, and abruptly found himself in a deep grotto with a high, inverted V-shaped ceiling. Ahead of him, Broadmoor slowed and glided to a stop beside a small rock landing, where he jumped off his machine, tore off his coat and began stuffing it with a bundle of dead kelp that had washed into the grotto. Pitt immediately saw the wisdom of the Indian's scheme. He hit the stop switch on the handlebar and matched Broadmoor's actions.

Once the coats were filled to simulate headless torsos, they were thrown in the water at the entrance to the grotto. Pitt and Broadmoor stood there watching as the dummies were swept back and forth before being carried by the backwash into the maelstrom outside.

"You think that will fool them?" asked Pitt.

"Guaranteed," answered Broadmoor confidentially. "The wall of the cliff slants out, making the opening to the grotto impossible to see from the air." He cocked an ear at the sound of the helicopter outside. "I'll give them another ten minutes before they head back to the mine and tell Dapper John Merchant, if he's regained consciousness, that we bashed our brains out on the rocks."

Sure enough, the sound of the helicopter echoing into the grotto gradually died and faded away. He checked the fuel tanks of the watercraft and nodded comfortably. "If we run at half speed we should have just enough fuel to reach my village."

"I suggest we relax till after sunset," said Pitt. "No sense in showing our faces in case the pilot of the helicopter has a suspicious disposition. Can you navigate home in the dark?"

"Blindfolded in a straitjacket," Broadmoor said indisputably. "We'll leave at midnight and be in bed by 3:00 A.M."

They departed the grotto long after dark as insurance against chance discovery by Dorsett security patrol boats. Broadmoor draped the chain of a small shaded penlight around his neck so that it was hanging on his back.

Pitt followed the tiny beam through the surf and around the rocks, amazed at the ease with which Broadmoor navigated in the dark without mishap.

The image of Maeve, forced to work as a spy under the boot of her father, blackmailed by his seizure of her twin sons, made him boil with anger. Driven by a determination to stop Arthur Dorsett no matter the cost and consequences, he gripped the handlebars till his knuckles gleamed white under the light from a quarter-moon as he forged through the cataract from Broadmoor's wake.

25

PITT SAT BEHIND THE DESK IN HIS OFFICE FOR THE FIRST TIME in nearly two months, his eyes distant, his hand toying with a Sea Hawk dive knife he used as a letter opener. He said nothing, waiting for a response from Admiral Sandecker who sat across from him.

He had arrived in Washington early that morning, a Sunday, and gone directly to the empty NUMA head-quarters building, where he spent the next six hours writing up a detailed report on his discoveries on Kung-hit Island and offering his suggestions on how to deal with the underwater acoustics.

He swung around in his chair and gazed out the window at the Potomac River and envisioned Maeve standing on the deck of *Ice Hunter,* the look of fear and desperation in her face. He felt furious with himself for deserting her. He was certain Deirdre had divulged the kidnapping of Maeve's children by her father on board *Ice Hunter.* Maeve had reached out to the only man she could trust, and Pitt had failed to recognize her distress. That part of the story Pitt had left out of his report.

Sandecker closed the report and laid it on Pitt's desk. "A remarkable bit of fancy footwork. A miracle you weren't killed."

"I had help from some very good people," Pitt said seriously.

"You've gone as far as you can go on this thing. I'm ordering you and Giordino to take ten days off. Go home and work on your antique cars."

"You'll get no argument from me," said Pitt, massaging the bruises on his upper arms.

"Judging from your narrow escape, Dorsett and his daughters play tough."

"All except Maeve," said Pitt quietly. "She's the family outcast."

"You know, I assume, that she is working with NUMA in our biology department along with Roy Van Fleet."

"On the effects of the ultrasound on sea life, yes, I know."

Sandecker studied Pitt's face, examining every line in the weathered yet still youthful-looking features. "Can we trust her? She could be passing along data on our findings to her father."

Dirk's green eyes registered no sign of subtlety. "Maeve has nothing in common with her sisters."

Sensing Pitt's reluctance to discuss Maeve, Sandecker changed the subject. "Speaking of sisters, did Boudicca Dorsett give you any indication as to why her father intends to shut down his operations in a few weeks?"

"Not a clue."

Sandecker rolled a cigar around in his fingers pensively. "Because none of Dorsett's mining properties are on U.S. soil, there is no rapid-fire means to stop future killings."

"Close one mine out of the four," said Pitt, "and you drain the sound waves' killing potency."

"Short of ordering in a flight of B-1 bombers, which the President won't do, our hands are tied."

"There must be an international law that applies to murder on the high seas," said Pitt.

Sandecker shook his head. "Not one that covers this situation. The lack of an international law-enforcement organization plays in Dorsett's favor. Gladiator Island belongs only to the family, and it would take a year or more to talk the Russians into closing the mine off Siberia. Same with Chile. As long as Dorsett pays off high-ranking government officials, his mines stay open."

Maeve put on a good face through her ordeal. At first she had wept whenever she was alone in the small colonial house in Georgetown that her father's aides had leased for her. Panic swept her heart at thoughts of what might be happening to her twin boys on Gladiator Island. She wanted to rush to their sides and sweep them away to safety, but she was powerless. She actually saw herself with them in her dreams. But the dreams of sleep became nightmares on awakening. There wasn't the least hope of fighting the incredible resources of her father. She never detected anyone, but she knew without doubt that his security people were watching her every move.

Roy Van Fleet and his wife, Robin, who had taken Maeve under her wing, invited her to join them in attending a party thrown by a wealthy owner of an undersea exploration company. She was loath to go, but Robin had pushed her, refusing to take no for an answer and insisting she put a little fun in her life, never realizing the torment Maeve was going through.

"Loads of capital bigwigs and politicians will attend," Robin gushed. "We can't miss it."

After applying her makeup and pulling her hair tightly back in a bun, Maeve put on a brown Empire-waist dress of silk chiffon and embroidered net with beaded bodice and a short three-tier skirt.

She peered through the curtains at the street outside. There was a light layer of snow on the ground, but the streets were clear. The temperature was cold but not frigid. She put on a long black coat that came down to her ankles and waited for the Van Fleets to pick her up.

Pitt showed the invitation he'd borrowed from the admiral at the door of the country club and was passed through the beautiful wooden doors carved with the likenesses of famous golfers. He dropped off his topcoat at the cloakroom and was directed into a spacious ballroom paneled in dark walnut. One of Washington's elite interior decorators had created a stunning undersea illusion in the room. Cleverly designed paper fish hung from the ceiling, while hidden lighting gave off a soft wavering blue-green glow that provided an eye-pleasing watery effect.

The host, president of Deep Abyss Engineering, his wife and other company officials stood in a receiving line to greet the guests. Pitt avoided them and surveyed the room.

There must have been close to two hundred people present. An orchestra was playing a medley from motion picture musical scores. He recognized several congressmen and four or five senators, all on committees dealing with the oceans and the environment. Many of the men wore white dinner jackets. Most were in the more common black evening clothes, some with vividly patterned cummerbunds and bow ties. Pitt preferred the old look. His tux sported a vest with a heavy gold chain draped across the front, attached to a pocket watch that had once belonged to his great-grandfather, who had been a steam locomotive engineer on the Santa Fe Railroad.

The women were dressed elegantly, some in long dresses, some in shorter skirts complemented by brocaded or sequined jackets.

Pitt was easily bored at parties like this and seldom stayed more than an hour before heading back to the apartment above his aircraft hangar. Tonight was different. He was on a quest. Sandecker had informed him that Maeve was coming with the Van Fleets. His eyes wandered the tables and the crowded dance floor but found no sign of her.

Either she changed her mind at the last minute or hadn't arrived yet, he figured.

It was then that Maeve walked into the ballroom. The entire room seemed to blur, and everyone in it faded into a gray mist, leaving Maeve standing alone in the center of a radiant aura.

He came back down to earth as she stepped away from the receiving line ahead of the Van Fleets and paused to gaze at the crowded mass of partygoers. Then she was walking with the Van Fleets to a table, where they all sat down and ordered from a waiter. Maeve was no sooner settled in her chair when men, both young and old enough to be her grandfather, came up and asked her to dance. She politely turned down every request. He was amused to see that no appeals moved her. They quickly gave up and moved on, feeling boyishly rejected. The Van Fleets excused themselves to dance while they waited for the first course. Maeve sat alone.

He walked directly across the dance floor through the swaying couples without stepping left or right. Maeve was people-watching out of sheer boredom when she became vaguely aware of a man striding purposefully in her direction. At first she paid him little notice, thinking he was only another stranger who wanted to dance with her. In another time, another place, she might have been flattered by the attention, but her mind was twenty thousand kilometers away. Only when the intruder approached her table, placed his hands on the blue tablecloth and leaned toward her did she recognize him. Maeve's face lit with inexpressible joy.

"Oh, Dirk, I thought I'd never see you again," she gasped.

"I came to beg your forgiveness for not saying goodbye when Al and I abruptly left the *Ice Hunter.*"

She was both surprised and pleased at his behavior. She thought he held no affection for her. Now it was written in his eyes. "You couldn't have known how much I needed you," she said, her voice barely audible above the music.

He came around the table and sat beside her. "I know now," he said solemnly.

Her face turned to avoid his gaze. "You could not begin to understand the scrape I'm in."

Pitt took Maeve's hand in his. It was the first time he had deliberately touched her. "I had a nice little chat with Boudicca," he said with a slight sardonic grin. "She told me everything."

Her poise and grace seemed to crumble. "You? Boudicca? How is that possible?"

He stood and gently pulled her from her chair. "Why don't we dance, and I'll tell you all about it later."

As if by magic, here he was, holding her tightly. Suddenly, she pushed him back slightly. "You know about my sons?"

"What are their names?"

"Sean and Michael."

"Your father is holding Sean and Michael hostage on Gladiator Island so he can extort from you information on any breakthroughs by NUMA on the slaughter at sea."

Maeve stared up at him in confusion, but before she could ask any further questions, he pulled her close again. After a few moments, she began to cry softly. "I feel so ashamed. I don't know where to turn."

"You can turn to me," Pitt said softly.

They kept moving around the dance floor, still holding each other as the band finished one number and began another.

It was a full minute before Pitt spoke. "I need your help in consolidating my plans," he said.

"Plans for what?"

He looked at her as if he was surprised she asked. "To sneak onto Gladiator Island, of course, snatch your boys and make a clean getaway."

"You'd do that?" Maeve gasped. "You'd risk your life for me?"

"And your sons," Pitt added firmly.

"But why?"

He had an overpowering urge to tell her that he harbored feelings of deep affection for her. True to form, he swerved to the light side.

"Why? Because Admiral Sandecker gave me ten days off, and I hate to sit around and not be productive."

A smile returned to her face. "That's not even a good lie."

"Why is it," he said as he pulled her closer just before the song ended, "that women always see right through me?"

PART III

DIAMONDS . . . THE GRAND ILLUSION

◆ MARVELOUS MAEVE ◆

January 30, 2000
Gladiator Island, Tasman Sea

26

THE DORSETT MANOR HOUSE SAT IN THE SADDLE OF THE island, between the two dormant volcanos. The front overlooked the lagoon, which had become a bustling port for the diamond mining activities. The style was based on the classical layout—a central courtyard surrounded by verandas from which doors opened onto thirty rooms, all furnished in English colonial antiques. The only visible modern convenience was a large satellite dish, rising from a luxuriant garden, and a modern swimming pool in the center courtyard.

Arthur Dorsett hung up the phone, stepped out of his office-study and walked over to the pool where Deirdre was stretched on a lounge chair, in a bikini, carefully absorbing the tropical sun into her smooth skin.

"I have just gotten off the phone with Washington," he said heavily. "It seems your sister has vanished."

Deirdre sat up, startled, and lifted a hand to shade her eyes from the sun.

"I'll bet my share of Dorsett Consolidated you know where to find her." She smiled archly at him. "What is our timetable?"

"I suspect that Mr. Pitt and Maeve have already left Washington."

Her eyes squinted at him under the sun. "So soon?"

"Since Maeve hasn't been seen at her house, nor has Pitt set foot in his NUMA office for the past two days, it goes without saying that they are together and on their way here for the twins."

"A mistake, thinking we could trust Maeve," Deirdre said reproachfully. "You should have guessed she would come chasing after her brats the first chance she got."

"I'll arrange for her never to see them again," Dorsett said.

"A great pity," Deirdre said.

Dorsett looked at her. "Pity? Who am I supposed to pity, Maeve or the twins?"

"Neither."

"Who then?"

Deirdre wore a sardonic grin. "The millions of women around the world, when they find out their diamonds are as worthless as glass."

27

ADMIRAL SANDECKER HAD GIVEN PITT'S MISSION HIS VERY reluctant blessing with grave misgivings. He considered Arthur Dorsett a very threatening man, a greedy sociopath who killed without a shred of remorse. The admiral cooperated by authorizing a NUMA aircraft for Pitt and Giordino to fly, with Maeve, to New Zealand and take command of a research ship as a base of operations for the rescue, but with the strict condition that no lives be risked in the attempt. Pitt gladly agreed, knowing the only people at risk, once the *Ocean Angler* stood a safe distance off Gladiator Island, would be the three of them. His plan was to use an underwater submersible to slip into the lagoon, then land and help Maeve reclaim her sons before returning to the ship. It was, Pitt thought bemusedly, a plan without technicalities. Once on shore, everything hinged on Maeve.

He looked across the cockpit at Giordino, who was piloting the executive Gulfstream jet. His burly friend was as composed as if he were lounging under a palm tree on a sandy beach.

Pitt rose from his seat, moved back into the main cabin and stared down at Maeve. She had slept fitfully during the long and tedious flight from Washington, and her face looked tired and drawn. Even now her eyes were closed, but the way she constantly changed position on the narrow couch indicated she had not yet crossed over the threshold into unconscious slumber. He reached over and gently shook her. "We're about to land in Wellington," he said.

Giordino flared the aircraft, dropping smoothly till the tires touched and smoked briefly on contact with the ground. He taxied off the runway onto the flight line toward the parking area for transient and privately owned aircraft. "You see a NUMA vehicle?" he shouted over his shoulder at Pitt in the back.

The familiar turquoise and white colors were not in sight. "Must be late," said Pitt. "Or else we're early."

Pitt opened the passenger door and set a small step at the end of the stairs. Giordino passed out their traveling bags, locked up the aircraft and took cover with Pitt and Maeve under one wing while a sudden rain squall passed over the airport. Almost as quickly as it appeared, the storm moved across the bay, and the sun broke through a rolling mass of white clouds. A few minutes later, a small Toyota bus with the words HARBOR SHUTTLE painted on the sides splashed through the puddles and stopped. The driver stepped to the ground and jogged over to the aircraft. He was slim with a friendly face and dressed like a drugstore cowboy.

"One of you Dirk Pitt?"

"Right here," Pitt acknowledged.

"Carl Marvin. Sorry I'm running late. The battery went dead in the shore van we carry aboard the *Ocean Angler,* so I had to borrow transportation from the harbormaster. I do hope you weren't inconvenienced."

"Not at all," said Giordino sourly. "We enjoyed the typhoon during intermission."

The sarcasm flew over the driver's head. "You haven't been waiting long, I hope."

"No more than ten minutes," said Pitt.

Marvin loaded their bags in the back of the shuttle bus and drove away from the aircraft as soon as his passengers were seated. "The dock where the ship is moored is only a short drive from the airport," he said cordially. "Just sit back and enjoy the trip."

Pitt and Maeve sat together. Giordino settled into the seat in front of them and directly behind the driver. He spent most of the drive studying an aerial photo of Gladiator Island that Admiral Sandecker had borrowed from the Pentagon.

Time passed quickly and they soon turned off the main road into the bustling dock area, which was quite close to the city. A fleet of international cargo vessels, representing mostly Asian shipping lines, were moored beside long piers flanked by huge storage buildings. No one paid any attention to the wandering course taken by the driver around the buildings, ships and huge cargo cranes. His eyes watched the passengers in the rearview mirror almost as often as they were turned on the piers ahead.

"The *Ocean Angler* is just on the other side of the next warehouse," he said, vaguely gesturing at some unseen object through the windshield.

"Is she ready to cast off when we board?" asked Pitt.

"The crew is standing by for your arrival."

Giordino stared thoughtfully at the back of the driver's head. "What's your duty on the ship?" he asked.

"Mine?" said Marvin without turning. "I'm a photographer with the film crew."

"How do you like sailing under Captain Dempsey?"

"A fine gentleman. He is most considerate of the scientists and their work."

Giordino looked up and saw Marvin peering back in the rearview mirror. He smiled until Marvin refocused his attention on his driving. Then, shielded by the backrest of the seat in front of him, he wrote on a receipt for aircraft fuel that was pumped aboard in Honolulu before they headed toward Wellington. He wadded up the paper and casually flipped it over his shoulder onto Pitt's lap.

Talking with Maeve, Pitt had not picked up on the words that passed between Giordino and the driver. He casually unfolded the note and read the message:

THIS GUY IS A PHONY.

Pitt leaned forward and spoke conversationally without staring suspiciously at the driver. "What makes you such a killjoy?"

Giordino turned around and spoke very softly. "Our friend is not from the *Ocean Angler*."

"I'm listening."

"I tricked him into saying Dempsey is the captain. Paul Dempsey skippers the *Ice Hunter*. Joe Ross is captain of the *Angler*."

True to their fears, the driver swung the bus through the gaping doors and between two men in the uniforms of Dorsett Consolidated security guards. The guards quickly followed the bus inside and pushed the switch to close the warehouse doors.

There wasn't time for any drawn-out conference. The bus was passing deeper into the darkened warehouse. "Dump our buddy Carl and let's bust out of here."

Giordino did not wait for a countdown. Four quick steps and he had a choke hold on the man who called himself Carl Marvin. With unbelievable speed, Giordino swung the man from behind the steering wheel, opened the entry door of the bus and heaved him out.

As if they had rehearsed, Pitt jumped into the driver's seat and jammed the accelerator to the carpeted floorboard. Not an instant too soon, the bus surged forward through a knot of armed men, scattering them like leaves in the wake of a tornado.

Pitt swung a broadside turn down a wide aisle separating tiers of stacked crates of merchandise, took aim at a large metal door and crouched over the steering wheel. With a metallic clatter that sent the door whirling from its mountings, the Toyota bus roared out of the warehouse onto the loading dock, Pitt twisting the wheel rapidly to keep from clipping one leg of a towering loading crane.

This part of the dockyard was deserted. No ships were moored alongside, loading and unloading their cargo holds. A party of workers repairing a section of the pier were taking a break, sitting elbow to elbow in a row on a long wooden barricade that stretched across an access road leading from the pier as they ate their lunch. Pitt lay on the horn, spinning the wheel violently to avoid striking the workers, who froze at the sight of the vehicle bearing down on them. As the bus slewed around the barricade, Pitt almost missed it entirely, but a piece of the rear bumper caught a vertical support and spun the barricade around, slinging the dockworkers about the pier as if they were on the end of a cracked whip.

"Sorry about that!" Pitt yelled out the window as he sped past.

A long truck and trailer pulled in front of him, blocking off his exit. He frantically cramped the steering wheel in a crazy zigzag to avoid smashing into the huge truck. There was a loud metallic crunch, followed by the smashing of glass and the screech of tortured metal as the bus sideswiped the front end of the truck. The right tire was blown and the front suspension knocked out of alignment.

"Do you have to hit everything that comes across your path?" Giordino asked irritably. He sat on the floor on the undamaged side of the bus, his huge arms circled around Maeve.

"Thoughtless of me," said Pitt. "Anyone hurt?"

"Enough bruises to win an abuse lawsuit," said Maeve bravely.

Giordino rubbed a swelling knot on one side of his head and gazed at Maeve woefully. "Your old man is a sneaky one. He knew we were coming and threw a surprise party."

"Someone at NUMA must be on his payroll." Pitt spared Maeve a brief glance. "Not you, I hope."

"Not me," Maeve said firmly.

Giordino made his way to the rear of the bus and stared out the window for signs of pursuit. Two black vans careened around the damaged truck and took up the chase. "We have hounds running up our exhaust pipe. They have Dorsett Consolidated Mining logos painted on their doors."

"Not exactly the news I wanted to hear," Pitt said dryly.

"You'd think we'd have left enough wreckage to have a dozen cop cars on our tails by now," grumbled Giordino. "Why aren't they doing their duty and patrolling the docks? I think it only fitting they arrest you for reckless driving."

"If I know Daddy," said Maeve, "he paid them to take a holiday."

With no coolant, the engine rapidly heated up and threw clouds of steam from under the hood. Pitt had almost no control over the demolished vehicle. The front wheels, both splayed outward, fought to travel in opposite directions. A narrow alleyway between two warehouses suddenly yawned in front of the bus. Pitt hurled the bus into the opening. His luck was against him. Too late he realized the alleyway led onto a deserted pier with no exit except the one he passed through.

"The end of the trail," Pitt sighed.

Giordino turned and looked to the rear again. "The posse knows it. They've stopped to gloat over their triumph."

"Maeve?"

Maeve walked to the front of the bus. "Yes?" she said quietly.

"How long can you hold your breath?"

"I don't know; maybe a minute."

"Al? What are they doing?"

"Walking toward the bus, holding nasty-looking clubs."

"They want us alive," said Pitt. "Okay, gang, take a seat and hold on tight."

"What are you going to do?" asked Maeve.

We, my dear, are going for a swim. Al, open all the windows. I want this thing to sink like a brick."

"I hope the water's warm," said Giordino as he unlatched the windows. "I hate cold water."

To Maeve, Pitt said, "Take several deep breaths and get as much oxygen as you can into your bloodstream. Exhale and then inhale as we go over the side."

"I bet I can swim underwater farther than you," she said with gutsy resolve.

"Here's your chance to prove it," he said admiringly. "Don't waste time waiting for an air pocket. Go out the windows on your right and swim under the pier as soon as the water stops surging inside the bus."

Pitt reached behind the driver's seat, unzipped his overnight bag, retrieved a nylon packet and stuffed it down his pants.

"What in the world are you doing?" asked Maeve.

"My emergency bag," explained Pitt. "I never leave home without it."

"They're almost on us," Giordino announced calmly.

Pitt slipped on a leather coat, zipped it to his collar,

turned and gripped the wheel. "Okay, let's see if we can get high marks from the judges."

He revved up the engine and shifted the automatic transmission into LOW. The battered bus jerked forward, right front tire flapping, steam billowing so thick he could hardly see ahead, gathering speed for the plunge. There was no railing along the pier, only a low, wooden horizontal beam that acted as a curb for vehicles. The front wheels took the brunt of the impact. The already weakened front suspension tore away as the wheelless chassis ground over it, the rear tires tearing rubber as they spun, pushing what was left of the Toyota bus over the side of the pier.

The bus seemed to fall in slow motion before the heavier front end dropped and struck the water with a great splash. The last thing Pitt remembered before the windshield fell inward and the seawater surged through the open passenger door was the loud hiss of the over-heated engine as it was inundated.

The bus bobbed once, hung for an instant and then sank into the green water of the bay. All Dorsett's security people saw when they ran to the edge of the dock and looked down, was a cloud of steam, a mass of gurgling bubbles and a spreading oil slick. The waves created by the impact spread and rippled into the pilings beneath the pier. They waited expectantly for heads to appear, but no indication of life emerged from the green depths.

28

PITT GUESSED THAT IF THE DOCKS COULD ACCOMMODATE
large cargo ships the water depth had to be at least fifteen
meters. The bus sank, wheels down, into the muck on the
bottom of the harbor, disturbing the silt, which burst
into a rolling cloud. Pushing away from the wheel, he
stroked toward the rear of the bus to make sure Maeve
and Giordino were not injured and had exited through a
window. Satisfied they had escaped, he snaked through
the opening and kicked into the blinding silt. When he
burst into the clear, visibility was better than he had
expected, the water temperature a degree or two colder.
The incoming tide brought in fairly clean water, and he
could easily distinguish the individual pilings under the
pier. He estimated visibility at twenty meters.

He recognized the indistinct shapes of Maeve and
Giordino about four meters in front, swimming strongly
into the void ahead. He looked up, but the surface was
only a vague pattern of broken light from a cloudy sky.
And then suddenly the water darkened considerably as
he swam under the pier and between the pilings. He
finally surfaced in the midst of a small sea of floating
litter. He sucked in several breaths of salty air and swung

around to find Maeve and Giordino bobbing in the water a short distance behind him.

They swam over, and his regard for Maeve heightened when he saw her smiling. "Show-off," she whispered, aware that voices could be heard by the Dorsett men above. "I bet you almost drowned trying to outdistance me."

"I don't think anyone saw us," muttered Giordino. "I was almost under the dock before I broke free of the silt cloud."

Pitt motioned in the general direction of the main dock area. "Our best hope is to swim under the pier until we can find a safe place to climb clear."

"What about boarding the nearest ship we can find?" asked Giordino.

Maeve looked doubtful. Her long blond hair floated in the water behind her like golden reeds on a pond. "If my father's people picked up our trail, he'd find a way to force the crew to turn us over to him."

Giordino looked at her. "You don't think the crew would hold us until we were under the protection of local authorities?"

Pitt shook his head, flinging drops of water in a spiral. "If you were the captain of a ship or the commander in charge of dock police, would you believe a trio of half-drowned rats or the word of someone representing Arthur Dorsett?"

"Probably not us," Giordino admitted.

"If only we could reach the *Ocean Angler*."

"That would be the first place they'd expect us to go," said Maeve.

"Once we were on board, Dorsett's men would have a fight on their hands if they tried to drag us off," Pitt assured her.

"A moot point," Giordino said under his breath. "We

haven't the foggiest idea where the *Ocean Angler* is berthed."

Pitt stared at his friend reproachfully. "I hate it when you make so much sense," he teased.

"Has she a turquoise hull and white on the cabins above like the *Ice Hunter?*" asked Maeve.

"All NUMA ships have the same color scheme," Giordino answered.

"Then I saw her. She's tied to Pier 16."

"I give up. Where's Pier 16 from here?"

"The fourth one north of here," replied Pitt.

"How would you know that?"

"The signs on the warehouses. I noticed number 19 before I drove off of Pier 20."

"Now that we've fixed our location and have a direction, we'd best get a move on," Giordino suggested. "If they have half a brain they'll be sending down divers to look for bodies in the bus."

"Stay clear of the pilings," cautioned Pitt. "Beneath the surface, they're packed with colonies of mussels. Their shells can cut through flesh like a razor blade."

"Is that why you're swimming in a leather jacket?" asked Maeve.

"You never know who you'll meet," Pitt said drily.

Without a visual sighting, there was no calculating how far they had to go before reaching the research ship. Conserving their strength, they breaststroked slowly and steadily through the maze of pilings, out of sight of Dorsett's men on the dock above. They reached the base of Pier 20, then passed beneath the main dockyard thoroughfare, which connected to all the loading docks, before turning north toward Pier 16. The better part of an hour crept by before Maeve spotted the turquoise hull reflected in the water beneath the pier.

"We made it," she cried out happily.

"Don't count your prize money," Pitt warned her. "The dock might be crawling with your father's muscle patrol."

The ship's hull was only two meters from the pilings. Pitt swam until he was directly beneath the ship's boarding ramp. He reached up, locked his hands around a cross member that reinforced the pilings and pulled himself out of the water. Climbing the slanting beams until he reached the upper edge of the dock, he slowly raised his head and scanned the immediate vicinity.

The area around the boarding ramp was deserted, but a Dorsett security van was parked across the nearest entry onto the pier. He counted four men lined across an open stretch between stacks of cargo containers and several parked cars alongside the ship moored in front of the *Ocean Angler*.

He ducked below the edge of the dock and spoke to Maeve and Giordino. "Our friends are guarding the entrance to the pier about eighty meters away, too far to stop us from making it on board."

No more conversation was necessary. Pitt pulled both of them onto the beam he was standing on. Then, at his signal, they all climbed over the beam that acted as a curb, dodged around a huge bollard that held the mooring lines of the ship, and with Maeve in the lead, dashed up the boarding ramp to the open deck above.

When he reached the safety of the ship, Pitt's instincts began working overtime. He had erred badly, and the mistake couldn't be undone. He knew when he saw the men guarding the dock begin walking slowly and methodically toward the *Ocean Angler* as if they were out for a stroll through the park. There was no shouting or confusion. They acted as though they had expected their quarry to suddenly appear and reach the sanctuary of the ship. He knew when he looked over decks devoid of human activity that something was very, very wrong. He knew when a door opened from a companionway leading to the bridge and a familiar figure stepped out onto the deck that the unthinkable had happened.

"How nice to see you again, Mr. Pitt," said John Merchant, snidely. "You never give up, do you?"

29

PITT, IN THOSE FIRST FEW MOMENTS OF BITTER FRUSTRATION, felt an almost tangible wave of defeat wash over him. It was all too painfully obvious that with advance warning from their agent inside NUMA, Dorsett's men had arrived at the *Ocean Angler* first, subdued the captain and crew, and taken over the ship just long enough to trap Pitt and the others. Pitt felt he should have predicted it and come up with an alternate plan, but he'd underestimated the shrewd diamond tycoon.

When he saw a small army of uniformed men appear from their hiding places, some with police clubs, a few leveling rubber-pellet guns, he knew hope was lost. But not irretrievably lost. Not so long as he had Giordino at his side. He looked down at Giordino to see how he was reacting to the terrible shock. As far as he could tell, Giordino looked as though he was enduring a boring classroom lecture.

Pitt put his arm around Maeve, whose brave front began to crumble. She bowed her head and placed it in her hands as her shoulders sagged. Her fear was not for herself but for what her father would do to her boys now that it was painfully obvious she had deceived him.

"What have you done with the crew?" Pitt demanded of Merchant, noting the bandage on the back of his head.

"The five men left on board were persuaded to remain in their quarters."

Pitt looked at him questioningly. "Only five?"

"Yes. The others were invited to a party in their honor by Mr. Dorsett, at Wellington's finest hotel. Hail to the brave explorers of the deep, that sort of thing. As a mining company, Dorsett Consolidated has a vested interest in whatever minerals are discovered on the seafloor."

"You were well prepared," said Pitt coldly. "Who in NUMA told you we were coming?"

"A geologist, I don't know his name, who keeps Mr. Dorsett informed of your underwater mining projects. He's only one of many who provide the company with inside information from businesses and governments around the world."

"A corporate spy network."

"And a very good one. We've tracked you from the minute you took off from Langley Field in Washington."

The guards who surrounded the three made no move to restrain them. "No shackles, no handcuffs?" asked Pitt.

"My men have been commanded to assault and maim only Miss Dorsett should you and your friend attempt to escape." Merchant's teeth fairly gleamed under the sun between his thin lips. "Not my wish, of course. The orders came direct from Ms. Boudicca Dorsett."

"A real sweetheart," Pitt said acidly. "I'll bet she tortured her dolls when she was little."

"She has some very interesting plans for you, Mr. Pitt."

"I can't stand the suspense. Where do we go from here?"

"Mr. Dorsett will arrive shortly. You will all be transferred to his yacht."

"I thought his floating villa was at Kunghit Island."

"It was, several days ago." Merchant smiled, removed his glasses and meticulously polished the lenses with a small cloth. "The Dorsett yacht has four turbocharged diesel engines connected to water jets that produce a total of 18,000 horsepower that enable the 80-ton craft to cruise at 120 kilometers an hour. You will find Mr. Dorsett is a man of singularly high taste."

"What does he do for laughs besides count diamonds?"

Just for a moment, Merchant's eyes blazed at Giordino and his smile faded, then he caught himself and the lifeless look returned as if it had been applied by a makeup artist.

"Humor, gentlemen, has its price. As Miss Dorsett can tell you, her father lacks a fondness for satiric wit. I venture to say that by this time tomorrow you will have precious little to smile about."

Arthur Dorsett was nothing like Pitt had pictured him. He expected one of the richest men in the world, with three beautiful daughters, to be reasonably handsome, with a certain degree of sophistication. What Pitt saw before him in the salon of the same yacht he'd stood in at Kunghit Island was a troll from Teutonic folklore who'd just crawled from an underworld cave.

Dorsett stood a half a head taller than Pitt and was twice as broad from hips to shoulders. This was not a man who was comfortable sitting behind a desk. Pitt could see from whom Boudicca had gotten the black, empty eyes. Dorsett had weathered lines in his face, and the rough, scarred hands indicated that he wasn't afraid of getting them dirty. The mustache was long and scraggly with a few bits of his lunch adhering to the strands of hair. But the thing that struck Pitt as hardly befitting a man of Dorsett's international stature was the teeth that looked like the ivory keys of an old piano, yellowed and badly chipped.

He was positioned in front of the driftwood desk with the marble top, flanked by Boudicca, who stood on his left, and Deirdre, who sat in a patterned-silk chair. The sinister eyes examined every detail of Pitt and Giordino like needles, probing every centimeter from hair to shoelaces. He turned to Merchant, who was standing behind Maeve, his hand resting inside a tweed sport coat on a holstered automatic slung under one arm.

"Nicely done, John." He beamed. "You anticipated their every move." He lifted a matted eyebrow and stared at the two men standing before him, wet and bedraggled, turned his eyes to Maeve, stringy damp hair sticking to her forehead and cheeks, grinned hideously and nodded at Merchant. "Not all went as you expected, perhaps? They look like they fell in a moat."

"They delayed the inevitable by trying to escape into the water," Merchant said airily. The self-assurance, the pomposity, were mirrored in his eyes. "In the end they walked right into my hands."

"You and your men are to be commended." Dorsett nodded approvingly. "A liberal bonus will be forthcoming to all involved."

"That is most kind of you, sir," Merchant purred.

"Please leave us now."

As soon as Merchant was gone, Maeve lashed out at her father. "I demand you tell me if Sean and Michael are all right, unharmed by your rotten mine superintendent."

Without a word, Boudicca stepped forward, reached out her hand in what Pitt thought was a show of affection, but brought it viciously across Maeve's cheek, a blow with such force it almost knocked her sister off her feet. Maeve stumbled and was caught by Pitt as Giordino stepped between the two women.

Shorter by half, Giordino had to look up into Boudicca's face as if he were staring up at a tall building. "There's a homecoming for you," he said drolly.

Boudicca hit Giordino hard, harder than most Olympic boxers. Her balled fist caught Giordino on the side of the cheek and the jaw. It was a savage blow, a damaging roundhouse blow, not one that was expected from a woman, and it would have knocked most men off their feet, cold. Most men would have been unconscious for twenty-four hours. Giordino's head snapped to one side and he took a step backward, shook his head as if to clear it and then spat out a tooth onto the expensive carpet. Incredibly, against all comprehension, he stepped forward again.

"You are one stupid man," she said coldly.

Her hands lashed out and clamped around Giordino's neck. He stood with his fists clenched at his sides, making no move to stop her. His face drained of all color and his eyes began to bulge and still he made no effort to defend himself. He stared at her without any malice at all.

"Release him!" Arthur Dorsett snapped. "Do not soil your hands on a rat."

Giordino still stood like a statue in a park, when Boudicca released her grip around his throat and stepped back, rubbing the knuckles she had scraped on his face.

"Next time," she snarled, "you won't have my father to save your filthy hide."

"Did you ever think of turning professional?" Giordino rasped hoarsely, tenderly touching the growing discoloration marks around his neck. "I know this carnival that could use a geek—"

Pitt put his hand on Giordino's shoulder. "Let's hear

what Mr. Dorsett has to say before you sign up for a rematch."

"You're wiser than your friend," said Dorsett.

"Only when it comes to averting pain and associating with criminals."

"Is that what you think of me? That I'm a common criminal?"

"Considering that you're responsible for murdering hundreds of people, an unqualified yes."

Dorsett shrugged imperviously and sat down behind his desk. "Regrettably, it was necessary."

Pitt found himself staring at stark, unfettered madness. "You have a sick, warped philosophy of life."

"So far it has served me very well."

"What's your excuse for not stopping the mass killing caused by your ultrasonic mining operations?"

"To mine more diamonds, what else?" Dorsett stared at Pitt as though he were studying a specimen in a jar. "In a few weeks I will make millions of women happy by providing them with the most precious of stones at a cost a beggar can afford."

"What percentage is there in dominating a depressed market?"

"I'm not interested in dominating the market, Mr. Pitt. I want to kill it for all time."

Pitt noticed that Dorsett didn't gaze right at him but fixed his eyes impassively on a point behind Pitt's head as if seeing a vision only he could see. "If I read you correctly, you're cutting your own throat."

"It sounds that way, doesn't it?" Dorsett lifted a finger at Pitt. "Exactly what I wanted everyone to think, even my closest associates and my own daughters. The truth of the matter is that I expect to make a great sum of money."

"How?" Pitt asked, his interest aroused.

Dorsett allowed a satanic grin to display his grotesque

teeth. "The answer lies not in diamonds but in the colored gemstone market."

"Now I see what this is all about," said Maeve as if witnessing a revelation. "You're out to corner the market on colored stones."

She began to shiver from her wet clothing and a sweeping dread. Pitt removed his soggy leather jacket and draped it around her shoulders.

Dorsett nodded. "Yes, Daughter. During the last twenty years, your wise old father has stockpiled his diamond production while quietly buying up claims to the major colored gemstone mines around the world. Through a complex formation of front corporations I now secretly control eighty percent of the market."

"By colored gemstones," said Pitt, "I assume you mean rubies and emeralds."

"Indeed, and a host of other precious stones, including sapphire, topaz, tourmaline and amethyst. Almost all are far more scarce than diamonds. The deposits of tsavorite, red beryl or red emerald, and the Mexican fire opal, for example, are becoming increasingly difficult to find. A number of colored gemstones are so rare they are sought by collectors and are very seldom made into jewelry."

"You will pay for your crimes, Dorsett," Pitt said calmly but with a cold edge in his voice. "You will surely pay for the unbearable grief and agony you have caused."

"Who will be the angel of my retribution?" Dorsett sneered. "You, maybe? Mr. Giordino here? I do not believe there will be ordained retaliation from the heavens. The possibility is too remote. The only certainty I can bank on, Mr. Pitt, is that you won't be around to see it."

"Execute the witnesses by shooting them in the head and throwing their bodies overboard, is that your policy?"

"Shoot you and Mr. Giordino in the head?" There was no trace of emotion, of any feeling in Arthur Dorsett's voice. "Nothing so crude and mundane, nor so merciful. Thrown in the sea? Yes, you may consider that a foregone conclusion. In any event, I will guarantee you and your friend a slow but violent death."

30

AFTER THIRTY HOURS OF POUNDING THROUGH THE SEA AT incredible speeds, the powerful turbodiesels fell off to a muffled throb, and the yacht slowed and began to drift amid a sea of gentle swells. The last sight of the New Zealand shoreline had long since disappeared in the yacht's wake. To the north and west dark clouds were laced with forks of lightning, the thunder rumbling dully across the horizon. To the south and east there were no clouds and thunder. The skies were blue and clear.

Pitt and Giordino had spent the night and half the next day locked in a small supply compartment aft of the engine room. There was barely enough room to sit on the deck with knees drawn up to their chins.

Now, they were being escorted out onto the stern deck, surrounded by a small army of guards armed with a variety of weapons designed to inflict bodily harm but not kill. Both men blinked in the fading sunlight just as the first few raindrops fell, carried ahead of the advancing clouds by a light breeze.

Dorsett sat protected under an overhang in a chair at a table laden with several savory dishes laid out in silver serving bowls. Boudicca and Deirdre, seated on their father's left and right, didn't bother looking up from their food as Pitt and Giordino were brought into their divine presence. Pitt glanced around for Maeve, but she wasn't to be seen.

"I regret that you must leave us," said Dorsett between bites of toast heaped with caviar.

Dorsett rubbed food from his mouth with a napkin with the savoir-faire of an auto mechanic wiping his greasy hands. "I apologize for providing such a small craft, one without an engine, I might add, but it's all I have to offer."

"I see," Pitt said quietly. "I see indeed. You plan to set us adrift."

"You should be grateful that I'm giving you a chance to live."

"Adrift in a part of the sea devoid of maritime traffic, directly in the path of a storm." Pitt scowled. "The least you should do is supply pen and paper to make out our last wills and testaments."

"Our conversation has ended. Good-bye, Mr. Pitt, Mr. Giordino, bon voyage." Dorsett nodded at John Merchant. "Show them to their craft."

Merchant pointed to a gate in the railing that was swung open.

Pitt stepped to the edge of the deck and stared down at the water. A small semi-inflatable boat bobbed in the water beside the yacht. Three meters in length by two meters wide, it had a fiberglass V-hull that appeared sturdy. The craft had mounted an outboard engine at one time, but that had been removed. The control cables still dangled from a center console. The interior was empty except for a figure in Pitt's leather jacket huddled in one end.

Cold rage swept Pitt. He took Merchant by the collar of his yachting jacket and cast him aside as easily as if he'd been a straw scarecrow. He stormed back to the dining table before he could be stopped. "Not Maeve too," he said sharply.

Dorsett smiled, but it was an expression completely lacking in humor. "She took her ancestor's name, she can suffer as her ancestor did."

"You low-down, dirty scab!" Pitt snarled with animal hate. That was as far as he got. One of Merchant's guards rammed the butt of his automatic rifle viciously in Pitt's side, just above the kidney.

A tidal wave of agony consumed Pitt, but sheer wrath kept him on his feet. He lurched forward, grabbed the tablecloth in both hands, gave a mighty jerk and wrenched it into the air. Glasses, knives, forks, spoons, serving dishes and plates filled with gourmet treats exploded over the deck with a great clatter. Pitt then threw himself across the table at Dorsett, not with the mere intent to strike him or choke him to death. He knew he'd have one, and only one, chance at maiming the man. He extended his index fingers and jabbed just as he was smothered in guards. A maddened Boudicca slung her hand down in a ferocious chop to Pitt's neck, but she missed and caught him on the shoulder. One of Pitt's fingers missed its target and scraped over Dorsett's forehead. The other struck home, and he heard an agonized primeval scream. Then he felt the blows raining on him in every bone of his body, then nothing as the crazy melee snapped into blackness.

Pitt woke and thought he was in some bottomless pit or a cave deep in the earth. Or at least in the depths of some underground cavern where there was only eternal darkness. Desperately, he tried to feel his way out, but it was like stumbling through a labyrinth. Lost in the throes of a nightmare, doomed to wander forever in a black maze, he thought vaguely. Then suddenly, for no more than the blink of an eye, he saw a dim light far ahead. He reached out for it and watched it grow into dark clouds scudding across the sky.

Every square centimeter of his body throbbed with pain. From his skull to his knees, it seemed every bone was broken. He tried to sit up, but stopped in mid-motion and groaned in agony. Maeve touched his cheek and cradled his shoulders with one arm. "It will hurt less if you don't try to move."

He looked up into her face. "Well, I certainly made a mess of things, didn't I?" he murmured.

She slowly shook her head, the long blond hair trailing across his cheeks. "No, no, don't think that. You wouldn't be here if it wasn't for me."

"Merchant's boys worked you over pretty good before throwing you off the yacht. You look like you were used for batting practice by the Los Angeles Dodgers."

Pitt struggled to a sitting position. "Dorsett?"

"I suspect you may have fixed one of his eyes so he'll look like a real pirate when he slips on his eye patch. Now all he needs is a dueling scar and a hook."

"Boudicca and Deirdre carried him inside the salon during the brawl," said Maeve. "If Merchant had realized the full extent of Father's injury, there is no telling what he might have done to you."

Pitt's gaze swept an empty and ominous sea through eyes that were swollen and half closed. "They're gone?"

"Tried to run us over before they cut and ran to beat the storm," said Giordino. "Lucky for us the neoprene floats on our raft, and without an engine that's all you can call it, rebounded off the yacht's bows. As it was, we came within a hair of capsizing."

Pitt refocused his eyes on Maeve. "So they left us to drift like your great-great-great-grandmother, Betsy Fletcher."

She stared at him oddly. "How did you know about her? I never told you."

"I always investigate the women in my life."

"And a short life it'll be," said Giordino, pointing grimly to the northwest. "Unless my night-school class in meteorology steered me wrong, we're sitting in the path of what they call in these parts a typhoon, or maybe a cyclone, depending how close we are to the Indian Ocean."

The sight of the dark clouds and the streaks of lightning followed by the threatening rumble of thunder was enough to make Pitt lose heart as he peered across the sea and listened to the increasing wind. The margin between life and death had narrowed to a paper's thickness. Already the sun was blotted out and the sea turned gray. The tiny boat was minutes away from being swallowed in the maelstrom.

Pitt hesitated no longer. "The first order of the day is to rig a sea anchor." He turned to Maeve. "We'll need my leather jacket and some line and anything that will help create a drag to keep us from capsizing in heavy seas."

Without a word, she slipped out of the coat and handed it to him while Giordino rummaged in a small storage locker under a seat. He came up with a rusty grappling hook attached to two sections of nylon line, one five meters, the other, three meters. Pitt laid open the jacket and filled it with everyone's shoes and the grappling hook, along with some old engine parts and several corroded tools Giordino had scrounged from the storage locker. Then he zipped it up, knotted the sleeves around the open waistband and collar and tied the makeshift bundle to the shorter nylon line. He cast it over the side and watched it sink before tying the other end of the line solidly to the walk-around console mounted with the useless controls for the missing outboard engine.

"Lie on the floor of the boat," ordered Pitt, tying the

remaining line around the center console. "We're in for a wild ride. Loop the line around your waists and tie off the end so we won't lose the boat if we capsize and are thrown in the sea."

He took one last look over the neoprene buoyancy tubes at the menacing swells that swept in from a horizon that lifted and dropped. The sea was ugly and beautiful at the same time. Lightning streaked through the purple-black clouds, and the thunder came like the roll from a thousand drums. The tumult fell on them without pity. The full force of the gale, accompanied by a torrential rain, a drenching downpour that blocked out the sky and turned the sea into a boiling broth of foam, struck them less than ten minutes later. The drops, whipped by a wind that howled like a thousand banshees, pelted them so hard it stung their skin.

Spray was hurled from wave crests that rose three meters above the troughs. All too quickly the waves reached a height of seven meters, broken and confused, striking the boat from one direction and then another.

Miraculously, the sea anchor was not torn away. It did its duty and exerted its drag, preventing the sea gone berserk from capsizing the boat and throwing everyone into the murderous waters from which there was no return. The gray waves curled down upon them, filling the boat's interior with churning foam, soaking them all to the skin, but tending to pull the center of gravity deeper in the water, giving an extra fraction of stability. The twisting motion and the choppy rise and fall of the boat whirled their cargo of seawater around their bodies, making them feel they were being whipped inside a juice blender.

In a way, the size of the tiny craft was a blessing. The neoprene tubes around the sides made it as buoyant as a cork. No matter how violent the tempest, the durable hull would not burst into pieces, and if the sea anchor held, it would not capsize. Like the palms that leaned in the wind from gale-force winds, it would endure. The next twenty-four minutes passed like twenty-four hours, and as they hung on grimly to stay alive, Pitt found it hard to believe the storm had not overwhelmed them. There was no word, no description for the misery.

The never-ending walls of water poured into the boat, leaving the three of them choking and gasping until the boat was thrust up and onto the crest of the next swell. There was no need for bailing. The weight of the water filling the interior helped keep them from capsizing. One second they were struggling to keep from floating over the sides of the tubes, the following second preparing for the next frenzied motion, as they fell into a trough, to keep from being slung into the air.

Darkness came and passed, a night of torment that never seemed to end. They were numbed by the cold and constantly soaked. The chill cut through their flesh like a thousand knives. Dawn was a deliverance from hearing the waves roar and break without seeing them. With a sunrise shrouded by the convulsive clouds, they still grimly hung onto life by the barest of threads. They longed for daylight, but it finally came in a strange gray light that illuminated the terrible sea like an old black-and-white motion picture.

Despite the savagery of the turbulence, the atmosphere was hot and oppressive, a salty blanket that was too thick to breathe. The constant effort to keep from drowning had taken all they had to give. The fight had been against all odds, and total exhaustion was just around the corner. And yet, Pitt refused to see the futility of it all. He clung to life, drawing on his dwindling reserve of strength, holding tight as the next wave engulfed them, knowing their time to die was fast approaching.

31

BUT PITT, MAEVE AND GIORDINO DID NOT DIE.

By early evening, there was an easing of the wind, and the jumbled seas began to diminish shortly after. Unknown to them, the typhoon had veered off its earlier course from the northwest and suddenly headed southeast toward the Antarctic. In another hour, the sky was clear of clouds, and the wind was hardly strong enough to sail a sloop in. It was as if the storm were a bad dream that struck in the night and vanished with the soft light of day. They had won only one battle in a war with the elements. The savage seas and the cruel winds had failed to take them into the depths.

Their first task was to pull in the steadfast sea anchor and remove their shoes and the tools and other items from Pitt's jacket. Afterward, they took an inventory of every single item, seemingly useless or not, that might come in handy for the long haul ahead. At last, Pitt removed the small packet that he had shoved down his pants just before driving the bus over the side of the dock.

"What did you find with the boat?" he asked Giordino.

"Not enough hardware to hang a barn door. The

245

storage compartment held a grand total of three wrenches of various sizes, a screwdriver, a fuel pump, four spark plugs, assorted nuts and bolts, a couple of rags, a wooden paddle, a nylon boat cover and a handy-dandy little number that's going to add to the enjoyment of the voyage."

"Which is?"

Giordino held up a small hand pump. "This, for pumping up the flotation tubes."

"How long is the paddle?"

"A little over a meter."

"Barely tall enough to raise a sail," said Pitt. He opened the small waterproof packet and laid out a Swiss army knife, a very old and worn Boy Scout compass, a small tube of matches, a first aid kit no larger than a cigarette package, and a vest-pocket .25 caliber Mauser automatic pistol with one extra clip.

Maeve stared at the tiny gun. "You could have shot John Merchant and my father. Do you always carry a survival kit?"

"Since my Boy Scout days."

"Who do you intend to shoot in the middle of no-where?"

"Not who, but what. A bird, if one comes close enough."

"You'd shoot a defenseless bird?"

Pitt looked at her. "Only because I have this strange aversion to starving to death."

While Giordino pumped air into the flotation tubes before working on a canopy, Pitt examined every square centimeter of the boat, checking for any leaks or abrasions in the neoprene floats and structural damage to the fiberglass hull. He dove overboard and ran his hands over the bottom but found no indication of damage. The craft appeared to be about four years old and had apparently been used as a shore boat when Dorsett's

yacht moored off a beach without a dock. Pitt was
relieved to find it slightly worn but in otherwise excellent
shape. The only flaw was the missing outboard engine
that no longer hung on the transom of the boat.

Climbing back on board, he kept them busy all day
with odd little jobs to take their minds off their predica-
ment and growing thirst. Pitt was determined to keep
their spirits up. He had no illusions as to how long they
could last. He and Giordino had once trekked through
the Sahara Desert without water for nearly seven days.
That was a dry heat; here the heavy humidity sucked the
life out of them.

Giordino rigged the nylon cover as a shield from the
burning rays of the sun, draping it over the paddle he
had mounted on the control console and tying it down
over the high sides of the flotation tubes with short
lengths cut from the nylon line. He sloped one edge so
that any rainwater it caught would flow and drop into an
ice chest Maeve had found under one seat. She cleaned
the grime from the long unused ice chest and did her best
to straighten up the interior of the boat to make it
liveable. Pitt used his time to separate the strands from a
section of nylon line and knot them into a fishing line.

The only food source within two thousand kilometers
or more was fish. If they didn't catch any, they would
starve. He fashioned a hook from the prong of his belt
buckle and tied it to the line. The opposite end was
attached to the center of one of the wrenches so he could
grip it in both hands. The quandary was how to catch
them. There were no earthworms, trout flies, bass plugs
or cheese around here. Pitt leaned over the flotation
tubes, cupped his hands around his eyes to shut out the
sunlight and stared into the water.

Schools of herringlike fish, no larger than Pitt's little
finger, darted and wiggled under the boat. He recognized
pompano, dolphins, not to be confused with the por-

poise and their larger cousins, the dorado, with their high foreheads and long fin running down the top of their multicolored iridescent bodies. A couple of large mackerel glided in circles, occasionally striking at one of the smaller fish. There was also a small shark, a hammerhead, one of the strangest inhabitants of the sea, each of his eyes perched on the end of a wing that looked like it was jammed into his head.

"What are you going to use as bait?" asked Maeve.

"Me," said Pitt. "I'm using myself as a gourmet delight for the little fisheys."

"Whatever do you mean?"

"Watch and learn."

Maeve stared in undisguised awe as Pitt took his knife, rolled up a pant leg, and calmly carved off a small piece of flesh from the back of his thigh. Then he put it on the improvised hook.

"You got that screwdriver handy?" Pitt asked Giordino.

Giordino held it up. "You want me to operate on you too?"

"There's a small shark under the boat," Pitt explained. "I'm going to entice it to the surface. When I grab it, you ram the screwdriver into the top of his head between the eyes. Do it right and you might stick his pea-sized brain."

Maeve wanted no part of this business. She crawled to the stern of the boat and crouched behind the console, happy to get out of the way. "Mind you don't offer him anything to bite on."

As Pitt worked the hook slowly toward the boat, Giordino, his upraised arm poised with the screwdriver held dagger-fashion, peered into the deep. Then the shark was alongside, ashen gray on the back, fading to white on the belly, his dorsal fin coming out of the sea like a submarine raising its periscope. The screwdriver swung in an arc and struck the tough head of the shark as he rubbed his side against the flotation tubes. In the hand of most other men, the shaft would never have penetrated the cartilaginous skeleton of the shark, but Giordino rammed it in up to the hilt.

Pitt leaned out, clamped his arm under the shark's belly behind the gills and heaved just as Giordino struck again. He fell backward into the boat, cradling the one-and-a-half-meter hammerhead shark in his arms like a child. He grabbed the dorsal fin, wrapped his legs around the tail and hung on.

The savage jaws were snapping but found only empty air. Maeve cringed behind the console and screamed as the bristling triangular teeth gnashed only centimeters away from her drawn-up legs.

As if he were wrestling an alligator, Giordino threw all his weight on the thrashing beast from the sea, holding down the body on the floor of the boat, scraping the inside of his forearms raw on the sandpaperlike skin.

"You'll have to cut him," Pitt gasped to Giordino. "I feel as weak as a kitten."

"Rest easy," Giordino said. There was a patience, a warm understanding in his voice. "After the beating you took on the yacht and the pounding from the storm, it's a wonder you're not in a coma."

Although Pitt had honed the blades on his Swiss army knife to a razor edge, Giordino still had to grip the handle with both hands and exert a great deal of muscle in slicing through the tough underbelly of the shark. Under Maeve's guidance as a professional marine zoologist, he expertly cut out the liver and made an incision in the stomach. Then Maeve showed him how to slice the flesh from inside the skin efficiently.

"We should eat the liver now," she advised. "It will begin decaying almost immediately, and it is the most nutritious part of the fish."

"What about the rest of the meat?" asked Giordino, swishing the knife and his hands in the water to remove the slime. "It won't take long to spoil in this heat."

"We've got a whole ocean of salt. Slice the meat into strips. Then string it up around the boat. As it dries, we take the salt that has crystallized on the canopy and rub it into the meat to preserve it."

"I hated liver when I was a kid," said Giordino, somewhat green around the gills at the thought. "I don't think I'm hungry enough to eat it raw."

"Force yourself," said Pitt. "The idea is to keep physically fit while we can. We've proven we can supply our stomachs. Our real problem now is lack of water."

Nightfall brought a strange quiet. A half-moon rose and hung over the sea, leaving a silvery path toward the northern horizon. They heard a bird squawking in the star-streaked sky, but couldn't see it. The cold temperatures common to the southern latitudes came with the disappearance of the sun and eased their thirst a little, and their minds turned to other things. The swells beat rhythmically against the boat and lulled Maeve into thoughts of a happier time with her children.

After resting most of the afternoon, Pitt was wide awake and felt revitalized enough to work out their drift and forecast the weather by observing the shape of the clouds, the height and run of the waves and the color of the sunset. After dusk he studied the stars and attempted to calculate the boat's approximate position on the sea. Using his old compass while locked in the storage compartment during the voyage from Wellington, he noted that the yacht had maintained a southwest heading of two-four-zero degrees for twenty minutes short of thirty hours. He recalled John Merchant saying the yacht could cruise at 120 kilometers an hour. Multiplying the speed and time gave him a rough distance traveled of

3,600 kilometers from the time they left Wellington until they were set adrift. This he estimated would put them somewhere in the middle of the south Tasman Sea, between the lower shores of Tasmania and New Zealand.

The next puzzle to solve was how far were they driven by the storm? This was next to impossible to estimate with even a tiny degree of accuracy. All Pitt knew for certain was that the storm blew out of the northwest. In forty-eight hours it could have carried them a considerable distance to the southeast, far from any sight of land. He knew from experience on other projects that the currents and the prevailing winds in this part of the Indian Ocean moved slightly south of east. If they were drifting somewhere between the fortieth and fiftieth parallels, their drift would carry them into the desolate vastness of the South Pacific, where no ship traveled. The next landfall would be the southern tip of South America, nearly thirteen thousand kilometers away.

Pitt stared up at the Southern Cross, a constellation that was not visible above thirty degrees north latitude, the latitude running across North Africa and the tip of Florida. Described since antiquity, its five bright stars had steered mariners and fliers across the immense reaches of the Pacific since the early voyages of the Polynesians. Millions of square miles of loneliness, dotted only by the islands, which were the tips of great mountains that rose unseen from the ocean floor.

However he figured it, no matter how strong their desire to survive, and despite any good luck they might receive, the odds were overwhelming against their ever setting foot on land again.

32

IT WAS SUNDAY AND HIRAM YAEGER WORKED ALONE ON THE tenth floor of the deserted NUMA building. After nine straight hours of staring steadily at his computer monitor, Yaeger leaned back in his chair and rested his tired eyes. He had finally put the finishing touches on a complex program he had created using image-synthesis algorithms to show the three-dimensional propagation of sound waves through the sea. With the unique technology of computer graphics, he had entered a world few had traveled before. The computer-generated drama of high-intensity sound traveling through water had taken Yaeger and his entire staff a week to calculate. Using special-purpose hardware and a large database of sound-speed variations throughout the Pacific, they had perfected a photorealistic model that traced the sound rays to where convergence zones would occur throughout the Pacific Ocean.

The underwater images were displayed in extremely rapid sequence to create the illusion of motion in and around actual three-dimensional sound-speed contour maps that had been accumulated over a thirty-year study period from oceanographic data. It was computer imaging taken to its highest art form.

He kept an eye on a series of lights beginning with yellow and advancing through the oranges before ending in deep red. As they blinked on in sequence, they told him how close he was coming to the point where the sound rays would converge. A separate digital readout gave him the latitude and longitude. The pièce de résistance of his imagery was the dynamic convergence-zone display. He could even program the image to raise his viewpoint above the surface of the water and show any ships whose known courses were computed to bisect that particular sector of the ocean at a predictable time.

The red light farthest to his right flashed, and he punched in the program to bring the image out of the water, revealing a surface view of the convergence point. He expected to see empty horizons of water, but the image on the viewing screen was hardly what he'd imagined. A mountainous landmass with vegetation filled the screen. He ran through the entire sequence again, beginning from the four points around the ocean that represented Dorsett Consolidated's island mines. Ten, twenty, thirty times he reran the entire scenario, tracing the sound rays to their ultimate meeting place.

Finally satisfied there was no mistake, Yaeger sagged wearily in his chair and shook his head.

When the compact Motorola Iridium wireless receiver in his pocket beeped, Sandecker paused, washed down a bite of filet mignon and answered the call. "This is Sandecker."

"Hiram Yaeger, Admiral. Sorry to bother you."

"No need for apologies, Hiram. I know you wouldn't contact me outside the office if it wasn't urgent."

"Is it convenient for you to come to the data center?"

"Too important to tell me over the phone?"

"Yes, sir. Wireless communication has unwanted ears.

Without sounding overdramatic, it is critical that I brief you in private."

"I'm dining with Rudi Gunn. He and I will be there in half an hour." Sandecker slipped the phone back into the pocket of his coat and resumed eating.

"Bad news?" asked Gunn.

"If I read between the lines correctly, Hiram has gathered new data on the acoustic plague. He wants to brief us at the data center."

"I hope the news is good."

"Not from the tone of his voice," Sandecker said soberly. "I suspect he discovered something none of us wants to know."

Yaeger was slouched in his chair, feet stretched out, contemplating the image on an oversized video display computer terminal when Sandecker and Gunn walked into his private office. He turned and greeted them without rising from his chair.

"What do you have for us?" Sandecker asked, not wasting words.

Yaeger straightened and nodded at the video screen. "I've arrived at a method for estimating convergence positions for the acoustic energy emanating from Dorsett's mining operations."

"Good work, Hiram," said Gunn, pulling up a chair and staring at the screen. "Have you determined where the next convergence will be?"

The image on the viewing screen displayed a chart of the Pacific Ocean, with four green lines, beginning at the locations of the Dorsett mines and intersecting at Seymour Island in the Antarctic.

"If conditions are stable for the next three days, the latest death spot should be about here."

The lines, this time in yellow, met nine hundred kilometers south of Easter Island.

"Not much danger of it striking a passing ship in that part of the ocean," mused Sandecker. "Just to be on the safe side, I'll issue a warning for all ships to detour around the area."

Gunn moved in closer to the screen. "What is your degree of error?"

"Plus or minus twelve kilometers," answered Yaeger.

"And the circumference where death occurs?"

"We're looking at a diameter anywhere from forty to ninety kilometers, depending on the energy of the sound rays after traveling great distances."

"The numbers of sea creatures caught in such a large area must be enormous."

"How far in advance can you predict a convergence-zone intersection?" Sandecker queried.

"Ocean conditions are tricky to predict as it is," replied Yaeger. "I can't guarantee a reasonably accurate projection beyond thirty days into the future. After that, it becomes a crapshoot."

"Have you calculated any other convergence sites beyond the next one?"

"Seventeen days from now." Yaeger looked at the admiral, a polar-cold expression on his face. "I was saving the worst till last." His fingers played over the keyboard. "Gentlemen, I give you February twenty-second and a catastrophe of staggering magnitude."

They were not prepared for what flashed on the screen. What Sandecker and Gunn saw on the video screen was an unthinkable event they had no control over, an encircling web of disaster that they could see no way to stop. They stared in sick fascination at the four purple lines that met and crossed on the screen.

"There can be no mistake?" asked Gunn.

"I've run my calculations over thirty times," said Yaeger wearily, "trying to find a flaw, an error, a variable that will prove me wrong. No matter how I shake and bake it, the result always comes out the same."

"No," whispered Sandecker. "Not there, not of all places in the middle of a vast and empty ocean."

"Unless some unpredictable upheaval of nature alters the sea and atmosphere," said Yaeger quietly, "the convergence zones will intersect approximately fifteen kilometers off the city of Honolulu."

33

THIS PRESIDENT, UNLIKE HIS PREDECESSOR, MADE DECISIONS quickly and firmly without vacillating. Sandecker's request to see the President hadn't impressed White House Chief of Staff Wilbur Hutton. Even members of the President's own cabinet had difficulty in arranging a face-to-face meeting. Hutton pursued his job as Executive Office gatekeeper overzealously.

Now he greeted Sandecker warmly despite the fact that the admiral showed up unannounced. "Your request to see the President sounded urgent, but I'm afraid he has a full schedule. You needn't have made a special trip for nothing."

Sandecker smiled, then turned serious. "My mission is too delicate to explain over the phone, Will. There is no time to go through channels. The fewer people who know about the danger, the better."

Hutton motioned Sandecker to a chair as he walked over and closed the door to his office. "Forgive me for sounding cold and heartless, but I hear that story with frequent regularity."

"Here's one you haven't heard. Sixteen days from now every man, woman and child in the city of Honolulu and on most of the island of Oahu will be dead."

Sandecker felt Hutton's eyes delving into the back of his head. "Oh, come now, Jim. What is this all about?"

"My scientists and data analysts at NUMA have cracked the mystery behind the menace that's killing people and devastating the sea life in the Pacific Ocean." Sandecker opened his briefcase and laid a folder on Hutton's desk. "Here is a report on our findings. We call it the acoustic plague because the deaths are caused by high-intensity sound rays that are concentrated by refraction. This extraordinary energy then propagates through the sea until it converges and surfaces, killing anyone and anything within a radius up to ninety kilometers."

Hutton said nothing for a few moments. "Wait right here," he commanded. He stepped through a doorway that led to the Oval Office and disappeared for a solid ten minutes. When he reappeared, Hutton motioned Sandecker inside. "This way, Jim. The President will see you."

Sandecker looked at Hutton. "Thank you, Will. I owe you one."

As the admiral entered the Oval Office, the President graciously came from around President Roosevelt's old desk and shook his hand. "Admiral Sandecker, this is a pleasure."

"I'm grateful for your time, Mr. President."

"Will says this is an urgent matter concerning the cause of all those deaths on the *Polar Queen*."

"And many more."

"Tell the President what you told me," said Hutton, handing the report on the acoustic plague to the President to read while the admiral explained the threat.

Sandecker presented his case with every gun blazing. He was forceful and vibrant. He believed passionately in his people at NUMA, their judgments and conclusions. He paused for emphasis, then wound up by requesting military force to stop Arthur Dorsett's mining operations.

The President listened intently until Sandecker finished, then continued reading in silence for a few more minutes before looking up. "You must admit, Admiral, acoustic energy is not a threat the government is prepared to guard against. This is completely new to me. I'll need time for my advisers on the National Science Board to investigate NUMA's findings."

"The convergence will occur in sixteen days," said Sandecker darkly.

"I'll be back to you in four," the President assured him.

"That still leaves us plenty of time to carry out a plan of action," said Hutton.

The President reached out his hand. "Thank you for bringing this matter to my attention, Admiral," he said in official jargon. "I promise to give your report my fullest attention."

"Thank you, Mr. President," said Sandecker. "I couldn't ask for more."

As Hutton showed him out of the Oval Office, he said, "Don't worry, Jim. I'll personally shepherd your warning through the proper channels."

Sandecker fixed him with a blistering glare. "Just make damned sure the President doesn't let it fall through the cracks, or there won't be anyone left in Honolulu to vote for him."

34

FOUR DAYS WITHOUT WATER. THE SUN'S UNRELENTING HEAT and the constant humidity sucked the perspiration from their bodies. Pitt would not let them dwell on the empty vastness that could depress all physical energy and creative thought. The monotonous lapping of the waves against the boat nearly drove them mad until they became immune to it. Ingenuity was the key to survival. Pitt had studied many shipwreck accounts and knew that too many shipwrecked mariners expired from lethargy and hopelessness. He drove Maeve and Giordino, urging them to sleep only at night and keep as busy as possible during daylight hours.

The old tried-and-true method devised by castaways and early navigators of chewing the moisture out of the raw fish was a feature of meals, along with the shark meat dried into jerky by the sun. Their sushi bar was also enhanced by two fair-sized flying fish they found flopping in the bottom of the boat during the night. The oily flavor of fresh, raw fish did not win any gourmet awards with their taste buds, but it went a long way in diminishing the agony of hunger and thirst. Their empty stomachs were appeased after only a few bites.

The need to replenish their body fluids was also

lessened by dropping briefly over the side every few hours while the others kept a sharp eye out for sharks. The cooling sensation generated by lying in wet clothes under the shade of the boat cover helped fight the misery of dehydration as well as the torment of sunburn. It also helped to dissolve the coating of salt that rapidly accumulated on their bodies.

The elements made Pitt's job of navigating fairly simple. The westerly winds out of the Roaring Forties were carrying them east. The current cooperated and flowed in the same direction. For determining his approximate position, a rough estimate at best, he relied on the sun and stars while using a cross-staff he'd fashioned of two slivers of wood cut from the paddle.

The cross-shaft was a method of determining latitude devised by ancient mariners. With one end of the shaft held to the eye, a crosspiece was calibrated by sliding it back and forth until one end fit exactly between either the sun or star and the horizon. The angle of latitude was then read on notches carved on the staff. Once the angle was established, the mariner was able by crude reckoning to establish a rough latitude without published tables for reference. To determine his longitude—in Pitt's case, how far east they were being driven—was another matter.

The night sky blazed with stars that became glittering points on a celestial compass that revolved from east to west. After a few nights of fixing their positions, Pitt was able to record a rudimentary log by inscribing his calculations on one end of the nylon boat cover with a small pencil Maeve had fortuitously discovered stuffed under a buoyancy tube. His primary obstacle was that he was not as familiar with the stars and constellations this far south as he was with the ones found north of the equator, and he had to grope his way.

"Here we are drifting rudderless like jetsam and

flotsam over the great sea of life," Giordino muttered through salt-caked lips. "Now all we have to do is figure out a way to steer this thing."

"Say no more," said Pitt, using the screwdriver to remove the hinges on a fiberglass seat that covered a storage compartment. In less than a minute, he held up the rectangular lid, which was about the same size and shape as a cupboard door.

"How do you plan to attach it?" asked Maeve.

"By using the hinges on the remaining seats and attaching them to the lid, I can screw it to the transom that held the outboard motor so that it can swing back and forth. Then by attaching two ropes to the upper end, we can operate it the same as any rudder on a ship or airplane."

"So now that we've got a particle of control, great navigator, what's our heading?"

"That's up to the lady," said Pitt. "She's more familiar with these waters than we are."

"If we head straight north," Maeve answered, "we might make Tasmania."

"Do you know if there are landfalls on that course?" Giordino asked Maeve.

"Not many," she answered flatly. "The islands that lie south of New Zealand are few and far apart. We could easily pass between them without sighting one, especially at night."

"They may be our only hope." Pitt held the compass in his hand and studied the needle. "Do you recall their approximate whereabouts?"

"Stewart Island just below the South Island. Then come the Snares, the Auckland Islands, and nine hundred kilometers farther south are the Macquaries."

"Miss any one of them and it's open sea all the way to South America," Giordino said discouragingly.

Pitt shielded his eyes and scanned the empty sky. "If

the cold nights don't get us, without rain we'll dehydrate long before we step onto a sandy beach."

Maeve wiped the wet strands of blond hair out of her eyes. "Thankfully, our boat hasn't capsized and none of us was thrown out."

"How's the rudder?" Pitt asked Giordino.

"Why are you asking?"

"I almost don't want to tell you," Pitt said tautly.

Maeve stared around the seemingly uninjured boat. "I don't see any obvious damage that can't be repaired."

"Nor I," Giordino agreed after examining the integrity of the buoyancy tubes.

"You didn't look down."

In the bright sunlight they could see the grim tension that was on Pitt's face. They stared in the direction he gestured and suddenly realized that any hope of survival had rapidly vanished.

There, running the entire length of the bottom hull, was a crack in the fiberglass that was already beginning to seep water.

35

"WHAT IS THE RECORD FOR SOMEONE ADRIFT AT SEA?" ASKED Sandecker as he adjusted a sweatband around his head. He was jogging through Potomac Park; Rudi Gunn was riding a bicycle alongside him.

"Steve Callahan, a yachtsman, survived 76 days after his sloop sank off the Canary Islands," answered Gunn, "the longest for one man in an inflatable raft. The Guinness World Record holder for survival at sea is held by Poon Lim, a Chinese steward who was set adrift on a raft after his ship was torpedoed in the South Atlantic during World War Two. He survived 133 days before being picked up by Brazilian fishermen."

"Was either adrift during a force ten blow?"

Gunn shook his head. "Neither Callahan nor Poon Lim was hit with a storm near the intensity of the typhoon that swept over Dirk, Al and Miss Fletcher."

"Going on two weeks since Dorsett abandoned them," said Sandecker between breaths. "If they outlasted the storm, they must be suffering badly from thirst and exposure to the elements."

"Pitt is a man of infinite resourcefulness," said Gunn indisputably. "Together with Giordino, I wouldn't be surprised if they washed up on a beach in Tahiti and are relaxing in a grass shack."

Both men turned at the honk of a horn from a car with NUMA markings. The driver pulled to a stop in the street opposite the jogging path. He leaned out the passenger's window and shouted. "I have a call from the White House for you, Admiral."

As the admiral stepped over to the car, the driver handed him a portable phone. "Wilbur Hutton on a safe line, sir."

"Will?"

"Hello, Jim, I'm afraid I have discouraging news for you."

Sandecker tensed. "Please explain."

"After due consideration, the President has postponed any action regarding your acoustic plague."

"But why?" Sandecker gasped. "Doesn't he realize the consequences of no action at all?"

"Experts on the National Science Board did not go along with your theory. They were swayed by the autopsy reports from Australian pathologists at their Center for Disease Control in Melbourne, which conclusively proved that the deaths on board the cruise ship were caused by a rare form of bacterium similar to the one causing Legionnaires' disease."

"That's impossible!" Sandecker snapped.

"Fortunately or unfortunately, depending on how you look at it, you're in a minority in that belief."

Sandecker muttered darkly, "I know you did your best, Will, and I'm grateful."

"Please contact me if you come upon any further information, Jim. My line is always open to you."

"Thank you."

"Good-bye."

Sandecker handed the phone back to the driver and turned to Gunn. "We've been sandbagged."

Gunn looked shocked. "The President is ignoring the situation?"

Sandecker nodded in defeat. "Dorsett bought off the pathologists. They turned in a phony report claiming the cause of death of the cruise ship passengers was contamination from the heating system."

"We can't give up," Gunn said, furious at the setback. "We must find another means of stopping Dorsett's madness in time."

"When in doubt," Sandecker said, the fire returning to his eyes, "bank on somebody who is smarter than you are." He retrieved the phone and punched in a number. "There is one man who might have the key."

Asking Dr. Sanford Adgate Ames to come to Washington for a high-level conference was no different from praying to conjure up a wind to melt the polar ice cap. Neither was likely to respond. Ames hated New York and Washington with equal passion and absolutely refused to visit either place. Offers of testimonial dinners and awards wouldn't budge him from his hideaway on Camelback Mountain in Arizona.

Sandecker needed Ames, needed him urgently. Biting the bullet, he requested a meeting with the soundmeister, as Ames was called among his fellow scientists. Ames agreed, but with the strict provision Sandecker bring his golf clubs, as all discussion would take place on the links.

Now they stepped into a golf cart and started off after their balls with Ames at the wheel. "How can I help you, Admiral?" he asked.

"Are you aware of NUMA's efforts to track down and stop what we call an acoustic plague?" responded Sandecker.

"I've heard rumors."

"What do you think?"

"Pretty farfetched."

"The President's National Science Board agrees," Sandecker growled.

"So now I know why you've come. I am your final court of appeals. You want me to come up with a practical solution to your problem."

"Our problem," Sandecker gently corrected him.

"Yes," Ames said heavily, "I can see that now. I worked out a blueprint of sorts before you left the ground in Washington. It's far from perfect, mind you. The chance of success is less than fifty-fifty, but it's the best I can devise without months spent in serious research."

Sandecker looked at Ames, masking his excitement, his eyes alight with a hope that wasn't there before. "You've actually conceived a plan for terminating Dorsett's mining operations?" he asked expectantly.

Ames shook his head. "Any kind of armed force is out of my territory. I'm talking about a method for neutralizing the acoustic convergence."

"How is that possible?"

"Simply put, sound-wave energy can be reflected," said Ames.

"The simplest answer is preferred over the complex."

"There you have it. My advice, for what it's worth, is for NUMA to build a reflector similar to a satellite dish, lower it into the sea at the point of convergence and beam the acoustic waves away from Honolulu."

Sandecker kept his face from showing any emotion, but his heart pounded against his ribs. The key to the enigma was ridiculously uncomplicated. True, the execution of a redirection project would not be easy, but it *was* feasible.

"If NUMA can build and deploy a reflector dish in time," he asked Ames, "where should the acoustic waves be redirected?"

A wily smile crossed Ames' face. "The obvious choice would be to some uninhabited part of the ocean, say south to Antarctica. But since the convergence energy slowly diminishes the farther it travels, why not send it back to the source?"

"The Dorsett mine on Gladiator Island," Sandecker said, tempering the awe in his voice.

Ames nodded. "As good a choice as any. The intensity of the energy would not have the strength to kill humans after making a round trip. But it should give them one huge headache. You know," he added as he stepped onto the ninth green, "I've developed some of my most creative concepts while relaxing on a golf course."

36

THIS WAS THE END OF THE LINE, PITT THOUGHT BITTERLY. This was as far as any human was expected to go. Their end would come in the water as food for the fish. The little boat that had carried them so far through so much chaos was literally coming apart at the seams. The crack along the bottom of the hull lengthened fractionally with every wave that carried the boat over its crest.

For the moment the sea was fairly calm. From crest to trough, the waves rolled just under a meter. But if the weather suddenly became unsettled and the sea kicked up, death would do more than merely stare them in the eyes.

Pitt hunched over the rudder in the stern, listening to the now familiar scrape and splash of the bailer. His intense green eyes, sore and swollen, scanned the horizon as the orb of the morning sun flushed from a golden-orange glow to flaming yellow. He searched, hoping against hope that a hint of land might rise above the clean straight horizon of the sea surrounding them. He searched in vain. No ship, aircraft or island revealed itself. Except for a few small clouds trailing to the southeast a good twenty kilometers away, Pitt's world was as empty as the plains of Mars, the boat little more than a pinprick on a vast seascape.

After catching enough fish to start a seafood restaurant, hunger was not an anxiety. Their water supply, if conserved, was good for at least another six or seven days. It was the fatigue and lack of sleep caused by the constant bailing to keep the boat afloat that was taking a toll.

At first they labored in four-hour shifts, because Maeve demanded she carry her share of the exertion. As the seam split farther and farther apart, the water no longer seeped, but rather spurted like a long fountain. Their peril sharpened Pitt's mind. In a final desperate attempt, he lowered the sail, laid it flat in the water, then slipped it under the hull and tied the lines to the buoyancy tubes. The nylon sheet, pressed against the crack by the pressure of the water, slowed the advance of the leakage by a good fifty percent, but at best it was only a stopgap measure that bought them a few extra hours of life. Unless the sea became perfectly calm, the physical breakdown of the crew and the splitting apart of the boat, Pitt figured, would occur shortly after darkness fell. He glanced at his watch and saw that sunset was only four and a half hours away.

Pitt bailed into the afternoon, mechanically, losing all sense of time, barely noting the passage of the brutal sun, never wilting under its punishing rays. He bailed like a robot, not feeling the pain in his back and arms, his senses completely numbed.

Maeve had roused herself out of a state of lethargy. She sat up and peered dully at the horizon behind Pitt's back. "Don't you think palm trees are pretty," she murmured softly.

"Yes, very pretty," Pitt agreed, giving her a tight smile, believing her to be hallucinating. "You shouldn't stand

under them. People have been killed by falling coco-
nuts."

"Don't you think you should steer more to starboard?" she said listlessly.

"Starboard?"

She stared as if in a trance. "Yes. You don't want to
miss the island by sailing past it."

Pitt's eyes narrowed. Slowly, he turned and peered
over his shoulder. After nearly sixteen days of taking
position sightings from the sun and suffering from the
glare on the water, his eyes were so strained that he could
only focus in the distance for a few seconds before
closing them. He cast his eyes briefly across the bow but
saw only blue-green swells.

He turned back. "We can no longer control the boat,"
he explained softly. "I've taken down the sail and placed
it under the hull to slow the leakage."

"Oh, please," she pleaded. "It's so close. Can't we land
and walk around on dry ground if only for a few
minutes?"

She said it so calmly, so rationally in her Australian
twang, that Pitt felt his spine tingle. Could she actually
be seeing something? Reason dictated that Maeve's
mind was playing tricks on her. But a still-glowing spark
of hope mixed with desperation made him rise to his
knees while clutching a buoyancy tube for stability. At
that moment the boat rose on the crest of the next swell
and he had a brief view of the horizon.

The trees, clearly visible, were clustered on the small
areas of sand that filled the cracks of the rocks. Pitt now
realized the island was much closer than it had seemed
at first view. It lay no more than eight or nine kilometers
away.

"The little lady wins a prize," Pitt announced. "We're
within sight of land."

Both Maeve and Giordino struggled to their feet, clung to Pitt and gazed at their distant hope of refuge. "She's no mirage," said Giordino with a big grin.

Pitt did not allow himself to be carried away by elation. "We're not there yet. We'll have to replace the sail and bail like crazy if we're to land on its shore."

Giordino judged the distance separating them from the island, and his expression sobered considerably. "Our home-away-from-home won't make it," he predicted. "She'll split in two before we're halfway."

37

THE SAIL WAS RAISED, AND ANY LENGTH OF LINE THAT COULD be spared was used to tie the splitting hull together. With Maeve at the rudder, Giordino bailing like a crazy man and Pitt sloshing the water in sheets over the side with his bare hands, the ruptured boat set its bow directly toward the small, low-lying island a few kilometers distant. At long last they had visible proof that Pitt's navigation had paid off.

The mind-drugging fatigue, the overwhelming exhaustion had dropped from Pitt and Giordino like a heavy rock. They entered a zone where they were no longer themselves, a psychological zone where another world of stress and suffering had no meaning.

As Pitt and Giordino fought the incoming water, they became conscious of a sullen thunder that seemed to grow louder. A quick pause, and their eyes locked as they realized that it was the unique sound of surf pounding against rock cliffs. The waves had turned murderous and were drawing the boat ever closer into a fatal embrace. The castaways' happy anticipation of setting foot on dry land again suddenly turned to a fear of being crushed in a thrashing sea.

Instead of a safe haven, what Pitt saw was a forbidding

pair of rocks jutting abruptly from the sea, surrounded and struck by the onslaught of massive breakers. These were not tropical atolls with inviting white sand beaches and waving friendly natives. There was no sign of habitation on either island, no smoke, no structures of any kind to be seen. Barren, windswept and desolate they seemed a mysterious outpost of lava rock, their only vegetation a few clusters of low nonflowering plants and strange-looking trees whose growth appeared stunted.

He could not believe that he was in a war with unyielding stone and water for the third time since he had found and rescued Maeve on the Antarctic Peninsula. For a brief instant his thoughts raced back to the near escape of the *Polar Queen* and the flight from Kunghit Island with Mason Broadmoor. Both times he had mechanical power to carry him clear. Now he was fighting a watery burial on a little waterlogged boat with a sail not much bigger than a blanket.

Pitt studied the cadence of the waves as friction with the bottom slope caused them to rise and slow down, measuring the break of the crests ahead and astern and timing their speed. The wave period shortened to roughly nine seconds and was moving at approximately twenty-two knots.

He turned to Maeve. "Try and keep us in the darkest blue of the water."

"I'll do my best," she replied bravely.

The roar of the breakers came with a steady, rolling beat, and soon they saw as well as heard the hiss of the spray as it burst into the sky. Without direct and manual control, they were helpless; the whims of the restless sea took them wherever it desired. The surge was building ever higher now. On closer inspection the slot between the rock outcroppings seemed like an insidious trap, a silent siren beckoning them to a false refuge. Too late to sail out to sea and around the islands. They were committed and there could be no turning back.

The seas became more nervous the nearer they approached. So did Pitt when he calculated the crest of the waves to be almost ten meters in height when they curled and broke. Maeve struggled with the rudder to control their course, but the boat did not answer her helm and quickly became unmanageable. They were totally caught in the surge.

"Hold on!" Pitt shouted.

They were under a literal wall of hydraulic pressure. It felt as though the boat were being transported underwater by an out-of-control elevator. The total submersion seemed to take minutes, but it could not have lasted more than a few seconds.

Three or more seas rolled over them with diminishing force, and then they were through the breakers and into calmer water. Pitt snapped his head around, spitting out the saltwater he had taken in by not closing his mouth tightly, his wavy black hair whipping off the water droplets in glistening streaks.

"We're through the worst!" he yelled happily. "We've gained the channel!"

Amazingly, the boat was still afloat and in one piece. Giordino had never stopped bailing, even when he was sitting in water up to his chest. He sputtered and wiped the salt from his eyes and continued throwing water over the side like there was no tomorrow.

The hull was now completely cracked in two and barely held together by the hurriedly attached nylon lines and the clamps connecting the buoyancy floats. Giordino finally conceded defeat as he found himself sitting up to his armpits in seawater. He looked around dazedly, his breath labored, his mind deadened by exhaustion. "What now?" he mumbled.

Before Pitt answered, he dipped his face in the water and peered at the bottom of the channel. The visibility was exceptional, though blurred without a face mask, and he could see sand and rock only ten meters below. Schools of vividly colored fish swam about leisurely, taking no notice of the strange creature floating overhead.

"No sharks in here," he said thankfully.

"They seldom swim through breakers," said Maeve through a spasm of coughing. She was sitting with her arms stretched out and draped over the stern buoyancy tube.

The current through the channel was carrying them closer to the northern island. Solid ground was only thirty meters away. Pitt looked at Maeve and broke into a crooked grin. "I'll bet you're a strong swimmer."

"You're talking to an Aussie," she said coolly, and then added, "Remind me sometime to show you my butterfly and backstroke medals."

"Al is played out. Can you tow him to shore?"

"The least I can do for the man who kept us out of the mouths of sharks."

Pitt gestured toward the nearest shoreline. There was no sandy beach, but the rock flattened out into a shelf as it met the water. "The way looks clear to climb on firm ground."

"And you?" She pulled back her hair with both hands, wringing away the water. "Do you want me to come back for you?"

He shook his head. "I saved myself for a more important effort."

"What effort?"

"Club Med hasn't built a resort here yet. We still need all the food supplies we have in hand. I'm going to tow what's left of the boat and the goodies therein."

Pitt helped roll Giordino over the half-sunken buoyancy tubes into the water, where he was grasped under the chin lifeguard-style by Maeve. She stroked strongly to shore, pulling Giordino behind her.

Splicing and knotting the rigging back into one long nylon line, Pitt attached it to the half-sunken boat and tied the other end around his waist. Then he swam toward shore. The current helped by nudging the boat around in an arc. After traveling twenty meters, he finally felt firm ground beneath his feet. Now he could use the added leverage to pull the boat onto the rock shelf. He was wearily grateful when Maeve and Giordino both waded in and helped him tow it ashore.

Pitt sat down and rested, too tired to dance for joy at being off the water. He slowly rose to his knees before standing up. For a few moments he had to hold onto the ground to steady himself. The motion of nearly two weeks bobbing about in a small boat had affected his balance. The world spun, and the entire island rocked as if it floated on the sea. Maeve immediately sat back down, while Giordino planted both feet firmly on the rock and clutched a nearby tree with thick foliage. After a few minutes, Pitt rose shakily to his feet and made a few faltering steps. Not having walked since the abduction in Wellington, he found his legs and ankles were unfeeling and stiff. Only after he'd staggered about twenty meters and back did his joints begin to loosen and operate as they should.

They hauled the boat farther onto the rocks and rested for a few hours before dining on their dried fish, washed down by rainwater they found standing in several concave impressions in the rock. Their energies restored, they began to survey the island.

Giordino paced off the width from shore to shore and announced that their refuge was only 130 meters across.

The highest point was a flattened plateau no more than 10 meters in height. Surrounded by natural seawalls that defied the swells, the island had the appearance of a fortress under constant attack.

A short distance away, they discovered the shattered remains of a boat that lay high and dry in a small inlet that was carved out of the rock by the sea, evidently driven there by large storm waves. She was a fair-sized sailboat, rolled over on her port side, half her hull and keel torn away from an obvious collision with rocks. She must have been a pretty boat at one time, Pitt imagined. Her upperworks had been painted light blue with orange undersides. Though the masts were gone, the deckhouse looked undamaged and intact. The three of them approached and studied it before peering inside.

"A grand, seaworthy little boat," observed Pitt, "about twelve meters, well built, with a teak hull."

"A Bermuda ketch," said Maeve, running her hands over the worn and sun-bleached teak planking. "A fellow student at the marine lab on Saint Croix had one. We used to island-hop with it. She sailed remarkably well."

Giordino stared at the paint and caulking on the hull appraisingly. "Been here twenty, maybe thirty years, judging by her condition."

"I hope whoever became marooned on this desolate spot was rescued," Maeve said quietly.

Hoisted by Giordino, Pitt climbed aboard the canted hull and crawled through the hatch into the deckhouse. "She's been stripped clean," he called out from the inside. "Everything that wasn't screwed down has been removed. Check the transom and see if she has a name."

Maeve walked around to the stern and stared up at the faded letters that were barely readable. *"Dancing Dorothy.* Her name was *Dancing Dorothy."*

Pitt climbed down from the yacht's cockpit. "A search is in order to locate the supplies taken from the boat.

The crew may have left behind articles we can put to use."

Resuming their exploration, it took little more than half an hour to skirt the entire coast of the tear-shaped little island. Then they worked their way inland. They separated and strung out in a loose line to cover more territory. Maeve was the first to spot an axe half buried in the rotting trunk of a grotesquely shaped tree.

Giordino pulled it loose and held it up. "This should come in handy."

They continued to search around carefully. A few minutes later Pitt came to a jumbled stack of logs in the form of a hut, with a boat's mast standing beside it. The structure was about three meters wide by four meters long. The roof of logs intermixed with branches was undamaged by the elements. The unknown builder had raised a sound dwelling.

Outside the hut was a wealth of abandoned supplies and equipment. A battery and the corroded remains of a radio-telephone, a direction-finding set, a wireless receiver for obtaining weather bulletins and time signals for rating a chronometer, a pile of rusty food cans that had been opened and emptied, an intact teakwood dinghy equipped with a small outboard motor and miscellaneous nautical hardware, dishes and eating utensils, a few pots and pans, a propane stove and other various and sundry items from the wrecked boat. Strewn around the stove, still discernible, were bones of fish.

"The former tenants left a messy campground," said Giordino, kneeling to examine a small gas-driven generator for charging the boat's batteries, which had operated the electronic navigational instruments and radio equipment scattered about the campsite.

"Maybe they're still in the hut," murmured Maeve.

Pitt smiled at her. "There's only one way to find out." He bent under the low doorway and stepped inside.

After being exposed to bright light for days on end, Pitt's eyes took a minute or two to become accustomed to the interior darkness of the hut. Except for the shaft of sun through the doorway, the only illumination came from the light seeping through the cracks between the logs. The air was heavy and damp with the musty smell of dirt and rotted logs.

There were no ghosts or phantoms lurking in the shadows, but Pitt did find himself staring into the empty eye sockets of a skull attached to a skeleton.

It lay on its back in a berth salvaged from the sailboat. A tattered pair of shorts covered the pelvis, and the bony feet still wore a pair of rubber-soled deck shoes. The skeletal hands were crossed above the rib cage and clutched a leather logbook.

Pitt leaned over the skeleton, gently removed the logbook and left the hut.

"What did you find?" asked Maeve with burning curiosity.

"Let me guess," said Giordino. "A humongous chest full of pirate treasure."

Pitt shook his head. "Not this trip. What I found was the man who sailed the *Dancing Dorothy* onto the rocks. He never made it off the island."

Giordino stepped to the doorway and peered inside the hut at the remains. "I wonder how he came to be so far off the beaten track."

Pitt held up the logbook and opened it. "The answers should be in here."

Maeve stared at the pages. "Can you make out the writing after all this time?"

"Yes. The log is well preserved, and the hand wrote boldly." Pitt sat down on a rock and scanned several pages before looking up. "His name was Rodney York, and he was one of twelve yachtsmen entered in a solo nonstop race around the world, beginning in Portsmouth, England, and sponsored by a London newspaper. First prize was twenty thousand pounds. York departed Portsmouth on April the twenty-fourth, 1962."

"Poor old guy has been lost for thirty-eight years," said Giordino solemnly.

"On his ninety-seventh day at sea, he was catching a few hours' sleep when the *Dancing Dorothy* struck"—Pitt paused to glance up at Maeve and smile—"what he calls the 'Miseries.'"

"York must not have studied Australian folklore," said Giordino.

"He quite obviously made up the name," Maeve said righteously.

"According to his account," Pitt continued, "York made good time during his passage of the southern Indian Ocean after rounding the Cape of Good Hope. He then took advantage of the Roaring Forties to carry him on a direct course across the Pacific for South America and the Strait of Magellan. He figured he was leading the race when his generator gave out and he lost all contact with the outside world."

"What does he write after being marooned?" demanded Maeve.

"He wasn't exactly a Robinson Crusoe. He lost most of his food supplies when the yacht struck the rocks and capsized. When the boat was later washed up on shore after the storm, he recovered some canned goods, but they were soon gone. He tried to fish, but caught barely enough to stay alive, even with whatever rock crabs he could find and five or six birds he managed to snare. His final entry reads: 'Can no longer stand or move about. Too weak to do anything but lie here and die. How I wish I could see another sunrise over Falmouth Bay in my native Cornwall. But it is not to be. To whoever finds this log and the letters I've written separately to my wife and three daughters, please see they get them.'"

"Hard to believe he lay here for decades without a curious crew from a passing ship or a scientific party coming ashore to set up some kind of weather data gathering instruments," Giordino said.

Tears rolled down Maeve's cheeks as she wept unashamedly. "His poor wife and children must have wondered all these years how he died."

"York's last land bearing was the beacon on the South East Cape of Tasmania." Pitt stepped back into the hut and reappeared a minute later with an Admiralty chart showing the South Tasman Sea. He laid it flat on the ground and studied it for a few moments before he looked up. "I see why York called these rocks the Miseries," said Pitt. "That's how they're labeled on the Admiralty chart."

"How far off were your reckonings?" asked Giordino.

Pitt produced a pair of dividers he'd taken from the desk inside and measured off the approximate position he had calculated with his cross-staff. "I put us roughly 120 kilometers too far to the southwest."

"Not half bad, considering you didn't have an exact fix on the spot where Dorsett threw us off his yacht."

"Yes," Pitt admitted modestly, "I can live with that."

"Where exactly are we?" asked Maeve, now down on her hands and knees, peering at the chart.

Pitt tapped his finger on a tiny black dot in the middle of a sea of blue. "There, that little speck approximately 965 kilometers southwest of Invercargill, New Zealand."

"It seems so near when you look at it on a map," said Maeve wistfully.

Giordino pulled off his wristwatch and rubbed the lens clean against his shirt. "Not near enough when you think that no one bothered to drop in on poor Rodney for almost forty years."

"Look on the bright side," said Pitt with an infectious grin. "Pretend you've pumped thirty-eight dollars in quarters into a slot machine in Las Vegas without a win. The law of averages is bound to catch up in the next two quarters."

"A bad analogy," said Giordino.

"How so?"

Giordino looked pensively inside the hut. "Because there is no way we can come up with two quarters."

"Nine days and counting," declared Sandecker, gazing at the unshaven men and weary women seated around the table in his hideaway conference room.

"Time is against us," said Dr. Sanford Adgate Ames. "It is physically impossible to construct a reflector unit and deploy it before the deadline."

The sound expert and his student staff in Arizona intermingled with Sandecker's NUMA people in Washington as if they were sitting at the same table in the same room. The reverse was also true. Sandecker's experts appeared to be sitting amid the student staff in Ames' work quarters. Through the technology of video holography, their voices and images were transmitted across the country by photonics, the transference of sound and light by fiber optics. By combining photonics with computer wizardry, time and space limitations disappeared.

Sandecker looked across the table at a tired Rudi Gunn. "Any ideas, Rudi?"

"I've run through every logical possibility," Gunn answered. "Dr. Ames is right—it is out of the question to consider fabricating a reflector in time. Our only prospect is to find an existing one and transport it to Hawaii."

"You'll have to break it down, ship it in pieces and then put it back together," said Hiram Yaeger, turning from a laptop computer that was linked to his data library on the tenth floor. "No known aircraft can carry something of such a large surface area through the air in one piece."

Sandecker drummed his fingers on the table thoughtfully. "Which puts us back in the starter's gate before the race."

A woman in her forties, fashionably dressed in a conservative blue suit, stared contemplatively at one of the admiral's paintings, the one illustrating the famous World War II aircraft carrier *Enterprise* during the battle for Midway. Her name was Molly Faraday, and she was a former analyst with the National Security Agency who had jumped over to NUMA at Sandecker's urging, to be his intelligence agency coordinator.

"I think I might have the solution to our problems," she said in a quiet voice.

The admiral nodded. "You have the floor, Molly."

"As of yesterday," she lectured, "the Navy's aircraft carrier *Roosevelt* was docked at Pearl Harbor, taking on supplies and making repairs to one of her flight-deck elevators before joining the Tenth Fleet off Indonesia."

Gunn looked at her curiously. "You know that for certain?"

Yaeger jumped right to the heart of the matter. "How large is the parabolic reflector?"

Molly buried her head in her hands a moment before looking up. "I seem to recall that it was eighty meters in diameter."

"More than the surface area we require," said Ames.

"Do you think the NSA will let us borrow it?" asked Sandecker.

"They'd probably pay *you* to carry it away."

There was a brief silence as everyone in the room turned to face Sandecker, including Ames, who was sitting at a desk thirty-two hundred kilometers to the west. Abstractedly, Sandecker toyed with an unlit cigar. What most did not know was that his mind wasn't on the possible destruction of Gladiator Island. His mind was saddened and angered at the same time over the abandonment of his best friends in a raging sea by Arthur Dorsett. In the end, hate won out over any humane consideration.

He stared at the image of Sanford Ames. "Compute your calculations, Doc, for aiming the reflector at Gladiator Island. If we don't stop Dorsett Consolidated, and stop them in the shortest time possible, no one else will."

38

TWO DAYS OFF THE SEA AND EVERYONE FELT AS IF RAISED from the dead. York's campsite was tidied up and every article and object inventoried. Maeve refused to go in the hut even after they buried Rodney York in a small ravine that was partially filled with sand. A tentlike shelter was built from the old Dacron sails found inside the hut, and they settled down to the day-to-day routine of existence.

To Giordino, the greatest prize was a toolbox. He immediately went to work on the radio and the generator but finally gave up in frustration after nearly six hours of futile labor.

"Too many parts broken or too badly corroded to repair. And without a generator to charge them, the radio-telephone, direction-finding set and wireless receiver are useless."

"Can replacements be fabricated with what we've got lying about?" asked Pitt.

Giordino shook his head. "General Electric's chief engineer couldn't fix that generator, and even if he could, the engine to turn it over is completely shot. There's a crack in the crankcase. York must not have seen it and run the engine after the oil leaked out, burning the bearings and freezing the pistons. It would take an automotive machine shop to put it back in running order."

Pitt's first project as resident handyman was to find three small blocks of wood that were straight grained. These he split from a side board on the berth that had served as Rodney York's final resting place. Next, he made a template of everyone's forehead just above the eyebrows from the stiff paper jackets of novels he found on York's bookshelf. He marked the template lines on the edge of the wood blocks and trimmed accordingly, cutting out an arched slot for the nose. Holding the blocks tightly between his knees he gouged and smoothed hollows on the inner curl of the wood. Then he removed the excess outer wood and cut two horizontal slits in the hollowed walls. With oil from a can sitting beside the outboard engine, he stained the thinly curled finished product before cutting two holes in the ends and attaching nylon cord.

"There you are, ladies and gentlemen," he said, passing them out. "Colonel Thadeus Pitt's spectacular sun goggles, from a secret design revealed on the lips of a dying Eskimo just before he rode off across the Arctic Ocean on the back of a polar bear."

"Can you pull any other tricks out of your hat besides the goggles?" asked Maeve whimsically.

Pitt lay back on the sand with his hands behind his head. "I'm glad you brought that up. After a strenuous afternoon of intense thought, I've arrived at the conclusion that we should move on to a more receptive climate."

Maeve gave him a look of utter skepticism. "Move on? We have two badly damaged boats that can't sail across a swimming pool. Just what do you suggest we use for our all-expenses-paid cruise to nowhere?"

"Elementary, my dear Fletcher," he said expansively. "We build a third boat."

"Build a boat?" demanded Maeve. "With what materials?"

"A flotation tube from our boat here, the upper works from York's boat there, throw in a few logs, and pretty soon you've got a vessel fit for an ocean voyage."

"This I have to see," said Maeve.

Their vessel to escape the island was built on a flat section of rock in a small valley protected from the breeze, thirty meters from the water. They laid out rail-like ways of beech logs to slide their weird creation into the relatively calm waters between the two islands. For the most part, construction went smoothly without major setbacks. The closer they got to completion, the more their fatigue fell away.

Maeve threw herself into weaving two sails from the leafy branches. The first few hours were spent experimenting, but by late afternoon she began to get the hang of it and could weave a square meter in thirty minutes. By the third day, she was down to twenty minutes. Her matting was so strong and tight, Pitt asked her to make a third sail, a triangular jib to set forward of the mainmast.

Together, Pitt and Giordino unbolted and lifted the ketch's upper deckhouse and mounted it over the forward part of the steering cockpit. This abbreviated section of the ketch was then lashed on top of the buoyancy tubes from their little boat, which now served as the center hull. When finished, the hybrid craft had the appearance of a sailboat perched on a hovercraft.

As they sat around the fire at dawn, warding off the early morning chill of the southern latitudes, Pitt pored over York's navigational and plotting charts.

"Think you can hit Gladiator Island on the nose?"

Maeve asked him over dinner on the second evening before the launch.

"If not the nose, then the chin," Pitt said cheerfully. "Which reminds me, I'll need a detailed map of the island."

"How detailed?"

"Every building, every path and road, and I'd like it all to scale."

"I'll draw you a map from memory as accurately as I can," Maeve promised.

The day before the launch was one of feverish activity. Final preparations included the manufacture of Pitt's mystery kite, which was folded and stowed in the deckhouse along with 150 meters of light nylon line from York's boat that had retained its integral strength. Then their meager supplies of foodstuffs were loaded on board along with the navigational instruments, charts and books. Cheers erupted over the barren rocks when the outboard motor coughed to life after four decades and nearly forty pulls on the starter rope by Pitt, who felt as if his arm was about to fall off.

"You did it!" Maeve shouted delightedly.

Pitt spread his hands in a modest gesture. "Child's play for somebody who restores antique and classic automobiles. The main problems were a clogged fuel line and a gummed-up carburetor."

"Nice going, pal," Giordino congratulated him. "A motor will come in handy during our approach to the island."

"We were lucky the fuel cans were airtight and none of the contents evaporated after all these years. As it is, the gas has almost turned to shellac, so we'll have to keep a sharp eye on the fuel filter. I'm not keen on flushing out the carburetor every thirty minutes."

"How many hours of fuel did York leave us?"

"Six hours, maybe seven."

Later, with Giordino's help, Pitt mounted the outboard motor to brackets on the stern section of the cockpit. For a final touch, the steering compass was installed just forward of the tiller. After the woven-mat sails were attached to the mast, gaffs and booms with spiral lacing, the sails were raised and lowered with only a minor bind or two. Then they all stood back and stared at their creation. Pitt doubted whether any boats that ever sailed the seven seas were as bizarre as this one.

"She's not exactly what you'd call sleek and elegant," mused Giordino.

"Nor will she ever be entered in the America's Cup Race," added Pitt.

"You men fail to see her inner beauty," said Maeve fancily. "She must have a name. It wouldn't be fitting if she wasn't christened. What if we call her the *Never Say Die?*"

"Fitting," said Pitt, "but not in keeping with mariners' superstitions of the sea. For good luck she should have a woman's name."

"How about the *Marvelous Maeve?*" offered Giordino.

"Oh, I don't know," said Pitt. "It's corny but cute. I'll vote for it."

Maeve laughed. "I'm flattered, but modesty dictates something more proper, say like *Dancing Dorothy II.*"

"Then it's two against one," Giordino said solemnly. *"Marvelous Maeve* she is."

"Now comes our fitness exercise," said Pitt. He passed out lines attached to the forward section of the middle hull. Everyone looped one end of a line around their waist, dug in their feet and leaned forward. Slowly, stubbornly, the boat began to slide over the tree trunks laid on the ground like railroad tracks. Still weakened from a lack of proper food and their ordeal, the three quickly used up their depleted strength dragging the boat toward a two-meter precipice rising from the water. Soon the boat teetered on the edge of the ends of two beech-log ways that angled down and under the low rolling waves.

Several minutes passed. The sun was a quarter of the way past the eastern horizon, and the sea was innocent of any sign of turbulence. Pitt slipped the rope loop from around his waist and threw it on the boat. "I guess there's no reason to put off the inevitable any longer." He climbed into the cockpit, swung the outboard motor down on its hinges and pulled at the starter rope. This time it popped to life on the second try.

Giordino held Maeve by her wrists and gently lowered her down onto the roof of the deckhouse. Then he jumped and landed on his feet, as agile as a gymnast, beside her.

"That concludes the entertainment part of the program," said Pitt, reversing the outboard. "We'll motor around to the leeward side of the island where the sea is calmer before we test the wind."

Giordino helped Maeve step past the deckhouse and into the cockpit. They sat down to rest a moment while Pitt steered the boat through the channel and into the swells sweeping around the north and south ends of the two deserted islands.

Pitt took a final look at the islands. Then he looked at the packet wrapped in a piece of Dacron sail that held Rodney York's logbook and letters. He vowed that if he somehow lived through the next several days and managed to rescue Maeve's sons, he would get York's final testament to his living relatives, trusting that they would mount an expedition to bring him home again to be buried beside Falmouth Bay in his beloved Cornwall.

PART IV

CATASTROPHE IN PARADISE

GLADIATOR ISLAND

39

THERE WAS NO MOON. THE WIND HAD VEERED AND SWEPT IN from the south, driving the *Marvelous Maeve* hard to the northwest. Pitt had never imagined that the ungainly looking craft could sail so well. She would never win a trophy, but he could have closed his eyes and envisioned himself on a first-class yacht, skimming over the sea without a care in the world.

The swells no longer had the same hostile look nor did the clouds look as threatening. The nightly chill also diminished as they traveled north into warmer waters. The sea had tested them with cruelty and harshness, and they had passed with flying colors. Now the weather was cooperating by remaining constant.

Maeve and Giordino no longer felt as though they were struggling to stay alive. Their few moments of warmth and pleasure, nearly drowned by adversity, were becoming more frequent. Pitt's unshakable optimism, his contagious laughter, his unrelenting grasp of hope, his strength of character sustained and helped them face the worst that nature could throw at them.

"At first light I'll mark our course and figure the distance separating us from Gladiator Island," Pitt told the others.

"I can't believe I'll actually see my boys again," Maeve murmured thankfully.

Pitt said nothing for a moment, thinking of the unknown that lay ahead of them. Then he said gently, "You'll see them, and you'll hold them in your arms. I promise you."

Shortly after midnight, Pitt took his final sighting of the stars and marked his chart under the light of a half-moon. If his calculations were in the ballpark, they should be sighting Gladiator Island within the next few hours. He instructed Maeve and Giordino to keep a lookout ahead while he allowed himself the luxury of an hour's sleep. It seemed to him that he had barely drifted off when Maeve gently shook him awake.

"Your navigation was right on the button," she said, excitement in her tone. "The island is in sight."

"A beautiful job of navigating, old buddy," Giordino congratulated him. "You beat your estimated time of arrival."

Pitt stared into the night but only saw the splash of stars and moon on the sea. He opened his mouth to say he couldn't see anything when a shaft of light swung across the western horizon, followed by a bright red glow. "Your island has a beacon?" he asked Maeve.

"A small lighthouse on the rim of the southern volcano."

"At least your family did something to aid marine navigation."

Maeve laughed. "Thoughts of lost sailors never entered my great-grandfather's mind when he built it. The purpose has always been to warn ships to steer clear of the island and not to come ashore."

"I make landfall in about three hours," said Pitt. "Can you guide us into the narrow channel with the roomy beach?" he asked Maeve.

"You might as well climb Mount Everest with an ice pick. And then there are the security guards. They patrol the bluffs every hour," Maeve said flatly.

"At night too?"

"Daddy leaves no door open for diamond smugglers," she said as if explaining to a schoolchild.

"How large is the patrol?"

"Two men, who make one complete circuit of the island during their shift. They're followed by another patrol on the hour."

"Is it possible for them to see the beach from the edge of the bluff?" Pitt grilled her.

"No. The cliff is too steep to see straight down." She looked at Pitt, her eyes in the moonlight wide and questioning. "Why all the interrogation about the backside of the island? The lagoon is the only way in."

Pitt gazed on the rocks that had had a long roll of fatalities, rocks where the shipwrecked men who survived wished they had drowned rather than suffer untold miseries as slaves in the Dorsett diamond mines. For a long time, as the cliffs of Gladiator Island loomed up out of the darkness, no one on the *Marvelous Maeve* moved or spoke. Pitt saw Maeve's back as she lay in the bow, acting as lookout for any offshore rocks. He glanced at Giordino and caught the white blur of his friend's face and the slow nod as he stood poised to start the outboard motor.

"How far to the inlet?" he called to Maeve softly.

"I think it's about a kilometer up the shore from the lighthouse," she answered without turning.

The boat had lost considerable way after swinging east to north along the shoreline, and Pitt was finding it difficult to maintain a steady course. He raised a hand as a signal to Giordino to start the outboard motor. Three heartbeats slowed and then suddenly increased as Giordino pulled on the starter rope, ten, twenty, thirty times without success.

Giordino paused, massaged his tiring arm. Then he took a firm grip on the pull handle and gave a mighty heave. The motor snorted and its exhaust puffed a few moments before settling down to a steady snarl. Giordino wiped the sweat from his face and grinned.

Now that Giordino steered the craft with the outboard, Pitt lowered the sails and removed his kite from the deckhouse. He deftly looped a coil of thin line on the deck of the boat. Then he tied a small grappling hook, found at York's campsite, to the line slightly below where it attached to the kite. Then he sat and waited, knowing in his heart of hearts that what he had in mind had only one chance of succeeding out of too many to count.

"Maeve, see anything yet?" asked Pitt.

"I can't be certain. I never had to find the inlet in the dark before," she replied testily.

Pitt studied the swells. They were growing steeper and closer together. "The bottom is coming up. Another thirty meters and we'll have to turn for open water."

"No, no," Maeve said in an excited voice. "I think I see a break in the cliffs. I'm sure of it. That's the inlet that leads to the largest beach."

"How far?" Pitt demanded.

"Sixty or seventy meters," she answered, rising to her knees and pointing toward the cliffs.

Then Pitt had it too. A vertical opening in the face of the palisades that ran dark in the shadows out of the moonlight. Pitt wetted his finger and tested the wind. It held steady out of the east. "Ten minutes," he begged under his breath. "All I need is ten minutes." He turned to Giordino. "Al, can you hold us in a steady position about twenty meters from the entrance?"

"It won't be easy in the surge."

"Do your best." He turned to Maeve. "Take the tiller

and aim the bow head-on into the swells. Combine your efforts with Al's on the outboard to keep the boat from swinging broadside."

Pitt unfolded the struts on his homemade kite. When extended, the Dacron surface measured nearly two and a half meters high. He held it up over the side of the boat, pleased to see it leap up out of his hands as the breeze struck its bowed surface. He payed out the line as the kite rose and dipped in the predawn sky.

Maeve suddenly saw the genius behind Pitt's mad plan. "The grappling hook," she blurted. "You're trying to snag it on the top of the bluffs and use the line to climb the cliffs."

"That's the idea," he replied as he focused his gaze on the obscure shape of the kite, just slightly visible under the half-light from the moon.

Adroitly jockeying the throttle of the outboard and the Forward/Reverse lever, Giordino performed a masterful job of keeping the boat in one spot. He neither spoke nor took his eyes off the sea to observe Pitt's actions.

Pitt had prayed for a steady wind, but he got more than he bargained for. The onshore breeze, meeting resistance from the rising palisades, curved and rushed up their steep face before sweeping over the summit. The big kite was nearly pulled from his grip. He used a sleeve of his battered leather jacket as a protective glove, holding it around the line to keep the friction from burning his hands. The immense drag was nearly pulling his arms out of their sockets. He clamped his teeth together and hung on.

He brushed off all thoughts of failure as he taxed his depth perception to the limit. In the black of night, even with the moon's help, he could not begin to accurately judge when the grappling hook had risen beyond the top of the bluffs. He felt the knot he'd tied to indicate when the line had payed out a hundred meters slip under the leather jacket. He roughly figured another twenty meters before loosening his grip on the line. Released from its resistance to the wind, the kite began to seesaw and fall.

Pitt felt as if a great pressure was released from his mind and body as he gave a series of tugs on the line and felt it go taut. The grappling hook had dug its points into the rock on the first attempt and was holding firm. "Take her in, Al. We've got our way to the top."

Giordino had been waiting for the word. Gladly, he eased the motor into Forward, opened the throttle and threaded the *Marvelous Maeve* between the rocks into the eye of the cove under the cliffs.

Maeve returned to the bow and acted as lookout, guiding Giordino through the black water that seemed to grow calmer the deeper they penetrated the inlet. "I see the beach," she informed them. "You can just make out a light strip of sand fifteen meters ahead and to starboard."

In another minute the bow and outriggers touched the strip of beach and ran up onto the soft sand. Pitt looked at Maeve. The cliffs shadowed the light from the moon, and he saw her features only vaguely. "You're home," he said briefly.

40

PITT GAVE THE LINE A HARD TUG. "WE'D BETTER GET MOVING before a patrol comes along."

"I should go first," said Giordino. "I'm the strongest." With a nod, he grabbed at the thin line and gave it a sharp pull to test its immovability. "This thing strong enough to take my weight?"

Pitt shrugged. "We'll have to hope so, won't we?"

Giordino gave him a sour look and started up the side of the cliff. He quickly vanished in the blackness while Pitt grasped the end of the line and held it taut to take up the slack.

"Find a couple of protruding rocks and tie off the boat fore and aft," Pitt ordered Maeve. "If worse comes to worst, we may have to rely on *Marvelous Maeve* to carry us away from here."

Maeve looked at him curiously. "How else did you expect to escape?"

"I'm a lazy sort. I had it in the back of my mind that we could steal one of your father's yachts, or maybe an aircraft."

"Do you have an army I'm not aware of?"

"You're looking at half of it."

Further conversation died as they gazed unseeing in

the darkness, speculating on Giordino's progress. Pitt's only awareness of his friend's movements was the quivering on the line.

After thirty minutes, Giordino stopped to catch his breath. His ascent had been fairly rapid considering the unevenness of the rocks. Climbing without the line would have been impossible. Even with the proper gear, having to make his way in the dark a meter at a time, groping for toeholds, driving in pitons and securing ropes, the climb would have taken the better part of six hours.

He paused to look upward at the shadowy lip of the summit, lined against the stars. Five meters, he estimated, five meters to go. His breath was heaving in aching gasps, his chest and arms bruised from scraping against unseen rock in the darkness. His immense strength was down to the bottom of its reserves. He was climbing the last few meters on guts alone. Indestructible, as hard and gritty as the rock on which he climbed, Giordino kept going, refusing to stop again until he could climb no more. Then suddenly the ground at the top of the cliff opened before his eyes and spread out on a horizontal level. One final heave over the edge and he lay flat, listening to his heart pound, his lungs pumping like bellows, sucking air in and out.

For the next three minutes Giordino lay without moving, elated that the agonizing exertion was over. He surveyed his immediate surroundings and found himself stretched across a path that traveled along the edge of the cliffs. A few paces beyond, a wall of trees and underbrush loomed dark and uninviting. Seeing no sign of lights or movement, he traced the line to the grappling hook and saw that it was firmly imbedded in a rock outcropping.

Pitt's zany idea had worked incredibly well.

Far below, Pitt turned to Maeve. "Your turn."

"I don't know if I'm up to this," she said nervously. "Heights scare me."

He made a loop, dropped it over her shoulders and cinched it tight around her waist. "Hold tight to the line, lean back from the cliff and walk up the side. Al will haul you up from above."

He answered Giordino's signal by jerking three times on the line. Maeve felt the slack taken up, followed by the pressure around her waist. Clamping her eyes tightly shut, she began walking like a fly up the vertical face of the cliff.

Far above, his arms too numb to elevate Maeve by hand, Giordino had discovered a smooth slot in the rock that would not damage or cut into the nylon fibers. He inserted the line and laid it over his shoulders. Then he bent forward and staggered across the path, dragging Maeve's weight up the cliff behind him.

In twelve minutes, Maeve appeared over the edge, eyes tightly closed. "Welcome to the top of the Matterhorn," Giordino greeted her warmly.

"Thank goodness that's behind me," she moaned gratefully, opening her eyes for the first time since leaving the beach. "I don't think I could ever do it again."

Giordino untied Maeve. "Keep watch while I hoist Dirk. You can see a fair distance along the cliffs to the north, but the path south is hidden by a big group of rocks about fifty meters away."

"I remember them," said Maeve. "They have a hollow interior with natural ramparts. My sister Deirdre and I used to play there and pretend we were royalty. It's called the Castle. There's a small rest station and a telephone inside for the guards."

"We've got to bring Dirk up before the next patrol comes along," said Giordino, carefully dropping the line again.

303

To Pitt, it felt as if he were being hauled topside in the time it took to fry an egg. But less than ten meters from the rim, his ascent abruptly stopped. No word of warning, no word of encouragement, only silence. It could only mean one thing. His timing was unlucky. A patrol must be approaching. Unable to see what was occurring on the ledge above, he pressed his body into a small crevice, lying rigid and still, listening for sounds in the night.

Maeve had spotted the beam of light as it swung around one wall of the Castle and immediately alerted Giordino. Quickly, he secured the line around a tree to maintain tension so Pitt wouldn't be dropped back onto the beach. He brushed dirt and dead leaves over the section of rope that showed but had no time to conceal the grappling hook.

"What about Dirk?" Maeve whispered frantically. "He might wonder what happened and call up to us."

"He'll guess the plot and be as quiet as a mouse," Giordino answered with certainty. He shoved her roughly into the underbrush beside the path. "Get in there and stay low till the guards pass by."

The unswerving single beam of light grew larger as it approached. Giordino's pulse jumped at seeing that the guards were studying every inch of the path as they walked. These men took their work seriously. They spied something and stopped directly in front of Maeve and Giordino.

"Hello, here's something the last patrol missed, or wasn't here an hour ago."

"What do you see?" asked his partner.

"Looks like a grappling hook off a boat." The first guard dropped to one knee and brushed away the hurried camouflage. "Well, well, it's attached to a line that drops down the cliff."

The other guard pulled out a knife and made ready to

cut the line. "If any are waiting to come up from below, they're about to be awfully disappointed."

Maeve sucked in her breath as Giordino stepped out of the bushes onto the path. "Don't you characters have anything better to do than wander around at night?"

The first guard froze, his knife hand raised in the air. The second guard spun around and leveled his Bushmaster M-16 assault rifle at Giordino. "Freeze in your position or I'll fire."

The guard with the flashlight beamed it at Maeve. He stood in silent surprise, peering intently into her face before finally mumbling, "Miss Dorsett?"

"Fletcher," she corrected him. "Maeve Fletcher."

"I . . . we were told you drowned."

"Do I look like I've been floating in the sea?" Maeve, in her ragged blouse and shorts, wasn't sure how she appeared to the guards. But she knew without doubt that she didn't look like the daughter of a billionaire diamond tycoon.

"May I ask what you're doing here this time of the morning?" the guard asked politely but firmly.

"My friend and I decided to take a walk."

The guard with the knife wasn't buying it. "You'll excuse me," he said, grabbing the line in his free hand in readiness to slice it with his left, "but there is something very wrong here."

Maeve stepped over and abruptly slapped the man with the leveled rifle across the cheek. The startling display of supremacy surprised both guards, and they hesitated. Swift as a coiled rattler, Giordino sprang at the nearer guard, brushing away the assault rifle and smashing his head into the man's stomach. The guard grunted in a violent convulsion before crashing to the ground on his back. Giordino, losing his footing, toppled across the fallen guard.

Unnoticed, a hand with an arm attached snaked over

the edge of the cliff, reached up and snatched the rifle, jerking it out of the guard's hands. Before the guard drew another breath, he was yanked into space. His final scream of terror echoed throughout the black void until it became muffled and died.

Then Pitt's head, lit by the flashlight on the ground, raised above the cliff's edge. The eyes blinked in the glare of the light and then the lips turned up in a slight grin.

"I believe that's what you call *flying* in the face of adverse opinion."

Maeve hugged Pitt. "You couldn't have arrived at a more opportune moment."

With Maeve as a guide, they set off along the cliff path. After traveling about five hundred meters, Maeve held up a hand and gestured into the thick underbrush. "We'll cross the island here," she informed them. "A road curves to within thirty meters of where we stand. If we're careful and remain out of sight of any traffic, we can follow the road into the central housing area for Dorsett employees."

"Where are we in relation to the volcanoes that anchor each end of the island?" asked Pitt.

"We're about halfway between and opposite the lagoon."

"Where do you think your boys might be held?" Giordino put to her.

"I wish I knew," she said distantly. "My first guess is the manor house, but I wouldn't put it past my father to keep them under guard in the security compound, or worse, they're kept by Jack Ferguson."

"Not a good idea to wander around like tourists looking for a restaurant," said Pitt.

"I'm with you," Giordino agreed. "The proper thing to do is find someone in authority with the answers and twist his arm."

Pitt fastidiously straightened the jacket of his stolen

uniform and brushed off the shoulders. "If he's on the island, I know just the man."

Twenty minutes later, after traveling over a road that wound in a series of hairpin turns over the spine of the island, they approached the compound that housed the mining engineers and the security guards.

In another hundred meters, Maeve stopped and gestured for Pitt and Giordino to drop behind a low hedge that bordered a concrete thoroughfare. One end of the road ended at a driveway that passed through a large arched gate to the Dorsett family manor house. A short distance in the opposite direction, the road split. One broad avenue trailed down a slope to the port in the center of the lagoon, where the docks and warehouses reflected a weird appearance under the eerie yellow glow of sodium-vapor lamps. Pitt took an extra minute to study the big boat tied beside the dock. Even at this distance, there was no mistaking the Dorsett yacht. Pitt was especially pleased to see a helicopter sitting on the upper deck.

"Point out the chief of security's house," Pitt said to Maeve.

"The house you want sits on the southeast corner of the security guards' compound. Its walls are painted gray."

"I see it." Pitt drew a sleeve across his forehead to wipe away the sweat. "Is there a way to reach it other than the road?"

"A walkway runs along the rear."

"Let's get moving. We don't have a whole lot of time before daylight."

They stayed in the shadows behind the hedge and the neatly trimmed trees that stretched alongside the paved shoulders of the road. Tall streetlights were spaced every fifty meters, the same as most city streets. Except for the soft rustle of wild grass and scattered leaves beneath their feet, the three of them moved quietly toward the gray house at the corner of the compound.

Pitt stepped out of the shadows and slipped up to one side of the back door and peered through a window. The interior was lit only by a dim light over a hallway that ended at a stairwell leading to the second floor. Cautiously, he reached over and gently twisted the latch. There was a barely audible click as the shaft slipped from its catch. He took a deep breath and cracked the door slightly. It swung on its hinges noiselessly, so he pushed it wide open and stepped into a rear entryway that opened into a small kitchen. He stepped across the kitchen and quietly closed a sliding door leading to a hallway. Then he turned on the light. At the signal, Maeve and Giordino followed him in.

"Warm air," Maeve whispered happily. "I haven't felt warm air in weeks."

"I can taste the ham and eggs already," said Giordino.

"First things first," Pitt said quietly.

Turning the light out again, he slipped the hallway door open. He cocked his head and listened, hearing only the soft noise of a heater fan. Flattening himself against the wall, he moved along the hallway under the muted light before starting up the carpeted stairway, testing each step for a squeak before setting his weight on it.

At the landing at the top of the stairs, he found two closed doors, one on either side. He tried the one to his right. The room was furnished as a private office with computer, telephones and file cabinets. The desk was incredibly orderly and free of clutter, the same as the kitchen. Pitt smiled to himself. Sure of himself now, he stepped over to the left door, kicked it open and switched on the light.

The man lay on his side. Pitt would have missed the

fractional movement but for the apparent indifference of the man. He lightly pulled the trigger, sending two quick shots into the pillow. The muzzle blast was muffled by the gun's suppressor and came like a pair of hand claps. Only then did the man in bed bolt upright and stare at a hand that was bleeding from a bullet through the palm.

"Good morning, Chief," said Pitt cheerfully. "Sorry to inconvenience you."

John Merchant blinked in the light and focused his eyes on his intruders.

"This has to be a nightmare," Merchant gasped. "I saw you cast adrift with my own eyes, before the storm struck. How is it possible you all survived?"

"We were swallowed by a whale," said Giordino, pulling the window curtains closed. "We upset his tummy, and you can guess what happened next."

"You people are crazy. You'll never get off the island alive."

Pitt gave a casual shrug. "I'd venture to say that one of your guards, the one I threw over the cliffs about half an hour ago, would disagree."

Pitt moved quickly and placed the muzzle against one of Merchant's elbows. "I'm in a hurry. Unless you wish to be doubly maimed, I suggest you speak, and speak the truth or you'll have a tough time brushing your teeth from now on. Tell me where Miss Fletcher's sons are being held."

"Miss Fletcher's sons work in the mines with the other laborers. They're kept with the others in the guarded camp."

Pitt turned to Maeve. "It's your call."

Maeve looked into Merchant's eyes, her face taut with emotion. "He's lying. Jack Ferguson, my father's overseer, is in charge of the boys. They would never be out of his sight."

"Where does he hang out?" asked Giordino.

"Ferguson lives in a guest house beside the mansion so he can be at my father's beck and call," said Maeve.

Pitt smiled coldly at Merchant. "Sorry, John, wrong answer. That will cost you an elbow."

"No, please, no!" Merchant muttered through teeth clenched from the pain. "You win. The twins are kept in Ferguson's quarters when they're not working in the mines."

Maeve stepped forward until she was standing over Merchant, distraught and grieved at envisioning the suffering her sons were enduring. Her self-control crumbled as she slapped him sharply, several times across the face. "Six-year-old boys forced to work in the mines! What kind of monsters are you?"

Pitt's face reflected sorrow and anger. He moved the muzzle to within a millimeter of Merchant's left eye, then lowered the gun.

Pitt nodded and smiled knowingly at Giordino. "He's not worth wasting a bullet." He looked about the room and nodded toward the closet. "We'll leave him in there."

Merchant's fear was obvious from the tic at one corner of his mouth. "I'll suffocate in there."

"I can shoot you now. Take your pick."

Merchant said no more and offered no resistance as he was bound with the bed sheets, torn into strips, and pushed into the closet. Giordino moved half the furniture in the bedroom against the door to keep it from being forced open from the inside.

"We've got what we came for," said Pitt. "Let's be on our way to the old homestead."

41

IT WAS A NORMAL DAY LIKE MOST DAYS IN THE TROPICAL waters off the Hawaiian Islands, warm with more than a trace of humidity and a light breeze, generally referred to as the trade winds. It was a Saturday, a day when the beaches at Waikiki and the windward side of the island were slowly coming alive with early birds awake for an early morning dip. Soon they would be followed by thousands of local residents and vacationers looking forward to leisurely hours of swimming in surf subdued by offshore reefs, and sunbathing on heated sand later in the day. Lulled by the relaxing atmosphere, none were remotely aware that this might be their last day on earth.

The *Glomar Explorer,* only one of her big twin screws driving under full power, pushed steadily toward the site of the deadly acoustic convergence, the sound waves already hurtling through the sea from the four sources. She should have been running a good half hour late, but Chief Engineer Toft had pushed his crew to and beyond the edge of exhaustion. Up on the starboard wing of the bridge, Sandecker peered through binoculars at a commercial version of the Navy's SH-60B Sea Hawk helicopter, with NUMA markings, as it approached the ship from bow-on, circled once and dropped on the big ship's stern landing pad. Two men hurried from the aircraft and entered the aft superstructure. A minute later, they joined Sandecker on the bridge.

"Did the drop go well?" Sandecker asked anxiously.

Dr. Sanford Adgate Ames nodded with a slight smile. "Four arrays of remote acoustical sensing instruments have been deployed under the surface at the required locations thirty kilometers distant from the convergence zone."

"We laid them directly in the four estimated paths of the sound channels," added Gunn, who had made the flight with Ames.

"They're set to measure the final approach and intensity of the sound?" Sandecker asked.

Ames nodded. "The telemetry data from the underwater modems will be relayed by their surface flotation satellite link to the onboard processor and analyst terminal here on board the *Explorer*. The system works similarly to submarine acoustic locating programs."

"Fortunately, we have a weather and current window working in our favor," said Gunn. "All things considered, the sound waves should come together as predicted."

"Warning time?"

"Sound travels underwater at an average of fifteen hundred meters per second," replied Ames. "I figure twenty seconds from when the sound waves pass the modems until they strike the reflector dish under the ship."

"Twenty seconds," Sandecker repeated. "Very little time to mentally prepare for the unknown."

"Since no one without some kind of protection has survived to describe the full intensity of the convergence, my best estimate of its duration before it is totally deflected toward Gladiator Island is approximately four and a half minutes. Anyone on board the ship who does not reach the dampened shelter will surely die."

Sandecker turned and gestured at the vivid green mountains of Oahu, only fifteen kilometers distant. "Will any effects reach the people on shore?"

"They might feel a brief but sharp pain inside their heads, but no permanent harm should come to them."

Sandecker stared out the bridge windows at the huge mass of machinery soaring skyward in the middle of the ship. Infinite miles of cable and hydraulic lines ranged over the deck from the derrick and cranes. Teams of men and women, sitting and standing on platforms suspended in the air like those used by skyscraper window cleaners, worked at reconnecting the seemingly unending number of links on the enormous reflector shield. The giant derrick held the main frame of the shield, while the surrounding cranes lifted the smaller numbered pieces into their slots where they were then joined. Thanks to Rudi Gunn's foresight in cleaning and oiling the connectors, all parts fit quickly and smoothly. The operation was going like clockwork. Only two more parts were left to install.

Sandecker looked at the man studying the digital numbers on the ship's computerized navigation system. "Captain Quick."

The master of the *Glomar Explorer* looked up. "Admiral Sandecker."

"How far to the site?"

"Less than five hundred meters and another twenty minutes until we begin pinpointing the ship over the numbers your people computed for the Global Positioning System."

"Which leaves us only forty minutes to deploy the reflector shield."

The long minutes passed with everyone in the wheelhouse keeping one eye on the clock and the other on the red digital numbers of the Global Positioning System as they diminished finally to a row of zeros, indicating the ship was over the precise site where the sound rays were calculated to converge and explode with unparalleled intensity.

Teams of engineers and technicians, electronics systems experts and scientists worked simultaneously to put the reflector shield in the precise path of the sound waves. The NUMA team, working on platforms far above the deck, made the final connections and attached the shield to the drop hook of the derrick.

Far below, one of the most unique sections of the ship stirred to life. Taking up the middle third of the ship, the 1,367 square meter Moon Pool, as it was called, filled with water as two sections of the center hull, one fore, the other aft, retracted into specially designed sleeves. The dredging hose would be extended thousands of meters deep to the minerals carpeting the ocean's bottom and where the vast reflector shield would be lowered into the sea.

The engineering systems on board the *Glomar Explorer* were originally constructed to raise heavy objects from the seafloor, not to lower lighter but more expansive objects downward. Procedures were hurriedly modified for the complex operation. Minor glitches were quickly overcome. Every move was coordinated and performed with precision.

"Six minutes and ten seconds to convergence," Captain Quick's voice droned over the ship's loudspeakers. "All ship's personnel will go to the engine-room storage compartment at the aft end of the ship and enter as you have been instructed. Do this immediately. I say immediately. Run, do not walk."

Suddenly, everyone was dropping down ladders and scaffolding, hurrying in unison like a pack of marathon runners toward the propulsion and pump room deep in the bowels of the ship. Here, twenty ship's crew members had been busily sound-isolating the supply compartment with every piece of dampening material they could lay their hands on. The ship's towels, blankets, bedding and mattresses, along with all cushions from lounge chairs and any scraps of lumber they could scrounge were placed against ceiling, deck and bulkheads to deaden all intruding sound.

As they rushed down the passageways belowdecks, Sandecker said to Ames, "This is the agonizing part of the operation."

Sandecker and Ames found the NUMA team members settled in one corner of the compartment and joined them, moving beside Rudi Gunn and Molly Faraday, who had preceded them. They immediately gathered around monitoring systems that were integrated with the warning modems and other underwater sensors. Only the admiral, Ames and Gunn held off using the sound deadeners so they could confer right up to the final few seconds.

The compartment quickly filled amid a strange silence. Unable to hear, no one spoke. Captain Quick stood on a small box so he could be observed by all in the room. He held up two fingers as a two minute warning.

Five seconds passed, then ten. Sandecker began to feel the prickle of disaster in the nape of his neck. Then suddenly, ominously, the acoustic sensors, thirty kilometers distant, began registering the incoming sound waves along their predicted paths.

"Good Lord!" muttered Ames. "The sensors have gone off the scale. The intensity is greater than I estimated."

"Twenty seconds and counting!" snapped Sandecker. "Get your ear mufflers on."

The first indication of the convergence was a small

resonance that rapidly grew in magnitude. The dampened bulkheads vibrated in conjunction with a hum that penetrated the sound-deadening ear protectors. The crowded people in the confined room sensed a mild form of disorientation and vertigo. But no one was struck by nausea and none panicked. The discomfort was borne stoically. Sandecker and Ames stared at each other, fulfillment swamping them in great trembling waves.

Five long minutes later it was all over. The resonance had faded away, leaving an almost supernatural silence behind it.

Gunn was the first to react. He tore off his sound deadeners, waved his arms and shouted at Captain Quick. "The door. Open the door and let some air in here."

Quick got the message. The mattresses were cast aside and the door thrown open. Sandecker's reaction time was almost inhuman. He ran up the companionways to the wheelhouse in a time that would have broken any existing record, if there had been one. He snatched up a pair of binoculars and rushed out onto the bridge wing. Anxiously, he focused the lenses on the island, only fifteen kilometers distant.

Cars were traveling routinely on the streets, and busy crowds of sunseekers moved freely about the beaches. Only then did he expel a long sigh and sag in relief over the railing, totally drained of emotion.

"An utter triumph, Admiral," Ames said, pumping Sandecker's hand. "You proved the best scientific minds in the country wrong."

Overcome with exhilaration, Gunn and Molly both hugged Sandecker, an act considered unthinkable on any other occasion. "You did it!" said Gunn. "Nearly two million lives saved, thanks to your stubbornness."

Gunn's expression suddenly turned sober. "A great pity Dirk wasn't here to see it."

Sandecker nodded solemnly. "His concept was the spark that ignited the project."

Ames studied the array of instruments he had set up during the voyage from Molokai.

"The reflector positioning was perfect," he said happily. "The acoustic energy was reversed exactly as intended."

"Where is it now?" asked Molly.

"Combined with the energy from the other three island mining operations, the sound waves are traveling back to Gladiator Island faster than any jet plane. Their combined force should strike the submerged base in roughly ninety-seven minutes."

"I'd love to see his face."

"Whose face?" asked Ames innocently.

"Arthur Dorsett's," answered Molly, "when his private island starts to rock and roll."

42

THE TWO MEN AND THE WOMAN CROUCHED IN A CLUMP OF bushes off to one side of the great archway that broke the middle of a high, lava-rock wall enclosing the entire Dorsett estate. Beyond the archway, a brick driveway circled around a large, well-trimmed lawn through a grand porte cochere, a tall structure extending from the front of the house to shelter people getting in and out of cars. The entire driveway and house were illuminated by bright lamps strategically spaced about the landscaped grounds. Entry was barred by a thick iron gate that looked like it came from a castle out of the Middle Ages. Nearly five meters thick, the archway itself housed a small office for the security guards.

"Is there another way in?" Pitt asked Maeve softly.

"The arched gate is the only way in or out," she whispered back.

"No drainage pipe or small ravine conveniently running beneath the wall?"

"Believe me, when I think of all the times I wanted to run away from my father when I was a young girl, I'd have found a passage leading from the grounds."

"Security detectors?"

"Laser beams along the top of the wall with infrared

body-heat sensors installed at different intervals about the grounds. Anything larger than a cat will cause an alarm to sound in the security office. Television cameras automatically come on and aim their lenses at the intruder."

"How many guards?"

"Two at night, four during the day."

"No dogs?"

She shook her head in the darkness. "Father hates animals. I never forgave him for stomping on a small bird with a broken wing I was trying to nurse back to health."

Pitt stared at the gate thoughtfully, carefully gauging visible activity by the guards. They seemed content to stay inside and monitor the security systems. Finally, he rose to his feet, rumpled his uniform and turned to Giordino.

"I'm going to bluff my way inside. Hang loose until I open the gate."

He slung the assault rifle over his shoulder and pulled his Swiss army knife from a pocket. Extending a small blade he made a small cut in one thumb, squeezed out the blood and smeared it over his face. When he reached the gate, Pitt dropped to his knees and gripped the bars in both hands. Then he began to shout in a low moaning tone, as if in pain.

"Help me. I need help!"

A face appeared around the door, then disappeared. Seconds later, both guards ran out of the security office and opened the gate. Pitt fell forward into their waiting arms.

"What happened?" demanded a guard. "Who did this to you?"

"I was coming up the road from the dock when two men jumped me from behind."

"We'd better alert the main security compound," blurted one of the guards.

"Help me inside first," Pitt groaned. "I think they fractured my skull."

The guards lifted Pitt to his feet and slung his arms over their shoulders. They half carried, half dragged him into the security office. Slowly, Pitt moved his arms inward until the guards' necks were in the crooks of his elbows. As they pressed together to pass through the doorway, he took a step backwards, hooked the guards' necks in a tight grip and exerted every bit of strength in his biceps and shoulder muscles. They both crashed to the floor, unconscious for at least the next two hours.

Safe from detection, Giordino and Maeve hurried through the opened gate and joined Pitt inside the office. Giordino picked up the guards as if they were straw scarecrows and sat them in chairs around a table facing a row of video monitors. "To anyone walking by," he said, "it'll look like they fell asleep during the movie."

A quick scan of the security system, and Pitt closed down the alarms, while Giordino bound the guards with their own ties and belts. Then Pitt looked at Maeve. "Where's Ferguson's quarters?"

"There are two guest houses in a grove of trees behind the manor. He lives in one of them."

"I don't suppose you know which one?"

She shrugged. "This is the first time I've returned to the island since I ran away to Melbourne and the university. If I remember correctly, he lives in the one nearest the manor."

"Time to repeat our break-in act," said Pitt. "Let's hope we haven't lost our touch."

They moved up the driveway at a steady, unhurried pace. They were too weakened from an inadequate diet and the hardships of the past weeks to run. They reached what Maeve believed was the living quarters of Jack

Ferguson, superintendent of Dorsett's mines on Gladiator Island.

The sky was beginning to lighten in the east as they approached the front door. The search was taking too long, Pitt thought. With the coming of dawn, their presence would most certainly be discovered. They had to move fast if they wanted to find the boys, reach the yacht and escape in Arthur Dorsett's private helicopter before the remaining darkness was lost.

There was no stealth this time, no slinking quietly into the house. Pitt walked up to the front door, kicked it in with a splintering crunch and walked inside. A quick look around with the flashlight taken from the guards at the cliff told him all he needed to know. Ferguson lived there all right. There was a stack of mail on a desk that was addressed to him and a calendar with notations. Inside a closet, Pitt found neatly pressed men's pants and coats.

"Nobody home," he said. "Jack Ferguson has gone. No sign of suitcases, and half the hangers in the closet are empty."

"He's got to be here," said Maeve in confusion.

"According to dates he's marked on his calendar, Ferguson is on a tour of your father's other mining properties."

She stared at the vacant room in futility and growing despair. "My boys are gone. We're too late. They're dead."

Pitt put his arm around her. "They're as alive as you and I. It goes without saying that your father wouldn't harm your sons. He may threaten, but I'll bet they're in your old room, where they've been all along, playing with a room full of toys, courtesy of their old granddad."

Maeve looked at him in confusion. "He didn't force them to work in the mines?"

"Probably not. Merchant turned the screws on your

maternal instincts to make you think your babies were suffering so he could make you suffer."

Maeve looked at Pitt for a long moment, her expression turning from disbelief to understanding, then she shivered. "Well, it certainly worked."

"I hate to dampen good news, but this time the people of the house are stirring about." He gestured at lights shining in the windows of the manor house.

"My father always rises before dawn," said Maeve. "He never allowed my sisters and me to sleep after sunrise."

"What I wouldn't give to join them for breakfast," moaned Giordino.

"Not to sound like an echo chamber," said Pitt, "but we need a way in without provoking the inhabitants."

"All rooms of the manor open onto interior verandas except one. Daddy's study has a side door that leads onto a squash court."

"What's a squash court?" inquired Giordino.

"A court where they play squash," answered Pitt. Then to Maeve, "In what direction is your old bedroom?"

"Across the garden and past the swimming pool to the east wing, second door on the right."

"That's it then. You two go after the boys."

"What will you do?"

"Me, I'm going to borrow Daddy's phone and stick him with a long-distance call."

The atmosphere on board the *Glomar Explorer* was relaxed and partylike. The NUMA team and the ship's personnel that were gathered in the spacious lounge next to the galley celebrated their success in repelling the acoustic plague. Admiral Sandecker heaved himself out of his chair after being informed by the ship's communications officer that he had an important call from his chief geologist, Charlie Bakewell. He walked to a quiet part of the lounge and pulled a compact satellite phone from his pocket. "Yes, Charlie."

"I understand congratulations are in order." Bakewell's voice came clearly.

"It was a close thing. We barely positioned the ship and dropped the reflector shield before the convergence occurred. Where are you now?"

"I'm here at the Joseph Marmon Volcanic Observatory in Auckland, New Zealand. I have an update for you from their staff of geophysicists. Their most recent analysis of the sound ray energy's impact on Gladiator Island isn't very encouraging."

"Can they compute the repercussions?"

"I'm sorry to say the predicted magnitude is worse than I originally thought," answered Bakewell. "The two volcanos on the island, I've since learned, are called Mount Scaggs and Mount Winkleman, after two survivors from the raft of the *Gladiator*. What we neglected to consider was Dorsett's mining operations making the volcanos most susceptible to outside tremors. Even a minor seismic disturbance could trigger volcanic activity from Mounts Scaggs and Winkleman. In short, if Dorsett doesn't stop digging, it's only a matter of time before his miners uncork the central conduit, releasing an explosion of molten lava."

"An explosion of molten lava," Sandecker repeated mechanically. "What have we done? Hundreds of lives will be lost."

"There are no women and children known to be on Gladiator Island. What is Dr. Ames' estimate of the sound wave's arrival at Gladiator?" inquired Bakewell.

Sandecker glanced at his watch. "Twenty-one minutes to impact."

"There's still time to warn the inhabitants to evacuate the island."

"My people in Washington have already tried to alert Dorsett Consolidated Mining management of the potential danger," said Sandecker. "But under orders from Arthur Dorsett, all communications between his mining operations and the outside have been cut off."

"It sounds almost as if Dorsett wanted something to happen."

"There is still a possibility no eruption will happen. The sound ray's energy might dissipate before impact. I'll get back to you when I know more," said Bakewell. "Hopefully, I've given you the worst, and all news from now on will be good."

"Thank you, Charlie. I hope so too."

Sandecker switched off the phone and stood there thoughtfully. Anxiety and foreboding did not show on his face, not a twitch of an eyelid, not even a tightening of the lips, but there was a dread running deep beneath the surface. He did not notice Rudi Gunn approaching him until he felt his shoulder tapped.

"Admiral, there is another call for you. It's from your office in Washington."

Sandecker switched on the phone and spoke into it again. "This is Sandecker."

"Admiral?" came the familiar voice of his longtime secretary, Martha Sherman. Her normally formal tone was nervous with excitement. "Please stand by. I'm going to relay a call to you."

"Is it important?" he asked irritably. "I'm not in the mood for official business."

"Believe me, you'll want to take this call," she informed him happily. "One moment while I switch you over."

A pause, then, "Hello," said Sandecker. "Who's this?"

"Good morning from Down Under, Admiral. What's this about you dawdling around blue Hawaii?"

Sandecker was not the kind of man to tremble, but he

trembled now and felt as if the deck had fallen from under his feet. "Dirk, is it you?"

"What's left of me," Pitt replied. "I'm with Al and Maeve Fletcher."

"I can't believe you're all alive," Sandecker said as if an electrical surge was coursing through his veins. "Tell me how you survived all this time."

"A long story," said Pitt. "I'd rather you brought me up-to-date on the acoustic plague."

"A story far more involved than yours. I'll give you the particulars when we meet. Where are the three of you now?"

"We managed to reach Gladiator Island. I'm sitting in Arthur Dorsett's study as we speak, borrowing his telephone."

Sandecker went numb with disbelief. "You can't be serious."

"Dead serious. We're going to snatch Maeve's twin boys and make our getaway across the Tasman Sea to Australia." He said it in such a way as to sound like he was walking down the street to buy a loaf of bread.

Cold fear replaced Sandecker's earlier anxiety, but it was the shocking fear of helplessness. The news struck with such unexpectedness, such suddenness, that he was incapable of words for several seconds until Pitt's inquiring voice finally penetrated his shock.

"Are you still there, Admiral?"

"Pitt, listen to me!" demanded Sandecker urgently. "Your lives are in extreme danger! Get off the island! Get off now!"

There was a slight pause. "Sorry, sir, I don't read you—"

"I've no time to explain," Sandecker interrupted. "All I can tell you is a sound ray of incredible intensity will strike Gladiator Island in less than twenty minutes. The impact will set up seismic resonance that is predicted to blow off the volcanos on opposite ends of the island. If the eruption takes place on the western side, there will be no survivors. You and the others must escape to sea while you still can. Talk no further. I am cutting off all communications."

Sandecker switched off his phone, capable of nothing but the realization that he had unknowingly and innocently sealed a death warrant on his best friend.

43

THE SHOCKING KNOWLEDGE STRUCK PITT LIKE THE THRUST of a dagger. He stared through a large picture window at the helicopter sitting on the yacht moored to the pier in the lagoon. He estimated the distance at just under a kilometer. Burdened by two young children, he figured they would need a good fifteen minutes to reach the dock. Without means of transportation, a car or a truck, it would be an extremely close timetable. The time for caution had flown as if there had never been such a time. Giordino and Maeve should have found her sons by now. They had to have found them. If not, something must have gone terribly wrong.

He turned his gaze first toward Mount Winkleman, and then swept the saddle of the island, his eyes stopping on Mount Scaggs. They looked deceptively peaceful. Seeing the lush growth of trees in the ravines scoring the slopes, he found it hard to imagine the two mounts as menacing volcanos, sleeping giants on the verge of spewing death and disaster in a burst of gaseous steam and molten rock.

Briskly, but not in a hurried panic, he rose out of Dorsett's leather executive chair and came around the desk. At that instant, he halted abruptly, frozen in the

327

exact center of the room as the double doors to the main interior of the house swung open, and Arthur Dorsett walked in.

He was carrying a cup of coffee in one hand and a file of papers under an arm. He wore wrinkled slacks and what had once been white but was now a yellowed dress shirt with a bow tie. His mind seemed elsewhere. Perceiving another body in his study, he looked up, more curious than surprised. Seeing the intruder was in uniform, his first thought was that Pitt was a security guard. He opened his mouth to demand the reason for Pitt's presence, then stiffened in petrified astonishment. His face became a pale mask molded by shock and bewilderment. The file fell to the floor, its papers sliding out like a fanned deck of cards. His hand dropped to his side, spilling the coffee on his slacks and the carpet.

"You're dead!" he gasped.

"You don't know how happy I am to prove you wrong," Pitt commented, pleased to see that Dorsett wore a patch over one eye. "Come to think of it, you *do* look like you've seen a ghost."

"The storm . . . there is no way you could have survived a raging sea." A flicker of emotional repossession showed in the one black eye and slowly but surely grew. "How was it possible?"

"A lot of positive thinking and my Swiss army knife." This guy is big, Pitt thought, very glad he was the one pointing a gun.

"And Maeve . . . is she dead?" He spoke haltingly as he studied the assault rifle in Pitt's hands, the muzzle aimed at his heart.

"Just knowing that it causes you great annoyance and displeasure makes me happy to report she is alive and well and at this very moment about to make off with your grandsons." Pitt stared back, green eyes locked with black. "Tell me, Dorsett. How do you justify murdering your own daughter? Did one single woman who was simply trying to find herself as a person pose a threat to your assets? Or was it her sons you wanted, all to yourself?"

"It was essential the empire be carried on after my death by my direct descendants. Maeve refused to see it that way."

"I have news for you. Your empire is about to come crashing down around your head."

Dorsett failed to grasp Pitt's meaning. "You intend to kill me?"

Pitt shook his head. "I'm not your executioner. The island volcanos are going to erupt. A fitting end for you, Arthur, consumed by fiery lava."

Dorsett smiled faintly as he regained control. "What sort of nonsense is that?"

"Too complicated to explain. I don't know all the technicalities myself, but I have it on the best authority. You'll just have to take my word for it."

"If you're going to shoot," said Dorsett, cold anger glaring from his coal-black eye, "do it now, clean and quick."

Pitt grinned impassively. Maeve and Giordino had yet to make an appearance. For the moment he needed Arthur Dorsett alive in case they had been captured by security guards. "Sorry, I haven't the time. Now please turn around and go up the stairs to the bedrooms."

"My grandchildren, you can't have my grandchildren," he muttered as if it was a divine statement.

"Correction, Maeve's children."

"You'll never get past my security guards."

"The two at the front gate are—what's the word?—incapacitated."

"Then you'll have to murder me in cold blood, and I'll wager everything I've got that you don't have the guts for it."

"Why is it people keep thinking I can't stand the sight of blood?" Pitt touched his finger against the trigger of the assault rifle. "Get moving, Arthur, or I'll shoot off your ears."

"Go ahead," Dorsett lashed out. "You already took one of my eyes."

At that instant Boudicca walked into the study, not recognizing Pitt in the guard's uniform, and not realizing her father was in immediate danger.

"We have unwelcome visitors, Daughter," said Dorsett. Almost as if he had eyes in the back of his head, he knew that Pitt's attention was focused briefly on Boudicca. It was the distraction Dorsett had prepared for. In a violent twisting motion, he whirled around, one arm striking the gun barrel and knocking it aside.

Pitt instinctively pulled the trigger. A spray of bullets blasted into a painting of Charles Dorsett over a fireplace mantel. Physically weakened and dead on his feet from lack of sleep, Pitt's reaction time was a fraction longer than it should have been. The strain and exhaustion of the past three weeks had taken their toll. He watched in what seemed slow motion as the assault rifle was torn from his hands and sent flying across the room before smashing through a window.

Dorsett was on Pitt like a maddened rhino. Pitt clutched him, struggling to stay on his feet. But the heavier man was swinging his huge fists like pile drivers. Pitt twisted his head but a fist caught him on the side of the head above one ear. Fireworks burst inside his brain, and he was swept by a wave of dizziness. Desperately, Pitt crouched and rolled to his side to escape the rain of blows.

He jumped in the opposite direction as Dorsett lunged at him. The old diamond miner had sent many a man to the hospital with only his bare hands, backed by arms and shoulders thick with muscle. During his rough-and-tumble youth in the mines, he had prided himself on never having to resort to knives and guns. His bulk and power were all he required to put away anyone with the nerve to stand up to him. Even at an age when most men turned to flab, Dorsett retained a body as hard as granite.

Pitt shook his head to clear his sight. He felt like a battered prizefighter, desperately holding on to the ropes until the bell for the end of the round, struggling to bring his mind back on track. Few were the martial-arts experts who could put down Dorsett's irresistible mass of sheer muscle. Pitt was beginning to think the only thing that would slow the diamond merchant was an elephant gun.

"What now, old man? Are you going to bite me with your rotting teeth?"

The insult had the desired effect. Dorsett roared insanely and leaped across the desk. Pitt calmly took one step back, snatched up a metal desk lamp and swung it with strength renewed by wrath and hatred.

Dorsett tried to lift an arm to ward off the blow, but he was a fraction slow. The lamp caught him on the wrist, snapping it before hurtling on against the shoulder and breaking the collarbone with a sharp crack. He bellowed like a stricken animal and came after Pitt again with a look of malevolence heightened by pain and pure savagery. He threw a vicious punch at Pitt's head.

Pitt ducked and jammed the base of the lamp downward. It connected somewhere below Dorsett's knee on the shin, but the momentum of the flying leg knocked the lamp from Pitt's hand. There was a clunk on the carpet. Now Dorsett was coming back at him almost as if he were completely uninjured. The veins were throbbing on the sides of his neck, the eye blazed and there were dribbles of saliva at the ends of his cracked, gasping mouth. He actually seemed to be laughing. He had to be mad. He mumbled something incoherent and leaped toward Pitt.

Dorsett never reached his victim. His right leg collapsed, and he crashed to the floor on his back. Pitt's swing of the lamp base had broken his shin bone. This time Pitt reacted like a cat. With a lightning move, he sprang onto the desk, tensed and jumped.

Together, Pitt's feet hurtled downward into Dorsett's exposed neck. An agonized animal sound burst from his throat, a horrible gurgling sound that came through his crushed windpipe. Then Dorsett's body collapsed as all life faded away and the sadistic light in his eye blinked out.

Pitt somehow managed to remain standing, panting through clenched teeth. He stared at Boudicca, who strangely had made no move to help her father. She looked down at the dead body on the carpet with the uncaring but fascinated expression of a witness at a fatal traffic accident.

"You killed him," she said finally in a normal tone of voice.

"Few men deserved to die more," Pitt said, catching his breath while massaging a growing knot on his head.

Boudicca turned her attention away from her dead father as though he didn't exist. "I should thank you, Mr. Pitt, for handing me Dorsett Consolidated Mining Limited on a silver platter."

"To the adoring daughter go the spoils. What about Maeve and Deirdre? They're each entitled to a third of the business."

"Deirdre will receive her share," Boudicca said matter-of-factly. "Maeve, if she is still alive, will get nothing. Daddy had already cut her out of the business."

"And the twins?"

She shrugged. "Little boys have accidents every day."

"I guess it isn't in you to be a loving aunt."

Deep inside him he knew he was no match for Boudicca, but he had to act while he had the slight advantage of surprise. The thought was still in his mind when he sprinted forward, head down, across the room, crashing shoulder first into Boudicca's stomach. Boudicca was caught off guard, but it made little difference, almost no difference at all. She took the full force of the blow, grunted from the sudden shock, and although she reeled back a few steps, she remained standing. Before Pitt could recover his own balance, she clutched him with both arms under his chest, swung around in a half circle and threw him against a bookcase, his back shattering the glass doors. Incredibly, he managed somehow to remain erect on wobbly legs instead of crashing to the floor.

Pitt gasped in agony. His whole body felt like every bone was broken. He fought off the pain and charged again, catching Boudicca with a bruising uppercut with his fist that drew blood. It was a blow that should have knocked any woman unconscious for a week, but Boudicca simply wiped away the blood streaming from her mouth with the back of one hand and smiled horribly. She doubled her fists and moved toward Pitt, crouched in a boxer's stance.

He stepped in, ducked under a savage right-hand slash and hit her again with the last of his remaining strength. He felt his fist drive home against flesh and bone, and then he was pounded by a tremendous blow that caught him in the chest. Pitt thought his heart had been mashed to pulp. He couldn't believe any woman could hit so hard. Vaguely, he saw Boudicca lean down, take him by one leg and hurl him crazily across the floor, where he collided with the open door. Pitt lay there, teetering on the edge of unconsciousness, swimming in pain, sensing but not really feeling the blood flowing from a gash above his left eye.

Boudicca stood there beside the body of her father, smirking with anticipation. Complete mastery was etched in her face. "Time for you to join my father," she said. Her tone was deep, icy and compelling.

"There's a nauseating thought for you." Pitt's voice came thick and slurred.

Then Pitt saw the malice slowly fade in Boudicca's face and felt a hand gently ease him aside as Giordino entered the Dorsett family study.

He stared at Boudicca contemptuously and said, "This one is mine."

At that moment Maeve appeared in the doorway, clutching a pair of blond-haired little boys by the hands, one on either side of her. She looked from Pitt's bleeding face to Boudicca to her father's body on the floor. "What happened to Daddy?"

"He caught a sore throat," muttered Pitt.

"Sorry I'm late," said Giordino calmly. "A couple of nannies proved overly protective. They locked themselves in a room with the boys. It took me a while to kick in the door." He handed Pitt the nine-millimeter automatic taken from John Merchant.

Gone was any display of confidence in Boudicca's eyes. Gone too was any anticipation of merely hurting her opponent. This time she was fighting for her life, and she was going to use every dirty street-fighting trick she'd been taught by her father. This was to be no civilized boxing or karate match. She moved wolflike to position herself to deliver a killing blow, mindful of the gun in Pitt's hand.

"So you came back from the dead too," she hissed. "A pity you survived only to die in my house—"

A mistake. Boudicca wasted the half second with

unnecessary talk. Giordino was on her like a cattle stampede, legs bent, feet extending as they came in contact with Boudicca's chest. The impact doubled her over with a gasp of agony, but incredibly, she somehow retained her stance and clamped her hands around Giordino's wrists. She hurled herself backward over the desk, pulling him with her.

The evil grin came back on her lips as she held her victim helpless in a steel grip. She increased the pressure and bent his wrists with the intention of breaking them with her Amazon strength. It was a shrewd move. She could render Giordino disabled while shielding herself with his body until she could retrieve a revolver Arthur Dorsett kept loaded inside a bottom desk drawer.

Giordino seemed to lie there immobile, as if accepting defeat without fighting back, while Boudicca kept bending his wrists slowly backward.

Then slowly, as if he'd been conserving his strength, Giordino pulled his wrists and hands upward as if curling a set of weights. Incomprehension followed on the heels of shock in Boudicca's face. Then came disbelief, and her body quivered as she exerted every trace of strength to stop the relentless force. Suddenly, she could grip his wrists no more, and her hold was broken. Before Boudicca could recover, Giordino was across the desk and pressing her arms to the floor. Held immobile by strength she had never expected, Boudicca thrashed in frantic madness to escape. Desperately, she tried to reach the desk drawer containing the revolver, but Giordino's knees kept her arms effectively pinned against her sides.

Giordino flexed his arm muscles, and then his hands were around her throat. "Like father, like daughter," he snarled.

Boudicca realized with sickening certainty that there would be no release, no mercy. She was effectively imprisoned. Her body convulsed in terror as Giordino's massive hands squeezed the life from her.

"We've got to leave," Pitt said without wasting a second. "The whole island is about to go up in smoke and cinders."

"Come again?" Giordino asked dumbly.

"I'll draw you a picture later." Pitt looked at Maeve. "What have you got for transportation around the house?"

"A garage on the side of the house holds a pair of minicars Daddy uses—used for driving between the mines."

Pitt swept one of the boys up in his arms. "Which one are you?"

Frightened of the blood streaming down Pitt's face, the youngster mumbled, "Michael." He pointed to his brother, who was now held by Giordino. "He's Sean."

"Ever flown in a helicopter, Michael?"

"No, but I always wanted to."

"Wishing will make it so," Pitt laughed.

As Maeve hurried from the study, she turned and took one last look at her father and Boudicca. There was no time to mourn them now.

44

THEY FOUND DORSETT'S ISLAND VEHICLES, COMPACT MODELS of a car built in Australia called a Holden, in a garage adjoining the manor. The cars had been customized by having all the doors removed for easy entry and exit and were painted a bright shade of yellow. Pitt was eternally thankful to the late Arthur Dorsett for leaving the key in the ignition of the first car in line. Quickly, they all piled in, Pitt and Giordino in the front, Maeve and her boys in the back.

The engine roared to life, and Pitt shoved the floor shift into first gear. He pressed the accelerator pedal as he released the clutch, and the car leaped forward.

Giordino leaped out at the archway and opened the gate. They had hardly shot onto the road when they passed a four-wheel-drive open van filled with security men traveling in the other direction.

"Everybody wave and smile," directed Pitt. "Make it look like we're all one big happy family."

The uniformed driver of the van slowed and stared curiously at the occupants of the Holden, then nodded and saluted, not sure he recognized anyone but assuming they were probably guests of the Dorsett family. The van was stopping at the archway as Pitt poured on the power

337

and raced the Holden toward the dock stretching out into the lagoon.

"They bought it," said Giordino.

Pitt swerved off the main road serving the two mines and headed toward the lagoon. They had a straight shot at the dock area now. No cars or trucks stood between them and the yacht. Pitt didn't take the time to look at his watch, but he knew they had less than four or five minutes before Sandecker's predicted cataclysm.

"They're coming after us," Maeve called out grimly.

Pitt didn't have to look in the rearview mirror to confirm, nor be told their run for freedom was in jeopardy because of the guards' quick reaction in taking up the chase. The only question running through his mind was whether he and Giordino could get the helicopter airborne before the guards came within range and shot them out of the sky.

Pitt hit the stoutly built wooden dock at better than 120 kilometers per hour, then jammed his foot on the brake pedal, sending the car into a long skid aimed directly toward the security office. The startled guard, unsure which way to jump, froze for an instant and then leaped off the side of the dock into the water to escape being crushed against the front grill of the car.

"Neatly done," Giordino said admiringly, as Pitt straightened out and braked sharply beside the yacht's gangway.

"Quickly!" Pitt shouted. "Al, run to the helicopter, remove the tie-down ropes and start the engine. Maeve, you take your boys and wait out of sight in the salon. It will be safer there if the guards arrive before we can lift off. Wait until you see the rotor blades begin to turn on the aircraft. Then make a run for it."

"Where will you be?" asked Giordino, helping Maeve lift the boys out of the car and sending them dashing up the gangway.

"Casting off the mooring lines to keep boarders off the boat."

Pitt was sweating by the time he pulled the yacht's heavy mooring ropes from their bollards and heaved them over the side. Then, in almost the exact same instant, the helicopter's engine coughed into life followed by the crack of a gunshot from inside the yacht.

He sprinted up the gangway, fear exploding inside him, hating himself for sending Maeve and her boys on board the boat without investigating. He reached for the nine millimeter, but then remembered he had given it to Giordino. He ran across the deck, tore open the door to the salon and ran inside.

His mind reeled at the shock of hearing Maeve plead, "No, Deirdre, no, please, not them too!"

Pitt's eyes took in the terrible scene. Maeve on the floor, her back against a bookcase, her boys clutched in her arms, both sobbing in fright. A blood-red stain was spreading across her blouse from a small hole in her stomach at the navel.

Deirdre stood in the center of the salon, holding a small automatic pistol aimed at the twin boys. She nodded slowly at Pitt, her gun hand white and as firm as marble. "The servants Maeve and your friend locked in a closet knew I was sleeping on the boat and called me. Now you will die as my father died, but not before I've finished with Maeve."

Pitt turned slowly. "Maeve is already dead," he lied.

Deirdre leaned sideways and tried to examine her sister around Pitt's body. "Then you can watch as I shoot her precious twins."

"No!" Maeve cried out from behind Pitt. "Not my babies!"

Deirdre was beyond all reason as she lifted the gun and stepped around Pitt for a clear shot at Maeve and her sons.

White rage overcame any shred of common sense as Pitt leaped, hurling himself toward Deirdre. He came out fast, saw the muzzle of the automatic pointing at his chest. Pitt hardly felt the impact from the two bullets as they struck and penetrated into his flesh. He pounded Deirdre off her feet with a crushing impact that distorted her delicate features into an expression of agony. She toppled backward over a coffee table. There was a horrible sound like a dried branch snapping as her spine fractured in three places.

"You'll pay . . ." she moaned wrathfully, staring up at the growing circles of blood on Pitt's side and upper chest.

"Maybe," he said slowly. "But it's better than being paralyzed for the rest of my life."

He stumbled over to Maeve. Bravely, she ignored her wound and was consoling the little boys.

"It's all right, my darlings," she said softly. "Everything will be all right now."

Pitt knelt in front of her and examined her wound. There was little blood, just a neat hole that looked like nothing more than a slight stab wound from a small object. She was bleeding internally, and unless she received immediate medical treatment, death was only minutes away.

Pitt's heart felt as if it had fallen into a chasm filled with ice. He instinctively wanted to cry in bitter grief, but no sound came from his throat, only a moan of sorrow that rose from deep inside him.

Giordino couldn't stand the delay any longer. Dawn had arrived, and the eastern sky above the island was already glowing orange from the sun. He jumped from the helicopter to the deck, ducking under the rotating blades as a van carrying security guards raced onto the dock. What had happened to Pitt and Maeve? he wondered anxiously.

Haste was vital. The only reason the guards had not fired on the helicopter or yacht was because they were afraid to damage Dorsett property. Now the guards were only a hundred meters away and closing in.

Giordino was so engrossed in keeping his eyes on their pursuers and his mind on what was delaying his friends that he failed to notice the sound of dogs barking from all parts of the island or the sudden flight of birds ascending and flying in confused circles in the sky. Nor did he sense an odd humming sound or feel the quivering on land and see the sudden agitation of the lagoon's waters as the sound waves of staggering intensity, driven by an immense velocity, slammed into the subterranean rock of Gladiator Island.

Only when he was within a few steps of the door to the main salon did he glance over his shoulder at the guards. They were standing transfixed on the dock whose planking was curling like waves across a sea. They had forgotten their quarry and were pointing to a small cloud of gray smoke that had begun to rise and spread above Mount Scaggs. Giordino could see men pouring like ants from the tunnel entrance in the volcano's slope. There seemed to be some activity inside Mount Winkleman as well. Pitt's warning about the island going up in smoke and cinders came back to him.

He burst through the doorway of the salon, then stopped dead. "What happened?" he gasped as he surveyed the scene.

Pitt looked up at him without answering. "The eruption, has it started?"

"There's smoke coming from the mountains, and the ground is moving."

"Then we're too late."

Giordino immediately knelt beside Pitt and stared at Maeve's wound. "This looks bad."

She looked up at him, her eyes imploring. "Please take my boys and leave me."

Giordino shook his head heavily. "I can't do that. We'll all go together or not at all."

Pitt reached over and clutched Giordino's arm. "No time. The whole island will blow any second. I can't make it either. Take the boys and get out of here, get out now."

As if he had been struck by a bombshell, Giordino went numb with disbelief. Nothing in his entire life had primed him to desert his best friend of thirty years to a certain death. His expression was one of agonized indecision. "I can't leave either of you." Giordino leaned over and slipped his arms under Maeve as if to carry her. He nodded at Pitt. "I'll come back for you."

Maeve brushed his hands away. "Don't you see Dirk is right?" she murmured weakly.

Pitt handed Rodney York's logbook and letters to Giordino. "See that York's story reaches his family," he said, his voice hard with glacial calmness. "Now take the kids and go!"

Giordino shook his head in torment. "You never quit, do you?"

Outside, the sky had suddenly vanished, replaced by a cloud of ash that burst from the center of Mount Winkleman with a great rumbling sound that was truly terrifying. Everything went dark as the evil black mass spread like a giant umbrella. Then came a more thunderous explosion that hurled thousands of tons of molten lava into the air.

Giordino felt as if his soul was being torn away. Finally, he nodded and turned his head, a curious understanding in his grieved eyes. "All right." And then

one last jest. "Since nobody around here wants me, I'll
go."

Pitt gripped him by the hand. "Good-bye, old friend.
Thank you for all you've done for me."

"Be seeing you," Giordino muttered brokenly, tears
forming in his eyes. He looked like a very old man who
was shrouded in solemn and heart-wrenching shock. He
started to say something, choked on the words and then
he snatched up Maeve's children, one boy under each
arm, and was gone.

45

Seconds after he was sure Giordino had lifted the helicopter off the yacht and was safely in the air, Pitt pushed himself to his feet, wetted a towel from the sink in the bar and wrapped it around Maeve's head. Then he began piling cushions, chairs, every piece of furniture he could lift over Maeve until she was protected from the approaching sea of fire. He stumbled into the wheelhouse, clutching his side where one bullet had plunged. The other bullet had glanced off a rib, bruised and deflated one lung and passed out through his back muscles. Fighting to keep from falling into the black, nightmarish pool clouding his eyes, he studied the instruments and controls of the boat's console.

Pitt found the proper switches and kicked over the big Blitzen Seastorm turbodiesel engines. They had no sooner rumbled to idling rpms when he engaged their Casale V-drives and pushed the throttles forward. The deck beneath his feet shuddered as the bow lifted and the water behind the stern whipped into foam. He took manual control of the helm to steer a course toward the open sea.

Hot ashes fell in a thick blanket. He could hear the crackling and the growling of the approaching tempest of fire. Flaming rocks fell like hail, hissing in clouds of steam as they hit the water and sank beneath the surface. They dropped endlessly out of the sky after having been thrown a great distance by the tremendous pressures coming out of Mount Scaggs. The column of doom engulfed the docks and seemed to take off in pursuit of the yacht, rolling across the lagoon like an enraged monster from the fiery depths of hell. And then it was on top of him in full fury, descending over the yacht in a whirling convoluted mass two hundred meters high before Pitt was able to clear the lagoon. The boat was pitched forward as it was struck a staggering blow from astern. The radar and radio masts were swept clean away, along with the lifeboats, railings and deck furniture. The boat struggled through the blazing turbulence like a wounded whale. Flaming rocks crashed on the superstructure roof and decks, smashing the once beautiful yacht into a shattered hulk.

The heat in the wheelhouse was searing. Pitt felt as if someone had rubbed his skin with a red hot salve. Breathing became agonizingly difficult, especially so because of the collapsed lung. He prayed that Maeve was still alive back in the salon. Gasping for air, clothing beginning to smolder, hair already singed, he stood there desperately gripping the helm. The superheated air forced its way down his throat and into his lungs till each intake of breath was an agony. The roar of the firestorm in his ears combined with the pounding of his heart and the surge of his blood. His only resources to resist the blazing assault were the steady throb of the engines and the sturdy construction of the boat.

When the windows around him began to crack and then shatter, he thought he would surely die. His whole mind, his every nerve was focused on driving the boat forward as though he could by sheer willpower force her ahead faster. But then abruptly the heavy blanket of fire thinned and dropped away as the yacht raced into the clear. The dirty gray water went emerald green and the sky sapphire blue. The wave of fire and scalding mud had finally lost its momentum. He sucked in the clean salt air like a swimmer hyperventilating before making a free dive into the depths. He did not know how badly he was injured, and he did not care. Excruciating pain was stoically endured.

At that moment, Pitt's gaze was drawn by the upper head and body of an immense sea creature that rose out of the water off the starboard bow. It appeared to be a giant eel with a round head a good two meters thick. The mouth was partially open and he could see razor-sharp teeth in the shape of rounded fangs. If its undulating body were straightened out, Pitt estimated its length at between thirty and forty meters. It traveled through the water at a speed only slightly slower than the yacht. Once through the channel, it rolled forward into the depths, and with a wave of his huge tail, disappeared.

Pitt had heard of this sea creature but never thought he would see it with his own eyes. "So Basil exists," he muttered. He nodded a good-bye and turned his attention back to the console.

The navigational instruments were no longer functioning. He tried sending a Mayday over both the radio and satellite phone, but they were dead. Nothing seemed to function except the big engines that still drove the yacht through the waves. Unable to set the boat on an automatic course, he tied the helm with the bow pointed west toward the southeastern coast of Australia and set the throttle a notch above idle to conserve what little fuel remained. A rescue ship responding to the catastrophe on Gladiator Island was bound to spot the crippled yacht, stop and investigate.

He forced his unsteady legs to carry him back to Maeve. With great trepidation, he stepped over the threshold separating the salon from the wheelhouse. The main salon looked like it had been swept by a blowtorch. The thick, durable fiberglass skin had kept much of the heat from penetrating the bulkheads but the terrible heat had broken through the glass windows. Remarkably, the flammable material on the sofas and chairs, though badly scorched, had not ignited.

Uncaring of his pain and injuries, he furiously threw aside the furniture he had heaped over Maeve. She had to be still alive, he thought desperately. She had to be waiting for him in all her pain and despair at once again losing her children. He pulled off the last cushion and stared down with mounting fear. Relief washed over him like a cascade as she lifted her head and smiled.

"Maeve," he rasped, falling forward and taking her in his arms. Only then did he see the large pool of blood that had spread on the deck carpeting.

"You're not going to die," he said, unable to control the fabric of his heart as it tore in pieces. "We're going to live a long life together, cruising the sea while we raise a boatload of kids who swim like fish."

"Thank you," she said in a low whisper. Then her eyes fluttered and closed. Her body seemed to wilt like a flower under a frigid blast of cold. Her face became serene like a peacefully sleeping child's.

"No!" he cried, his voice like a wounded animal baying in the night.

All life seemed to flow out of Pitt too. He no longer clung to consciousness. He no longer fought the black mist closing in around him. He released his hold on reality and embraced the darkness.

PART V

THE DUST
SETTLES

BASIL

46

Giordino's plan for a quick, turnaround flight to Gladiator Island had been dashed almost from the beginning.

After using the Agusta's state-of-the-art satellite communications system to brief Sandecker on board the *Glomar Explorer* in Hawaii, he contacted air-and-sea rescue units in both Australia and New Zealand and became the first person to announce the disaster to the outside world.

Upon approaching the capital city of Tasmania, Giordino flew along the steep foothills bordering Hobart, whose commercial district was located on the west bank of the Derwent River. Locating the airport, he called the tower. The flight controllers directed him to set down in a military staging area half a kilometer from the main terminal. He was stunned to see a huge crowd of people milling about the area as he hovered over the landing site.

Once he shut down the engine and opened the passenger door, everything was accomplished in an orderly manner. Immigration officials came on board and arranged for his entry into Australia without a passport. Social services authorities took custody of Maeve's young sons, assuring Giordino that as soon as their father was located, they would be placed in his care.

Then as Giordino finally set foot on the ground, half starved and exhausted almost beyond redemption, he was attacked by an army of reporters shoving microphones under his nose, aiming TV cameras at his face and shouting questions about the eruption.

The only question he answered with a smile on his face was to confirm that Arthur Dorsett was one of the first casualties of the holocaust.

Pitt had been lucky, as every nurse on the floor of the hospital in Hobart, Tasmania, never ceased telling him. After a bout of peritonitis from the perforated colon, and the removal of the bullet from his pelvic girdle, where it had made a nice dent in the bone, he began to feel as if he had rejoined the living. When his lung reinflated and he could breathe freely, he ate like a starving lumberjack.

Giordino and Sandecker hung around until they were assured by the medical staff that Pitt was on the road to recovery. Then they escorted Maeve's boys to Melbourne, to their father, who had flown in from his family's sheep station in the outback for Maeve's funeral. A big man with a university degree in animal husbandry, he promised Sandecker and Giordino to raise the boys in good surroundings. He wisely retained attorneys to watch over the twins' best interests. Satisfied the boys were in good hands and that Pitt would soon be ready to return home, the admiral and Giordino flew back to Washington, where Sandecker received a tumultuous welcome and a round of ceremonial banquets as the man who fought a one-sided battle to save Honolulu from a tragic disaster.

The doctor walked into the room and found Pitt standing at the window, gazing longingly down at the Derwent River flowing through the heart of Hobart. "You're supposed to be in bed," said the doctor.

Pitt gave him a hard look. "I've laid on a mattress a three-toed sloth wouldn't sleep on for five days. I've served my time. Now I'm out of here."

The doctor smiled slyly. "You have no clothes, you know. The rags you were wearing when they brought you in were thrown out in the trash."

"Then I'll walk out of here in my bathrobe and this stupid hospital gown."

"I can see arguing with you is wasting my other patients' time." The doctor shrugged. "Go if you must. I'll see the nurse finds you some decent street clothes so you won't be arrested for impersonating an American tourist."

No NUMA jet this trip. Pitt flew a commercial plane home. As he shuffled onto the aircraft, still stiff and with a grinding ache in his side, the flight attendants stared at him in open curiosity, watching him search the overhead numbers for his seat.

One attendant, brown hair neatly coiffed, eyes almost as green as Pitt's and soft with concern, came over to him. "Are you Mr. Pitt?" she asked as she motioned to an empty seat by the window.

"At the moment I wish I were someone else, but yes, I'm Pitt."

"You're a lucky man," she said smiling.

"So a dozen nurses kept telling me."

"No, I mean you have friends who are very concerned about you. The flight crew were told you would be flying with us and were requested to make you as comfortable as possible."

How did Sandecker know he'd escaped the hospital, left directly for the airport and purchased a standby ticket to Washington, he wondered.

As it turned out, the flight attendants had little to do for him. He slept most of the trip, coming awake only to eat. He did not even know the plane was approaching Dulles International until the wheels thumped down and woke him up.

He came off the shuttle bus from the aircraft into the terminal, mildly surprised and disappointed that no one waited to greet him. If Sandecker had alerted the airline's flight crew, he certainly knew when the plane was scheduled to arrive. Not even Al Giordino was waiting at the curb when he walked haltingly toward a taxi stand. A clear case of out-of-sight, out-of-mind, he told himself as his mood of depression deepened.

It was eight o'clock in the evening when he exited the cab, punched his code into the security system of his hangar and walked inside. He turned on the lights that reflected in the mirrored finish and chrome of his collector cars.

A tall object that nearly touched the ceiling stood in front of him, an object that hadn't been there when he left.

For several moments, Pitt stared in rapt fascination at the totem pole. A beautifully carved eagle with spread wings graced the top. Then, in descending order, came a grizzly bear with its cub, a raven, a frog, a wolf, some type of sea creature and a human head at the bottom that remotely resembled Pitt. He read a note that was pinned to the ear of the wolf.

Please accept this commemorative column in your honor from the Haida people as a token of their appreciation for your efforts in removing the disfigurement on our sacred island. The Dorsett mine has been closed, and soon the animals and plants will reclaim their rightful home. You are now an honored member of the Haida.

Your friend,
Mason Broadmoor

Pitt was deeply moved. To be given a masterwork of such eminent significance was a rare privilege. He felt grateful beyond measure to Broadmoor and his people for their generous gift.

Then he walked around the totem and felt his heart stop beating. Disbelief clouded his opaline green eyes. Then astonishment was replaced with emptiness followed by sorrow. Directly behind, sitting in the aisle between the classic cars, was the *Marvelous Maeve*.

Tired, worn and the worse for wear, but there she sat in all her sea-ravaged glory. Pitt could not imagine how the faithful boat had survived the eruption and had been transported thousands of kilometers to Washington. It was as if someone had performed a miracle. He walked over, and reached out his hand to touch the bow to see if he wasn't hallucinating.

Just as his fingertips met the hull's hard surface, people began emerging from the back of the Pullman railroad car parked along one wall of the hangar, the rear seats of the automobiles and from his upstairs apartment, where they had been hiding. Suddenly, he was surrounded by a crowd of familiar faces shouting "surprise" and "welcome home."

Giordino embraced him gently, well aware of Pitt's injuries. Admiral Sandecker, never one for emotional display, warmly shook Pitt's hand, turning away as tears welled in his eyes.

Rudi Gunn was there, along with Hiram Yaeger, and over forty of his other friends and fellow employees at NUMA. His parents were there to greet him too. His father, Senator George Pitt of California, and his mother, Barbara, were shocked at his gaunt appearance, but bravely acted as though he looked healthy and fit. St. Julien Perlmutter was there, directing the food and drink. Congresswoman Loren Smith, his close friend for ten years, kissed him hello, saddened at seeing the dull, world-weary look of pain and exhaustion in his normally glinting eyes.

Pitt stared at the little boat that had performed so faithfully. He turned without hesitation to Giordino. "How did you ever manage it?"

Giordino smiled triumphantly. "After the admiral and I flew you to the hospital in Tasmania, I returned to the island with another load of relief supplies. A quick pass over the eastern cliffs revealed that *Marvelous Maeve* had survived the eruption. I borrowed a couple of Aussie engineers and lowered them into the ravine. They secured the boat to the cable from the helicopter. I hoisted it to the top of the bluffs, where we disassembled the hull and outriggers. The operation took some doing, but the parts we couldn't load inside the helicopter we attached underneath the fuselage. Then I flew back to Tasmania, where I talked the pilot of a commercial cargo plane that was headed for the States into transporting the beast home. With the help of a team from NUMA, we put it back together barely in time for your arrival."

"You're a good friend," said Pitt sincerely. "I can never repay you."

"It is I who owe you," Giordino responded.

"I deeply regret that I was unable to attend Maeve's funeral in Melbourne."

"The admiral and I were there along with her boys and the father."

"Who gave the eulogy?"

"The admiral delivered the words you wrote," said Giordino sadly. "There wasn't a dry eye in the house."

"And Rodney York, our marooned sailor?"

"We sent York's logbook and letters to England by courier," said Giordino. "York's widow is still living by Falmouth Bay, a sweet little lady in her late seventies. I talked to her by phone after she received the log. There is no expressing how happy she was to learn how York died, even if it was thirty-eight years later. She and her family are making plans to bring his remains home."

"I'm glad she finally knows the story," said Pitt.

"She asked me to thank you for your thoughtfulness."

The surprise over, the party took off in full swing until

after midnight. Friends came and went until Pitt was talked out and fighting to stay awake. Finally, Pitt's mother insisted her son get some rest. They all bid him a good night, wished him a speedy recovery and began drifting out the door for the drive to their homes.

"Don't come to work until you're fit and able," counseled Sandecker. "NUMA will struggle along without you."

"There is one project I'd like to pursue in about a month," said Pitt, the old buccaneer gleam briefly flashing in his eyes.

"What project is that?"

Pitt grinned. "I'd like to be on Gladiator Island when the water clears in the lagoon."

"What do you expect to find?"

"His name is Basil."

Sandecker stared, puzzled. "Who is Basil?"

"He's a sea serpent. I figure he'll return to his breeding ground after the lagoon is free of ash and debris."

Sandecker placed a hand on Pitt's shoulder and gave him a look usually reserved for a child who has claimed to have seen the bogeyman. "Take a nice long rest, and we'll talk about it."

The admiral turned and walked away, shaking his head and mumbling something about no such things as sea monsters.

Sandecker offered to drive Loren to her townhouse, and she gladly accepted, having arrived at Pitt's welcome-home party in a cab. They sat in reflective silence until the car passed over the bridge into the city.

"I've never seen Dirk so down," said Loren, her face sad and thoughtful. "I never thought I'd ever live to say it, but the fire has gone out of his eyes."

"He'll mend," Sandecker assured her. "A couple of weeks of rest, and he'll be champing at the bit again."

"Don't you think he's getting a little old to play the daring adventurer?"

"I can't think of him sitting behind a desk. He'll never stop roving the seas, doing what he loves to do."

"What drives him?" Loren wondered aloud.

"Some men are born restless," Sandecker said philosophically. "To Dirk, every hour has a mystery to be solved, every day a challenge to conquer."

Loren looked at the admiral. "You envy him, don't you?"

Sandecker nodded. "Of course, and so do you."

"Why is that, do you think?"

"The answer is simple," Sandecker said wisely. "There's a little of Dirk Pitt in all of us."

After everyone had left and Pitt was standing alone in the hangar amid his collection of mechanical possessions, each of which had in some way touched his past, he walked stiffly to the boat he and Maeve and Giordino had built on the Misery rocks and climbed inside the cockpit. He sat there a long time, silently lost in his memories.

He was still sitting there in the *Marvelous Maeve* when the first rays of the morning sun brushed the rusting roof of the old aircraft hangar he called home.